About the Authors

Margaret Way was born in the City of Brisbane. A Conservatorium trained pianist, teacher, accompanist and vocal coach, her musical career came to an unexpected end when she took up writing, initially as a fun thing to do. She currently lives in a harbourside apartment at beautiful Raby Bay, where she loves dining all fresco on her plant-filled balcony, that overlooks the marina. No one and nothing is a rush so she finds the laid-back Village atmosphere very conducive to her writing.

Carol Marinelli recently filled in a form asking for her job title. Thrilled to be able to put down her answer, she put writer. Then it asked what Carol did for relaxation and she put down the truth – writing. The third question asked for her hobbies. Well, not wanting to look obsessed she crossed the fingers on her hand and answered swimming but, given that the chlorine in the pool does terrible things to her highlights – I'm sure you can guess the real answer.

Kandy Shepherd swapped a career as a magazine editor for a life writing romance. She lives on a small farm in the Blue Mountains near Sydney, Australia, with her husband, daughter and lots of pets. She believes in love at first sight and real-life romance – they worked for her! Kandy loves to hear from her readers. Visit her at kandyshepherd.com

With Love From
COLLECTION

January 2020
With Love From Las Vegas

February 2020
With Love From Cape Town

March 2020
With Love From Sydney

April 2020
With Love From Florence

May 2020
With Love From Athens

June 2020
With Love From London

With Love From Sydney

MARGARET WAY

CAROL MARINELLI

KANDY SHEPHERD

MILLS & BOON

First Published in Great Britain 2020
By Mills & Boon, an imprint of HarperCollins*Publishers*
1 London Bridge Street, London, SE1 9GF

ISBN: 978-0-263-28106-4

MIX
Paper from responsible sources
FSC™ C007454

This book is produced from independently certified FSC™ paper to ensure responsible forest management.

For more information visit: www.harpercollins.co.uk/green

Printed and bound in Spain
by CPI, Barcelona

IN THE AUSTRALIAN BILLIONAIRE'S ARMS

MARGARET WAY

CHAPTER ONE

SUCH a beautiful young woman would always turn heads, Holt thought. Stares were guaranteed, and he was a man who automatically registered the physical details of anyone who crossed his path, whether business or social. He never forgot faces. He never forgot names. It was a God-given asset. Now his eyes were trained on the mystery woman as she entered the banquet room on the arm of Marcus Wainwright, the fifty-plus member of one of the richest and longest established families in the country. The combined impact brought the loud buzz of conversation in the huge room to an abrupt halt.

"I don't *believe* it!"

His date for the evening, Paula Rowlands, of Rowlands shopping malls fame, sounded as if she was on the verge of freaking out. "For crying out loud, Holt, that proves it! The gossip is *true*." For added emphasis, she dug her long nails into the fine cloth of his dinner jacket. "Marcus has brought her to the social event of the year."

That was enormously significant. "At least she didn't sneak in," he said dryly, "though I'm sure the toughest bouncer wouldn't have asked for ID. He'd have ushered her through with a 'wow!'"

Paula swung to face him. "Holt, really!" she chided. "She works in a *florist shop*!"

"There goes the neighbourhood!"

"God yes!" Paula moaned.

It was obvious Paula thought they were on the same page. It didn't occur to her he was being facetious. Paula was a snob. No doubt about it, but he liked her none the less. Snobbery was a minus, but Paula had a few pluses going for her. She was glamorous and generally good company both in and out of bed. The biggest plus for her among her wider circle of men friends was her billionaire father, George Rowlands. George was a genuine first-generation entrepreneur and a really decent guy. It was the Rowlands women, mother and daughter, Marilyn and Paula, neither of whom had worked a day in their lives apart from strenuous workouts in the gym, who suffered from delusions of grandeur.

"She *owns* the business, I believe," he tacked on. "Aunt Rowena told me only the other day when the rumours began to fly, she's a genius at handling flowers."

Paula stared at him with dumbstruck eyes. "Handling flowers, Holt? Darling, you can't be serious?"

He laughed. "Is that you in your Queen Victoria mode? Actually I am. I didn't say she pinched bucketloads from over neighbourhood fences and stacked them in the boot of her car. She apparently has a great talent for arranging flowers."

Paula continued to eye him incredulously. "How difficult is *that*?"

"Oh, believe me, it's an art form. It really is." Hadn't he pondered over what precisely had gone wrong with Marilyn Rowlands's many unsuccessful attempts at the Rowlands mansion?

"Joe the goose can arrange flowers," Paula said complacently, supremely unaware she had inherited her mother's "eye". "The trick is to buy lots, then shove them in fancy vases."

"Too easy!" He continued to track the progress of Marcus and the beauty on his arm. She might have walked out of a bravura late nineteenth century painting, he decided, his attention well and truly caught. Singer Sargent or Jacque Emile Blanche perhaps? A lover of beauty in all its forms, for a moment he damned nearly forgot where he was. Small wonder Marcus had become infatuated.

"Your great-aunt here tonight?" Paula asked, hoping the answer was no. Rowena Wainwright-Palmerston rather intimidated Paula, though she knew it wasn't deliberate. "She looks great for her age," she said in an unconsciously patronising voice.

"Rowena looks great for *any* age," Holt clipped off smartly, though his attention was fully employed studying the blonde vision.

"Holt, baby?" Paula elbowed him in the ribs, trying to draw his attention back to her.

He had to grimace. "What are you trying to do, maim me?"

"Never!" She began to rhythmically smooth his back with her hands.

"She's extremely beautiful." He felt a stab of alarm. He was very fond of Marcus. Protective as well. Whatever he had expected of Marcus's shock lady friend, it wasn't this, though his great-aunt had warned him.

"She's quite a remarkable young lady and, without question, well bred. Cool old-style beauty, if you know what I mean. Very Mittel Europa. Not a modern look at all. That would appeal to Marcus. There's a story there, mark my words!"

"I hope you noticed the *hair*?" A bridling Paula jolted him out of his thoughts again.

"You're not going to tell me *you* were born with copper hair?"

Paula's eyes flashed with resentment. "Just a few foils," she lied. "Hers can't be real! Where do you get that *white* blonde except from a bottle?"

"Scandinavia, maybe?" he suggested. "Her surname is Erickson, I believe. Sonya Erickson. Bit of a clue. Norwegian background perhaps? Norway the Land of the Midnight Sun, birthplace of Ibsen, Grieg, Edvard Munch, Sigrid Undset, and, as I recall, the infamous Quisling."

Paula frowned. She didn't know half those people. She'd seen Ibsen's *Hedda Gabler* at the Sydney Theatre Company and thought it a dead bore, even if Cate Blanchett was as always brilliant. So far as she was concerned the play had little or no relevance to modern life. And what sort of a solution was suicide? "I never thought Marcus could be such a fool," she said with surprising bitterness. "Neither did Mummy."

"Ah, Mummy!" The *terrible* Mummy who had a Chihuahua called Mitzi that greeted male visitors in full Rottweiler mode. Marilyn Rowlands, who had been brought up to believe if a girl wasn't married by twenty-four she was doomed to live and die alone. Marilyn was therefore desperate to marry off her twenty-eight-year-old daughter.

To *him*.

Even if Paula were the last woman left in the world, he feared he would remain a bachelor.

"You were at the dinner party Mummy arranged to get Marcus and Susan Hampstead together, remember?" Paula took condemnatory eyes off Ms Ericksen to shoot him a glance. "They'd both lost their partners."

His reply was terse to the point of curtness. "Susan Hampstead. *Three* marriages? *Three* divorces? Marcus lost his dearly loved wife." There was a world of difference between the late Lucy Wainwright and Susan Hampstead, a living, breathing, career courtesan, and he wasn't going to let Paula forget it.

"Yes, yes, I *know*." Paula resumed rubbing his back in a conciliatory and, it had to be said, irritatingly *proprietary* fashion. He couldn't embarrass her in public by shrugging her off. He had to stand there and take it. They weren't an Item. He had been up front about it all. *No* commitment, but try as he did he couldn't stop Paula and her mother thinking there was or there would very soon be.

His mood turned pensive. "Marcus has been a very sad man for a long time. It's good to see him out and about." Only the *last* thing the Wainwright clan would want for Marcus was to make a dreadful and inevitably painful mistake. The girl was too young. Too beautiful. Too everything. She mightn't have Susan Hampstead's cobra-like attack, but in real terms she could prove far more dangerous.

"Marcus obviously footed the bill for her dress." Paula glanced down at her own stunning designer gown, which suddenly appeared to her less stunning. "I can imagine just how much that evening dress cost. No florist could possibly afford it. It's couture. Vintage Chanel, I'd say. The jewellery too. Surely I've seen the pendant before?"

Mummy certainly would have, he thought, but he didn't enlighten Paula. The pendant necklace, an exquisite Colombian emerald surrounded by a sunburst of diamonds, that hung around the girl's white swan neck had belonged to Lucy. So too had the chandelier-style diamond earrings. The set had been Marcus's wedding gift to his beautiful green-eyed wife. They hadn't been seen for the best part of six years, which was roughly the time lovely little Lucy had taken to die of bone cancer.

"Ah, well, mistresses never go out of date." His own

surge of resentment towards the newcomer shocked him. *Lucy's emeralds, God!* Would Lucy mind? Would she turn over in her grave? No, Lucy had been a beautiful person. Shouldn't he at least give this young woman a chance? But his male intuition had gone into overdrive. She was one of those life altering women. Needless to say she would be very clever. Manipulative, as a matter of course. He noted she had matched her gown, not only to the jewel, but to her beautiful emerald eyes. They were set at a fascinating slant. Her eyes rivalled the precious gemstone. It dipped into the perfectly arched upper swells of her breasts. Her skin was flawless, lily white. One rarely saw such porcelain skin outside Europe. Her beautiful, thick, white-blonde hair, which he was prepared to bet a million dollars was natural with that white skin, was arranged in an elegant chignon interwoven with silver and gold threads that stood out like a glittering sunburst. It was incredibly effective. They could have had a young goddess on the scene.

Rowena as usual was spot on. A young woman who owned and worked in a florist shop looked like Old World aristocracy, so regal was her demeanour. She didn't appear in the least overawed by her lavish surroundings, the fashionable crowd, the seriously rich, the celebrities and socialites, or troubled by the full-on battery of stares. She moved with confidence showing no sign she was aware of the effect she was having on the room full of guests. Royalty couldn't have pulled it off better.

"And she's got inches on Marcus," Paula pointed out, as though it were absolutely *verboten* for a woman to be taller than her escort.

"Very likely her high heels." She was certainly above average height for a woman. As a couple, they were a study in contrasts. Marcus, medium height, worryingly thin, dark, grey-flecked hair, grey eyes, an austere scholarly face, and a knife sharp brain. He looked more like a university don than a captain of industry. His companion was ultra slender, but not in that borderline anorexic way Holt so disliked. She was *willowy*. She moved beautifully with the grace of a trained dancer. Lovely arms, neck and small high breasts. Her legs, hidden by the full-length silk gown, would no doubt be just as spectacular.

That as may be, she couldn't be the defunct European aristocrat she appeared. More likely a hard-nosed gold-digger lurking beneath the surface. A woman as beautiful as that could have any man she wanted. Obviously topping her list of requirements for potential suitors was considerable *wealth*. That would decimate the numbers. Though Marcus was by no means the richest member of the Wainwright family—that was the family patriarch, Julius—Marcus had at least a hundred and forty million dollars. A fortune that size assured any man up to ninety years of age blue-chip eligibility. A hundred and forty million dollars should just about cover any girl-on-the-make's lifetime expenses.

Paula got another steely grip on his arm.

"Hey, Paula, those sessions at the gym are really paying off."

"Sorry." She relaxed the pressure. "You're not usually so testy. But I guess you're upset for poor Marcus. She's obviously an adventuress."

"A lot of women have that streak."

Paula gave a nervous laugh. At least she was an heiress. That let her off the hook. "Look out," she warned, clearly perturbed. "They're coming *our* way."

He gave her a sardonic glance. "Why not? Marcus is my uncle, after all."

She recognised him from his photographs. David Holt Wainwright. They didn't do him justice. In the flesh he was the embodiment of vibrant masculinity. Oddly enough a lot of handsome men were lacking in that department. He had it in spades. A kind of devilish dazzle, she thought. Handsome was too tame a word. She took in the height, the splendid physique, that look of high intelligence he shared with his uncle, the infinite self confidence only the super-rich had, plus an intrinsic sexiness that from all accounts drew women in droves. His thick crow-black hair, worn a little longer than usual, was cut into deep crisp waves that clung to his well-shaped skull. His brilliant dark eyes, so dark a brown they appeared black, dominated his dynamic face. He photographed well. A flashing white smile that lit a dark face to radiance was a big asset for anyone in the public eye. But the glossy images were as nothing to the man.

And he had already arrived at the conclusion she was an adventuress looking for a rich husband. It was there in that brilliant assessing gaze. What greater legitimacy could there be for a working girl than to marry a millionaire?

"David's friend is Paula Rowlands," Marcus was murmuring quietly in her ear. "Her father owns a good many shopping malls. Don't let her rattle you."

"Does it matter what she thinks of me?" she asked calmly, grateful she had mastered the art of hiding her true feelings to a considerable degree. It had been a struggle concealing her vulnerabilities, but she had learned to her cost to be very wary of trusting people, let alone sharing her innermost thoughts. Marcus, a lovely man, was the outstanding exception.

"No, it doesn't." Marcus laughed.

"Well, then." She hugged his arm. Being here tonight had everything to do with her respect and affection for Marcus Wainwright. She knew in accepting his invitation she was making a big shift out of obscurity into the limelight. It didn't sit comfortably with her but Marcus had insisted her appearance would be remarked on and bring in a whole lot of new customers. For some time now she had started to number the rich among her regulars. Most had lovely manners, others were unbelievably pretentious. Marcus's aunt Rowena, Lady Palmerston, widow of the distinguished British diplomat of the late seventies early eighties, Sir Roland Palmerston, was among the former. She frequently called into the shop, saying delightedly she found Sonya's arrangements "inspiring".

"But she'll try, my dear," Marcus warned. "The Rowlands women are frightful snobs. *Money* is their aristocracy."

"Your nephew must see something in her? She's very attractive and she has a real flair for wearing clothes."

Marcus gave a dry laugh that turned into a cough. "My nephew wants and needs a great deal more than that in a woman. It's Paula and her mother who hang in there."

"Well, he *is* seriously eligible," she put forward with a smile.

"David got the best of all of us," he said with very real pride.

The cautionary voice always at work inside Sonya's head was issuing warnings. Not of the smug-faced Paula Rowlands, heiress, but David Holt Wainwright, Marcus's dearly loved nephew. *He* was the one who was going to cause her grief. She had learned to rely on her intuition. David Wainwright was a very important figure in Marcus's life. He was already querying the exact nature of her friendship with Marcus. And friendship was all it was. She had her suspicions Marcus wanted more of her. He could offer her a great deal, not the least of it blessed *safety*, but at this point she was allowing the friendship plenty of time to go where it would.

* * *

Afterwards it seemed to Holt that Sonya Erickson had entered his life in a kind of blaze. Very few people did that. It wasn't just her beauty, ravishing though it was, it was the inbred self-confidence. Beauty alone didn't guarantee that kind of self-assurance. Paula didn't have it for all her privileged background. This young woman was the very picture of patrician ease. There had to be a whole file on her somewhere with many secrets lodged therein. Paula was still whispering in his ear, for all she was worth, even though Marcus and his beautiful companion were almost upon them.

"Do me a favour, Paula, okay?" He put a staying hand on her arm.

"Of course, darling. Whatever you say!"

"Then kindly shut up. It's damned rude."

Holt made the move forward, his hand extended, a natural smile of great charm on his face. "Uncle Marcus."

"David." A matching expression of deepest affection lit the older man's face.

The two shook hands, then moved into their usual hug. Marcus and Lucille Wainwright had not been blessed with children, though they had longed for them. Holt had been very close to both from childhood as a result. They loved him. He loved them. In a way he had been the son they never had.

Marcus began the introductions the moment they broke apart. "Sonya Erickson." No further explanation. Just Sonya Erickson. No more was offered. But it was painfully obvious Sonya Erickson had become extremely important to him. If not, why the emeralds?

Remember Lucy's emeralds.

"*Sonya*, please," the young woman invited as she gave Holt her hand. It was done so gracefully—hang on, so *regally*—he was a beat away from raising her elegant hand just short of his lips. That caused a moment of black amusement. Yet there wasn't the merest hint of seduction in her beautiful green eyes when so many women tried it on. There wouldn't be a woman in the country who didn't know he had a few bob. But Ms Erickson's glorious green eyes revealed nothing beyond an aristocratic interest and a cool speculation to match his.

Up close she was even more beautiful. Paula, brightly chatting now to Marcus—Step Two in Paula's plan was to charm all his relatives—must be *hating* her. Beautiful women were a major stumbling block to their less fortunate sisters. Another man might have been overwhelmed. Not he. He had his head well and truly screwed on. But admittedly he was a man who recognised the fact a woman's beauty was immensely powerful. The beautiful Sonya had gained Marcus's attention. No mean feat. Marcus wasn't the kind of man who'd had passing affairs after Lucy's death. Rather Marcus had turned into something of a recluse.

Now this! Ms Erickson had mesmerized him. If Holt stood looking into her green eyes much longer, it might well happen to him, such was her spectacular allure.

"Marcus speaks of you often," she was saying, snapping him back to attention.

"If I need someone to speak well of me I go to Marcus," he said.

"I wondered if perhaps I should have curtsied?" Sonya smiled at him with aloof charm.

"Maybe I would have returned a bow. Here's to beauty!"

"No wonder Marcus loves you," she murmured.

He couldn't resist. "And he obviously finds you special."

That self-confidence, the patrician air, just *had* to be inbred. He began to wonder about her background. Might be an idea to check it out. Who *was* she? She had a lovely speaking voice to add to her assets. A faint accent. He couldn't pick it up. Surely indicated a gracious background? Or an intensive course in elocution. Did they still call it that? *Elocution, art of speech?*

His hand, he found to his mild self-disgust, was still feeling the effect of its contact with her skin. It was like a brief but searing encounter with electricity. It sent sparkles racing up his arm and a stir through his body. He had to take note. The lady was dangerous. She rated attention.

"Marcus is very dear to me," he said, taking just enough care that it didn't sound like a warning.

"Then you are both blessed."

She turned away from him to Marcus, a hint of sadness in her face.

A woman of mystery indeed!

And didn't she know how to play the part! In fact she was so good it was all he could do not to applaud.

Paula, momentarily sidelined, pushed herself back into the conversation with a smile. "May I say how beautiful you look, Ms Erickson." She couldn't quite pull genuine sincerity off.

"Thank you." A slight inclination of the white-blonde head.

Paula had to be an idiot if she didn't realize the mysterious Ms Erickson had summed her up on the spot and decided to shrug off the underlying hostility and dislike. Wise move, he thought. Play it cool.

"And the necklace!" Paula, big on jewellery, threw up both hands. "It's absolutely *glorious*! You must tell me how you came by it. A family heirloom perhaps?"

Zero tact on Paula's part. She might as well have shouted: *As though that's possible!*

Just as he was debating abandoning Paula for the

evening or perhaps treading on her expensively shod toe, Ms Erickson put her long-fingered white hand very lightly to the great glittering emerald. "My family lost everything at the end of World War Two," she offered very gravely.

God, that woman, Anna Andersen, claiming to be the Grand Duchess Anastasia couldn't have done it any better, Holt thought. Why on earth would she want to be a florist? She had everything going for her to be a big movie star.

"Really?" Paula exclaimed, incredulously.

He could read Paula's thoughts. Ms Erickson was only making it up.

"That *can't* be true! I feel you're kidding me."

"Too true." Sonya Erickson's reply was so quiet she might have been talking to herself.

High time to step in. The last thing he ever wanted was to offer the slightest embarrassment to his uncle.

"Shall we go to our table?" he suggested. His voice was as smooth as molasses, when his blood was heating up.

Marcus, who had tensed, gently took hold of the exquisite Sonya's arm. "Lead the way, David," he murmured.

He did so, shouldering responsibility like a man.

Since Marcus had pressed her to accompany him to this gala evening Sonya had wondered what it would be like. Now her gaze swept across the spacious room. Everything sparkled under the big chandeliers: glittering sequins, beading, crystals, expensive jewellery, smiling eyes. And the dresses! Strapless, one-shouldered, backless, daringly near frontless. A kaleidoscope of colour. She had known she would be mixing with the super rich, people in the public eye, and perhaps she would be meeting a member or two of Marcus's family, although she knew his parents were currently in New York. She knew all about David Holt Wainwright. She had gleaned quite a lot from magazines and business reviews. He was very highly regarded, brilliant in fact, the man to watch even though she knew he wasn't yet thirty. His mother was Sharron Holt-Wainwright, heiress to Holt Pharmaceuticals. Money married money. That was the way of it. Marcus always referred to his nephew as David. Mostly he got *Holt* from his mother's family and just about everyone else, Marcus had explained. It was his uncle Philip, his mother's brother, who had hit on the nickname. It had stuck, probably because the arresting good looks and the superior height had come from the Holt side of the family.

She felt Marcus's family would be against her. The age difference would be a big factor although rich men married beautiful young women all the time. Whether such marriages were for love or not, young wives were rarely given the benefit of the doubt. That was the way of the world. The gossip would have gone out. She worked in a florist shop, a good one, but she wasn't someone from their social milieu. She was a working girl. No one of any account. No esteemed family. No connections. No background of prestigious schools and university. Worse yet, she was twenty-five. Marcus was almost three decades on, not to mention his wealth. By and large, she had accepted the invitation against her better judgment. She knew her blonde beauty, inherited from her mother and maternal grandmother, gave her a real shot at power, but she had never entertained the notion she could land herself a millionaire.

Marcus was different. She had sensed the unresolved grief in him from the very first time he had wandered into her shop. He had been lingering outside, a distinguished older man, impeccably dressed, looking in the window, enticed apparently by an arrangement of lime-green lilium buds and luxurious tropical leaves, figs on branches, and some wonderful ruby-red peonies she had arranged in an old Japanese wooden vase. Just the one arrangement. No distractions.

She had smiled at him, catching his eyes. A moment later he came into the shop filled with beautiful flowers and exquisite scents. A shyly elegant, courtly man. She had taken to him on the spot. Trace memories, she supposed. The *friendship* had flourished. These days he allowed her to "work her magic" in his very beautiful home. It was way too big for a man on his own—a mansion. He employed a married couple, housekeeper and chauffeur/groundsman, who lived in staff quarters in the grounds but he had long refused to sell the house when many spectacular offers had been made. The house he had shared with his late wife. It held all his memories.

She knew all about memories. It had cemented their bond. It was just one of those things that happened in life. Like called to like. Marcus had later directed his aunt, Lady Palmerston, to her shop. Lady Palmerston in turn had directed many of her friends. She owed them both a lot. She realized for any young woman, especially one in her position, Marcus Wainwright would be a great catch. His age wouldn't come into it. He was a handsome, highly intelligent and very interesting man. He was also the type of man who liked making the people in his life happy. Self-gratification wasn't his thing. Marcus was a fine man. The first time she had met him he had commented on her green eyes.

"My late wife had wonderful eyes too. Green as emeralds."

Poor Marcus with all his dreams of happiness shot down in flames. Similar tragedies had happened to her.

"What are you thinking about?"

Sonya turned her head towards that vibrant, very sexy voice. It was pitched low for her ears only. All through the lavish four-course dinner she had listened with fascinated attention to his contributions to the conversation. It volleyed back and forth between highly educated, professional people. Even so, it was Holt Wainwright who carried their table of eight along effortlessly. He had a wide range of interests about which he was very knowledgeable. He was highly articulate and quick witted. He effortlessly commanded an impressive company. And here was a man, easily the youngest man at the table, totally at ease and in control of himself. She had to give him full marks for that.

She had been seated between Marcus and Holt. Marcus was busy answering a flurry of questions from one of the women guests, Tara Bradford, a top executive with a merchant bank, a formidable looking woman in her well-preserved early fifties. Sonya caught the vibes. Not that it was difficult. Tara Bradford, a divorcee, tall, thin, handsome more than attractive, was very interested in Marcus. She showed it in every look, every gesture. Tara had been a close friend of Marcus's late wife. She had directed only a few words Sonya's way, but with a smooth courtesy. Public relations were important. Tara gave the strong impression she already knew Marcus would come to his senses. May-November matches were just so unsuitable. Besides, the mature woman had so much more to offer.

Sonya, for her part, had been intensely aware of Holt Wainwright. Nothing extraordinary about that. He was a very charismatic man. Scores of women would have felt his attraction. She wasn't about to become enmeshed in such madness. But one couldn't control chemical reactions. Mercifully caution had been inbred in her. Getting too close to Holt Wainwright would be like playing with fire. Any resultant conflagration could pull the life she had so carefully constructed for herself down on her head. That kind of insight lent an edge of fear, like a glittering sword poised over her head.

Holt sat in silence watching the gentle tenderness of her expression gradually change. It lost its warmth, became almost shuttered. "I was recalling how I first met Marcus," she told him lightly.

"He came into your florist shop." His smile was urbane, but his instincts were every bit as keen as hers. He knew at some level they could hurt one another badly. Hurt Marcus. A little danger always excited him, but that couldn't happen with Marcus involved. He cared far too much about his uncle.

Sonya wasn't about to allow his brilliant fathoms-deep dark gaze faze her. "But you *know*. Marcus was attracted to one of my arrangements in the window."

"I'm told you're a genius at work."

"A quiet achiever!" she said, finding it difficult to unlock her glance from his. They had become almost duel-like in quality. "Lady Palmerston?"

"Another one of your admirers."

"Thankfully." Her expression relaxed into a smile. "I run a business. I need customers. Good customers who appreciate what I do."

"Then you must have been thrilled Marcus and my great-aunt walked through your door," he returned suavely.

She looked directly into his clever, probing eyes. "Perhaps I can help *you* at some time, David. I've begun arranging the flowers for luncheons, dinner parties, parties of all kinds, weddings. I've had to take on staff."

As if he'd be rash enough to make a booking! "I'll make note of that," he said, knowing full well he would never contact her. Too dangerous. Better to lie awake thinking about it. "Tell me about yourself," he invited.

And wouldn't there be lots to tell, said the cynical voice in his head.

"Little to tell." She had no difficulty with the lie. "Anyway, I'm sure you'll run a few checks."

"I'm your man," he said with cool amusement.

"There is such a thing as minding your own business." She drew back a little, picking up her wine glass.

"The thing is, Sonya, beautiful exotic women usually have a few skeletons in the cupboard."

"A cynical view."

"Truer than you think."

"Then it's a great comfort to me to know, if I do have a few skeletons lurking in my cupboard, *you* won't find them." There was a blend of mockery and disdain in her voice.

"Is that a dare?"

"What can I say?" She shrugged her white shoulders.

Beautiful shoulders. He could learn to appreciate that shrug. Even wait for it. And that little gesture with her hands? Pure *Europa*. "Yes, or no," he said.

She dared turn her head knowing he was baiting her. His eyes were as dark as hers were full of light. "No dare. It's a promise," she replied, keeping her voice as low pitched as his.

At the same moment Marcus turned his attention back to Sonya with what looked like an expression of relief on his face. Surely Tara knew she would never land Marcus? Holt thought. Lucy and Tara had been friends. It was clear poor Tara thought that guaranteed her next in line. Though even Tara would be far more suitable than Ms Erickson of the emerald-green eyes. If he had panicked her in any way she hid it supremely well. How did she manage such aplomb at twenty-five years of age?

He knew in his bones he was right. Ms Sonya Erickson had a *past.*

Right now she was looking to a rosy future with Marcus. He hadn't a single doubt if she wanted marriage she would get it. She was already wearing the jewels. He needed to ask Marcus in a diplomatic way if he had lent them to her for the night. Or had he gone totally overboard and given them to her? That idea plagued him. He imagined the sort of conversation that might have gone on.

"You're wearing an emerald silk dress, Sonya? I have in mind a particular necklace and matching earrings. They need an airing, after being locked away in the safe."

Did she protest? *"Really, no, Marcus!"*

"It would please me so much."

To be strictly fair it was hard to resist Marcus. Maybe she was the sort of young woman who lived to please. Dear Marcus, so long faithful to the memory of his beautiful Lucy, appeared to have fallen deeply in love.

Alas!

No wonder writers used the verb *fall.* The feeling was exactly like a free fall through space. The profound worry was the beautiful Sonya could be the best heartbreaker of them all. She must have trodden a path littered with admirers. *Lovers?* Despite himself he thought it would be quite an experience to share a bed with Ms Erickson. He was only human, but he was having none of taking Ms Erickson on trust. The beautiful Ms Erickson was wearing a mask. He would check on her discreetly. Clarify the situation.

The voice in his head said wryly, *It's already too late.*

CHAPTER TWO

MIDWEEK Holt had lunch with Rowena. Usual place, Simone's. The food was so good even Gordon Ramsay would have to wax lyrical. He and Rowena had things to discuss. Namely Marcus's future. Marcus was very dear to both of them and now they realized Marcus for the second time in his life was totally enraptured and could be at that very moment seriously considering marrying a woman young enough to be his daughter.

Okay, was that a bad thing? It happened all the time with beautiful clever girls. Most often they were blonde. Rich men married blondes for choice. He didn't exactly know why. Beauty came in many guises. But he had to say blonde was good.

He was nearly ten minutes late, having to work hard at winding up a meeting with a lot of guys in business suits and one woman executive with really Big Hair. With the light behind her he had the unsettling sensation he was talking to a balloon. If he lived to be one hundred he would still be amazed by what women did to their hair. The incredible colours they tried out. One of the girls in the office, Ellie, had gone briefly pink and purple. Maybe it was to attract his attention? He had stumbled over her so often, he had come to the conclusion she deliberately lay in wait.

A majestic-looking Rowena waved when she saw him, her face lighting up.

"Sorry I'm late." He threaded his way through the tables, acknowledging friends along the way. Simone's did a roaring trade with the big end of town. He bent to kiss Rowena's velvet cheek. He loved everything about her. Her wit and her wisdom. She always wore the same perfume like a signature note. Roses softened by iris, musk and, he thought, vanilla? It was so wonderfully subtle and evocative of Rowena, who could blame her for sticking to one sublime perfume? Most of the women in his circle ran the gamut. The beautiful Sonya had worn a serenely beautiful fragrance he was not familiar with. But it had been heaven to inhale.

"What are we having?" Once seated, he picked up the menu.

Rowena glanced across at him, delighting in his handsomeness. "I hope I did the right thing, dear. I've already ordered for both of us. I know how little time you have."

"You also know my tastes. So what is it?" He put up his hand to signal the drinks waiter. He and Rowena always shared a bottle of wine. Just enough. Not too much. He had plenty of work to do. Rowena, after a long successful life as a top diplomat's wife and hostess, knew exactly her limits. He only wished Paula did. She had become very argumentative after the gala night, claiming Sonya Erickson had not only sunk her claws in Marcus but had fascinated *him* as well. Of course he had denied it. Not strenuously.

To go with the fine Riesling Rowena had chosen seared scallops, white truffle butter, Tasmanian salmon with a creamy crab sauce and niçoise vegetables; he said he'd pass on dessert. Rowena elected to stay with the chocolate and mandarin parfait. Rowena was one of those fortunate women who loved her food but never put on a pound.

"So, you think Marcus is in love with her?" Rowena got right down to business.

"I wouldn't say it if I didn't. She's extremely beautiful. Well spoken. And nobody's fool."

"But you don't trust her?" Rowena had the Wainwright piercing grey eyes.

"What do *you* think?"

"I haven't seen them together, dear."

"Excuse me, do you have to? She was wearing *Lucy's emeralds*! Not something I'd expect of Marcus."

"Maybe she promised to take them off when the night was over." Rowena gave him an arch smile.

"Do you suppose she *stayed* over?" The idea dismayed him. Not a good sign.

"Come on, my dear. You sound dismal. It's the twenty-first century. Marcus is still a fine-looking man. She could well have."

"Then he's a lucky son of a gun," he said, with a twist in his smile.

"Sure you weren't a bit taken yourself?" She reached out to touch his hand.

"I'm a *man*, Rowena," he said very dryly.

"Very much so. What about that Paula of yours?"

He ran a hand over his brow. "Rowena, you *know* perfectly well Paula is a long-time friend. It's not serious."

"God, I hope not!" Rowena heaved a grateful sigh. "And that mother of hers!" She closed her eyes. "I bet she never gets off her knees praying for a match. But enough of the Rowlands. No wonder poor George spends his entire time at work."

"I like him."

"So do I." Rowena smiled. "A diamond in the rough."

"Ms Erickson is no rough diamond," he pointed out. "She has the aristocrat down pat. She's highly intelligent.

And ultra cool. But she doesn't love Marcus. That's the big worry."

"How would *you* know?" Rowena's gaze sharpened on his face.

"I *know*," he said and glanced away.

"So you're worried where this is going?"

"The short answer, Rowena, darling, is *yes*. I'd be a fool not to be wary of Ms Erickson."

"For what it's worth, I like her. I *really* like her."

"Your opinion is worth a lot. But what's her story?" he asked tersely. "She has one, of course."

Rowena nodded sagely. "One wouldn't have to be a mastermind to sense that. She has a very graceful flow of conversation. Pick a subject. Any subject. She speaks fluent French. I once put a question to her in French about the extraordinary arrangement she was working on at the time, a blend of burgundy and pale pink calla lilies. She answered, switching automatically from English to French. Polished accent. Better than mine. The one thing she doesn't talk about is herself. She appears so self-contained yet I feel she's terribly *alone*. There's a sadness there, don't you think?"

"Maybe that's part of her role of woman of mystery?" His tone was highly sceptical. "She could be a consummate actress."

Rowena negated that with a shake of her silver-streaked head. "She's genuine."

"But genuine what, Rowena dear? I've made a few enquiries on the side. Couldn't come up with anything much. I might try Interpol." It was only half a joke.

"She's only been in the country for around five years," Rowena supplied.

"Yes, I found out that much. There's a trace of an accent that isn't French."

"Hungarian," Rowena said with some certainty.

"Hungarian?" He set down his wine glass to give her a long look. Rowena and her husband had lived for many years in Europe. "The land of Liszt, Bela Bartok, Kodaly, Franz Lehar? I've even heard of the gorgeous Gabor sisters and their equally gorgeous mother. You know I haven't visited Budapest, which you assure me is one of the most beautiful cities in Europe, but you and Sir Roland knew it well. Or did you ask her straight out?"

"No, love." Rowena sat back. "But I have an excellent ear for accents. Besides, Sonya is a very private young lady. Her inbuilt cautions, insecurities if you like, have something to do with her former life. Somehow she has developed—"

"A mask?" he supplied. "So what is the mask hiding?"

Rowena sighed. "I'm having one of my buffet luncheons next Sunday. I'm asking Sonya. Would you care to come?'

He decided on the spot to *seize* on the invitation. Worry about the collateral damage later. "Is Marcus coming?"

"I wanted to speak to you first, before giving him a call. I always ask Marcus. He comes if he likes the people."

"Oh, God, Rowena," he groaned. "I advise extreme caution. I have the feeling the beautiful Sonya is going to wheel out a trolley full of tricks."

"Possibly," Rowena considered. "But I like her and I do love a mystery. So do you."

"If only she were older!" he lamented. "More suitable."

"No, no, *no* to Tara Bradford." Rowena threw up her hands in horror.

"Tara wouldn't break his heart," he pointed out rather grimly.

"What a blessing." Rowena allowed herself a touch of malice. "Only Marcus has no romantic interest in poor old

Tara. Wishful thinking on her part. She's a splendid woman in many ways, but she does have thunderous legs."

"All the better to hold her up," he offered vaguely. "I haven't seen Sonya's legs yet. I bet they're perfect."

Rowena nodded. "I have and they *are*."

The following afternoon he stopped by Marcus's house with its millions-plus view of Sydney Harbour. He'd been extremely busy all week with meetings plus endless piles of paperwork his father usually handled. His father, a notoriously secretive man, and CEO of Wainwright Enterprises, trusted few people outside his immediate family. These days he was leaving more and more to his only son and heir, adding to his already heavy workload. As a consequence he hadn't had a chance to catch up with his uncle, who headed up the property department. Considering the properties owned by Wainwright Enterprises, it was a huge job in itself. As well, he and Marcus, both of them holding Law and Economics degrees with first-class honours, sat in on major meetings with the legal department. They did work in the same building, Wainwright Towers, but not on the same floor. Made a surprising difference as it happened.

The house Marcus and Lucy had lived in for so many years had been left to Lucy by her maternal grandmother, Lady Marina Harnett, a great philanthropist and art collector. To Holt's eye it was one of the prettiest houses in the city. Not grand like the Wainwright ancestral home he had been raised in, but smaller and more welcoming to his eye, especially in the days when Aunt Lucy had been alive. She was the sweetest, kindest woman imaginable and she had to die. That was the trouble with life; there was always death at the end. The enemy that couldn't be overcome. Death did despicable things. He remembered his mother had been grief stricken when at long last Lucy had passed away. She and Lucy had been great friends. The family had taken Lucy to their hearts. No one could take her place.

So what *now*, with a very possible candidate for the second Mrs Marcus Wainwright on the scene? Would it be seen by the family as a betrayal of Lucy? Everyone wanted Marcus's happiness, but a beautiful young woman like Sonya Erickson could only inspire suspicion. God help him, he was already dealing with his mistrust of her.

He stepped out of the car, glancing briefly at a small blue hatchback nosed into a corner. Looked as if the estate had bought the housekeeper a new little runabout. The gardens were looking superb, ablaze with flowers. He started across the paved circular drive to the sandstone house. It had been built in the mid-1850s to a very high standard. Regency in design, it was perfectly symmetrical. The only concession to the Australian climate was the broad verandah with its series of white elegant pillars and fretwork. A lot of the original land had been sold off over the years—too valuable for one family to keep to themselves—but the original servants' quarters, beautifully maintained and updated, were still at the rear of the house along with storerooms that looked more like bungalows. He had spent such a lot of time here, for a moment he was overwhelmed by nostalgia.

"David, darling."

Pulled tight by little Aunt Lucy—a bare inch or so over five feet—feeling the great affection she had for him break over him in waves. No wonder Marcus had turned into himself after he lost her. Life could be very cruel. Sometimes it appeared as though the best went early. It would take for ever for the Wainwright clan to accept someone like Sonya if the worst came to the worst. A beautiful young woman's motives for marrying a man old enough to be her father could *not* be pure. He had felt her affection for

Marcus. That was genuine enough. The huge worry was it would take a miracle for that affection to turn to love. At least romantic love. Didn't every young woman want that? Didn't every young man? He was moving fast towards thirty. Many attractive young women had come his way but no one who engaged him in every possible way. He really wanted that. He wanted passion. He wanted magic. He wanted a woman to capture his imagination. Sadly no one ever had. He was beginning to wonder if anyone ever would.

That was what he wanted. He wanted the right woman to bring fulfilment to his existence. Not that he didn't have a good life. A very busy life, a privileged life, but he knew what he was missing. His mother and father had been greatly blessed with a love match. He had grown up in a happy, stable household fully aware of how much his parents loved one another and him. It greatly disturbed him now to realize he was only a nudge away from maybe wanting to be where Sonya Erickson was. No use telling himself it was because he needed to check her out for Marcus's sake. So where did that leave him?

In an impossible position, pal.

There lay the answer. His love for his uncle was deep. He could never be the one to hurt him. As for Sonya? Wouldn't it be natural for any young woman to be flattered by the attentions of an older, rich and distinguished man? Even have her head temporarily turned? The worrying thing was Ms Erickson revealed no such excitements. She was entirely in possession of herself when excitement, even joy, fitted much better. He was well advised to mistrust her. His allegiance was to Marcus.

The front door was open. He was about to call a hello when a young woman came into sight carrying a large crystal bowl filled with a profusion of beautiful flowers.

He didn't register the full array of blossoms, gerberas, lush roses, peonies, he was too busy concentrating on the young woman. She wore fitted jeans that showed off her lovely lissom figure and the length of her legs. A simple vest-type top did the same for her breasts. Her shimmering long hair, centre parted, fell down her back in thick sinuous coils.

Rapunzel.

She came to a halt, so clearly startled he might have been wearing a balaclava over his head.

"Don't drop it," he warned, swiftly moving towards her. The Ice Princess for some reason had totally lost her cool. "Hold on. I'll take it. Just don't *drop* it," he repeated the warning.

A visible shiver passed through her.

At least his tone was effective. "Let me have it."

He seemed to tower over her. *"David,"* she said, dismayed by the fact her normally composed voice was wavering.

His alternative name had never sounded so good, so intimate to his ears. He took the bowl from her, turning to place it on the rosewood library table that graced the entrance hall. "I startled you. I'm sorry." They were so close, barely a foot apart. He could see every little ripple along her throat as she swallowed. "Are you okay?' he asked. She appeared disorientated. This was a completely different Sonya from the one he had previously seen. Impossible as it seemed, she also looked frightened. Perhaps endangered was a better word?

Feeling very exposed, she tried to force herself back to attention. Her reaction had been a big mistake.

David, too, was feeling a degree of perturbation. His hand went to her sloping white shoulder. He meant only to steady her, but his fingers were bent on caressing her white skin, warm to his touch. This was no beautiful statue.

This was a living breathing woman. His eyes fell to the long heavy silk lock of her hair as it slid across his hand. He wanted to grasp a handful of it, pull her to him. He wanted to lower his head to capture her beautiful mouth that was surprisingly aquiver. He wanted to pick her up in his arms and carry her off like some caveman. Within seconds temptation after temptation was playing itself out. All common sense was getting away from him. This was mania. *Magic*, definitely black. She obviously had sirenlike powers. Fascinating men was a form of control. She could deliberately be luring him into her territory.

He stood back from her, the barriers springing back into place. "I'm sorry if I startled you. What are you doing here?" Given how he had *felt*, his voice sounded unnecessarily harsh. Was it guilt for slipping momentarily from his standards of behaviour?

For a moment she said nothing, giving her own protective shields a chance to get back into place. "Marcus has given me the job of doing the flowers for the house." She felt enormous relief some of her habitual cool composure had come back into her voice.

"I see. Where is Marcus?" he asked, looking down the spacious hallway with its beautiful parquetry floor towards the library. Marcus's favourite room.

"He's not here. But he should be home soon."

The way she spoke drove home the hurt. Did she think she could take Lucy's place? "I'll wait." The rush of sexual desire was replaced by hard distrust.

"Would you like a drink?" she asked, turning to lead him into the drawing room. "Coffee, something stronger?"

"I'm fine." He sounded just short of curt. "*You're* the one who looks like you could do with a stiff drink."

"You startled me, that's all."

"I might have been an intruder," he said, with more than a hint of sarcasm.

"Perhaps it was the quality of your own surprise," she returned. "You don't like or trust me." There was straightforward challenge in her voice.

"It's not a question of liking, Ms Erickson. It's more to do with your *role*."

"Back to Ms Erickson, no Sonya?" She arched her fine brows.

"Sonya is a lovely name." He shrugged. "Tell me, is it your *real* name?"

"What an extraordinary question."

She had come to stand beneath a nineteenth century Russian chandelier, one of a matched pair in the yellow, gold and Wedgwood blue drawing room. In front of the white Carrara marble fireplace he noted she had placed a huge Chinese fish bowl filled with a wealth of sweet-smelling flowers. To add to the impact the beautiful pastel colours mimicked the colours in the magnificent nineteenth century Meissen porcelain clock that took centre place on the mantelpiece beneath a very valuable landscape. Other small arrangements were placed around the large room, rivalling the treasures on display.

"And?"

"Of course it's my real name," she said, one hand pushing a thick lock of hair back off her shoulder.

The drawing room was all too feminine for his taste, too *opulent*, silks and brocades, but Sonya Erickson could have been made for it. Even in tight sexy jeans and designer vest-top she fitted in. It occurred to him with her hair worn long and loose and very little make-up she looked hardly more than a girl of nineteen or twenty.

He released a tense breath. "But what about the Erickson? Would you believe I actually knew a woman who changed her name four times? She's in jail now for fraud. She managed to extract the life savings from God knows how many fools of men."

"Please, don't make me weep!" she exclaimed. "Men *are* fools. But it's hardly fraudulent to change one's name by deed poll."

"Are you saying *you* have?'

She ignored his question. "Why don't you sit down?" she invited, with an elegant gesture of her hand.

"You might be in your own house," he answered, tightly. *Lucy's house.*

"Marcus has made me very welcome here." Her answer was equally pointed. "So you can't find out much about me. How disappointing for you. Is this what it's all about?"

"I came to see Marcus," he said. "I wasn't expecting *you*. Why don't you take the sofa?" he suggested. "I'll take the armchair. I know you're highly intelligent so we can cut to the chase. It's obvious my uncle has come to care deeply for you. And in a very short space of time. That presents problems, don't you agree?"

"Problems for *you*? I don't see the problem for me. Marcus is a lovely man. Was I supposed to submit my credentials to you? I might tell you Marcus has never asked anything of me. He trusts me."

His brilliant dark eyes flashed. "That's what I'm worried about. Who and what are you really, Sonya? What is it you want?"

"Who said I wanted anything?" she responded with an imperious lift of her brows. She took not the gold sofa, but a gilded armchair opposite him.

Sunlight was falling through the tall windows, filtered by the sheer central curtain. It illuminated her figure, making her hair and her beautiful skin radiant. "You were wearing

Aunt Lucy's diamond and emerald jewellery at the gala function," he said, the words freighted with meaning.

A flush like pink roses on snow warmed her cheeks. "Is there anything shameful about that? You're far too quick to place blame. Marcus *wanted* me to wear them. I could say insisted. He'd asked me the colour of my dress. When I said emerald green, he suggested a set of jewellery that needed an airing. I assure you the set is safely back in his safe."

It was too hard to resist. "Do you happen to know the combination?"

"Do *you*?" she shot back.

"I could open it blindfolded. I really don't want to offend you, Sonya."

"Then you couldn't be doing a better job," she said coldly, sitting very straight, long legs crossed neatly at the ankles.

Excellent deportment lessons there. "Your dress was exquisite, by the way. Did Marcus buy it for you?"

"Ah, the direct approach!" she said, looking down her finely cut nose at him. "I wore it because I had nothing better. Nor could I buy better. The dress is many years old."

He sat studying her. She appeared to be telling the truth.

"Vintage haute couture." She waved a hand.

"It looked it," he said, wanting to pierce her defences.

She shrugged a shoulder. "But you are not here to discuss my evening dress, which I might tell you belongs to me." She remembered her beautiful mother wearing it. But that was another time, another place, another world. A time when she had been happy.

"Actually I'm here to catch up with my uncle," he said,

breaking into her sad thoughts. "My love and loyalty is with him. You must understand that?"

She gave a light sceptical laugh. "Come now, you have no real right to interfere in his life, David. Marcus is a man in his fifties, a highly intelligent man."

"Who in all his adult years has never looked at another woman outside Lucy. Until now," he retorted sharply. "My big concern, Sonya, is that he doesn't get hurt. Extraordinarily enough Marcus is an innocent in his way. His health isn't all that good either. For years the whole family has been concerned he might simply die of a broken heart. That's how devoted he was to Lucy, his wife."

She flicked a platinum tendril off her heated cheek. "I understand the great pain of his loss. Marcus has told me many things about his beloved Lucy." She could tell him something of her own losses but her rigid sense of caution stopped her.

"Has he?" Another highly significant thing, he thought.

"Haven't you met anyone in your life you immediately identified with?" she asked, hostility in her beautiful green eyes.

He stared back at her, knowing he could never say he had identified with her. *On sight.*

"You won't be able to take Lucy's place, Sonya," he assured her. "No one will let you. You simply don't know what you're getting into. The Wainwright family is very powerful. You can't imagine how powerful. You wouldn't want to get them offside. You wouldn't want to embarrass them. *Family* is very important. So too is the Wainwright fortune. None of us would like to see a huge chunk of it going out of the family. We're all interconnected in business. You're far too young for Marcus. You know it. I know it. That said, many people would only see you in one way—as a woman on the make—and hate you for it."

"So what you're saying is, I couldn't possibly come up to your exalted standards?" she asked with surprisingly cool contempt. "Or is the fact Marcus is thirty years older the main objection?'

He showed his own anger. "If you were even twenty years older I doubt if I'd be saying any of this. You don't *love* Marcus, Sonya. Don't tell me you do."

"I wasn't about to tell you anything," she said icily. "The Wainwrights, who are they when it's all said and done? Billionaires? So what? That's not class, breeding, tradition. This nation is barely over two hundred years old. You're parvenus. Your English ancestor, Wainwright, only arrived in this country in the early eighteen hundreds, the flicker of an eyelid. Your family does *not* impress me."

"Evidently." He was somewhat taken aback by her remarks, yet amused. "So tell me about *your* illustrious family?" he challenged. "European aristocracy, were they? Counts and countesses a dime a dozen? Or haven't I given you sufficient time to get a really good story together? Maybe you're a fantasist? Where do you come from exactly? Is Erickson even your real name?"

"Maybe I change it," she said, sounding all of a sudden very foreign.

"Quite possible. My great-aunt Rowena thinks you have a slight Hungarian accent. She was married to a top British diplomat for many years. She knows Europe. She knows accents."

Her eyes blazed emerald. "Well, well, well! I can't find any other words."

"Surely it's not difficult for you to tell us something of your background? I'm ready to listen."

She stood up. "So sorry, David, but I'm not ready to

talk. Especially to *you.* You're very arrogant for so young a man."

He too rose to his feet, making her look small by comparison. "Beside you I'm an amateur," he said cuttingly.

Colour stained her high cheekbones. "You do not know the correct way to treat me."

"Or address you either. Should it be Contessa?" There was hard challenge in his strikingly handsome face.

"Who knows what might have been?" she said, then broke off abruptly, as if she had already volunteered too much. Her head tilted into a listening attitude. "That's Marcus now," she said thankfully, beginning to walk away from him. "I would not like him to find us arguing. Marcus is a very lonely man. He may think he's in love with me because I have green eyes. His Lucy had green eyes. I've no need to tell you that. Marcus loves you like his own son."

"So that gives me rights and obligations, doesn't it?" he answered tautly, tiring of her play-acting. "Lucy did have beautiful green eyes, but Lucy looked nothing like *you.* She didn't act like you either. She was a sweet, gentle woman, which by and large you *aren't.* What is it you're after?"

She turned to look at him with icy reserve. "I'm sorry, David. It seems to me that's none of your business. Now I must go and greet Marcus. You may not believe it, but I too want him to be happy."

He waited, resisting the urge to go to the window to witness the quality of the greeting. Moments later Marcus came into the living room, a spring in his step. He was looking better than he had looked for ages. There was colour in his skin, a brightness in his eyes. Marcus is a good man, he thought with a lunge of the heart. He deserves another chance at happiness. Only he wasn't going to stand by and allow a young woman who rebuffed any attempt to invade her privacy to damage their close loving relationship. What did she have to hide anyway? Ultimately her background would have to come out.

"David, I'm so glad you called in." Marcus bounded forward to seize his nephew's hand.

"I've missed seeing you," David responded. "Sonya has been looking after me."

"Wonderful. Wonderful!" Marcus enthused, drawing Sonya forward, his kind, distinguished face alight with pleasure. "I do so want you two to get to know each other better."

There was an unintended warning in that. He knew beyond doubt he had to forbid himself all and any erotic thoughts of Sonya Erickson. He couldn't possibly be the one to break his uncle's heart. On the other hand Ms Erickson, with all her barriers in place, would have to open up about her past.

Twenty minutes later Holt left. He had accepted one drink, Scotch over ice. He was driving and he was a guest at a dinner party that night. His emotions were in turmoil. He hadn't planned on any of this, but there was no avoiding the bitter truth now. Despite his very real concerns, he had become powerfully attracted to Sonya Erickson, if that was her real name. For the first time in his ordered life, he was losing his footing. No comfort to be drawn from that. The worst aspect was he knew he wouldn't give a damn who or what she was if she was the woman he wanted. She was in fact the *only* woman who had ever made such an impact on him. A different order altogether from his usual girlfriends. And there was Marcus looking better than he had looked in years. Marcus wanting he and Sonya to be *friends*.

God, what a mess!

If Sonya Erickson were truly in love with Marcus he would have to accept their marrying, whatever his private misgivings. But the beautiful Sonya, though obviously fond of Marcus—who could *not* be?—was *not* in love with him. Why was he so sure? Disturbing to know he could take her off Marcus whether she wanted it or not. Mutual attraction was very hard to hide. She was as attracted to him as he was to her. It hadn't crept up on them. In one of those sad ironies of life the attraction had been immediate. Neither had chosen the time. Now it was starting to take a heavy toll. Better they had never met. For an enigmatic young woman who presented herself as emotionally detached, what had drawn her to Marcus?

Apart from the money? said his cynical inner voice.

What had caused her to let down her guard? Marcus's essential goodness, his kindness, his courtly manner. More importantly Marcus would never pry. She had told him that herself. Did she want above anything a secure place in the world? Marcus could give her that. Did she fear being swept off her feet by some driving passion that could upset all her plans? She definitely had issues. Not a whole lot of trust in people. He'd already concluded it all had to do with her past life. Did a great need to be *safe* drive her? He was fast reaching the conclusion she was on the run from something. *Someone?* How would that impact on Marcus's plans?

There were too many question marks hanging over Ms Erickson's head. One thing was very clear. She was an extremely fast worker. She could be the second Mrs Marcus Wainwright if she so wanted. One heard of May/December marriages all the time. But in just about every case, the man was rich. He didn't like it. He didn't like it at all. He needed to talk to Rowena.

* * *

When he arrived at his apartment he rang Rowena to say he would be coming to Sunday lunch. Rowena always kept a marvellous table. More importantly, he and Rowena could keep an eye on proceedings and later confer.

"All right if I bring Paula?" he asked. "I know you're not fussed on her."

"Protection, dearest, is that it?"

He grimaced to himself. "I don't want to be seen to be using Paula. She'd actually love to be invited."

"Doesn't answer the question, dear."

"Marcus is madly in love with her, Rowena," he said firmly. "I was at the house this afternoon. Sonya was there, putting flowers all around the place."

"I bet they looked wonderful," Rowena's cultured voice fluted down the phone.

"She does have the genius touch. Did you know about this recent development?"

"Matter of fact I did. Sonia had some marvellous bromeliad stems for me. Wonderful to see with just a large green leaf hanging over the side."

"Rowena dear, I'm sure the bromeliads looked inspirational," he said edgily, "but what I most want to talk about is this. What is Sonya up to? She *knows* Marcus is in love with her. Can you really say with any degree of confidence a marriage between them might work, given the thirty-year leap? She could divorce him and get a hefty settlement. Break Marcus's heart. That's a huge worry."

"It's possible, my darling, but who is able to predict a marriage?"

"Now there's a cop out if ever there was one," he exclaimed. "She's won you over as well. You and Rolly had a great marriage. So do Mum and Dad."

"Ah, then, your mother had a great deal of money. So

did I. No one could ever have accused us of being fortune hunters. Makes things a lot easier."

"Mum is *four* years younger than Dad," he pointed out.

"My lovely Rolly was twelve years older than me."

"The perfect gentleman."

"He was indeed."

"You all brought a great deal to one another," he said. "What is Sonya going to bring to Marcus?"

Rowena chuckled. Over-long.

"Okay, okay, but is she in it for short term gain, Rowena? I'd love to look on the positive side, but I couldn't bear to see Marcus humiliated. She doesn't love him. That's the pity. But she does have him wrapped around her little finger. He's happy at the moment. Really happy. I have to say it's lovely to see."

Rowena abruptly sobered. "I'm as concerned as you are, David. For both of them. You know, dear, I've come to the conclusion Sonya is carrying a burden she can't lay down. Despite that poise of hers, the high-born air, she seems to me a little lost."

"Lost?" For a moment he thought he might lose it entirely. "She's as switched on as they come."

"Lighten up, love," Rowena advised. "I know how much you love Marcus. You've always looked up to him. You have heart. You're also very perceptive. I do realize the developing situation had to be taken very seriously. I'm with you there. Marcus, up until he met Sonya, has acted as though all happiness had passed him by."

"It's a dilemma, isn't it?" he said. "Marcus is the one who stands to be hurt. Even if a marriage did take place, marriages end. A beautiful young woman with a large settlement could move on. Marcus would not. We both know that."

"Yes indeed," Rowena quietly agreed.

"We can expect fireworks from Dad and Mum. Dad especially. He loves his brother. Dad will want Sonya thoroughly checked out. Even then he wouldn't approve. Neither would Mum. You know what they're like. You know what the family is like. They'll condemn her right off as a fortune hunter and a fake."

"Well, she's not faking the patrician air," Rowena said in strong defence of the young woman she had come to like and admire.

"She's a mystery woman indeed," David answered, very, very dryly.

"There's a story there, my darling. But not a happy one, I'm sure."

"It makes a lot of women happy marrying a millionaire," he pointed out.

"In a lot of cases it doesn't work out marrying for love," she countered. "I hear the Grantleys are divorcing. How long ago was it we were at the wedding?"

"Not long enough for them to open the wedding presents," he said. "So, see you Sunday."

"Looking forward to it."

Problems. Problems. Problems, Rowena thought as she hung up.

Was it possible beautiful young Sonya was in some way flawed? Had she a plan in mind? Marcus could offer her the good life, but would she be content for long with that? And what did Sonya think of David? She felt deeply troubled now. David was a marvellous young man. She couldn't count the number of women young and old who had succumbed to David's extraordinary charm. David had everything going for him. Sonya would be a rare woman if she didn't feel his attraction. So what *did* Sonya think of David? On Sunday she would make it her business to find out.

CHAPTER THREE

WHAT *am I doing? Where am I going with my life? I was coping well enough. Now I feel utter confusion.*

She often got caught up in conversations with herself. Sonya sat in front of her mirror while she put in her earrings. These days all she could seem to focus on was David Wainwright and the mounting tensions and difficulties springing up between them. She wanted to stop thinking about him, but his image was so compelling he broke again and again into her consciousness, no matter how hard she tried to keep up the barricades. She had the dismal feeling her past life with its tragedies had damaged her. Well, she was damaged, she admitted, but *for ever*? That was a frightening prognosis.

Maintain the distance. Maintain the emotional barriers. You need no more complications in life.

There was no getting away from the voice in her head. Everyone had one, but, her being so much alone in life since the tender age of sixteen, her inner voice only got stronger. David Wainwright's mental image was so persistent, so vivid, for the first time in her life she understood how dangerous powerful sexual attraction could be. It played havoc with one's control. And he was coming to Lady Palmerston's buffet lunch!

You'll be seeing him again! Oh, sweet Lord! Forget the man.

Only her senses were exquisitely, excruciatingly sharpened. She realized to her dismay it was affecting her normal behaviour. Only how did one stop the mix of excitement and panic that stormed through her? She needed to block both emotions. A woman's weakness only gave a man power. She didn't want any man to dominate her thoughts, let alone her life. She wanted peace, peace, *peace.* A mature man, who had suffered himself, could give her that. Peace was important, a sense of being protected. God knew she'd had little of it in her fraught life. At twenty-five, she was still in recovery. At least that was how she thought of it.

Recovery.

Her history was a tragic one. But no one must know it. Not yet. When it came down to it meeting the Wainwrights had only complicated her life. She had to decide what she needed to do next. In less than half an hour, Marcus would be picking her up in his chauffeured Bentley. Marcus was a true gentleman, noble of character, much as her father had been. It would be a sin to lead Marcus on yet she knew she could have a real life with Marcus. No dramas. No concealing her true identity. She would have security. The age difference didn't really bother her. Or it hadn't until she had met Marcus's nephew, David. Waves of emotion started to wash over her…

God, if you're up there, you have to help me! I've no one else to call on.

Her parents had died very tragically in a car crash, ten years before. Only the crash had been engineered. She knew by whom. He would never do it himself. He would never be brought to justice. He lived in far-off America. But he had the power, the connections and the money to organize a hit even across continents. There would never be a mention of his name in connection with the tragic event. Laszlo had many friends in high places, even if he had many more enemies. But they couldn't get to him. Like the Wainwrights, Laszlo was a billionaire with huge international interests in oil and steel.

And she had something he wanted very badly. The Andrassy Madonna. A precious icon that had been in the family since the seventeenth century. Up until recent times Laszlo had believed the Madonna, fashioned by medieval craftsmen—her robes and headpiece studded with diamonds, rubies, emeralds and seed pearls—had disappeared into the hands of the invading Russians when the estate was pillaged at the end of the Second World War. Laszlo's father, Karoly, had done the wise thing gathering up his family and what he could of his fortune and fleeing Europe for the United States and safety. There, he became enormously rich again.

Her great-grandfather had stayed to the death. His eldest son, Matthias, the heir, had elected to stay with his father, resisting all pleas to make his escape. It was her grandmother, Katalin, who, as a little girl, had been the one to escape with the help of a loyal family servant. Her great-grandfather and her great-uncle had been taken prisoners and never seen or heard of again. It was a tragic story repeated all over war-torn Europe and Russia.

But the Madonna believed to be lost for ever was in her possession. Proof of her identity. It gave her power, but offered no immunity against Laszlo. Rather the reverse. Possession put her in danger. After the Berlin Wall came down the estate had been returned to the Andrassy-Von Neumann family, albeit in ruins. Laszlo claimed to be the rightful heir and gained possession of the estate, when she was the rightful heir. Only she would never make her claim. Never be in a position to make it. Laszlo would get rid of her before he allowed her to take anything he considered belonged to him. She would be just another young woman to go missing never to be seen again. Laszlo was a powerful man with all the money and a team of lawyers. She had neither. She had long since learned Might was Right. Not the other way around. Laszlo had been pumping a great deal of money into the country of his birth, buying influence and friends in high places. Many of the valuable stolen paintings and artifacts had been returned to him, but the thing Laszlo most wanted was the Andrassy Madonna.

And she had it. The *one* thing her grandmother had been able to spirit out of a war-torn Hungary.

She shook herself out of her dark, disturbing memories. For a short but intense period of her life, she had found herself in enemy territory, struggling to get by with no one close to trust. The risks had been compounded by her sex. A good-looking young girl on her own was considered fair game. Here in this country of such peace and freedom she was getting herself together. She regretted some of the things she had said to David Wainwright, especially the bit about his family being parvenus. One of her tempestuous moments. She'd thought she had learned to override them, but contact with David only made her painfully aware the wide range of emotions of her preadolescent years, when she had such wonderful parental care, were reforming.

For the occasion she had mixed two pieces she liked and felt confident in: a lovely apricot silk shirt with the sleeves pushed up, tucked into a great pair of cream silk-cotton trousers. She had settled on a wide deep pink and cream leather belt to sling around her waist. The belt pulled the outfit together. Several long dangly necklaces, pretty but inexpensive, around her neck, a striking silk scarf patterned in apricot, pink and chocolate, to tie back her long hair at the nape. She had a good cream leather shoulder bag to go with the outfit. The latest in high-heeled sandals. She knew Paula Rowlands would be there. If the Valentino David's girlfriend had worn at the gala was anything to go on she knew how to dress. She wondered how serious the relationship might be. It wasn't intense or she would have noticed. But money married money. Everyone knew that. Passion waned. Money handled wisely just grew and grew.

Lady Palmerston's residence was situated in the most elite location in the entire country, nestling as it did between beautiful blue bays with breathtaking views of the Harbour Bridge and the Opera House. Marcus had told her on the drive over David had a penthouse apartment less than five minutes away. Maybe he often walked over to visit his great aunt. She realized if one had to enquire how much properties like these were worth, one didn't have and would never have the money to afford them. Now she had an extremely wealthy man as a good friend. She knew she could make something come of it. A lot of women regarded marrying a rich man as a goal in life. Could she? She and Marcus were moving inexorably into another stage of their relationship. Falling in love with his nephew was *unthinkable*.

Yet her grandmother had been born in a palace. No fantasy, the truth. Sonya had never dared visit the magnificent Andrassy-Von Neumann estate but she had been shown many old books and seen the photographs of it taken before the Second World War broke out in Europe. She had studied them over and over, awestruck. Her grandmother had been born in a fairy-tale palace? The palace looked like something out of a dream. But the dream had been destroyed. She knew the estate had been taken over by the advancing Russian army in 1945. The stately palace had been left a wreck and its great tracts of valley with its lake, trees and wonderful gardens and glorious statuary left in ruin and rubble. All of the statues of gods and goddesses, water nymphs and the like had been used for target practice. Many act of senseless revenge, the glass in all the windows smashed. Inside the great house the grand collections of family crystal, glass and handmade porcelains. The valuable paintings had been declared sacrosanct. They had been carefully wrapped up and taken away.

War.

Was there ever going to be an end to it? She thought, *Never.* Life took some momentous turns. There were countless stories of reversals of fortune down through the ages. The Czar and his family who had lived in splendour had died in horrifying circumstances. The last Emperor of China had lived out his life as a market gardener. Her beautiful dispossessed grandmother had died relatively early, with a broken heart that had never mended. Her mother, taught both Hungarian and German at her mother's knee, had sailed through her days like a swan on a lake, with perfect composure, but it was a composure that masked her deep, deep grief.

She had told Marcus none of this. Marcus didn't even know her real name. As she had told David, Marcus didn't pry. She knew he was waiting for her to confide in him, but she had built such walls of defence. Talking about her past would be accompanied by an inrush of pain. No one need know her traumas. All these long years no one outside her grandmother, her parents, now herself had laid eyes on the Madonna. She had not been allowed to see the Madonna herself until her sixteenth birthday. That had been two short weeks before her parents had been so cruelly killed.

Always remember Laszlo is out there to do you harm.

Memories of her mother's green eyes looking into hers,

her mother's patrician hand stroking her long blonde hair. Good blood was in the genes.

The man past his first youth who wanted her had given her the news of their death, trying to take her into his arms, but she had resisted wildly, even so young recognising the erotic undercurrent in the family relationship. It was a terrifying thing to be left so powerless. She had waited and planned. Then she had disappeared. From that moment on always on the run. It was the equivalent of being turned out on the streets.

The buffet tables set up in the air-conditioned indoors were draped in spotless white linen, and laden with delectable food. In passing Sonya saw whole seared salmons, ocean trout, stacks of oysters, prawns galore, sea scallops, lobsters and delicious little "bugs". There was also carved grain-fed lamb for those who liked a mix; warm salads, cold salads, potato salads, all the accompaniments. It could feed a Third World country.

The guest list was for a party of twenty. Four large glass-topped rectangular tables shaded by royal blue, white-fringed umbrellas were in place for al fresco dining. One could choose indoors or out, though the informal living room with its white marble floor and largely white furnishings was open to the broad terrace with its white canopy by way of a series of foldaway glass doors that brought the spectacular view in.

They were greeted warmly by Rowena, who led them out onto a sun-drenched terrace where the guests who had already arrived were assembled enjoying a glass of whatever they fancied, served by two handsome young man in jaunty uniforms that featured very dashing waist-length fitted jackets. Sonya recognised the logo of the excellent catering company Rowena had employed. She herself had provided the wealth of prize blooms, including some exquisite lotus blossoms, along with a generous amount of assorted leaves for Lady Palmerston to arrange herself. Lady Palmerston was as passionate about flowers as she was.

Smiles on all sides. Warm hellos. Nice to meet you. Some of the older ladies she knew. They were now her clients, thanks to their hostess. Mercifully Paula Rowlands's antagonism wasn't on display. Not yet anyway. Though Paula soon turned back to resume her conversation with her own kind of people.

Sonya watched as David Wainwright hugged his uncle. They were very close. There was no one to hug her like that any more. No family who had been out to look after her, just exploit her. When the moment came, David Wainwright all but shocked her by bending his handsome dark head to lightly brush her cheek. A couple of seconds only, yet she felt the thrill of it right down to her toes. When she looked up, his brilliant glance was hooded. It was obvious he wanted only happiness for his uncle, and just as obvious he didn't see her as any sort of a solution.

Marcus had been drawn away for a moment by two of his old chums, Dominic and Elizabeth Penry-Evans, one a Supreme Court judge, the wife an eminent barrister. David turned to her, his tone friendly, but laced with challenge. "How nice to see you here, Sonya."

"Very pleased to be here, David." She gave him a cool little smile. No need for him to know she was trying to slow her quickened breath. "This has to be one of the most glorious views on earth," she said, looking across the turquoise swimming pool to the sparkling blue harbour with its view of the famous Coat Hanger, the Sydney Harbour Bridge, and the world famous Opera House with its glittering white sails. "I believe you live only a short distance away?"

He was wrestling with an overpowering urge to pull at the silk scarf that tied back her beautiful hair. He wanted to see it loose and blowing, cascading around her face and over her shoulders. It was wonderful hair. "No doubt you will see my apartment some time," he said, adopting a careless tone.

"No urgency." She remained looking out over the spectacular view.

"I don't actually know where *you* live," he said. "But we can't forget you're something of a mystery woman."

She turned back, lifting her chin.

It was an amazingly imperious gesture, he thought. A simple lift of the chin? Who *was* this woman? One thing was certain: she had gone to great lengths to hide her background.

"Of course you do," she said. "It's a wonder I haven't stumbled over one of your spies."

He gave her a twisted smile. "Maybe spying is a very harsh word. Just a little checking."

"So you know I don't live in your part of town." The air around them seemed to be vibrating like the beating wings of a hummingbird.

"Well, maybe down a notch," he said lightly.

"How kind."

"You do admit to a chip on your shoulder, Sonya?" He knew he should move away from her. Only he couldn't. He really *couldn't.* He saw it as a blow to his self-control.

"I admit to a chip on *both* shoulders," she responded with mocking sweetness. "But it has nothing to do with not having a lot of money, or not moving in your illustrious circles, David."

How good his name on her lips sounded. No one else said it the same way. He got Holt from his mother. She *was* a Holt and never let anyone forget it. "Surely there's a strong possibility that's all going to change?"

"You'll be the first to know, David," she said scathingly.

"Marcus is already in love with you. But it's not *you*, Sonya, I'm worried about. You're obviously a young woman who knows how to look after herself."

Her emerald eyes flashed like jewels in the sunlight. "Is that so strange? Women have had to fight long and hard for independence, recognition. And the fight isn't over."

"And you've had to fight very hard to be strong?" It could explain so much about her.

"What woman doesn't?" she said scornfully, clearly on the defensive.

"Why so hostile, Sonya?" he asked. "Has some man really hurt you?" He found he badly wanted to know. She had presented her lovely profile so he couldn't look into her eyes. He had to face the fact he had an ever-growing need to discover all there was to know about this young woman.

For Marcus, or for yourself?

He felt shamed by the thought. For God's sake, she was here with Marcus.

"I have met threatening, difficult and a few terrifying men," she said, almost tonelessly. "Does that answer your question? I dare say there would be many women who could say the same. Battered, abused women who never saw it coming. I feel truly secure with Marcus."

His brows knotted in a frown. "And the feeling of security needs to be locked into your relationships?"

"Exactly." She stood motionless, her head turned away from him.

"So in a different situation where you could fall madly in love you would regard yourself as being under threat?"

She was startled by how he had hit on a problematic area. Her lack of trust in men. "Falling in love is a kind of madness, surely?" she parried. "Who can say being madly in love is essential to a good marriage? There are other very worthwhile things. So why don't you let Marcus worry about himself, David? He's a grown man. Or is it the *money*? Are you his heir?"

"Careful, Sonya," he warned.

"Touched a raw nerve, have I?" She turned back to him then, her beautiful eyes frankly mocking.

"If you're looking for raw nerves, you haven't found it," he said curtly. He was in fact the main beneficiary of Marcus's will.

"But then you're a man who doesn't get frazzled easily," she said. "But it's not nonsense entirely. It's often said, no one can have too much money."

"It's also said money can't guarantee happiness." He cut her off tersely.

"Maybe not, but it can guarantee wonderful houses to live in, superb views." She waved an elegant hand. "The best cars, yachts." Wonderful yachts with billowing sails were out on the sparkling blue water. "I'm told you're a fine yachtsman. Then there are clothes, jewels. You name it. Everything pretty well comes down to money."

"And you want it?"

"What I want is a pleasant day," she retorted, ultra cool.

"Of course you do," he said suavely. "I apologise. You must be pleased your fame with flowers has spread far and wide. Liz over there with Marcus has been into your shop. Two of Rowena's friends now present. Rowena, of course. She told me you provided all the very beautiful flowers for today?"

It was too much not to look at him. She felt compelled.

He was wearing a dark blue and white striped casual shirt of best quality cotton, beautifully cut white linen trousers, navy loafers on his feet. His polished skin was tanned to bronze, against which his fine teeth showed very white. He could have posed for a Ralph Lauren shoot, she thought wryly. "I've worked hard to secure the best sources," she said, with a touch of pride.

"I expect Paula will be next to pay you a visit." It was a taunt really. Unworthy of him.

"Please God, *no*!" she said with a charming little gesture of her hands.

"Hello? Does this mean you don't like her?"

"Do *you*?" She shot him a glance as cool and clear as crystal.

His expression turned sardonic. "I've adored her since childhood."

"Then clearly I've overestimated you."

He couldn't help it. He laughed aloud.

It was such an engaging laugh it caused the guests to look in their direction to smile. David Wainwright was a great favourite.

"That's very naughty of you, Sonya. And you the Ice Princess."

"I never said I was a nice person," she countered, not lightly, but with a hint of warning.

"Maybe I bring out the worst in you?" he asked. Her skin in the bright sunlight was as flawless as a baby's. One could become enslaved by a woman like this. He would do well to heed the warning.

"Well, you do give it your best shot." She paused, her tone changing. "Your girlfriend is on the way over."

He didn't turn his head. "I don't remember saying Paula was my girlfriend."

"I don't remember saying Marcus was my man friend," she returned sharply.

Paula Rowlands was not so much strolling as striding up to them. No doubt she was fuelled by the feline need to protect her territory, Sonya thought. "Here she comes. Hostility writ large upon her face. It must have been triggered by your laughing. It sounded too much like you were enjoying yourself."

He let his eyes run over her. "Actually, Sonya, I *was*."

Throughout the leisurely meal Rowena asked them to shift to different tables so everyone got an opportunity to speak to all the other guests. Sonya found herself having a delightful time. She had come prepared for undercover distrust; instead she might have been among friends. Of course she wasn't obviously paired with Marcus. On the contrary she was treated as a free spirit. That was exactly what she wanted. Every time she sat at table with David Wainwright every nerve in her body flared into life. It was as if she were made of highly flammable tissue paper and his nearness set her alight.

A very pretty, chic young woman called Camilla Carstairs was especially friendly. They arranged to meet up for coffee midweek. Camilla promised to come into the shop. "I've heard so much about it, Sonya. The flowers today are amazingly beautiful." Sonya found herself warming to such friendliness. She found out later, Camilla was the only daughter of "Mack" Carstairs, the trucking king.

After lunch the older couples retired to the house, while the younger guests remained outside or took strolls around the landscaped garden, an oasis of beauty and peace. A few ventured down to the turquoise swimming pool at the harbour's edge. Though Sonya had been seated at times with Paula Rowlands, Paula had had very little to say to her. Now Paula intended to change all that. She detached herself from a small group that did not include David Wainwright. He appeared to have gone inside. Meanwhile Paula made a beeline for Sonya, calling out her name.

"Yoo-hoo, Sonya, wait for me." She waved enthusiastically.

Here comes trouble, said the voice in Sonya's head.

And it wasn't wrong.

Paula, the very picture of friendliness, linked her arm through Sonya's as though they were bosom pals. Immediately it put Sonya back on guard.

"When did *this* happen?" she asked lightly, resisting the urge to pull away.

"What happen?" Paula widened her eyes.

"A big turnaround comes to mind." Sonya smiled.

Paula gave a laugh that was not reflected in her eyes. "Walk on with me," she said. "I *need* to talk to you."

"Sounds a bit like you need something to calm you more," Sonya offered wryly. She was well aware of Paula's seething jealousy.

"Ah, the little witticisms!" Paula tried to pull Sonya along.

Stand still. You could be looking at pandemonium here.

Sonya obeyed her inner voice. "I really think you can say whatever it is you want to say right here, Paula." The blue glitter of the water was all around them. A fairly strong breeze was blowing in, whipping at Sonya's silk scarf. "Is something the matter?"

Paula pealed another laugh. There they were, the two of them enjoying a jolly time. "You're becoming too friendly with Holt." Paula came right to the point, her voice pitched low, but her eyes brimming with strong emotion. "I'll go a step further. I believe you're deliberately trying to take him off me."

Some imp of mischief made her say, "I wish!" Unwise.

"Then you *are*?" Paula showed her outrage.

"I'm joking, Paula. Just a little joke." Sonya backed off. "Look, why don't you speak to David about your concerns?"

"David? *David*!" Paula sounded almost violent. "His name is Holt."

"Surely that's a nickname he was given as a child?" Sonya said. "I like David better."

"*You* like!" Paula's voice had turned into a croak. "Most people call him Holt. His mother is—"

"I know, the Holt heiress." Sonya nodded calmly. "I suppose if I did a quick whip around I'd find you're all staggeringly rich."

"Indeed we are!" Paula's face registered contempt. "And you the florist!"

"Is that meant to downgrade me? You merely sound a snob. I'm a very good florist as it happens. You can order over the phone. In fact, if you're looking for work in very pleasant surroundings, I might be able to put some your way. I understand you don't have a job." She was beyond anger. She just wanted to get away from this jealous young woman.

It took a decided wrench to get her arm back, though she tried not to make it obvious to anyone who might be watching. Her back to the pool, she didn't realize she was now standing too close to the edge. Paula kept her eyes so fixed on her, she might have been attempting hypnosis.

"The big difference between you and me, Ms Erickson, is I don't have to work. You envy me. I know you do. I can't blame you. I've got everything you want. Everything you'll never get." She spoke quite threateningly. "Remember, I'm watching you."

From long practice, Sonya was able to keep a rein on her own temper. "Do you suppose that bothers me?" she asked coolly.

Colour mottled Paula's cheeks. "It should! I'm in a position to make things go rather badly for you."

"I'm supposed to take that as a threat?"

"Take it any way you like," Paula said sharply. "Doesn't it make you happy you've got poor old Marcus wrapped around your little finger?"

"Happy? It makes me ecstatic." Sonya felt reduced to black humour. "Is *that* want you want to hear?"

Paula sucked in her breath, looking aghast. "So you admit it! I think it's absolutely loathsome what you're doing. You're nothing but a gold-digger."

"You should stop listening to gossip, Paula. And might I remind you I'm a guest here, just like you." How did she get rid of this woman? She was fully aware she was looking into the face of raw jealousy. Jealousy was a malignancy. It ate into the soul. "Do you think we might call a truce here and now, Paula?" she suggested, in a conciliatory voice. "You surely can't want a scene? You'll be upsetting Lady Palmerston."

"Like you're *not*?" Paula challenged, fiercely affronted by the suggestion they were equals. "Rowena and Holt are right onto you. That's why you've been invited. So they can keep an eye on you. Holt told me. He tells me everything. We all know who's doing the upsetting." Paula stepped nearer. Oddly there was a smile on her face.

A warning should have lit up like a neon sign. Sonya knew in an instant she had backed up dangerously close to the edge of the pool. But the speed with which she pitched backwards into the water stunned her. Gulps of it went down her throat. The pool water was surprisingly cold, to her shocked body near *freezing.* It closed over her head, locking her in its shining blue depths. The impact drained her whole body of strength. Panic flooded into her brain. She was flailing helplessly.

Her inner voice kicked in, giving her orders.

Lift up your arms. Kick your legs. Stroke upwards. Come on. You can do it.

She felt her sandals slide off her feet. Her clothes, even her long hair, were holding her down. With a huge effort she shot to the surface, water streaming off her head. She had time to catch an agonised half-breath, then she went down again, her heart pounding. This time she had the sense to clamp her mouth shut.

The embarrassing part was, she couldn't swim. How humiliating was that? She had never learned like any four-year-old Australian child how to swim.

Poolside, Paula, in tears now, was screaming for help. Sonya could hear the scream reverberating underwater. Paula hadn't pushed her. Paula hadn't touched her. Paula had simply manoeuvred her nearer the edge. Her high heels and loss of balance had done the rest. She couldn't possibly drown. There were too many people around. Anyone who said the drowning process was euphoric had it all wrong.

Next thing she knew a solid body was in the water with her. A strong arm arced out and grabbed her. The arm easily reeled her in. She clung to her rescuer, barely seeing him with the water in her eyes. But she knew who it was even before their heads hit the surface.

David.

Her chin was at water level.

"Spit it out. Spit the water out," he ordered, gripping her tight. "It's okay. I've got you."

She did as she was told.

"Good girl. You'll be fine now."

"Oh, my God!" She couldn't help herself. She moaned. Other guests crossed her vision. All wore anxious faces. No one was laughing.

"It's all right, Sonya," David assured her. "You can't swim?"

Instead of answering his question she found herself saying quite tartly, "I wasn't planning on going in the water."

His smile flashed. "Good. You sound more like yourself."

A young man called Raymond, who had been very attentive to Sonya during the afternoon, crouched over, reaching out an arm. "I'll take her from here, Holt."

"Thanks, Ray."

While Raymond and another young man hauled Sonya out of the water, Holt dived to the bottom of the pool to retrieve Sonya's high-heeled sandals. Then when he surfaced he passed them to a distressed Rowena while he heaved himself out. He had rid himself of his own shoes before taking his unscheduled dive.

Rowena and Marcus were on hand, both looking upset, holding up towelling robes. One pink. One navy. "Here, dear girl, put this on," Rowena urged, holding out the pink robe with such kindness tears sprang to Sonya's eyes. Marcus was busy helping his nephew into the navy robe, which David used to towel over his water-sleeked dark head.

"Come into the house," Rowena bid Sonya quietly. "We'll get you dry."

Sonya began apologizing. "I'm so sorry for spoiling such a lovely day, Lady Palmerston. I was standing too near the edge. I slipped. I can't swim unfortunately."

"I'll teach you," Ray called out with enthusiasm. Even

sopping, Sonya looked *glorious*. A real erotic turn-on. The silk shirt was plastered to her high breasts, revealing peaked nipples and darkish pink aureole.

"Poor old you!" Camilla moved in closer to rub Sonya's back consolingly. "But look at it this way. You're not the first person to take an unexpected header into that pool. Paula should have known better. Where is she anyway?" Camilla turned her glossy head.

"I expect she's upset," Sonya heard herself saying, modestly pulling her soaked shirt away from her breasts.

"Like we all care!" Camilla whispered in Sonya's ear. "Want me to come with you?"

Sonya tried a smile. "Thanks, Camilla, but I'll be fine once I'm out of these wet things."

Inside the house Marcus studied Sonya very intently. "I do so wish that hadn't happened to you, my dear. You slipped?"

He appeared so shaken, Sonya reached out a gentle hand to stroke his cheek. "A silly accident, Marcus. Not to worry."

"I wish I could believe that." His distinguished face looked decidedly unhappy.

"It was an accident, Marcus," she stressed, painfully aware she was dripping pool water all over the floor. "Let it go."

Marcus glanced over to where Rowena, head bent, was having a few quiet words with David. "I'll get you home," Marcus said.

"But you've been so enjoying yourself," she protested. "It's been a lovely afternoon. I like to see you so relaxed. You would have to call your chauffeur back."

Marcus shook his head. "That's not a problem. It's his job."

Rowena walked quickly over to them. "I've suggested to David he take you home, Sonya. He wants to go now. He'll take you if you're happy with that?"

David too moved back towards them, addressing his uncle. "It's no problem, Marcus, to drop Sonya off. I expect, like me, she wants to go. Your chauffeur will take a good thirty minutes to make the return journey. Rowena would like you to stay on a while longer."

Sonya began to finger comb her long wet hair. "Yes, please stay, Marcus," she urged, though Marcus looked most undecided. "The last thing I want is for a silly accident to ruin your day. I'll ring you this evening. Promise."

"Please," Marcus answered.

So it was arranged.

CHAPTER FOUR

THEY were out on the open road, the big car moving soundlessly except for the soft purr of the air conditioning. Neither of them had said anything for a full five minutes but all sorts of sparks were flying, each trying to envision what was on the other's mind. Sonya was wearing a brand-new pink tracksuit Lady Palmerston had provided her with. David's tracksuit was pearl grey. Obviously outfits like theirs were kept on hand for guests.

"I have an idea that wasn't an accident." David was the one to break the silence, his expression on the grim side. He had seen through Paula's Academy-Award-winning performance.

Sonya shook her head. Her hair was billowing madly from the dip in the pool water, but it was almost dry after a few minutes with a hairdryer. Lady Palmerston's Filipina maid, Maria, had attended her, taking charge of her wet clothes, except for her bra and briefs, which had been popped in the dryer so she could put them back on. "Entirely my fault," she said.

"Camilla told me you were standing with Paula."

"You can safely rule out any push." She had seen the accusation in Camilla's eyes, heard it in her voice, so it wasn't difficult to guess what Camilla had told him.

"Can I now?" he asked, tersely shooting a quick glance at her.

"What happened to Paula anyway? Surely you didn't leave her behind?"

"Paula came in her own car. She went home in it too. Very upset, or so she made it appear."

"Poor Paula!" she dryly commiserated.

"Give me a break!" he retorted. "Paula pushed you."

"Paula never laid a finger on me," she said firmly. "Though I certainly didn't make that spectacular jump on purpose. Paula and I had a few words. It made me less cautious around the pool."

"So, then, it was a planned manoeuvre?"

"I never said that at all."

"You're being very gracious," he offered.

"It comes very easily to me."

"Those aristocratic genes for sure," he pointed out sardonically. "Anyway, I must apologize."

She half smiled. "I enjoy hearing you apologize."

"I thought you might. What were you talking about anyway?"

She stared through the window at the beautiful day. People were out and about in their numbers, enjoying the sunshine and their naturally beautiful city with its magnificent blue harbour. They were passing a small park, a lovely sanctuary of mature shade trees and broad stretches of lush green grass. Children were playing around a central fountain, others had claimed the swings, attended by their doting parents. One little girl in a pretty dress patterned with delicate wildflowers waved joyfully at her. Sonya waved back, a tender smile on her face.

"*You*, would you believe?" she said and gave a faint laugh.

He groaned, shooting her another quick glance. She looked ravishing with her white-gold mane draped like luminous curtains around her face and falling down her back. The pink of the tracksuit was perfect against her white skin. "So are you going to tell me?"

"No."

He responded with a crooked smile. "If I say please?"

She shook her head. "You don't *need* to know. But I will tell you this. She believes I'm a *gold-digger*. Her words, echoing yours."

"A woman as beautiful as you doesn't have to do a damn thing. Much less dig," he said crisply. "Marcus is one thing. But why would *I* come into the conversation?"

"My dear David," she answered with supreme nonchalance, "the woman would *kill* for you."

"I assume you're joking?" There was a decided edge to his voice.

"You should have a word with her," she suggested. "It's not every day a girl has *two* Wainwrights to choose from. She said I was—wait for it—after *you* as well!"

"She *didn't*." He almost cringed. It was up to him now to put Paula straight. It hadn't worked before. It would now.

"Paula is suffering," Sonya pointed out, not without empathy. "If you don't love her, maybe you should put her out of her misery? Or is it the mother you're worried about? I understand she's the mother from hell."

He laughed. "Who told you that?"

"As if I'd reveal my sources!"

"Raymond." He hit on the answer. "Did he ask for your phone number?"

"He's coming into the shop. He's very attractive. I liked him."

"He obviously *loved* you." His tone was openly goading.

"Isn't that sweet? I'm so enjoying mixing with the mega-rich."

He slotted the Mercedes smoothly between two little run-abouts. "This will give the neighbours something to talk about," she said.

"Aren't you going to ask me up?" He turned his handsome face to her.

"I dare not," she said sharply.

He gave her a smile that would make the strongest-willed woman go weak at the knees. "Oh, come on, Sonya. Do you get many visitors?"

"Not too many."

"At the very least you can make me a cup of coffee. I want to see where you live."

"You *know* where I live," she said, in an off-putting tone. "In fact you never even asked for directions."

"Let's get out," he suggested.

"If you must."

The voice of caution kicked in. *This is going to be very, very tricky.*

The apartment complex wasn't the top end of the market, or anywhere near it, but it was attractive, a contemporary design, well maintained, and in a quiet suburban street. There were only four floors. Sonya's apartment was at the top. There was no one in the lift. Sonya didn't look at him on the way up. She was worryingly off balance, but determined to hide it. She knew if he touched her—even her hand—everything would change. So he must *not* touch her. And she couldn't afford to be too friendly. Her involuntary physical reactions to him were depleting her supply of self-control. There could be no winners here. Not him.

Certainly not her. For her there would be punishment of some kind.

They were inside the small two-bed apartment. Sonya had filled it with the sort of things that reminded her of her early life.

Holt looked around with pleasure. "You decorated this yourself?" He had already guessed the answer. "Where did you get all the old pieces?"

She watched in some wonderment as he moved around the living room. David Wainwright *here*! She almost felt like bursting into emotional tears. She had been so *lonely.* Marcus, lovely man that he was, couldn't hope to fill the sad void in her. *But David!* She berated herself for her weakness. "I picked them up from demolition yards, jumble sales, second-hand shops." She managed to sound perfectly calm. "It's amazing what people part with. I had to work on all my finds, of course. I love timber."

"So do I. This appeals to me greatly." He ran a hand over the back of a carved chair with very fine finials. It looked Russian.

"I'm absolutely delighted." She purposely spiked her tone.

Keep it light. Don't deepen the connection.

The living-dining area was the usual open plan, he saw. There was a galley-like small kitchen with granite bench tops and good stainless-steel appliances. The balcony had been made a relaxing green haven with luxuriant plants. But what she had done to an ordinary space was what impressed him.

"This has a lot of character." A beautiful scrap of tapestry had been used to cover the top of the cushion on its seat. "Not *our* sort of character where the emphasis is generally on exploiting the natural light, the sunshine and the indoor-outdoor lifestyle. This is a glimpse into a different world.

Neo-Gothic maybe?" He glanced across the room at her, his eyes touching on her face and lissom body.

"There's that," she agreed. "I like the way the timbers gleam so darkly against the white walls. The white-tiled floor I managed to cover with a really good rug, as you can see. That set me back a bit but it was worth it. I don't own the apartment. I rent it."

"And the big painting on the wall?" His interest was truly captured.

"Mine," she said. "Anyone can paint flowers."

"No, they *can't*!" He moved nearer the painting, an oil reminiscent of the Dutch school: dark background, lightly touched with green and mauve strokes, with massed flower heads, roses, peonies, lilies, others, taking up the entire central canvas. "This is very painterly," he said with genuine admiration.

"I can't resist flowers. I used a palette knife."

"Aren't you clever!" He was giving the painting his full attention. "Who taught you?"

"Oh, a relative," she said evasively.

"As forthcoming as usual?" His black eyes mocked. "You know, you could make a good living as an artist, Sonya. I could help you."

"You think that preferable to my capturing your uncle's heart and along the way a good slice of his fortune?" she retorted more sharply than she had intended. But she was made nervous by how easily he was getting under her skin. If he stayed too much longer she didn't think she could withstand his powerful aura. The very last thing she wanted was for a man to turn her whole world inside out. Contact was too dangerous. He would never give her what she needed. He would eventually marry some beautiful young woman within his own circle. She knew there would be a long list for him to choose from.

He sensed her concealed agitation. "Is that what you *really* want, Sonya?" The force of his gaze pinned her in place.

"What I want is perhaps something I will never get," she said enigmatically. "Now would you excuse me for a moment? I want to get out of this tracksuit." From the moment she had met him, every instinct had warned her not to allow him to come close. She knew she couldn't deal with emotions that could not be contained.

"Take your time," he called after her as she started to move down the narrow passageway. "I'm going to take a look at your books." He crossed to the large timber bookcase that stood against the end wall. It was jammed with books. "German, French, Russian, Hungarian, how weird is that?" he called after her. "No need to be in a rush to tell me."

"See how much you can work out on your own," she threw ironically over her shoulder.

When she returned she was wearing a long turquoise and lime-green dress that hung from shoestring straps over her bare shoulders. The bodice clung lovingly to her breasts, then fell in a fluid drop to her ankles. She wore little silver ballet shoes on her feet. Obviously she had run a brush through her hair, but the great thing was she had left it loose. "What languages do you speak?" he asked quietly, not taking his eyes from her. She looked so beautiful, so strangely *innocent*, he had to suck in his breath.

"A few." She moved quickly into the kitchen. There would now be a high barrier between them.

"You read Goethe and Schiller in the original? I saw that wonderful monument to them both when I was last in Germany. Then you have the French collection. A well-thumbed Flaubert's *Madame Bovary*, Victor Hugo, Dumas,

Gautier among others. A lot of Hungarian literature, Janos Arany, Kazinczy, Molnar, a very old chronical of Magyar affairs."

"You know perfectly well I have Hungarian blood."

"I know nothing of the sort," he lightly jeered. "Hungarian accent according to Rowena. Norwegian surname. Norwegian ancestry? What's the big secret anyway? What is it you're frightened of giving up? There has to be a better way, Sonya. Your manner, the extreme reserve, only adds fuel to the fire. It's as if you didn't exist up until five years ago."

"Maybe I'm on the run from villains," she suggested, preparing the coffee.

He shot her an impatient look. "I wouldn't be a bit surprised."

"Of course you wouldn't. You don't trust me one bit."

"How can I when you make yourself one-hundred-percent inaccessible? What sort of life have you had?"

He sounded as though it really mattered to him. That shook her. Her body was filling with shivery sensations.

"You must have had lovers?" How had they ever let her go?

She looked up very quickly from what she was doing, green eyes frosted. "Why make it sound as if I had a brigade of them? The truth is, I don't like men all that much."

"So you keep the ones you consider dangerous at a distance. It's the *why* I want to know. There's got to be an answer."

"Distance is effective," she said, pressing the button on the coffee machine.

"Generally speaking women who want distance don't give off high-octane sparks," he said dryly. "Not to men anyway. *You* do, Sonya. You know it. I know it."

She felt the heat that rushed into her cheeks. "How do you know I don't already hate *you*?"

"Okay, tell me," he invited. "*Do* you?"

She kept her eyes down. "Black or with cream?"

"All right, don't answer me," he said as though it was just what he expected. "Black, two sugars."

"Something with it?"

"No, thank you, Sonya. For God's sake come from behind that counter. There's not a lot of danger out here." How could he claim that, when the atmosphere was potentially explosive?

She gave him a cool look. "This *is* where I make the coffee."

"Looks more like you're barricading yourself in."

"I definitely am *not*."

"You definitely *are*," he contradicted.

"Well, we're enemies, aren't we? In a manner of speaking, of course."

He considered. "It might surprise you, Sonya, but I'm not gunning for you."

"What else would you call it?" She came around the counter, carrying the tray set with coffee things.

He stood up to take it from her, the brief touch of his hands on hers enough to soak her in warmth.

"On the coffee table, please," she said, trying to regain her habitual cool. "I hope it's the way you like it."

"What I'd like is for you to sit and talk to me," he said very seriously.

"I fancy our talk would turn into an interrogation." She shrugged. "You know my name, age, occupation, my address. What else do you need?"

"I have to say—*plenty*." His tone hardened somewhat. "You're getting yourself into something here, Sonya, as

I've already warned you. You should be prepared. You told Marcus you'd ring him this evening."

"I will. No need to make it sound like a duty." She sat down on the opposite sofa, leaving her coffee on the table.

"Do you fully understand how much he cares for you?" he asked.

"Well, I care for him," she replied with a touch of aggression. "His humour, his gentle nature, his generosity, the brilliance of his mind. There aren't many men as gentle and courtly as Marcus. I feel safe with him."

"Will you marry him if he asks you?" He put it to her bluntly.

Her emerald eyes flashed fire. "Are you really entitled to an answer?"

"Please don't be cute."

"Cute? *Cute*? You must be crazy!" Tempestuously she leapt to her feet, her hair flying. "I am not like that. Why don't you answer *my* questions."

"I might if you sit down again." He was having difficulty keeping his own emotional balance. He felt desire coiled deep within him like a tempting serpent. It was imperative he keep his distance, adjust his moral compass in the right direction.

"So don't make me angry." Sonya sank down again, reaching for a silk cushion as if she might throw it at any moment. "My question: are you serious about your Paula or are you just stringing her along?"

That rankled. "Paula and I go back a long way."

"No doubt to the cradle." She gave a tiny mocking yawn. "Only it's you who should be paying attention. You're not behind the door handing out unsolicited advice, so I tell you as a favour, she's madly in love with you."

He gave her a long, intense look. "Does this mean I'm

under some sort of obligation to return her love? I've never told her I was. I am *not* stringing her along as you're suggesting. In my experience one only has to press a woman's hand for her to start hearing wedding bells. I've dated a lot of attractive women. Not so many of late, I'm afraid. I'm too damned busy."

"Why wouldn't you be, as your father's heir?" she commented. "Why does Paula Rowlands want to hurt me? Why would she say such words? I very much resent I'm 'after' you. One would think it was a hunt."

"In a way it is." He gave a brief laugh. "We're all out there looking, searching, hunting for a soul mate."

"And you've rejected everyone so far?"

He levelled an intense stare at her. "Haven't you?"

She looked down, a glow in her cheeks. "I admit I have kept to myself as much as possible."

"A woman as tantalizing as you, Sonya, would pretty much have to keep up her guard. Is that the attraction with Marcus? You feel with Marcus you can control the relationship? Is that how you feel?"

She gave a sad little smile. "I've never been able to control anything in my life." Some of the old bitterness and frustration began to surface. She regretted it, but family ghosts were slipping by her. "Drink your coffee," she urged. "It's going cold." She picked up her own cup, trying to shake off her nerves. The best way to protect herself was to stay perfectly cool. Even detached. "When do your parents return?" she asked politely.

"They're enjoying themselves so much they'll probably take another month. We have many good friends in the US."

"Have you told them about me?" Her tone was now so cool it almost snapped.

He shook his dark head. "But someone is bound to have

let them know, Sonya. My parents know everybody. Most of them were at the gala. Women love to pass on gossip. You made quite an impact. But you would have known that. In fact you invited it. Which is a bit of a paradox, given your extreme reserve. Then if that weren't enough you were wearing Lucy's emeralds."

"As lovely as they are, they are not the most beautiful emeralds in the world," she said with one of her elegant shoulder shrugs.

More role playing! He wondered. At times when her composure threatened to fail her, her slight accent became more pronounced.

"You've worn better?" he asked, his expression frankly sardonic.

She had the foolish impulse to run down to her bedroom and take the Madonna from its hiding place. She would show it to him: diamonds, rubies, emeralds, pearls, extravagantly beautiful, extravagantly precious. The Wainwrights, for all their wealth, had nothing like that.

"Hard for you to believe but maybe I have seen better."

"In the display windows of leading European jewellers, no doubt. The problem is, Sonya, they belonged to Lucy. My mother loved Lucy. They were great friends. It was an extraordinary thing for Marcus to offer them to you to wear."

"I'd never contemplated he would do such a thing." She was driven to defend herself. "He made it almost impossible for me to refuse. He was intent on my wearing them. More to the point, he would have known what effect that would have on all of you."

His chiselled mouth tightened. "It's time they never looked better," he added ironically.

"I wish now I'd offered a strong refusal. So I must expect your parents will be predisposed to dislike me?"

"I'm afraid so, Sonya." He couldn't deny it. "And dislike is the least of it. We're all very protective of Marcus. My father, *extremely* so."

"So, it's a catastrophe if Marcus falls in love with me?" She issued the challenge.

"The perceived catastrophe would be *you* don't love him," he retorted. "He's thirty years your senior. We've been over this, Sonya."

"I very much dislike the way you treat me." Her green eyes turned stormy. "Is a big age difference all that important? Surely what is important is that Marcus finds happiness. All this emphasis on sex—a sex life surely isn't the be-all and end-all of a marriage?"

"Of course it isn't, but it's a great help to be hungry for each other." His vibrant voice deepened. "You don't get it, do you? A lot of people are going to hate you, Sonya."

"Well, I think you and they are very very stupid!" She spoke with sudden fire, rising to her feet again, her willowy back ramrod straight.

From where did this woman get her class, her style, her apparently natural air of superiority? Her previous life couldn't have been one of tranquillity. She was forever on her guard. "I wish you to go." She gave an imperious flourish of her hand towards the door.

"Certainly." He rose to his splendid height, torn between anger and amusement. "You can show me out."

"I *will*!" There was an extraordinary intensity in her green eyes. Her head was spinning. Her body was alive with excitements, hungers. She moved swiftly ahead of him, so swiftly the tiny bow on one of her silver ballet shoes hooked on the fringe of the rug. She pitched forward, cursing her haste, only he caught her up from behind.

His strong arms encircled her for the second time that day. *Surrounded* her like a force field. Her heart leapt into her throat as he pulled her back against him, both of them facing the door.

"Tell me again you hate me," he murmured in a dark velvety voice.

The polished skin of his cheek rasped thrillingly against hers. Every ounce of strength, physical and mental, seemed to be draining out of her body. "You *are* hateful!" He was reading her reactions, she knew it. He was taking her to a place she had never gone before. Man, the traditional manipulator of women!

"Don't lie to me," he whispered against her ear.

The very air was spitting, crackling, with tension. "Don't you realize what you're doing?" Her mind was crashing. Her heart was crashing. For these brief moments she was beset by intolerable yearnings, abruptly made aware of the passionate red blood in her.

"David?" She tried to wrest away from him, but he held firm.

A certain contempt he felt for himself was no match for his desire for her. The heady incense of sex was an inciting vapour that hung in the air. There had to be countless instances of overwhelming temptation but he had never felt anything remotely like this before. There were only two possible options available to him. Let her go. Or give into this furious passion. She was bent forward over his arm. His arms had effectively locked her in. The tips of his fingers were pressing into the undersides of her beautiful high breasts. Still he didn't release her. It was almost as though he were under a spell with all his senses inflamed.

Sonya was frantic to settle on a course of action. Her knees were buckling under the onslaught. Heat had turned to *scorch.* The delta between her legs had turned moist. "David, you mustn't do this."

True. True. True.

The two of them were locked into an impossible attraction. He could feel her trembling. "I know," he said harshly, turning her to face him. It was a mistake. He had her exactly where he wanted her, only he knew he had to let her go. The pity was he couldn't find the time or space to regain control. With a half-maddened exclamation, he brought his dark head down low over hers, furious with himself that he wanted her so *badly.* The voice of reason had quietened into nothingness…

His kiss was fierce. He had her beautiful body in his arms, their two bodies, male and female, connecting in an extravagantly erotic way. His strong male drive was urging him on, fuelling him with energy. At some point he realized she was having difficulty coping with such an onslaught. He lifted his mouth fractionally from hers, allowing her to take breath…only he was back to kissing her. He had never kissed a woman so passionately. He hadn't even known he *could* reach such a level of wanting, needing. He was desperate for her response. His fingers twined in a handful of her hair, holding her face up to him. Her mouth was so sweetly, so silkily *lush* he couldn't drag his own away.

Stop. You've got to stop. Or be damned.

The voice in his head had increased to a warning blast.

This is the woman Marcus has come to love.

Madness to continue to hold her, but he was losing the battling against this wild rage of emotion. He wanted to sweep her up and carry her down the corridor to her bedroom. He wanted to strip her dress from her, ablaze with the desire to feel skin on skin. He wanted to kiss and caress her all over her naked body with its satiny white skin. For minutes there it had felt so completely *right*.

But it was hopelessly *wrong*. The verdict cold and hard.

How could he see people hurt? The future of the three of them was in jeopardy. The eternal triangle. Marcus, himself and Sonya, the woman they both wanted. Yet hadn't it been inevitable from the first moment their eyes met?

With a monumental effort he forced himself to let her go, aware he was breathing as heavily as if he had run the four-minute mile. Her beautiful hair was in total disarray, fanning out like a halo around her emotion charged face. She looked so vulnerable, so young, his heart smote him.

"Sonya, forgive me. I hadn't meant that to happen." They were like a pair of conspiratorial lovers filled with as much agony as ecstasy.

Her voice shook so badly, it betrayed her. Could it be possible he had deliberately engineered this, seeking her reaction? "You rich people are so ruthless!" Her distressed mind turned to *tactics*. "Who are *you* to drag me into your arms? What is your agenda? We both know you have one." She had lost sight of her own.

"Agenda? Don't talk rubbish." His response was curt. "You know damned well I'm attracted to you." He could have laughed at the sheer inadequacy of the word. Magnetized? Mesmerized? Spellbound?

"Now this is very interesting." She was transformed into a state of the utmost hostility. "*You're* attracted to *me*!" The entrenched defence mechanisms were back in place.

"Neither of us sought it," he said. "Neither of us wanted it. It just happened."

"Just happened?" she cried. "Oh, you're very convincing."

"So were *you*, just then, beautiful Sonya. Okay, I admit

my mistake. I was the aggressor. But it's too late now to make a fuss. I'm sorry if I hurt you." His dark eyes moved slowly over her body.

She took a deep shaky breath, feeling weak and ashamed. "You are mad, mad, *mad*!"

"You're so damned right," he agreed tonelessly, his handsome face taut.

"You are leaving."

It was a statement, not a question.

Still he turned back. "You'd prefer me to stay?" There was hard mockery in his brilliant eyes when the temptation to stay was overwhelming.

"You are *leaving*," she repeated. 'This is not your finest hour, David Wainwright."

"I agree. I'm afraid I overestimated my powers of self-control. So how do I go about making reparation? I'm too much of a gentleman to ask you to account for *your* behaviour. There's a lot of passion dammed up behind the Ice Princess façade, isn't there, Sonya? Floods of it!"

She felt as if she were thrashing about in a cage. "I've had enough! I know what you're up to. You are *not* exonerated. You are wanting me to fall in love with you. That is your strategy. I should have been prepared. After all, men have been preying on the weakness of women since the dawn of time. Your precious Marcus would be safe from my greedy clutches. How could dear sweet Marcus compare to you? I can't deny your sexual power. But I can refuse to succumb to it. I've had no ordinary life. I've had years and years of—" She had to break off, sick with herself, sick with him. She took a strangled intake of breath. "Don't ever touch me again!"

"But we can't forget the here and *now*." Some demon was in him. The way she spoke to him. The combative glitter in her emerald eyes. Who did she think she was? She affected him so powerfully in all the right ways. And all the wrong ways. Anger engulfed him. He pulled her back into his arms, outrage overcoming his natural protective feelings towards women. *His* sexual power? he thought grimly. What about *hers*?

His kiss was like a brand. Sonya tried to grit her teeth, but his tongue forced entry into her mouth. An avalanche of dark pleasure had her near collapsing against him.

Equally furiously he drew back. "I'd say you returned my kisses, you little fraud."

Without a second's hesitation she lifted her arm, hell-bent on leaving the imprint of her fingers on his handsome, hateful face.

He caught her wrist mid-flight. "Don't mess with me, Sonya," he rasped.

"And blessings on you too!" she cried. "Maybe I will marry your Marcus. Outrage your entire family, Lady Palmerston who has been so kind to me, your friends, your whole circle, that witch of a Paula Rowlands. Go grab her if you want to grab a woman. She's desperate for you to do it. But you can't have *me*."

He shot out a hand to grasp the door knob. "You sure about that?" he asked with a lick of contempt. "Are you *sure* you can cross me?"

She laughed, throwing up her chin. "Trust me, David Wainwright. I've had plenty of experience of villains."

It was an admission that sobered him entirely. "I suggest if one shows up, Sonya, you give me a ring." He couldn't have been more serious.

"What use are you to me?" The stormy expression in her green eyes became uncertain.

He opened the door. "If you're in trouble—any kind of trouble—you had better contact me," he said. "Whatever else I am, Sonya, I'm no villain."

CHAPTER FIVE

SONYA had never thought to see Paula Rowlands come into her shop, given Paula's vehement promise that would never happen, but lo and behold there she was!

Another catastrophic day?

And the timing was terrible! She was having lunch with Camilla in just over a half-hour. Paula wasn't alone. An older woman was with her, both of them stern faced, dressed to the nines. This was the mother from hell obviously. Family resemblance was apparent; the expressions were identical. They might have been called as witnesses in an unsavoury court case involving her.

Sonya acknowledged them with a calm nod, although her stomach muscles were tensing. She finished off wrapping a large bunch of stunning yellow heliconias. She had added some ginger foliage that had very interesting yellow strips for effect. She passed them across to her valued customer with a smile. "There you are, Mrs Thomas. You might use a few dark philodendron leaves if you have them at home," she suggested. "See how it goes."

Maureen Thomas nodded, very happy with the unusual selection. "These are splendid, thank you so much."

"My pleasure."

Mrs Thomas glanced in pleasant fashion at the two very

uppity looking women as she walked to the door. She might have been invisible. It amused her.

Marilyn Rowlands swooped to the counter, a mother protecting her young. "Look here, young lady," she said without preamble, "it's wrong what you're doing. You're only creating serious problems for yourself."

"Do I know you?" Sonya's brows arched.

Breathe deeply. Keep calm.

Marilyn's face clouded. "You *know* me. I'm Paula's mother." She might have been as easily recognisable as the Queen of England.

"Paula can't speak for herself, then?" Sonya asked politely.

"No cheek, young lady," Marilyn Rowlands said, thinking this girl was a whole lot more than she had been led to expect. She was amazingly beautiful, with an ultra-refined look. "I take insolence from no one," she warned, placing a heavily be-ringed hand on the counter.

A blue cloisonne bowl full of exquisite gardenias jumped. Sonya settled it.

What was it the Buddhists intoned to calm them?

Om…om…om.

"Do I have a need for concern here, Mrs Rowlands?" she asked. "There *is* a security guard who patrols these shops."

Marilyn's coiffed head shot back in outrage. "Are you threatening me?"

"I have a perfect right to refuse service to difficult people who come into my shop, Mrs Rowlands."

Paula belatedly entered the fray. "No one speaks to my mother like that. My father could have you out of here in no time."

"I doubt that," Sonya said.

"You leave my husband out of this," Marilyn Rowlands ordered, not averse to a slanging match.

Sonya was. "Mrs Rowlands, I'm asking you quietly to leave."

Marilyn Rowlands stood her ground. "First I need you to promise me you'll stop your little games."

"What games exactly?'

"You know very well. You're an opportunist."

"So what's in it for me?" Sonya asked.

Paula threw up her hands in triumph. "I *knew* it! Didn't I tell you, Mummy?" she cried as though her low opinion of Sonya had been vindicated.

Marilyn opened her Chanel handbag, and then pulled out a cheque book. "Don't attempt to double cross me, young lady. How much?"

"What's the best you can offer?" Sonya asked.

"Why, you're no better than a con woman," Marilyn Rowlands said with an overlay of contempt.

"Five hundred thousand dollars!" Sonya named a ridiculous figure. Who cared?

Marilyn frowned ferociously. "That's a bit steep."

"David, or Marcus?" Sonya asked, covering up her sick feeling.

"Both. Holt adores Paula."

"So I can't have Marcus?"

Marilyn Rowlands frowned as if a massive migraine was coming on. "How long have you been on the make? I repeat, you can have *neither*. They're way out of your league."

"And I know for certain Holt is going to marry me," Paula threw in for good measure.

Her mother focused on Sonya with eyes as cold and round as marbles. "Two hundred and fifty thousand dollars, my last offer. It would be a fortune to someone like you.

Quit the flower shop. Get yourself an education. Move on. Take the money. Shut up shop. Head for sunny Queensland. Lots of lotus eaters up there. We want you gone." She looked in her bag, found her Mont Blanc pen. "A lot of people want you gone. Especially the Wainwright clan."

"Listen to me a moment, Mrs Rowlands." Sonya spoke very quietly, but with a note in her voice that stopped Marilyn Rowlands in her tracks. "I've been leading you on. I'm not interested in you or your money. I find this whole episode extremely distasteful. What I want you to do now is walk quietly out of my shop. And never return."

"Excuse me!" Marilyn Rowlands gave vent to a growl she could well have learned from her Chihuahua.

"You have my word I won't mention this visit or the offensive things you've said."

Paula broke in again. Seething with jealousy. "Why don't you go back to where you came from? Some dingy European dump, I expect."

"Perhaps I should call the security man."

Marilyn Rowlands put up her hand. "That's enough, Paula," she said sternly. "Wherever this young woman came from, it was no dump." She looked back to Sonya. "Turn my proposal over in your head, Ms Erickson. You're no fool. You could see the sense of it some time soon. Holt's parents are due home soon. I'm a pussy cat compared to Holt's mother. As for his father! You poor girl, it would be a horrendous thing to cross him. I highly recommend you don't do it. Holt is everything in the world to them. *You* have no chance in the world of gaining admittance to *that* family, believe me."

Sonya gave Marilyn Rowlands a straight look. "The question is do I *want* to gain admittance, Mrs Rowlands. I haven't as yet decided the answer."

* * *

At the weekend Marcus suggested she come out on his boat. Local weather was holding gloriously calm and fine. "It hasn't been out for ages," he told her. "You *must* come."

The "boat" turned out to be a svelte and racy 128 yacht designed years before by a famous ex-patriot who went on to become a world legend. Marcus, looking a good ten years younger in his tailored jeans and blue sports shirt beneath a gold buttoned navy blazer, showed her around the *Lucille Anne* with careless pride. "I used to be a good sailor in my day. Let it go. I'm sorry about that now. David is a brilliant sailor. He should take you out some time. You don't get seasick?'

"I'm sure one couldn't get seasick on this magnificent yacht." She smiled.

The *Lucille Anne* had three decks of cabins and saloons. The main saloon, marvellously comfortable, was panelled in walnut with touches of macassar ebony. Apart from the plush master suite there were four guest staterooms. On the teak laid aft deck reached by a gleaming stainless steel stairway with a balustrade, there was casual furniture and a swimming platform Sonya wasn't about to use any time soon.

"Lucy and I used to take it to the Mediterranean when young David was on holidays," Marcus told her with a smile of remembrance. "We looked on him as our own child. He was a remarkable boy. A remarkable young man."

"You love him?"

"Oh, yes!" Marcus confirmed quietly. "David is every inch the man we all wanted him to be."

It turned out to be a relaxing day spent in total luxury. A superb seafood lunch was served on the glass-topped oak table accented in ebony in the dining saloon. Afterwards they adjoined to the aft deck with its comfortable arrangements of chairs and wide teak table that held a low black bowl filled with pink and yellow hibiscus.

"You look happy." Marcus spoke in such a deep tender voice it was a clear giveaway. Sonya was wearing navy jeans with a navy and white T-shirt, white sneakers on her feet. A casual outfit on a beautiful young woman with a willowy body. She could have earned a fortune modelling clothes. Apparently that held little allure for her. She was seemingly content in her world of flowers.

Sonya turned her head lazily. "I am. You're lovely company, Marcus. Thank you so much for asking me."

"I want to do everything you want, Sonya," he announced, in a fervent voice. "And I want to do it *now.* I know you don't love me. I couldn't ask for that, but you are fond of me?"

Sonya sat straight, her heart thudding. This was an opportunity most women would give their eye teeth for. Only she wasn't at all sure she was one of them. It wasn't an everyday event to be proposed to by a millionaire. Some would be ecstatic. Only she had developed a taste of passion, shameful though the memory was. Affection was at the heart of her very real feelings for Marcus. Never passion.

Shove all thoughts of David Wainwright from your mind. Do it now, her inner voice instructed.

Marilyn Rowlands had made a point of telling her she would never fit into David Wainwright's world. In all probability she had spoken the truth. His parents would have their own ideas about their adored son's future.

"No, let me finish," Marcus said, sensing her perturbation. "I'm a rich man. But with no woman in my life to love, I might as well be dirt poor. I fell in love with you the instant I walked into your shop."

"Marcus!" She held out her hands like a supplicant,

palms up. How could she hurt this gentle man? He wanted her. More importantly he could protect her if ever the time came. She knew Laszlo wouldn't rest until he had tracked her down; made certain she wasn't in possession of the Andrassy Madonna. She had lived with the fear he would eventually find her. He could already be closing in.

"Please listen," Marcus begged. "You don't talk about yourself. In my experience people who have suffered deep traumas never talk. Maybe they can't. I know you have a story, but I'm content to wait until you're ready to tell me about it. I don't care what it is. I don't care what you've done—if indeed you've done anything. I want to marry you, Sonya. I want to look after you. There is still time for me to father a child. You will want for nothing."

Except passionate love.

Is that so bad? Don't you read the headlines, girl? Celebrities passionately in love one moment suddenly spitting venom and selling their stories to the magazines. They move on to someone else to fuel their tank. I ask you, what is love? Where does the love go?

"You don't have to answer me now. I can see I've stunned you. You can have all the time you want."

She had to control a desire to weep. "Marcus, you've *honoured* me." At the same time she couldn't help thinking maybe what he really wanted was a daughter. This man was terribly lonely.

Marcus must have guessed her thoughts. "Sonya, I love you as a *woman*," he said. "A beautiful, gifted woman, and most hopefully the mother of our child. You needn't fear I couldn't give you a child. My poor little Lucy couldn't get pregnant. She was never strong. Lucy would want me to be happy. She was the sweetest human being."

All sorts of emotions tugged at her. She had to remember what her life had been. Marcus could change all that. She spoke earnestly. “Marcus, your family might very well see me as an opportunist. You’re a rich man. You’re years older than I am. They would question that.”

“Let them!” he said scornfully. “As long as *you* don’t question it. I don’t give a damn what anyone thinks. I’m in love with you. I don’t even care David has his concerns. That’s how much I want you.”

So David, traitor, has spoken of his concerns!

“No Wainwright has power over me, Sonya,” Marcus said firmly. “You, however, *do*.”

Say something. Say something. Silence will give him hope.

He reached for her hand. “If you marry me I’ll do everything in my power to keep you safe and happy. That, I swear.”

It was an enormously touching moment. Would it be so terrible to marry Marcus?

Give yourself time to think. Marcus Wainwright is a good man. How many of them are about?

Days passed. She was kept very busy in the shop. She had an assistant, a single mother with two children, aged seven and nine, who did part-time work that fitted in with her mothering schedule. Penny had received some training in a suburban flower shop. She was very good with the customers, efficient at what she did and if she lacked a certain imagination it didn’t matter all that much to Sonya, who could always do a bit of tweaking. As a single mother Penny needed the work. Sonya had been happy to give it to her.

Midweek Marcus took her out to dinner in one of those restaurants where the price list would give the average person a heart attack. And that didn’t include the hefty tip. Marcus looked very handsome in his professorial fashion, his face radiating his pleasure and pride in her company.

His high spirits would have been apparent to all who gave him a little friendly wave as they passed, or those who bent closer over the table to make a comment, most probably acid.

The longer this goes on, the harder it gets. For you and him. You owe him an answer. You have to make up your mind what it's going to be.

The whole situation, so jubilant to Marcus, was weighing heavily on her mind.

The entrée, a selection of *teeny* morsels, delicious enough, but served in what was nearly a platter. It seemed to her ridiculously pretentious. She reached for her wine glass, noticing at that moment the maître d' showing a tall, stunningly handsome man and his extremely pretty companion to a table. Her decision was made for her.

It has to be a no. Of course it has to be a no. Married to a man you do not love with the prospect of seeing the man you're so powerfully drawn to on every family occasion. Sheer madness!

"Good Lord, it's David!" Marcus was saying delightedly as he stood up to attract his nephew's attention. "David!" he called. "He has Emma Courtney with him, Sonya. Lovely girl, Emma. She's nuts about him, as the saying goes. I should know. I'm nuts about you." He laughed, colour in his lean cheeks. "I'll introduce you."

It was the very last thing Sonya wanted. She sat back, desperate to achieve some semblance of calm.

David Wainwright will marry a young woman much like the one he's out with tonight.

Get that through your head.

His hand at Emma's elbow, Holt led the way to his uncle's table. The shock of seeing her again was as painful, as piercing as an arrow shot straight to the heart.

You fool!

His warning voice kicked in, determined on giving him hell. She was wearing the standard little black dress but her radiant beauty and her colouring made the dress look as if it were worth every last cent of a million dollars. Marcus was beaming with pride. It was obvious he would do anything for her. Lay down his life if need be. Not only was she far and away the most beautiful woman in the room, she was highly intelligent. If she was after position and security, a half-share of Marcus's money, it was as good as in her hand. From a florist shop to chatelaine of one of the most beautiful houses in a city full of beautiful houses. Money beyond her wildest dreams would be at her disposal. For all he knew the wedding date had already been set.

He had to bring all his concentration to bear just on saying hello.

Marcus gripped his shoulder. "What a surprise to see you, David. How are you, Emma? You look lovely as usual." Marcus moved a pace to kiss Emma's cheek. She was a true redhead with lovely bright blue eyes.

"Sonya." Holt acknowledged her with a slight bow. She gave him a cool smile.

Still playing the aristocrat for all she was worth. It was a sterling performance. He had to give her that. "I'd like you to meet a friend of mine, Emma Courtney. Emma, Sonya Erickson." He made the introduction.

Emma rated a real smile. It lit up Sonya's beautiful face like the sun sparkling off ice. "Nice to meet you, Emma."

"You too, Sonya. I've heard a lot about you." Emma was looking at Sonya with open admiration.

"I take it David is the one giving the information?" Sonya kept the smile on her face.

"All *good* things." Emma gave a tiny triangular smile. It

could have meant she'd had a few words with others, like Paula Rowlands, whom she no doubt knew.

A pleasantry or two more and they moved off. Emma glanced back and gave a little friendly wave.

"Lovely girl!" Marcus enthused, sitting down again. "I'm so glad David isn't serious about Paula. You have to be careful with those Rowlands women. Though I have to say Paula can be extremely nice when the mood takes her. Emma had better look out. Paula has always been wildly jealous of anyone who even looked sideways at David."

Tell me about it.

"Then she has a battle on her hands. Every woman in the room looked up the moment he walked in."

"You too?" Marcus shot her a quick intent look.

"Why not? I was enjoying it," she lied. "I had my own entry tracked."

"You'll have to get used to it, dearest girl." He relaxed. "It might be a nice idea to meet up with them after dinner. Go on somewhere. What do you think?"

No way could she handle that. "No nightclubs, Marcus," she said, pretending a modicum of regret. "I should be a good girl and go home. Early start at the markets tomorrow."

"Of course, my dear." His hand covered hers across the table. "Though I hope you'll find the time to pop into the house with me for ten minutes. I have something to show you. Jensen will drive you home, of course."

"Ten minutes, Marcus. No more."

"Splendid!" He raised his glass to her.

Whatever Marcus had in mind she thought she could deal with it.

Her arrangements, she noticed with satisfaction, were still amazingly fresh. There was such a glow about Marcus.

Unusual colour in his cheeks. For a very dignified, contained man, it was only too clear he was excited. Indeed he had come alive with exhilaration. He was a great collector. Perhaps he had acquired a new painting. Possibly for her? He knew she was passionate about good art.

"Sit down, my dear," he invited, pulling out an armchair covered in blue silk damask. "I had the most wonderful dream the other night. I dreamt you said yes to my proposal of marriage. Next day I went out and bought this." Slowly he withdrew from his inner breast pocket a small jewellery box. "Wasn't it Freud who said we should place great faith in our powerful dreams?" he asked, not waiting for her answer. "Sonya, dearest girl, I want you to wear this as a token of my everlasting love. Give me your hand, my dear. I'm sure it will be a perfect fit."

Was there any tactful way of offering a rebuff? *No*, was the short answer. Only for the life of her she couldn't seem to utter a word. Her mouth and throat had gone so dry she wanted to leap up to go and find a glass of water.

"There!" Marcus said with great satisfaction. "What did I tell you? Perfect. Don't you think so?"

Sonya was astounded. The diamonds were like chunks of Arctic ice. She stood up, feeling as though her heart had left her chest. "Marcus, is this what I think it is?"

"My dearest girl, you *know* it's an engagement ring," he said with loving indulgence. "I'm very serious about wanting to marry you. If I hesitate some other lucky man will sweep you up. I can't have that. You are my great chance at happiness."

Suddenly she wasn't at all sure he could withstand the shock of an abrupt refusal. He was so *happy*, even if he had rather jumped the gun. But then he would have lived a life when he could have just about anything he ever wanted.

"Were diamonds a mistake?" he asked, seeing her

confusion. "You will have the emeralds, my dear," he assured her. "But I thought *diamond* for the ring. They're the finest money can buy."

Distress flashed into her green eyes. "No, diamonds aren't the mistake, Marcus," she said slowly, reasoning she had best get this over with. "It's—" She broke off in horror as Marcus bent over, clutching his chest. "Marcus, what is it?" She flew up from her chair, to put her arms around him. She held him tight. "You're in pain."

"Nothing, nothing." Marcus tried to shrug off whatever ailed him. Only the high colour in his cheeks had turned to grey.

Sonya made her decision. "I'm going to call the ambulance. We need to get you to a hospital."

Marcus wasn't having that. "No, no, Sonya. I forbid it," he gasped. "A bit of chest pain. Not severe. Most probably heartburn. I don't normally eat dessert. It was too rich."

She wasn't convinced. "It's important you be checked out as soon as possible," she insisted, truly panicked and afraid for him. "Every moment counts. Let me call the ambulance."

"No," he said emphatically. "I'm feeling better already. I have a touch of anaemia, you know. Not enough iron."

"What about your doctor?" she persisted, not liking this one bit. "I could ring him. It's not late. I can't leave it like this, Marcus. Are you on any medication? I'll get you a glass of water."

By sheer will power Marcus pulled himself together. He sank back on the sofa. "You could try David. It's only discomfort, dear. Don't please panic. It's not a suspected heart attack, if that's what's worrying you. I know the symptoms. It's all the excitement, I suppose."

Please, God, let that be so!

Sonya ran to the kitchen, where she poured a glass of

water. “What’s David’s number?” she asked when she returned. Swiftly she unknotted Marcus’s tie, then the top button of his shirt. Next she put the glass into his hand. “Medication?”

“I’m fine, Sonya,” he insisted. “Please don’t fuss, my dear.” Marcus blew out his cheeks.

“I’ll get David.” Sonya ran to the landline in the kitchen and rang the number. Fear was pouring into her. She didn’t like the look of Marcus, no matter what he said. She should be ringing the ambulance whether he forbade it or not. David would most probably still be with Emma.

He answered on the fourth ring. “It’s Sonya,” she said, not trying to control her anxiety. “I’m at the house with Marcus. He’s taken a sick turn. He won’t let me ring the ambulance. He forbids it. He wants you. I’m going to ring his doctor.”

“Leave that to me,” he said in a clipped voice. “I’ll be there in under ten minutes. I’m not far away.”

When Sonya returned to the drawing room Marcus was still on the sofa, his torso slumped back, his right leg extended.

“Sit up straight, Marcus,” Sonya advised, going to him. “David is coming. He’s going to ring your doctor. They’ll be here shortly.” She held his hand within her own. “I love you, Marcus,” she found herself saying. “You’re a lovely man.”

They were still sitting, holding hands, when David strode in, followed by the doctor. David stood over them, his expression grave. The doctor went straight to his patient. He made a quick check. “I’m getting you to hospital, old man. Just to be sure.”

“I don’t want to go, Bart,” Marcus insisted. “I want to sit here with Sonya for ever.”

“Trust me, Marcus,” the doctor said. “You’re better off

in hospital. David has already called the ambulance. If I'm not mistaken it's turning into the drive."

"We'll follow in my car," David said, watching Sonya gently withdraw her hand from his uncle's. On the fourth finger of her left hand was a magnificent diamond engagement ring, a spectacular central stone flanked by dazzling smaller stones.

Acute anxiety for his uncle was overlaid by a bitter torrent of anger. He could hardly bear to look at her. There was the proof. She'd snagged Marcus hook, line and sinker.

"What are you all thinking of?" Marcus was trying hard to smile. "I'll be as right as rain in another half-hour."

"You've not been looking after yourself as well as you should have, Marcus," Bart Abbott said. "You'll have to spend the night. I want to run a few tests."

CHAPTER SIX

THEY were only granted a few minutes alone with Marcus before he was whisked away. Sonya was greatly heartened by the fact he looked a little better and he was safely in hospital where he belonged.

David completely ignored her.

"I can get a cab," she said, when they were out in the night air.

"You'll get mugged wearing *that ring*," he said curtly. "Come with me." He took hold of her arm.

The contempt in his voice made her blood boil. "Take your hand off me, David," she ordered.

He brought them both to an abrupt halt. "Don't start here. Don't start *now*," he warned. "I'm taking you home. I have no choice. I never leave a woman on her own at night. Besides, Marcus would confidently expect it of me to see you home. I need to do everything in my power to keep his fiancée safe."

"*No* fiancée," she flashed back.

"I would think that damned great ring is a sure sign of an engagement," he challenged harshly. "Once we're in the car I can take another look. Perhaps it's the grandest friendship ring of all time."

"Maybe it was meant that way." She was angry enough to say anything.

He hit the remote, unlocking his car. "Get in."

It was useless to protest. He meant business. "Aren't you interested in hearing *my* side of the story?" she asked as she tried to buckle her seat belt, all fingers and thumbs with nerves.

With a muffled exclamation he did it for her, then he started the engine, turning a taut profile. "What the hell is wrong with you?" he asked with severity.

"I might ask you the same question," she retorted, refusing to give him the psychological advantage. "You're all churned up and it isn't *only* Marcus's sick turn, upsetting as it is. It's the *ring* that's bugging you. So does he have a heart condition or what?"

He didn't answer until they were out onto the road. "Not that I know of," he said tersely. "Bart is right. Marcus hasn't looked after himself in years. We all thought he was committing a form of slow suicide after Lucy died. I know he's had to have a course of B12 injections. Iron. Ah, what the hell? The sick turn is bound to have happened because he's worked himself into a lather over *you*."

"That's right, blame me. It's not unexpected like Marcus giving me the ring was. You need a scapegoat. He's only fifty-five, isn't he?" she challenged angrily. "He isn't seventy or eighty!"

He threw her a scathing glance. "I ask you. Would seventy or eighty have been too much mileage on the clock for you? What about ninety? Would you have said yes, then?"

She drew in a ragged breath. "I haven't said yes now. I really don't appreciate being insulted. Marcus asked me in for a few minutes. We went into the drawing room. I sat down. Next thing, Marcus reached into his pocket, and before I could manage a word he's shoving a ring on my finger."

He made a sound of utter disbelief. "That must have shocked you out of your mind, Sonya darling."

The *darling* was a dark insult, but her heart gave a crazy jolt. "This is no time for us to fight, surely? I'm very fond of Marcus. He's a good, kind man, but I didn't ask him to fall in love with me. It took me a while to even see it coming."

"But you did see eventually, Sonya," he jeered. "You knew you had him in the palm of your hand. Now you've got the pay-off."

She was so angry she felt like jumping out of the car. "Here, have it!" she cried tempestuously as she wrenched off the ring. "It weighs a ton. You have it. It'll be a lot safer with you." She put it into the glovebox.

His smile was one of outright mockery. "You're lost to the stage, Sonya. But tell me, is there any history of psychotic behaviour in your family? You have to have one, even if they're tucked well out of sight."

"Oh, I've got one all right," she answered through clenched teeth. "You wouldn't know about the sort of people I've had to live with, David Wainwright with your life of privilege, loved and admired on all sides. You wouldn't know much about the kind of relatives *I* have."

"Professional con artists, I suspect," he said when it was cruel. "A crime family, maybe? Some in prison?"

"Why don't you just *drive*?"

She had the door of the Mercedes open before he had come to a complete stop.

"That was stupid," he reprimanded her, getting out. "I'll see you to your door."

"You stay here." Her hostility was in plain sight. "I'm in shock."

"Me too. But while Marcus is out of commission, I'm

responsible for the safety of his fiancée," he said with suave contempt.

She threw up her shining head. "What part of 'I'm in shock' don't you understand?"

"Let's go up," he said, moving purposefully towards her.

Had she resisted, she wouldn't have been in the least surprised had he thrown her over his shoulder.

A couple from the first floor was waiting for the lift. Good evenings were exchanged. The young woman could scarcely drag her eyes off Holt. Her partner was so busy staring at Sonya when the lift stopped at their floor he forgot to get out. His girlfriend gave him a sharp reminder.

"I don't think I'll lose my way if I walk myself to my door," Sonya said with heavy sarcasm. The lift had stopped at her floor. The door opened.

He held the diamond ring in his hand. He was staring down at it. "I can't keep this. It was given to you."

"Okay, I have to give it back!" Sonya's voice was a blend of anguish and anger. "I'm not making excuses for myself, David, but really Marcus presumed a great deal."

"Oh, wake up!" he exhorted her. "You knew what you were getting into." He took hold of her arm, walking her down the quiet corridor. "Give me the key."

"I won't let you in if it's the last thing I do," she said with vehemence.

"What are you frightened of?" His reply held a taunt.

"What are *you* frightened of?" She stared up into his fathomless dark eyes.

"Ruining everything for everybody, maybe," he said bleakly.

It shocked her. She stood back as he opened the door.

He pulled her in, shutting them into the quiet of the apartment. The fragrance she was wearing was swirling about in the air between them. It might have had the power of a drug. “Then there’s *this*!” He was caught up by an unstoppable surge. It had him pressing her slender body back against the closed door.

“Oh, yes, there’s *this*!” Colour lit her flawless white skin. The tension between them was palpable, electric. Once again they were in a dangerous place, the shadowy turbulence growing greater.

“I’m waiting for you to stop me,” he challenged. Adrenalin was flooding his veins. He manoeuvred his body ever closer to hers, the softness of a woman, the hard musculature of a man.

She turned her head from side to side, straining to keep some measure of control over the situation. “Even if I *screamed* it wouldn’t stop you.”

“Not that you’re about to scream,” he taunted, lifting his arms to position them on both sides of her blonde head. “You’re pinned in, Sonya.” She was staring up at him with her beautiful mesmeric eyes. “How long have I known you?” he asked, astonished by how little time had passed.

“Maybe you knew me in another life?” Her voice dropped low.

Another trick? Her voice was magic, the little foreign accent, the wide range of intonations, the pitch. That was the trouble with powerful attraction. The alarming way it took control.

“Strangely enough, I believe it.” He cupped the globe of her small breast in his hand. Then with a muffled exclamation he bent his head and crushed her captive silken mouth….

Sparks lit into a conflagration. Sensation was boundless; a wild clamouring in the blood that beat up waves of heat. It was as if every single light, every appliance in the apartment were turned on and *burning*, sucking in all the air. She gave a little moan, thinking nothing could ever be the same again. Her breasts were throbbing under his urgent caressing hands, the nipples gone cherry-hard when she felt her flesh were actually dissolving…

If the ringing phone had not penetrated the thickly meshed web they were caught into, he didn't know what would have happened. One minute they were mindlessly devouring each other, the next they were forced to break apart, breathless and trembling, trying to make the adjustment to the real world.

"That's the phone," she said, now humiliated by her headlong response to him.

He laughed at the sheer ridiculousness of it. "Don't answer it."

"I should." She shook her head, trying to clear it. Her legs were so weak it was an effort to reach the kitchen. When she picked up the receiver, she heard a woman's familiar voice, speaking with urgency.

"Sonya, it's Rowena. Would David be with you? I've had a call from the hospital. Marcus has been admitted."

"Then you know he had a sick turn, Lady Palmerston," Sonya said. "He gave us such a fright. I'll put David on. He brought me home."

"Thank you, dear."

She held out the phone to David. He took it, catching her around the waist and locking her into his grip. She freed herself none the less, moving away to allow him to speak in private. For years she had known the desperation of flight. Of always being on the run from those who would do her harm. She had never known the desperation of passion. He had felt it as much as she.

It was quiet on the balcony. She had filled it with a

luxuriant array of plants in large pots; flowering baskets she had attached to the brick wall. She stood in the night air, tears gathering in her eyes. She had long regarded crying as an intolerable indulgence. It had never helped her. Now she found herself on the verge of tears. For years she had told herself she wasn't scared of anything. But she *was* scared. She was scared of the depth of feeling she had for David Wainwright. She knew nothing would come of the violent attraction they felt for each other. It could only end badly. She was very worried about Marcus as well. Worried about what she would have to tell him. But when? For ghastly moments earlier that night she'd thought Marcus was about to suffer a heart attack. As it was, they wouldn't know the results of his tests for days.

You're in over your head, girl.

She had to give Marcus his ring back. There was faint conciliation in the thought Marcus should not have taken her acceptance as a given. But then the rich were different from everyone else. She put up a hand to pull the pins from her coiled hair. That done, she pressed her hands to her face. Sometimes life was merciless. She didn't love Marcus. Not in any romantic way. She did love David. In every way possible. Only it was Marcus who had given her the ring. Marcus who wanted to marry her. David didn't. He wanted nothing from her. But *sex.*

She still had her eyes closed when David came behind her, pulling her hands from her face. "You're crying." He flicked a salty tear off her cheek with his finger, placing it on his tongue. The cloud of erotica surrounding them was dense.

"It isn't with happiness," she said, turning to confront him. "What are we doing, David? I can see no way out of this short of disappearing."

"Isn't that what you've done before?"

His glittering eyes and his tone made her nerves jangle. "God, I hate you," she muttered.

"Just like I hate you," he returned in an openly self-mocking voice. "Isn't it better to hate me than love me if you're going to marry Marcus?"

"That will be *my* decision." Let him believe what he wanted to believe. It was a certain protection. "What is love really?" she asked.

He laughed briefly. "I have to let that one go at the moment, Sonya. But I can tell you a hell of a lot about wanting a woman."

"Marcus *wants* me but his kind of love I can't return," she said, torn by pity and sadness.

"Then you have to tell him."

His voice cut like a lash. "You want I should do it in the morning?" she challenged with a return of spirit. "Then you could all breathe a great sigh of relief. You don't fool me, David. It's not the time to upset Marcus. You know that as well as I do."

The truth of it made him angry. Yet desire for her was becoming something ungovernable. How could he be so uncaring of his uncle? "I have to go, Sonya," he rasped. "In another minute I'll pick you up and take you to bed."

"What, and betray Marcus?"

She threw up her head in a way now familiar to him. "That's *why* I'm going," he bit off. "I'm not proof against your witchcraft."

"So go, then." A soft poignancy replaced the anger in her voice. "How will it end, David?"

Abruptly the wild clamour that was in him turned to an even odder tenderness. He found himself turning back to cup her face in his hands. "I can't think about it right now, Sonya. I truly can't. We have to find out what's going on with Marcus."

"He was so excited! It was a flag signalling trouble."

She was the very image of lamentation. It caused his anger to flash back. "Has Marcus ever *kissed* you? I mean, *really* kissed you?" There was conflict here. The disloyalty associated with having to ask; the fear of how he would handle it if the answer was above and beyond *yes*.

She threw up her head. He would *never* give his trust. "This love affair is in Marcus's head. His life has been so lonely, for a woman, I mean. I know you all love him. It's extraordinary when you think about it. A kiss on the cheek, dinner, a few outings, one day on his yacht, and suddenly he can't part with me."

Holt forced his hands to drop to his sides. "Look at you! Why would he?" he asked harshly. "That's what falling in love is all about, Sonya." He moved with purpose to the door. He had to get away from her *fast*. Hunger for her was at cyclone-force, a headwind that could drive him back to her.

"I am *not* going to marry Marcus," she called after him.

"You need to marry someone." His retort was delivered with quick fire. "It doesn't do for a woman like you not to be safely contained."

They learned early the next morning Marcus had suffered a heart attack. He would be released in a few days, allowing time for the battery of tests. A top cardiac specialist had been called in. Sonya took flowers and fruit to the hospital. When she arrived at his private room she could see Lady Palmerston was there, looking, as ever, marvellous and so stylish in her tailored suit, slim black skirt, black and white jacket.

Marcus's face lit up. Lady Palmerston's did not. "Marcus

has just been telling me you're engaged?" she said, looking towards Sonya.

It was a far cry from the warm friendly tone Sonya had become used to. "I think Marcus has to give me time to catch my breath, Lady Palmerston," she said, moving to the bed to kiss Marcus's cheek. "How are you feeling, Marcus?"

"Much better," he said, his eyes dazzled by her youth and beauty. "Sorry I gave you and David such a fright. It was just a warning, the specialist said. I'm going to do *exactly* as he says. Life is too sweet."

"I'm sure the first thing is to put all excitements out of your mind, Marcus," Rowena said with a touch of severity. "A bit of quiet is called for."

"Now, now, Aunty dear." Marcus waved an affectionate hand at her. "I've had enough quiet all these years. The flowers are splendid, Sonya." He turned his head to admire them. Sonya had assembled six or seven red torch ginger flowers with some beautiful big glossy pinkish-red anthurium flowers and a few exotic tropical leaves. She intended to place them near the window.

"I have a vase with me," she said, lightly touching Marcus's hand. If only, if only he *hadn't* fallen in love with her. She did so want him as a friend. "I'll just fill it with water."

Less than ten minutes later a nurse came to the door. "Time for a rest now, Mr Wainwright," she said, crisply pleasant, but her eyes whipped over Rowena and Sonya with the message, *Time to leave*.

The lift to the ground floor was crowded, visitors, staff, a doctor in a pin-striped suit looking as though he was very important in the scheme of things. Noise and bustle everywhere. A hospital was never truly silent. Peace was hard to find. They were outside the hospital, walking to one of the parking areas, before Lady Palmerston spoke.

"You might tell me what this is all about, Sonya. An engagement?" She lifted her arched brows, her expression grave, but withholding judgment.

"I'm sorry, Lady Palmerston. I didn't see it coming."

"Call me Rowena, dear," Rowena said impatiently. "Marcus of all people to totally lose his head," she lamented. "Why, you're hardly more than a child."

"I'm twenty-five."

"A great age!" Rowena scoffed. "Marcus is thirty years older."

"So what should I have done?" Sonya implored. "I thought I had found a friend. I wasn't looking for a partner."

"Good Lord, Sonya, you must have had some idea where it was all going? An intelligent young woman like you."

"I regret I didn't speak out earlier. Initially it was the last thing I expected. I admire Marcus. He's a dear, distinguished man. Not an easy thing to tell him what he didn't want to hear. In my own defence I have to say I didn't encourage him. I didn't give him to understand our friendship was moving to another stage. Surely a smile isn't a big come-on? Enjoyment in good conversation? Sharing the things we have in common? I know all about loss, just as Marcus does. The trouble with rich people is they think they can have anything and *anyone* they want." She waved an agitated hand in front of her face.

Rowena considered. "There may be a touch of that," she frankly admitted. "But why, oh, why did you wear Lucy's emeralds, Sonya? That was a *huge* mistake. You've no idea how much gossip that caused."

"Gossip won't kill me," she said hardily. "People can say what they want." Sonya lifted her head to give Rowena a high mettled look. "Marcus was insistent. I had no idea the necklace would be so grand. There was such a look of pleasure in his eyes. For a moment I thought he was even on the verge of tears. I should have refused, but I was loath to take that light out of his face. My mistake."

"Well, it certainly put you in the line of fire," Rowena said quietly. "All of a sudden people are intensely interested in you. Who *are* you exactly? They all know now you're a florist. In my view the best florist in town, but a working girl."

"So, tough to be a working girl!" Sonya exclaimed with a satirical edge. "Naturally I masterminded a plan to land myself a millionaire."

Rowena took Sonya's arm. "My dear, you know as well as I do, it's every other young woman's goal to marry a millionaire."

"It is not mine." Sonya enunciated the words very clearly. "As it happens no one, including you, Lady Palmerston, knows the extent of my finances."

"How *would* I know?" Rowena asked in exasperation. "You never talk about yourself, Sonya. It's as though you're afraid to let anyone come near. I can see your attraction to Marcus. Marcus wouldn't have pressed you for information. I'm here for you, my dear. I like you. More, I've come to care for you. I readily understand how you've come to find a place in Marcus's heart. But your life before you came to this country appears to be a closed book. You're obviously well bred—" She broke off as if bewildered by Sonya's stand.

"I promise you, Lady Palmerston, I will tell you all about myself when I can." Sonya gently pressed her arm.

"So, no Rowena?" Rowena smiled.

Sonya's expression was intense. "I have such respect for

you, Lady Palmerston, I think I should work up to calling you Rowena."

"As you wish, my dear." Rowena glimpsed another Sonya, a young woman from a different background, a different world. Sonya gave such an impression of poise, of near regal self-assurance, then, out of the blue, a hint of a scared little girl. What did it all mean?

Two days after Marcus Wainwright was discharged from hospital he suffered, as others in similar circumstances had suffered before him, the one fatal heart attack. Even with a warning his death came as a pulverizing shock.

David received the news first from Marcus's distraught housekeeper, who found him lying on his side in bed. No sign of life, beyond any doubt. The housekeeper had once been a nursing sister.

From then on he took charge. News of the death of Marcus Wainwright couldn't be contained. His parents had to be advised. He fully expected them to return on the first available flight. He didn't tell them when he rang Marcus had fallen in love with a beautiful young woman decades his junior. He didn't divulge the fact Marcus had given her a magnificent diamond engagement ring. That definitely would have to wait. The entire Wainwright clan had to be advised. A hell of a thing. This was a tragedy that had been waiting to happen. Too late Marcus had come to a decision to take good care of himself.

Then of course there was Sonya.

Sonya was in for a very bad time unless he could control the media.

He knew from long experience he couldn't. The media would have a field day. And what of Marcus's will? If Marcus had been so sure he could persuade Sonya to marry him, wouldn't he have had the family solicitors draw up a new will? Sonya would surely be a beneficiary. He knew in the existing will he had been the principal beneficiary. Marcus had told him. If Marcus had had a new will drawn up it could be argued in court—if it ever came to that—Marcus was a sick man, indeed a dying man, infatuated by a young woman decades his junior. Marcus had been in a state of high confusion. How could a strange young woman of no background lay claim to what could very well be a substantial part of a considerable fortune? The inferences drawn would inevitably be that Sonya had worked on Marcus to change his will.

His mouth went dry at the thought of what his parents would make of it all. Both were formidable people to be approached with nigh on reverence. Grief might very well turn to outrage. Sonya might be an extremely beautiful, highly intelligent young woman with an unmistakable look of good breeding, but he and Rowena between them knew very little about her. One would have thought she was an orphan without family. Once the news broke she would go from an unknown to a high-profile woman. The woman in Marcus Wainwright's life.

By the time the press finished with her there would be nowhere to hide.

He didn't want to tell her over the phone. That would be too cruel. Though he couldn't spare the time he took a taxi to the trendy shopping conclave where she had her florist shop. No time for him to find a park for his own car.

Sonya knew, the instant she caught sight of David, something was very wrong. Her heart began a relentless banging against her ribs. No one was in the shop. She had been busy earlier on, now she was grateful for the lull.

"It's Marcus, isn't it?" She searched his brilliant dark

eyes. He was noticeably pale beneath his deep tan. "He's had a relapse?"

"Worse than that, Sonya." He held her eyes, feeling a heavy sense of guilt along with the grief. He wanted her as he had never wanted anyone before. "There's no easy way to tell you this. Marcus is dead."

"No, no, dear God, no!" She staggered, clutching at the counter for support. "How could this happen? They released him from hospital. I spoke to him last night."

"Heart attacks happen, Sonya, despite everything," he said with a heavy heart. "This one has been waiting to happen, I'm afraid. We can't delay. I want you out of here."

"I can't stay anyway." She was clearly in great distress.

"No, you can't." His emotions were so strong he found himself speaking too harshly. "You have to shut up shop. I'll help you. You'll have to make it until further notice or bring in staff. That can be worked out. *You* won't be able to come back once the news breaks."

"I'm so sorry. So sorry," she moaned. "You think I killed him?" She had gone whiter than white. Her whole body was trembling. She was near enough to breaking.

"Don't torture yourself with thoughts like that," he said quickly. Whatever else he was, he wasn't a savage. No way could he pull her into his arms and offer comfort. His whole being was filled with guilt. "Marcus was a sick man."

"Where did he die?" She was trying desperately not to cry.

"Get yourself together, Sonya," he urged, his whole body tense. "His housekeeper found him. He died peacefully in his sleep."

"Thank God! Does Lady Palmerston know?"

"Sonya, *everyone* will know if we don't get a move on. I have to get you out of here. *I* have to get out of here. People know me. I fear this is going to be a very big story." He couldn't think of a worse scenario.

Over the coming days several photographs of Sonia appeared in the papers and on the Internet. In all of them she looked movie-star glamorous.

A real knockout was the general opinion. All of the photographs, on Marcus's arm—Marcus looking very much older—standing with David, the two of them appearing to be staring into one another's eyes, sitting at the table with the rich and famous as they had been on that gala night. The night she had been wearing a vintage evening gown and Lucille Wainwright's glorious emerald and diamond necklace with the diamond chandelier drops. Her expression in all of them was of cool grace, as if she were to the manner born.

Sonya knew, if no one else, she was the image of her mother, Lilla. Her mother in turn had inherited Katalin's remarkable looks and colouring. Such physical beauty was a gift of the genes.

In New York on a piercingly cold day Laszlo Andrassy-Von Neumann stood in complete silence in Central Park as a tall burly man wearing a greatcoat and a thick dark hat with ear flaps approached him. The man came to a brief halt, withdrawing a manila folder from a deep pocket. Andrassy-Von Neumann had already seen the photographs. They were unmistakably of a woman of his family. To his intense triumph the photographs were of his lost cousin, Sonya. A few more photographs had been taken on the street where she appeared to be in flight from the paparazzi, the rest were the same photographs that had been splashed across the Australian press.

So that was where young Sonya had sought sanctuary!

In exchange for the folder he passed his informant a thick envelope containing a substantial wad of money. It was worth every penny. He had now ascertained Sonya was living in Sydney, under the name of Erickson. It was an enormous stroke of luck the man she had been involved with had been a public figure, otherwise it might have taken longer to find her. She had covered her tracks like a professional. In a way he couldn't help but admire her. America had been very good to his family and him. But he was Hungarian. He wanted to get back to his roots. He had poured so much into his country of birth he now had the estate back: the palace, the title deeds, every last contract signed and sealed.

He was the Andrassy-Von Neumann heir. Katalin and Lilla were dead. He had, however, no real wish to harm Sonya. All she had to do was hand over the Madonna. He would make her an offer she couldn't refuse. Ten million into her bank account? That should do it. Of course, if she were foolish enough to hold out against him? He didn't believe she would. From a penniless little florist to a millionairess in one bound. Her grandmother and her mother and father were dead. He was certain she would see the good sense in making a deal. The *only* sense. After all, they were *family*. He was Count Laszlo Andrassy-Von Neumann. The title to his mind would never be defunct. And Sonya must never be allowed to lay claim to being a countess and the rightful heir of an ancient family's estates. She couldn't possibly stand a chance against him. Katalin's true identity had been destroyed. All reference to her dropped like the plague. Like her father, the old count who had been fool enough to remain in his palace, and her brother, the heir, Katalin had become a victim of war. As for her daughter, Lilla, she was the child of little more than a peasant. The extraordinary thing was he would have recognised his cousin Sonya anywhere. She was without question an Andrassy-Von Neumann.

The phone was ringing as Sonya let herself into the apartment. She was breathing hard with outrage. She had been chased home from a local convenience store by one of the TV channels, a car with a man and a woman in it, on the lookout for a few words, no doubt. It was pretty much like being a hunted animal.

"You have to get out of there."

It was David issuing instructions. He skipped the niceties. Niceties had flown out of the window.

"I'm not going anywhere, David," she said, resisting his formidable tone. "Those media hounds would be onto me wherever I went. Your parents are home?" A photograph of the Wainwrights arriving at the airport had already hit the front pages. No comment from either of them. Both had looked gravely upset.

He gave in to a maddened sigh. "Neither of them wants you at the funeral, Sonya."

"What about *you*, David?" she questioned, very intent on the answer. If he said he didn't want her there, she would begin immediately to try to banish him from her heart and mind.

"You have a right to be there," he said. "The problem, of course, is that your presence will cause a considerable stir."

"Too bad!" she answered coldly. "Marcus would have wanted me to be there. Marcus *loved* me. Have you forgotten?"

"Listen, Sonya, I'm desperately tired," he admitted, with a decided edge. "I maybe damned near thirty but my dad still likes to bawl me out. My mother too is good at beating a drum."

"So you have to go along with them? I understand." Her heart dropped like a stone.

"Oh, come off it!" he bit off. "I can take the heat. The whole business, you must admit, is ghastly. The press must be giving you hell?" He hadn't willed or wanted falling in love with this woman. But he had. He had a terrible longing to be with her. But he couldn't shake the crush of guilt. Or the knowledge he knew so little about her. She hadn't been given an opportunity to make a final decision. It was possible she could have actually accepted Marcus's proposal. Lack of trust was a sharp knife in his chest.

"The press are doing their level best," she told him, aware of his ambivalent feelings towards her. "No wonder celebrities hate them. The hounding is appalling."

"That's why I want you to shift. I have an apartment lined up for you. Somewhere very secure."

"Thank you, David," she said with icy politeness, "but I can't take advantage of your kind offer. I'm staying here. And I'm coming to the funeral. Your parents can bawl you out all they like. They can bawl me out too if they want to. I have backbone. I know enough about you to believe you're every bit as tough as your illustrious parents. I *can* promise you I'll keep a low profile. I won't do a thing to draw attention to myself."

His discordant laugh echoed down the phone. "Sonya, you must have learned by now you only have to show your face to draw attention."

"Did I ask to have this face?" she burst out angrily. "Blonde women get too much attention, all of us bimbos. We both know I intend to pay my last respects to Marcus. If your family thinks they can try any stand-over tactics, they won't work. I've known some truly *horrible* people, David. Your parents would be the good guys compared to them."

"Don't you worry the press will uncover these *horrible* people?" he warned her. "They're pursuing you, and they're going to keep it up. I would think Marcus has taken care of you in his will."

"What, you don't know *already*?" she asked witheringly.

"It's the waiting game." A stinging heat assailed him. He so wanted to see her, despite all that was happening. "Sonya, I want to help you. You need protection. You're going to be hotly pursued in the days ahead."

Pain shot through her right temple. A bad headache coming on. "That seems to be my fate, David, to be pursued. I'll say goodbye now. You must do what you have to do. I know you mean well, but I refuse to be deterred. I will be at Marcus's funeral. I don't intend to disguise myself either, like don a black wig. I am who I am."

"Then let's get your damned name right!" he retorted.

"That would be a big mistake!" She slammed down the phone.

One minute later she was in floods of tears.

She had met a man who was perfect to her. But all wanted was to be rid of her.

CHAPTER SEVEN

SONYA had hoped the crowd would be so large she would have a good chance of slipping into the church unnoticed. As a necessary mark of respect to the Wainwright family she had done her best to look as inconspicuous as possible. Her giveaway white-blonde hair, she had all but concealed, fastening it in coils at the back, then topping it off with a wide-brimmed black hat. She had thought the inexpensive hat would be an excellent disguise. Unfortunately the result wasn't as low key as she had wished. The hat looked great on her. She already had a black dress and suitable accessories. Nothing ultra smart, but good quality. Part of the problem was, black suited her. It made a showcase of her colouring. Her hair wasn't on show, but she couldn't hide her white skin. But for this very sad occasion, black it had to be. She had no real status even if Marcus had given her that magnificent ring.

On and off for nights she had cried. She felt the tears coming now but she had to fight them back. She had to find and maintain her composure. A young woman in tears would only bring unwelcome attention. Mourners were everywhere. In its way it was a spectacular turnout. Among the dignitaries present, the State Premier, and a representative of the PM, who was out of the country. Marcus Wainwright had been a much respected man, a member of one of the richest and most influential families in the nation.

She made it up the stone steps on shaky legs and through the door of the cathedral. She looked to neither left nor right. A strong arm took hold of hers. She looked up quickly, anticipating trouble. What she saw was a heavily built man filling out a black suit. It was his job, she realized, to keep crowd control. He drew her aside. "Ms Erickson, isn't it?" he asked, very politely.

"Please take your hand off me," she said, keeping her tone low.

"You've done yourself no good coming here, miss." He was having difficulty not staring at her, she was so beautiful. "The family, I'm afraid, don't want you."

"I'm not here for the family, sir," Sonya said very quietly. "I'm here for Marcus Wainwright, my *dear* friend. Now, if you don't want me to raise my voice—I would regret the necessity, but I will—you'll take your hand away. Marcus would have wanted me here. Who do the other Wainwrights think they are, anyway?" Her green eyes flashed fire.

"Oh, they're Somebodies, Ms Erickson," he assured her, shaking his head. He could see the determination in her green eyes. He had to admire her for it. It was obvious he hadn't intimidated her in any way. Actually he didn't want to.

"Well, I'm a Somebody too," she said. "Please move away from me. I'm going to find a seat before they're all taken. I'll be as quiet as possible. I have no wish to cause offence but I refuse to be treated badly."

The security guard's eyes flickered. He dropped his arm and gave what came close to being a courteous bow. "Good luck to you, miss. I fear you're going to need it."

Every eye in the church turned as the Wainwright clan moved in procession to the front of the church. Sonya kept looking straight ahead. She couldn't see the casket. She didn't want to. She felt truly terrible. Three unimaginable things had happened. Marcus had fallen in love with her. Marcus was dead. David had accomplished what no other man had ever done. He had stolen her heart. Now he had as good as abandoned her. The service went on and on. She stood. She sat. She sang with the rest of them, not even knowing the words, but filling in as best she could. It was all so *unreal*. She listened to all the wonderful things family, close friends and dignitaries said about Marcus. David's contribution was the most beautiful and the most moving. She had to bite her lip hard the entire time he was speaking in his dark resonant voice. No one had dared mention the fact Marcus at the end of his life had been contemplating remarrying. The media wasn't any too sure of that. The Wainwright family was going to pretend she didn't exist.

Afterwards she stayed put until the church had almost been cleared before she made quietly for a side door, only to find the pathway outside had been blocked. That meant she had to go out of the front door. The Wainwrights, as was the custom, stood almost directly outside, receiving the long line of mourners who wished to express their sympathy. She would have to pass them. David was with them, tall, arresting and gravely formidable in his funereal clothes.

Looking straight in front of her, Sonya moved into the sunlight. It might have been a brilliant spotlight focused directly on her, because the buzz and hum of conversation among the huge crowd of mourners fell to a reverberating silence.

So much for the hat and the conservative clothes.

Her inner voice had kicked in.

Keep going. You can do it. Ignore all the curious and

condemnatory faces. Ignore the Wainwrights. David is one of them. Family solidarity is important. Think of yourself as someone special. You are!

She had herself under control, keeping her mind busy with the thought of what the family might have done had she been wearing Marcus's great diamond ring. Not only that, *flashed* it. She still had the ring. David had refused point blank to take charge of it, saying Marcus had wanted her to have it and that was that. How exactly did she return it? She was almost at the bottom of the stone steps when a young woman chose that precise moment to approach her, catching her by the arm.

Paula Rowlands moved right up into Sonya's face, muttering in a low contemptuous voice, "The hide of you! I don't believe it." She had been alerted Sonya was among the mourners so, during the service while appearing to be deeply saddened, she had decided on a strategy. She would ambush this infuriating woman who had been told not to show her face.

"Are you crazy?" Sonya asked. Disgust overcame any sense of alarm. "Don't bother to answer that. I'd like you to get away from me. And I mean *now*." She sounded far more positive than she felt.

Neither young woman saw Holt Wainwright move swiftly down the steps until he was towering over both young women. "I'll take you to your car, Sonya," he said, sounding as if he wouldn't tolerate any refusal. "You don't intend to go on?"

Of course he meant to the cemetery. "No." She put his mind at rest.

He turned his head to address Paula directly. His dark eyes were as glittery as black crystals. "I had no idea, Paula, you were so full of malice."

"Malice?" Deeply wounded, Paula stared up at him

incredulously. "*She's* the danger, Holt. *I'm* your friend, Holt, remember?"

"I'm trying to." He inclined his handsome head further towards her, still holding Sonya's arm. "Please do *not* offend my parents, Paula. Do *not* offend the memory of my uncle. Walk quietly away now."

Paula flushed scarlet. "Of course, Holt." She obeyed.

Those remaining of the huge crowd followed every step of their progress, across the road then down a side street to where Sonya had parked her car. That included press photographers and a television camera, although they'd had the common decency to keep their distance at this point.

"You were cruel to her, weren't you?" Sonya said on a distressed breath, but very glad of his supporting arm.

His handsome face was closed. "She deserved it. What was she saying anyway?"

"What you'd expect. Do *you* think I have a hide, David?"

"I think you've got a lot of guts," he answered tersely. "Not too many people stand up to my parents."

"*You* do. Otherwise you wouldn't be here with me now. Or this is one of your strategies? Get her away as quickly and as quietly as possible."

He could see her hurt. It registered in her beautiful eyes. Nothing but distress for the both of them. "All you need to know is *this*, Sonya. I won't have anyone attacking you. Whether it would have turned out well or a disaster, Marcus loved you."

"So you went for disaster? I guess you're with me now for Marcus's sake?"

"Sonya, right now I'm here for *you*." They had reached her small car, the roof and the bonnet lightly scattered with tiny yellow flowers from the overhead trees. "I need to talk to you, Sonya," he said.

He appeared to be studying every separate feature of her face.

"You're going straight home?"

"No, I'm taking off for parts unknown." She offered a dismal joke.

"Maybe that would be a good idea for a week or two." His forehead creased in concentration.

"So where do you suggest I go? Far North Queensland. Cape York?" She named a remote part of Queensland a few thousand miles away. "Or maybe across Bass Strait to Tasmania. That should be far enough."

"I can arrange Port Douglas." He named a famous Queensland beach resort. The aching hunger he felt for her was squeezing his chest.

"Problem is I'm not a sun worshipper like you. I'll think of something, David. I can see you're anxious to get rid of me."

He didn't deign to answer. *God, what do I do now?*

"Sonya Erickson, the girl who can't be found." She unlocked her car, sweeping the offending hat off her head and throwing it onto the seat. Then she shook her head, shaking her hair free of its tight, confining pins.

"How could you expect me to trust you, when you don't trust me, Sonya? You've told me nothing. At best you've thrown out a few clues. What could be so bad you keep it locked up? *Who* is looking for you, Sonya?" His tone was deadly serious. "Someone is. I'm convinced Erickson isn't your real name."

"I don't have a name," she said mournfully. No reason to tell him now. "I'm like my maternal grandmother. My identity has been lost."

He stared down at her, the waterfall of hair, her marvellous illuminated skin. "That doesn't make sense."

"It makes sense to me," she said.

"The will is going to be read this afternoon," he offered abruptly. "You're in it.'

"You're certain of that?" she asked scornfully. "So where am I—top of the list? Or second? God forbid I should rob you of your inheritance."

"Just once, Sonya. Be *yourself*."

"Good heavens, David. You sound as though you care?" She knew she had reached a crisis point in her life. She had to be strong. "If Marcus did remember me in his will I'm sure it'll be contested. This woman has exerted undue pressure on an ailing man might be the way to go." She knew she sounded bitter, but she had to make a final break.

"Marcus wouldn't have wasted any time seeing you were provided for," he said. God knew that would cause, not ripples, but a flood.

"Aren't the Wainwrights going to love that?" she scoffed.

Only her lovely mouth was quivering. Her desire to turn him away was in vain. "It's not the money, Sonya."

"Of course it's the money!" she said angrily, fighting tears. "Even billionaires don't knock back money. Money is everything to them. If Marcus has left me money I can refuse it. Or, better yet, give it away. Anyway, you could be *wrong*."

He very much doubted that. "I want to see you this evening," he said, tension in his entire body. "I can tell you then."

"But I don't want to see you." She slipped behind the wheel with natural grace, her eyes glittering with tears.

He looked in at her. "Yes, you *do*." Love was the best or the worst of spells. Once under it, one lost sight of common sense, even reason.

Sonya drove away without another word. On the one hand she believed she had Laszlo's people looking for her.

The big worry was her recent notoriety. She had never appeared in a newspaper before. She was exposed as never before. On the other hand, the Wainwrights, and their extended family, were all involved in some way in Wainwrights' numerous enterprises. They were the ones who wanted to slam the door in her face. David was powerfully attracted to her. She knew that just as she knew he didn't trust her. Who could blame him? She was acting as though she had a disreputable past and in some ways she had. She knew he was feeling a degree of guilt. She was feeling it too. When they had come together no thoughts of Marcus had stood in the way. She recognised too powerful parents had a way of having the last word.

Better you'd never come into his life.

Nor he into hers.

Every Wainwright face showed shocked disbelief. They were all gathered in the library while the family solicitor read out the will. Holt sat between his mother and father, from time to time taking his mother's hand. She might not be showing it, but he knew she was deeply shocked by Marcus's sudden death.

Charities dear to Marcus's heart were treated very generously, so too young members of the family. There were bequests to lifelong friends, tidy sums to staff present and past, Marcus's collection of valuable paintings—three of the most important to the National Art Gallery, the remainder to his mother, along with the bronze sculptures she had long admired. Chinese porcelains, jades and ivories went to Rowena, who was too upset to attend the will reading. A great windfall of shares went to his father, Robert, and many personal effects. The bulk of his uncle's fortune, including a hefty block of shares from Marcus's large portfolio went to him. Nothing unexpected about that. All the family knew he had been the apple of his uncle's eye. However, to everyone's stunned amazement twenty million dollars went to a Sonya Erickson, an unknown, for whom in Marcus's words he had, "a great affection".

His father and mother showed no emotion whatever throughout, but he could see his mother's cheeks were flushed and his father's strong jaw set. There was going to be a huge fuss later. Who *was* this Sonya Erickson?

"One thing," Sharron Holt-Wainwright said tersely. "She's very beautiful, very classy."

His mother never missed anything.

Everyone had gone home, most in a state of shock, to thrash out the ramifications of the will in private. Twenty million dollars to some young florist? She could buy a whole rainforest.

"Pour me a whisky and water, would you, David?" His father was down, down, down. The brothers had been very close.

"I'll have one as well," said his mother, who looked similarly drained. "I take a very dim view of all this." She looked across the room at her son. "How did this all happen, Holt? Surely you could have intervened in some way? It seems a terrible thing to say of darling Marcus, but he must have temporarily lost his mind. She's young enough to have been his daughter."

"Maybe he wanted a daughter," Robert Wainwright suggested. "Poor old Marcus was terribly lonely, no matter how hard we tried to bolster his spirits. He missed Lucy so. David, you're looking doubtful?"

"Marcus gave her a ring," Holt, well used to his parents using both names for him, responded bluntly. He handed a crystal tumbler to each of them. They would have to know. "An engagement ring."

"Good God!" Robert Wainwright's dark head fell back against the leather chair, as though for once he felt defeated.

"What can have been in Marcus's head?" his mother wailed. "He's been chased by plenty of women these past years. Suitable women his own age."

"He didn't *want* a woman his own age," David told her dryly. "He wanted Sonya."

"One needn't wonder why," Sharron said in a voice dry as ash. "Twenty million will make a big difference to a working girl."

"She doesn't know she's a rich woman yet," David said.

"A *very* rich woman." Robert Wainwright gave a hard cynical bark. "A woman as beautiful as that could wind any man around her little finger. We have to meet this girl, David. Make an effort to avoid any unpleasantness. At least she won't need to sell her story to some vapid woman's magazine. Not *now*. She's a florist?"

"Does she intend to return the ring or is she going to keep it as a souvenir?" Sharron asked, with heavy sarcasm.

"She did try to give it into my care."

"And?" Sharron fired up, staring back very closely at her son.

"I didn't take it," he replied flatly. "Marcus gave it to her. He wanted her to have it."

"It's the rare woman who gives anything back," said his father. "You must arrange some time for us to meet her."

"So does she just drop in or what?" He gave vent to a burst of anger.

His mother continued to stare at him. "Invite her to dinner," she said eventually. "I think my judgment might be more reliable than dear Marcus's. Or even *yours*, my darling. Make it this coming Saturday evening. I'm determined to get answers from this girl. If she's as smart as I think she is, she'll come. She must be made to understand no one trifles with this family."

It was a simple matter to follow his target back from the funeral of the bigwig she was alleged to have been involved with. A nice enough apartment complex, but nothing to speak about. Of course, she had been lying low. The count was certain she had no money to speak of. What she did have was a treasured icon that rightfully belonged to the count. It was his job to get it back. He could not fail. He would not fail. The count did not tolerate failure. He would keep her under surveillance, and then select the right moment. He was to offer her a great deal of money in exchange for the icon and her word that she would abandon any claim to the Andrassy-Von Neumann estate. There was to be no violence. Violence was a last resort. In the girl's place he would jump at the count's offer. The irony was she could have easily passed for the count's own granddaughter. The family resemblance was very strong.

CHAPTER EIGHT

HOLT arrived at Sonya's apartment around seven-thirty p.m., parking his borrowed car outside the building. His top-of-the-line Mercedes would be something of a give-away and he didn't want that. His nerves were strung tight. No way could he possibly *act* the way he felt. He was a man under considerable constraint. A man who was head over heels in love with a young woman his uncle had asked to be his wife. Moreover one neither of them had known much about. Now Marcus was no longer with them and he was left torn by feelings of guilt as though he had committed some serious transgression. It was largely irrational but it was there all the same. He felt the crush of it in his chest.

Today had been one of the worst days of his life. It took all his self control not to allow it to descend into chaos. Sonya, Ice Princess that she was, had been affected too. She could even feel some of his guilt. They had been caught up together, filled with a mad, uncaring rapture. There was even a possibility she mightn't want to see him again. Especially when she found out she was a very rich young woman. Real life beat fiction hands down, he thought.

She opened the door to him looking anything but an adventuress. Indeed she looked young and innocent. He took in at a glance the absence of her normal cool composure and the tantalising veil of sophistication. Her beautiful hair was hanging down her back in a thick plait, like a schoolgirl. The lovely colour was gone from her face. Her skin was as white as the petals of a rose. She was wearing a soft loose violet dress with some sparkly embroidery around the oval neckline and the long hem.

The opposite of the elation was despair. He wanted her so badly the pain was almost too fierce to be borne. But Marcus's sudden death had brought the barriers down. Could they ever come up? Suddenly, passionately, he reached for her hand. Their fingers entwined with a life of their own.

"Sonya, how are you?"

"Very shaky." She made no movement to pull away, though the shadow of Marcus loomed large.

There are rules, rules, rules. Self-esteem demands you stick to the rules.

What rules? She had discovered she had two inner voices. They went back and forth. Both in conflict. One haunted her in the early hours, castigating her for her inaction. The other told her she had made no positive commitment to Marcus. It was Marcus who had acted as though the relationship *he* had wanted were carved in stone. If she was to blame in any way—and she believed she was—it had been her inability to keep their friendship within bounds. The result, Marcus had steamed ahead with their friendship at the rate of knots. Fine man that he had been, Marcus had lived a life where he truly could have just about anything he wanted. The trade off for her was, he would give her a life of great privilege and comfort.

David's voice broke into her troubled thoughts.

"Have you eaten?"

"I'm not really hungry. Have you?" She risked staring up into his brilliant dark eyes. He was beyond handsome. But she registered his immense strain.

Such a short period of time since he had seen her, yet it felt like an eternity.

"I said have you eaten?" Sonya repeated, knowing he hadn't properly heard her.

He shook his dark head. "We could go out. On the other hand, we'd better stay in. I didn't even bring my own car. I stole one."

"You *didn't*!" She led him into the living room.

"Well, I took it without asking." He tried for a smile, but it was too much of an effort. Despondently he slumped onto one of the sofas.

"I could make us a sandwich," she offered, thinking she too could break under the pressure. He looked marvellous to her in the bright lights, his coal-dark eyes glittering in his finely sculpted face. "It won't take any time."

"Take all the time you like." He was daunted by the strength of his feelings for her. He knew he shouldn't be here. Not feeling like this. "How are you doing *really*?" he asked.

"I don't know." She moved into the galley kitchen. Her answer was very quiet. He had never thought to see her so subdued. "It all seems like a bad dream. I wanted Marcus in my life. But not as a husband, as my friend. Now I feel like I've somehow betrayed him."

He set his jaw. Didn't he share her feelings? "It wouldn't have worked, Sonya, even if the two of us hadn't become involved. I take the blame. I acted upon the attraction. Only Marcus didn't want you for a friend. He wanted you for a wife. You're telling me the truth? The relationship hadn't become sexual?"

She flared up so quickly, warmth rushed back into her body. "Think what you like!"

He sat forward, putting two hands to his dark head. "Sonya, I'm sick of *thinking*." He laid it out for her.

She could see the intolerable stress. It caused her to come from behind the counter. "I *told* you, David," she said in a calmer voice. "We're both upset. You've been with your parents, haven't you?"

"Of course I've been with my parents." His reply was decidedly edgy. "The will was read late this afternoon."

"Tell me you got the lion's share," she invited, hoping that was true.

"I did," he said, glancing up at her, desire pumping into him no matter what. "*You* got twenty million dollars."

"What?" She registered the steely expression on his face. The next moment she was overtaken by dizziness. "Twenty—" she began, then broke off. Oxygen wasn't reaching her brain. Her legs were starting to give. She told herself dazedly she had never fainted in her life, even when times were very bad, but the room was filling up with clouds of grey smoke.

David moved so fast he was near flying. He grabbed her before she hit the floor. "Sonya!" He felt intense anger at himself. Was he ever going to stop putting her to the test? He could at least have worked up to telling her of her inheritance, only he'd wanted her spontaneous reaction. Shame all around him. For what he had here was a genuine faint.

He arranged her on the rug that lay beneath her feet. Lying down was the fastest way to recovery. As a yachtsman, he had taken all the necessary first-aid courses. Anyone could faint given the right conditions. This was shock. Her eyes were open. She hadn't lost full consciousness. It was what was called a pre-syncope. He found it simple to diagnose. She was frowning as if irritated. After a moment she tried to sit up, but he held her down, grabbing a cushion off the sofa and putting it beneath her head.

"It's okay, Sonya. Lie there for a while. You'll be right in a moment or two."

It was all his fault. Angry with himself, he lowered himself onto the rug beside her, lying back. He was fed up with everything. Fed up with running the gauntlet of emotions. For a man who had been in control of his world he was floundering badly. He was thankful at least he hadn't *slept* with Sonya. Only, in kissing her with Marcus in the background, he felt as though he had given into a passion that had somehow diminished him. Betrayal wasn't in his nature. He had truly loved his uncle. Only he had wanted Sonya more.

You still want her.

His inner voice forced him to own up.

Neither of them spoke. Neither of them knew what to say. That was the full irony of it. They just lay there, side by side, each locked in their own thoughts that were remarkably similar.

Finally Sonya said, "I can't handle this, David. It's all too much. I don't want Marcus's money. A gift, a memento, maybe, I would have accepted, but never a fortune! I can't live with a gesture like that. I wasn't going to marry him."

"You're sure about that?" Jealousy exploded out of him. How ignoble!

She made a little keening sound, struggling not to turn to him.

Only David was compelled to turn to her. "Okay, I'm sorry. I didn't mean that."

"It will happen again," she told him bleakly. "Your efforts to bring me down."

"Or wait for you to bring *me* down," he said with black humour. "One of my fears is I know so little about you, Sonya. You have to accept Marcus's legacy. You can't give it back. No one will contest your right to have it. It was Marcus's wish."

"It's *my* wish he hadn't." How could he understand her, when she couldn't understand herself? From the age of sixteen she'd had no one close to advise her; no one to help her through her traumas, her never-ending grief at what had happened to her parents. Hadn't there been enough tragedy in their family life? What relatives she had, overnight changed. They wanted only to possess her, use her. Her heart had been cracked so badly she had thought it beyond repair. Yet under Marcus's benign influence, the mending had begun. But it was David who had brought her back to full blazing life.

"People will hate me," she said.

He answered quietly enough. "I thought you didn't care about what people thought?"

"It seems I was wrong. I'm ready to get up." From feeling unnaturally chilled, her blood was heating up. She knew the sensations for what they were: an automatic response to his nearness. They had always had this dynamic from the moment they met. There was small comfort in the fact neither of them had engineered a relationship. The only thing to blame was fate.

"Why bother?" The slightest trace of humour crept into his voice. "I'm liking it here." Compulsively, he reached out a long arm to put it beneath her head. So close to, he was inhaling her natural sweet fragrance like an aphrodisiac. "What am I going to do with you, Sonya?"

"What do you *want* to do with me?" There was a complete absence of provocation in her voice.

Yet it threw him into a kind of panic. "What I've wanted to do since I laid eyes on you," he said, feeling he was moving beyond all pretence.

"That *cannot* happen, David. You have lost your beloved uncle. I have lost a true friend." She continued to lie quietly beside the lean, splendid length of him. "What did your parents have to say?"

"They want to meet you, of course."

Her breath fluttered. "They want to find out exactly what kind of person I am? How did I scheme to get Marcus to fall in love with me?" She was too saddened for any show of indignation.

"Something like that," he said sombrely.

"Did you tell them he gave me an engagement ring?"

"I told them you tried to give it back into my keeping. I refused to take it."

"So they have serious business to attend to," she concluded. "They need to check this Sonya Erickson out?"

"*Someone* needs to, Sonya," he said bluntly. "I've told you, if there's anything worrying you, anything that could be called a problem, you'd be wise to tell me now."

She stared up at the white ceiling. "Perhaps you are overestimating your importance in my life, David. I am now an heiress, am I not?"

He gave a hard little grunt. "Yes, you are, but it doesn't help anyone when you spend your time trying to put me off. Don't you realize that? It's all going to come out, Sonya," he assured her with some force. "This legacy Marcus left you. It will be the talk of the town. Someone always spills the beans, no matter how many times they're told to keep their mouths shut. Your legacy far exceeds anything the minor beneficiaries received. People look to motivation, reasons. Why would a man like Marcus leave a young woman he knew for only a short time a small fortune?'

"*Small?*" she exclaimed in disbelief. "Twenty million dollars is *small*?"

"Well, it's hardly *big*!"

It was difficult to believe he was serious. Yet she knew he was. There was a *universe* of difference between them. She sat up, willing the strength to return to her legs. "So now I see you for exactly *who* you are. You're David Wainwright, heir to a great fortune."

"You're missing the bit about the huge responsibilities that go with it," he said bluntly. "No one talks about *them.* My father has always been under tremendous pressure. I am *now.* I expect a lot more in the future. It's not just a question of having a lot of money, Sonya. It's holding onto it for future generations. And I would remind you my family, through the Wainwright Foundation, does a lot of good."

"So I stand corrected. I think it might be a good idea if you left." Anger that could not be totally explained was a burning, smouldering trail towards dynamite. "Is it okay I get past you? Or do I have to go over the top of you?" Such sensations were coursing through her body, they were making her a little crazy.

He gave a deep groan, "God, yes, *do it*!" he invited.

"Maybe I will! You should not test me in this way." She began to lever her body over his.

It was a huge mistake.

His grip on her was so hard and strong his hands might have been made out of steel. "Why not? I'm not going to make it easy for you." The protective walls were imploding. A hunger more savage than anything he had ever known welled up inside him. He held her in place over his aroused body, then, when she moaned, he reversed their positions so he was half atop her, taking most of his weight on his upper arms.

"In one way I wish you hadn't done that," he said, staring into her emerald eyes, "and then again, I'm so glad you did."

"Always *my* fault?" Desire had all but knocked the breath out of her.

"Of course it's your fault," he mocked. "The little games you play." He displayed the strength and grace of a gymnast, holding his own weight while dropping taunting little kisses all over her face, her mouth, the line of her jaw and the length of her throat. Then he came back to run the tip of his tongue over the outline of her full mouth, tracing its contours.

It made her head spin. She wanted to pull him down on top of her. Press herself into him. Revel in the weight of his body on hers. She wasn't strong enough to withstand the tongues of flame licking at her. The little moans she kept hearing, pathetically, were hers. Her back was arching off the floor, her yearnings painfully clear. The stabbing sensations between her legs had become pain. At long last she was totally awakened to passion. Worse, her body, regardless of her mind, was demanding consummation.

"You're so...beautiful," he murmured.

It sounded as if he lamented the fact. His kisses, though long and deep, were taunting in their fashion. He *knew* she was desperate for more of him. She knew it as she knew his feelings of guilt. She shared them. Had dear, kind Marcus actually poisoned any hope of anything *real* between them? There was such turbulence in the air it was crowding the tiny space of common sense that remained in her head.

Don't let him know just how desperately you yearn for him. Don't do it. You will never meet his needs or the Wainwright expectations.

"How do I stop kissing you?" he muttered against her throat. "Is there a way?"

"You could let me up." She felt feverish with excitement, yet she found sufficient strength to speak coldly.

"I don't *want* to let you up. *Ever*!"

"Even when I want to be free?"

His answer cut to the truth. "You weren't free from the moment you looked into my eyes. Your will is falling short of your desires, Sonya," he mocked her.

"As is yours." She gave a broken laugh. "I thought, as you're always telling me, David, I'm expert at concealing myself?"

"It's high time we settled that. How many other men have kissed you?" He couldn't resist suckling her full lower lip. It was aquiver, so soft and lush.

"My father, long dead," she confessed, in a strange off-key whisper.

That sobered him. She had never mentioned her father. "Sonya, you must tell me about him." He swung back onto the floor, staring down at her, with such intensity in his eyes surely she would respond.

Only she didn't. "Let me up, David," she ordered.

"Certainly, my lady." He stood, drawing her to her feet, but keeping a steadying arm around her. He was acutely aware of the trembling in her body. He understood. *He* was a million miles away from being calm himself. "Why don't you lie on the sofa?" he suggested. "I won't bother you. I'll sit here." He pulled out an armchair. "You must talk, Sonya."

"It's rather terrible, the gift of love," she mused. She didn't take the sofa; she sat straight. "Rapture on the one hand. The real possibility it will be taken away on the other. In my experience love has meant loss. I'm not talking romantic love. I've shielded myself from that. I thought it wise. I have not been open with you and others, because I've found it so difficult to surrender my trust, David. Do you believe in heaven?" She looked at him, her heart in her eyes.

"If I did, Marcus will be there." Grief showed on his handsome face.

"So you don't?"

"One needs a whole lot of *faith*, Sonya. Faith is believing in something for which there's no proof. I keep an open mind on a possible afterlife. That's all."

"My parents were very good people," she said, looking down at her locked hands. "My grandmother. They believed in heaven."

"Do *you*?"

She arranged her thick plait over her shoulder. "How can I? Again, in my experience it's the good people who die. Bad people prosper."

"And the bad people are?" He kept his eyes trained on her, hoping her practised composure was about to crack open.

"My family."

"Family?" He frowned, thoroughly perplexed, but he stayed quiet. If he stayed quiet she might confide in him. David sat back in his chair, staring across at her.

She didn't speak again for a full minute. Her reticence was so well ingrained.

"Sonya, my parents want to meet you," he prompted her. "They'd like to ask you some questions. Surely you agree they're entitled to some answers? Marcus was my father's brother. They were very close. My mother loved Aunt Lucille. Marcus had asked you to be his wife. He gave you a magnificent ring. They know about that as they have to."

The emerald of her eyes darkened. "I tried to give it back."

"So where is it?" He suddenly thought to ask. "Valuable things need safekeeping."

A madness got into her. "You want to see something

to surpass your precious emeralds?" A blaze of challenge came into her face, her beautiful eyes flashed.

"So show me," he invited, wondering what this was all about.

"Wait and see." She sprang up, rushing down the corridor.

Moments later, she was back, holding something in her hands. A small book of some sort? he thought. An old photograph in a very unusual leather-bound case, dark green, gold-tooled. She sat down beside him breathing with enormous excitement. "You may look." She passed the case to him with very real reverence.

It was oddly heavy for its size and it had a tangible aura. It also gave off an aroma like woody incense. There were sparkling tears in her eyes.

"Sonya!" He set the case down a moment to stare at her. "Whatever *is* this?" There was such a look on her face it would make a strong man weep.

"Open it."

It was a command.

He didn't attempt any levity. He knew it would be a huge mistake. But as he took the case into his hands he felt a strange tingling. It ran up his arms, like shivers of electricity, and struck a chord in his body. He even had to bunch his hands. "What am I holding—a relic of some sort?" He knew she was deeply religious. Her background, of course.

"Come, open it." Her hand fell imperiously on his arm. "I have guarded it with my life."

She sounded *tortured.*

"Sonya, I'll do everything I can to help you." He felt such a protective surge she could surely feel it? "Are you in trouble?"

"David, I didn't *steal it,*" she told him, almost kindly.

He released a breath. "Thank God for that!"

Two sides of the case opened out, like a triptych. Very carefully, as though he was handling something precious and very rare, he opened one side, and then the other.

He possessed a good *eye*, refined as it was, growing up surrounded by beautiful things. Still he had to gasp, "God, is this *real*?" He was staring down in stunned amazement at what was an extremely old and valuable, if not priceless, icon of the Madonna.

"Not God, the Madonna," she announced, leaning into his shoulder.

Whatever scenarios he had imagined, it was never this. "But this is *extraordinary*! You must tell me about it." The Madonna's headdress and robe, the framing all around the icon, the ornamentation on both sides, were studded with precious stones—diamonds, rubies, sapphires, emeralds—and embellished with seed pearls. The halo around the Madonna's head was gold leaf. Her crown, studded with diamonds, had the unmistakable gleam of twenty-four-carat gold. The expression on the beautiful Byzantine face was mournful. The Madonna was not carrying The Child.

He shot her a piercing glance. "Are you sure some museum isn't after this as we speak? For pity's sake, Sonya, if *you* didn't steal it, and I believe you, did someone close to you?" Surely one wasn't allowed to carry a precious icon out of whatever country it came from, he thought. Poland, Hungary? It was obviously Roman Catholic.

"Be certain of it, David," she said, with a proud lift of her chin. "It was *not* stolen. The icon has been in my family for centuries. It was the only thing my grandmother could spirit out of Hungary in 1945 when the Russians were advancing." Her voice broke. She gave a little choking sob, which she quelled in an instant.

"Sonya, you've stunned me with this," he said slowly,

even if it did explain so much about her. "I regret I've sometimes taunted you about your aristocratic connections. Now it appears you have them. Could you tell me your grandmother's story? It sounds important."

She sank back against the sofa. "I don't share my secret with anyone," she said. "Now there is *you*." She began to speak in what seemed to him a trancelike voice. "My maternal grandmother's name was Katalin Andrassy-Von Neumann. She was the only one to escape the Russians under the protection of a family servant. My great-grandfather, Count Andrassy-Von Neumann, and Katalin's older brother, Matthias, remained at the palace. My great-grandfather's brother, Karoly, got together as much of his fortune as he could, then fled with his family to the United States. They all survived and became very rich. Maybe a lot richer than the Wainwrights." She shrugged ironically. "The Russians captured my great-grandfather and Matthias. They were never seen or heard of again. My grandmother lived the remainder of her life in far away Norway. She was forced into marriage with a member of the loyal servant's family after the old man died. My mother was married off too. She managed to escape. She found her saviour in my father. He was Austrian, of good family and thus a man of influence. I never knew the icon existed until I was sixteen. Not long after that, my parents were killed in a car crash." She stopped abruptly.

"Are you okay?" He spoke very quietly, concerned for her, but anxious not to stop the flow.

"Why not?" She gave a discordant laugh. "I'm speaking to you, aren't I? It is costing me an effort."

"I can see that. Sonya, I'm so sorry. We can stop now if you want to." It didn't seem right to upset her further.

Only she took up her story. "I am an orphan of the storm. I will go to my grave believing the crash that killed my parents was engineered by my cousin, Laszlo. He now calls himself Count Laszlo Andrassy-Von Neumann, though he is not entitled to." She was speaking with outright contempt. "I never feel safe even in this country of peace and freedom where everyone says exactly what they please. I *need* to feel safe, David."

"So you thought you would have been safe with Marcus?"

"He had so much to offer," she said mournfully. "I'm not talking about his money. I mean his kindness, his generosity, his protective feelings towards me. I wanted to let him into my life eventually. Only I found I couldn't marry a man I did not love in the romantic fashion. My feeling for Marcus was not like that. He would have been so perfect as the uncle I had long wished for."

He readily saw that. "Humour me, won't you? Start again and go slowly. Tell me about this Laszlo character. Where does he live?"

"Not here." She shuddered. "He has vast interests in the United States and in Hungary. The estate has been returned to him as the rightful heir along with many of the stolen paintings and so forth. He divides his time between the United States, a country so good to his father and him, and Hungary. He is Hungarian through and through. He wants the Madonna."

Why wouldn't he? "This is quite a story." Indeed his eyes were dazzled by the glitter given off by the many precious stones that decorated the icon. And Sonya had had it in her possession all this time. "One to marvel over really. Princess Michael of Kent and her mother took refuge here in Australia. Quite a few Jewish families, once immensely rich, came here to live out the rest of their shattered lives. Marcus knew one such lady. A great lady, he always said."

"Many European and Russian families have such stories," she said. "I should tell you Laszlo never does anything himself. He has people to carry out his wishes; do all his dirty work. He wasn't even in Germany when my parents were killed. The authorities said it was an accident. I *know* my mother went in fear of Laszlo. I can't talk any more about this." She bent her shining head.

"I'm grateful for what you have said, Sonya. It explains so much. But surely with all his resources this Laszlo was able to make contact with you?"

"Track me down, don't you mean?" She gazed at him, her eyes matching the glitter of the emeralds.

"Well—yes."

"He hasn't so far," she said. "I've been extremely careful. I train myself well. Who would think a young woman who worked in a florist shop would have a priceless icon in her possession anyway? Why should I be poor when I could be rich? Some people, heathens, might even pry out the stones. They would be worth a fortune. But that would be sacrilege. The icon remains with me. *I* am the rightful heir. Not Laszlo. I know it. He knows it."

There was big trouble brewing here, David thought. Sonya had long been under cover, but now that cover was blown. Ironically through her connection with his family. It was his family who now bore the responsibility of protecting her. "I think you should get out of this apartment," he said, decisively.

She faced him directly. *"No!"*

"Then you're not thinking straight," he told her, tersely. "You've had considerable exposure in the press. No country on earth is isolated these days. Our own press will be trying to find out all they can about you. *I* made an attempt that came to nothing. But it will all change. What is your *real* name?"

She smiled ironically into his eyes. "It matters?"

"Of course it matters." He spoke sternly, in an effort to get through to her.

"So, would you believe Von Neumann? I am Sonya Von Neumann. My father's family had connections with the Andrassy-Von Neumanns. That's how my mother met my father."

"Then surely after the tragedy there was some member of his family to protect you?" Even now he knew she wasn't giving him her complete trust.

"Never to *protect* me," she said with some bitterness. "To take me over. Control me. Marry me off to one of them. That wasn't going to happen. My grandmother was the heir, the only one remaining. She died. Next in line, my mother. You know her story. Now *me.* I am Countess Andrassy-Von Neumann under the old system, now defunct. Laszlo is *not* the count, but he doesn't care. He calls himself that. *Ergo*, it is!"

He frowned in concentration. "So tell me, Sonya, what is it *you* want? You obviously haven't resolved your burning issues. Is it your plan to oust your cousin? Are you now thinking of starting proceedings that could cost millions of dollars and drag on for years? You might have inherited real money from Marcus, but from what you tell me Laszlo is a very rich man with far greater resources to fight you. Most likely if he's poured money into the country of his birth he will have support in high places."

She sank small pearly teeth into her lower lip. "This I know. I can't fight him. I'd like to if only to prove he does not have a legitimate claim. It could take years out of my life. I don't want to go back to Hungary. I am happy here. He *is* family. He is male. I know he will have done everything in his power to restore the estate. He can even call himself the count. But he cannot have the Andrassy Madonna. That is *mine*!"

"But you fear he wants it very badly?"

"He wants it with a passion," she declared, very passionate about it herself. "It is supposed to have great spiritual powers. Laszlo holds himself to be head of the family. The family icon should be in *his* possession. The monetary value of the icon is not of importance to him, although it would be near priceless. The Madonna was always regarded as the family's most treasured possession."

He sat back. "And where exactly do you keep this priceless possession? Don't for God's sake tell me at the back of a drawer?"

"I am not going to say anything further."

"No, you're rather foolishly going to go back into your shell," he said shortly, pinning her narrow wrist. "You don't trust me?"

"I am not going to tell you," she repeated, sounding driven. "And you can give your parents a message. I will not be interrogated."

It took an effort to keep his tone level. "You need help, Sonya," he said quietly. "If you can only say so much to me, maybe you could speak to a professional? You've had to keep far too much bottled up. You've had to harden your heart."

"I didn't do such a good job with you," she pointed out with some hostility. "I try to not think of you but you get closer and closer."

"It works both ways, Sonya," he said, holding onto her. "I held my uncle very dear."

"And I did not?" She was suddenly furious. "Maybe you think I am telling you a fairy story?"

He held her stormy gaze. "The icon makes it real.

Everything about you falls into place. It must have been really bad living with the constant fear of discovery?"

She relaxed very slightly. "Laszlo had my parents killed. He will pay."

How? he wondered. "You could go public," he offered a suggestion with feigned seriousness. "You could never confront him yourself. Did you think that's where Marcus could step in?"

"No, no!" She shook her head. "Marcus was for protection. Laszlo will move heaven and earth to find me if he learns I'm here in Australia. He has dangerous people he can and will use."

"Not with me and my family in your life," he assured her. "Just tell me this. Could someone find the icon if they searched this place thoroughly? A professional, not a common or garden thief."

She swallowed. "They would have to be very, very good."

"Get real, Sonya!" he exclaimed. "If Lazlo sent someone he or she would be very, very good. That's why we need to get you out of here."

"To where, David?" she asked, clearly agitated. "Join you at your apartment? Join you in your bed?"

"You can stop that right now," he said. "Has anyone ever tried to force sex on you, Sonya? Someone in the past?"

"Men can be cruel!" she said.

He groaned, afraid of what she might explain. "Some are. Most aren't."

"The answer you require is *no.* I am—and you are hearing *correctly*—a virgin."

For a long moment he couldn't formulate a word. Was she telling the truth? She was an extremely beautiful young woman, twenty-five, but she did have that touch-me-not air. "I don't know if I should believe you," he said slowly. "How could you escape a love affair or two?"

"So?" She tilted her chin, looking at him disdainfully. "Twenty-five is good to be a virgin. I'll give myself only to the man I love."

He released a stifled breath. "Sonya, in my own defence I have to point out you've behaved like a very passionate young woman with me. Marcus wanted you to be his wife. Did you tell *him* you were a virgin?"

"None of his business," she said. "*My* business. I don't care if I *never* have sex."

He raised his hands in a gesture that said, *Enough!* "You'd better start learning to handle the truth. We've come pretty close to crossing the line."

"All right, I admit it!" Tears filled her eyes. "I wasn't looking for any of this. It just happened. I wish I could say I was a normal person, like your girlfriends. Paula Rowlands, however, is an exception. I am *not* normal. Because I have not had a normal life. I've lived with too much fear. I've lived with being greatly desired. For *sex*! There, now you know! Not *me*, who I am. My face, my body. Like my mother in her first disastrous marriage. But I was to be allowed time. I was the chosen one, always watched. I was a prize, you see. I was treated well in some ways. I wasn't beaten or starved or locked up. These were civilised people of good family. The intimidation was subtle but very real. I knew I had to escape after one frightening encounter. So I did."

He felt so greatly perturbed, he moved to cradle her in his arms. "These people, these relatives, have much to answer for. Did they by any chance know about the Madonna?"

She shook her head. "Of course not! They all believed it was lost along with so many other treasures. *I* was the treasure. The sixteen-year-old. So pretty! A pretty woman is always desirable, is she not?"

"Pretty doesn't say it," he said. "You had the money to run?"

"I did. Not a great amount, but enough to eventually get out of Europe. My father died without making a will, you see. He didn't know he was destined to die early. The money, of course, would have come to me in time, when I was eighteen, but meanwhile I had a guardian. It was the guardian who wanted me. He too was all of thirty years older."

"And he didn't come after you?" His voice hardened at the thought. Sixteen, robbed of her parents, and under tremendous fear of sexual abuse.

"I told you. I'm good at disappearing. I had protection. I had my father's gun."

He was surprised by how much that shocked him. "There are strict gun laws in the country, Sonya. Do you still have it?"

"Of course not!" she answered scornfully. "I threw it in a river as soon as I felt safe. I couldn't get into this country with a gun in my luggage. Guns are terrible things."

"I'm so glad you agree. Sonya, could you do something for me?" He looked down at her.

"I need to know what it is." She felt she ought to cry, she loved him so much.

"A sensible suggestion. I'll go back to my parents' home. You, I want safe in my apartment. It's a very secure building. This is *not*. Two girls in the lobby were only too pleased to let me through tonight. I could have been anyone."

"But you're not just anyone." She shrugged. "You're David Wainwright. I know the security on the building isn't tight. You Australians are so unsuspecting. I never let *anyone* through who appears to be waiting an opportunity."

"Very wise. And we Australians are not as unsuspecting as you think, though I concede we have been for a very long time. Do you want to pack a few things? I want you to bring the Madonna. I have a safe in the apartment. I think the icon should be transferred to a bank. Alternatively there's a strong room in my father's house. It could go there."

"It must stay with *me*," she maintained, her expression weighed down with a mix of powerful emotions.

"No one will take it from you, Sonya. But they very well could if you insist on keeping it here. Give it some thought now. If you truly believe Laszlo has never ceased searching for you, you've put yourself into the frame through association with Marcus. That makes us in our way responsible."

"You will go to your parents' house?" she questioned him, her green eyes searching his face.

"That's a promise. You have nothing to fear from me. I would never harm you."

"Maybe you harm me already," she confessed. "I'll go with you, David. Give me a few minutes to pack a bag."

He saw them the instant they came through the security door. His target and the tall, strikingly handsome young man who had been at the funeral and had walked her to her car. He knew who he was. David Wainwright. A member of a mega-rich, highly influential family. He looked superbly fit. He moved like a top athlete. Nevertheless he thought, if he had to, he could take him. He himself was as fit as any man could be, although he gave this Wainwright fellow a good ten and more years. Confrontation was clearly to be avoided. They were getting into a small nondescript car. Thousands of them on the road. He would follow them to their destination. They weren't going out for the evening. Wainwright was still wearing his dark suit but she was dressed in jeans and a white T-shirt. Even then she looked a countess.

CHAPTER NINE

DAVID had the entire top floor to himself. Sonya was coming to an understanding of what it meant to have a great deal of money. His harbourside apartment, a short distance from Lady Palmerston's, was sophisticated, clean lined, contemporary taste, stunning aboriginal art works glowing from the walls.

In the living room she saw several large sofas. The longest would comfortably seat six. It was positioned against the majestic backdrop of Sydney Harbour in its night-time dazzle. A half a dozen comfortable armchairs were covered in willow green; two bucket chairs upholstered in a complementary soft mustard suede.

The living room was divided from the dining room by a series of substantial wooden columns. The dining setting, with a rectangular mahogany table, meticulously crafted, was for ten. Adjacent another smaller setting for six, this time around a circular table. She could see he loved fine timbers as much as she did. The splendid mahogany flooring was bordered by a polished limestone inlay. It was all very impressive. A far cry from her apartment.

"You'll be safe here." David's eyes followed her slender, willowy figure as she wandered about.

"I love where you live, David. I love your style." She spoke calmly enough, but inside she was shaking. They were alone together inside his apartment. One part of her longed for him to sweep her up and make love to her. The other commanded her to hold herself together.

"That will do for a start," he said, his tone sardonic. "There are four bedrooms apart from the master suite. Come and see where you think you'll be most comfortable. All the guest rooms are made up, bed linens changed once a week whether I have guests or not. All of them have en suites. Sonya, come along." He knew he sounded in full possession of himself, but hunger for her was nearly bringing him to his knees.

"Where are we going to put the Madonna?" she asked.

"First things first, I see. I have a safe in my dressing room."

"May we put it away right now?" Her emerald eyes were fixed on him with great intensity.

"Of course. Follow me. I recommend you pick out your bedroom first. You get the icon out your bag. I'll go open the safe."

"You don't want me to know the combination?"

"If I give it to you, you have to guard it with your life," he returned.

The shorter the time they were inside the confines of his dressing room, off the bedroom, the better. One false move and she would be right into his arms. That couldn't happen. He had given his promise.

Sonya was so on edge she picked the first guest room they came to. He put out a hand to flick the panel that controlled the lighting. Immediately the room glowed with soft golden light. The room had an exceptional view of the harbour. There was a big king-sized bed, with a dark golden bedspread, a long, very interesting mahogany bench at its foot; a big comfortable armchair with a good-sized footstool. A long Japanese scroll framed in ebony over the bed; a plush coffee-coloured area rug imprinted with Japanese-style branches and blossoms in a soft chocolate.

"Your guests must count themselves very lucky," she said. "This will do me fine."

"Okay." He made himself walk away from her, fighting down urges that were mounting into a tremendous force.

"David?" she called, after a minute or two.

His name on her lips was a caress. "Are you lost? I'm down here at the end of the hallway."

He sounded so matter-of-fact she might have been a young cousin. These tumultuous emotions could well be on her side. She had to remember he would have had any amount of experience with women. She had had no sexual experience along the way. She moved slowly, almost pinning herself to the wall. She had to think of Marcus. There was no other way.

His bedroom was huge, again with the magnificent view and a spacious balcony beyond. The neutral colours were given considerable impact by a splendid dark crimson and gold bedspread. Matching cushions sat on the two big armchairs positioned on either side of a coffee table. On it stood a specimen vase, with a single pure white butterfly orchid with three delicate stems. A bronze bust of a beautiful woman was nearby.

"My mother," he said, following her gaze.

"She's very beautiful." Sonya moved closer to inspect it.

"That she is," he said. "I take after my mother's family, the Holts."

She stroked the sculpture with a gentle finger. "I can see *you* in the set of the eyes, the high cheekbones, even the mouth."

"I resemble my mother, yes. Come along, Sonya. We'll get this icon into safekeeping."

He spoke so crisply she had the dismal feeling she was holding him up and he wanted to be away from her. The dressing room was adjacent, beyond that the bathroom, all in keeping with the subdued opulence of the rest of the apartment.

She bent her head to kiss the case reverently, speaking a few words in Hungarian. It had been a source of family pride for her grandmother to teach her mother the language of her birth and for her mother in turn to pass that language on to her. Through her father she had learned to speak fluent French and German, just as her mother did. It had been nothing in her family to speak several languages. It had been encouraged. She passed the icon to David, watching him in silence as he put it into the safe, built into the floor of his mahogany wardrobe. The room had the smell of luxury, of leather and beautiful clothes.

"Thank you, David," she whispered.

"Let's get out of here."

There was a dark, intense look on his face. "You wanted to bring me here," she pointed out, turning about almost at a run. "Now you think you've made a mistake?"

"Maybe I have!" He moved after her.

"So the Madonna is safe! That's all that matters. I don't have to stay. I'm happy to go back home."

"Are you?" He swung her back to face him, as wound up as she. There was a fierce quaking locked up inside him that threatened to escape. A telltale shaking was travelling down his strong arms.

"I want to be as much away from you as you want to be away from me," she said fiercely. "Isn't that so?"

In her fury she looked incredibly beautiful, eyes blazing like precious gems, hot colour in her cheeks. "How many times do I have to tell you? I *want* you, Sonya. But I'm trying to do the right thing. Don't make it impossible for me. I hardly seem to know what I'm doing any more."

"And you hate it, don't you?" she accused "You want to fight it, this first time a woman has the better of you?"

"The better of me?" His handsome face tautened. "I'd advise you not to provoke me, Sonya." He felt panicked by his rush of anger. Only it wasn't anger at all. It was white-hot desire that was burning out of control.

Her eyes went huge in her emotion-charged face. She knew her behaviour was verging on the irrational, but she couldn't stop. "Why, would that give you an excuse to rape me?"

Shock and disgust froze his tall, elegant body. "I'm going to have to forget you said that, Sonya," he said, *too* quietly. "I'll go now. But before I do I'll show you how to lock up after me."

The words were barely out of her mouth before she realized how disgraceful they were. Some men wished to rape. David, never, never, never! She flew after him. "David, I'm sorry. So sorry. I didn't mean that. You are right to despise me."

"Good night, Sonya," he said curtly, without looking at her.

"Please, David, don't go in anger. I said I'm sorry." She had feared all evening she would cry. Now she did, seeking any measure of relief from the tightening knots of pain.

He swung back on her, looking incredibly tense, his eyes as black as night. "Don't *do* that. I don't want you to cry. Wait until I'm out of here."

"Yes, of course." Obediently she dashed the tears away with one hand, then perversely went back on the attack. Nothing made sense. "Who are you to give me orders?" she demanded. "I'm allowed to cry if I want to. Now, what is it you wish to show me?" She tilted her chin, wanting to prove her self-control hadn't gone with the wind.

Her dramatic volte-face got under his guard. Women! he thought in high frustration. "Come here." He motioned her towards a large panel of switches.

"I think I know how to handle a few switches," she told him with that infuriatingly blasé aristocratic air.

"You *don't* know." He gritted his teeth, feeling like a man lurching towards disaster. "Just listen and watch."

She didn't dare move a step closer. A step closer to this man she loved with all her heart. She had known little certainty in her life, but she knew *this*. "I fall in love with you," she burst out, flooded with all sorts of conflicting emotions. "It is all wrong, a catastrophe. I know you think that."

He felt like hitting something in his immense frustration. He knotted his fist, then hit the wall. "Sonya—"

"Every time I see you I fall deeper in love," she confessed, a writhing mass of nerves. The floodgates had well and truly opened. "A tragedy. I didn't want it. I don't even understand how it has happened."

"Sonya," he said very tightly indeed. "I *must* go."

"Go, then. Go, *go go*!" She was utterly beside herself, almost dancing on the spot. "I put up with you as long as I can!"

She was sounding more and more foreign, her excellent English failing her.

He couldn't afford to continue this argument. Didn't she know she was inciting him beyond control? "This one," he gritted, stabbing his finger to a switch. "Then this one." He pointed to a switch in the next line. The slightest spark would set him off.

"So you're going to abandon me?" she cried.

Was she a woman gone crazy sending out all these

mixed messages? He stared down into her overwrought face "Abandon you? Excuse me, you wanted me out!"

Do something, for God's sake. Do something for both of you. The voice inside his head shouted the warning.

"Don't go, David." Now she turned to pleading. "I hurt you. I am sorry."

"Sonya, if I stay—" He broke off, dragging breath into his lungs like a marathon runner.

"Stay," she whispered. "You want me. I want you. I want to lose my virginity to you. I promise you I won't regret it."

The drumming in his ears was so loud he had to put up his hands to cover them. The voice inside his head was no match for this heavy pounding. "Sonya," he groaned, under unbearable pressure.

"It's all right." She went to him, lifting her white slender arms to link them around his neck. "Kiss me, David."

It was a heartfelt plea. Yet her voice was more *alluring* than any woman's had the right to be.

"Hold me. Make love to me."

Such an invitation was like a galvanic electric charge. What man could deny himself promised rapture? He knew he was in thrall to her. Woman, the goddess. Man was right to fear her. Only he didn't hesitate to obey, not for a nanosecond. He swooped to lift her high in his arms.

For a moment as she opened her eyes Sonya was disorientated. She had no idea where she was. She was lying in a huge, wonderfully comfortable bed, stark naked. Then on a wave of heat it all came flooding back…

David!

She put a hand to a pink nipple. It throbbed. She found herself stroking her own skin with a sensuous hand. She had never felt more like a woman. She was a virgin no longer. She was in a state of euphoria.

David! She whispered his name. *David, her perfect lover!*

Rolling voluptuously onto her back, she stared up at the high plastered ceiling. The world felt like a different place. It was transformed. David had made love to her, starting so slowly, sweetly, gently, so exquisitely mindful of her, so when at long last, when she could stand no more, they joined together her deliriously excited body was ready for him.

"Forgive me," he had murmured, drawing back to stare at her, showing his distress.

Forgive? What was there to forgive? He had shown her unimaginable rapture. Afterwards both of them had sunk into a spent sleep, her naked body spooned into his, his strong arm around her. Both had awoken at dawn when they made love again, this time in an escalating desire that became a passionate fury. She had lost her heart totally. He had wrung the soul from her. Now her body was his. Every inch of it he had charted. She had thought sex something she could live without. She knew very differently now.

It was David who had now to take control of the situation. Could they become a couple? Could she ever be accepted? There were so many hurdles to be covered. But whatever happened in the future no one could take her night of nights from her. It had been a sublime experience. David had made it so. She wanted no other man.

He almost missed her coming out of the apartment building. She must have called a cab because she flagged it down as it approached the luxury complex. He had to be getting old. He had fallen asleep after he saw Wainwright drive away some hours before, in a big Mercedes.

She was on her own. That was good!

All he needed to do was follow her. He had a hunch she was returning to her own apartment. A hunch that was soon proved correct. No question the two of them were sleeping together. Why not? They were young, beautiful people. He didn't want to hurt this girl. He was Hungarian. He knew all about the tragedies of the Andrassy-Von Neumann family; the tragedies that followed after the war. He knew how the car crash that had killed the girl's parents had been engineered. He had never wanted such a job. He wasn't a murderer, but he did know the name of the man who had done the job. He had proof the count was a bad man. A scary man, even to him who had been given the job of scaring people. Only this young woman was the true countess, the rightful heir. Once all those things had mattered a great deal to him, but for years now he had been corrupted into becoming just another one of the count's pawns.

Sonya paid off the driver, then made for the entry to the building. She needed to pack more things if she was going to be away from her apartment for some time. David wanted her to stay at his apartment, but eventually they had decided it would be best for her to move in with Lady Palmerston, who had instantly agreed to having her.

Almost at the front door of the building she became aware of the footfall behind her. She turned, seeing a big, burly man, well dressed, advance towards her. His demeanour, however, was in no way threatening. He addressed her in Hungarian. Somehow she wasn't shocked. She had been expecting it.

"Good morning, Countess. At last I have found you."

His tone was respectful. Sonya replied in the same language. "What is it you want?" Her green eyes were cold and distant.

"Only to speak to you, Countess." He gave a half-bow. "Have no fear. I mean you no harm. There is no point in running away. I will always find you. Let us get this over. I come as an emissary from your cousin, Laszlo. He has a proposition to put to you. Allow me to put your mind at rest. He means you no harm."

She gave a bitter laugh. "Like he meant my mother and father no harm, I suppose?" At this time in the morning there was no one around. Most of the tenants, young people, would be at work. She was very much on her own.

"Please don't be frightened." He took a step back so as not to crowd her. "We will go up to your apartment. We will talk. I think you will be very happy to hear what the count wishes to offer you."

"There is *nothing* he could offer me," she said, with cold contempt.

"Please, Countess. Upstairs. You can't get away from him. I promise you I mean you no harm. Neither does the count. Violence is to be avoided at all costs."

"Only because he knows he wouldn't get away with it. I have spoken to important people about him."

"Upstairs, Countess," he insisted. "It is just a matter of delivering the count's proposal. Then I will leave."

Oddly she believed him. Perhaps some residual sense of decency, of honour remained.

It was just as she thought. Laszlo wanted the Madonna. In return he would pay into the bank of her choice, anywhere in the world, the equivalent of ten million dollars.

"It is a very good deal, Countess. You could be rich!"

Her expression was totally unimpressed. "Laszlo must be mad if he thinks *I've* got it."

The man shook his head. "But you have, Countess. Give

it up. You're a beautiful young woman, you have your whole life in front of you. Why should an icon mean so much?"

"You know very well," she reprimanded him, sternly. "You are Hungarian. Our religious icons mean a great deal to us. How do you know you won't be punished for trying to take it away?"

He laughed without humour. "I'll be punished if I *don't*!"

"Not if Laszlo is in jail."

He shook his head. "That won't happen, Countess. He has too much power. He will hunt you down wherever you go. Call him off. Let him have the icon."

"Perhaps I need the money first?" she said, with a cool lift of her arched brows.. "He *is* family, but a monster."

"So give him what he wants. Do you have it?"

"Certainly not *here*," she said. "I'm not a fool. Money first, then maybe we'll talk. He should be able to arrange an electronic transfer very easily. I can give you the name of my bank and the number of the account."

"A wise decision, Countess." The man stood up, a handsome man in his fashion, his blond hair almost sheared to the skull and penetrating blue eyes.

"How shall I contact you?" Sonya asked.

"Do not worry, Countess. I shall contact you. All that matters in life is to stay alive. It has been an honour to meet you. The Andrassy-Von Neumanns were once one of Hungary's greatest and most noble families."

When he arrived at the house, Angie, the housekeeper, told him his mother and father were enjoying a late breakfast.

"No need to announce me, Angie. I'll go through."

"I'll make fresh coffee," Angie said, hurrying away.

The informal dining room, well proportioned and expensively furnished, faced onto beautiful gardens of which his mother was enormously proud. "What is it, David?" his father looked up to ask. "You're on your way to work?' He studied his son's tall, lean figure. David was wearing one of his beautifully tailored business suits. He was well known for being a very smart dresser. "You needn't go in, you know. Nigel can hold the fort for a while."

"Have you had breakfast?" his mother asked, always happy to see her adored son.

"Angie's making me some coffee." He sat down, his briefcase on the floor beside him. "I have something to show you both. It needs to go into the safe room. It belongs to Sonya. I've also organized for her to stay with Rowena. She's not safe where she is."

His father regarded him with a puzzled frown. "Really, David, spare me the cops and robbers. What is it you've got? What could the girl have that needs to go into a strong-room?"

"You'll see in a minute." He reached into his briefcase. "What I'm going to show you has been in Sonya's family since the seventeenth century."

"Really? Sure she's not making it up as she goes along?" Sharron pursed her lips. Yet, Rowena, nobody's fool, trusted this girl.

"I think this will persuade you." He unwrapped the icon slowly, and then set it down gently on the table.

"And that's it?" His mother sat back, arching her fine brows. "An old case?" Only the binding had the patina of centuries.

He opened out one side, then the other. Sunlight was splashing through the tall windows into the breakfast room. He manoeuvred the case into a brilliant ray.

"Good God!" Robert Wainwright leaned forward, stunned. "A religious relic, obviously Roman Catholic."

"Where on earth did she get this?" His mother looked

every bit as stunned as her husband. "The diamonds are of the first water." She touched an exquisitely gentle finger to the array of diamonds in the Madonna's crown. "The precious stones are gorgeous too. The stones alone would be worth a great deal of money. How did a young woman who works as a florist come by this?" She searched her son's dark eyes.

"Go ahead, David. Tell us," Robert Wainwright said.

David did.

Afterwards his parents, their attitude greatly changed, made the decision to have Sonya's cousin investigated. "I'll make the necessary phone call right away," Robert Wainwright said. "There shouldn't be any difficulty tracking the Andrassy-Von Neumann family since 1945. Actually I know of the count. He's an industrialist and an extremely wealthy man."

David was back in his office when a phone call came through from Rowena. She sounded agitated, which wasn't like her. An involuntary spasm gripped the area around his heart. Surely Sonya was safely at home with Rowena? Even as he thought it he knew Sonya to be highly unpredictable. She had spent much of her life taking risks. He had been wrong to believe she would stay put.

"Sonya is here," Rowena told him at once. "She's had a rather frightening experience this morning."

He gripped the phone harder. "But she's okay? She hasn't been harmed in any way?"

"No, dear. I should have told you at once. But you must hear what she has to say. Is it possible for you to get away?"

He was already on his feet. "I'll be there shortly."

"Thank you, darling." Rowena made a sound of utter relief.

His first guess was Sonya's stalker was in town and had made contact with her. The Madonna was safe in his father's strongroom. His father had already started the investigative ball rolling. Not for the first time he was very grateful for the power and influence his father had.

His secretary came to the door, an anticipatory look on her face. She loved her job. "Have Prentiss bring the car around to the front of the building Liz," he said with some urgency.

"Onto it!" Liz moved off, never one to waste a moment.

They all sat in Rowena's garden room. A tense little group.

"Don't tell me, I can guess." David searched Sonya's face. "You've had a message from Laszlo via an intermediary."

She was enormously comforted by his presence, even if he was looking so formidable, such a tautness in his expression. "He treated me with respect," she said in an effort to allay his fears.

"Then he can count himself lucky," he clipped off. "My father has made a few phone calls. He knows of your cousin, Sonya. He's an important industrialist."

A lofty disdain came into her face. "Even important industrialists can be corrupt. Corruption is everywhere in high places. Massive fraud. Corporations with their meaner than mean streaks, robbing people, dismissing legitimate claims and getting away with it. It happens all the time."

"Well, you can leave the Wainwrights out of that," he said, leaning in closer to her.

"Hear! Hear!" Rowena piped up. "I've often wondered

what it would be like to be a victim I saw so many sad things in the old days. This Laszlo would seem to be a very bad boy indeed."

"He had my parents killed." Sonya started to rock herself, her arms crossed defensively across her body. "His man offered me ten million dollars for the Madonna. Blood money." Her voice broke.

"But S-Sonya!" Rowena was seriously taken aback.

Sonya met David's eyes. "No big thing! I already have twenty, don't I?"

He knew now to ignore the challenges she threw out. They were defence mechanisms. Her behaviour at different times was indicative of her perilous and erratic past life. "Indeed you have," he said in a calming voice. "So what is your thinking on this, Sonya? You get the money in, but you keep the Madonna."

"How did you guess?" She gave a little laugh. "Of course I keep the Madonna. It is *mine*! I give the money away to a just cause. Homeless young people, I think. You can help me there, David."

He sat studying her, an intent look on his face. "Do you like putting yourself deliberately in danger?" he questioned. "You don't seriously believe this Laszlo is going to let you get away with it?"

"He will just have to, won't he?" She gave the characteristic lift of her chin.

"My dear!" Rowena was starting to panic. She had come more and more to realize what a very difficult, even dangerous life Sonya had led.

Sonya could see neither of them was happy with her plan. "The man who visited me practically admitted Laszlo was responsible for the death of my parents." Tears stood in her eyes.

"How absolutely shocking!" Rowena was as astounded

by Sonya's story as David's parents had been, although she had known from the beginning Sonya was a young woman of breeding.

"I always knew it," Sonya told them painfully.

"But what is needed is hard evidence, proof, Sonya." Vertical lines appeared between David's black brows. "This man won't speak to the police. The last thing he needs is to have his cover broken. And what about Laszlo? He's a man who has long operated without ethical boundaries."

"So you're against me?"

He moved from his chair to where she was sitting on a two-seater sofa. He took her hand, keeping it within his own. "Listen, stay cool. You've had an upsetting experience. We're *all* on your side, Sonya. But I'm not about to tell you you've done the right thing pretending you were prepared to strike a bargain. How can you trust this man anyway? He's a hireling."

"He had nothing to do with the death of my parents, David," she cried. "He's Hungarian. I *knew* he did not intend to hurt me."

David was by no means certain of that. "But then he believed you, didn't he?" he countered. "He thought you had seen sense. How did he say he was going to contact you?"

"He didn't say. He's been watching me all along."

David's expression heightened to trigger alert. "So it's likely he knows you're here with Rowena?"

Her beautiful face showed her dismay. She looked across at Rowena. "I am so sorry, Lady Palmerston. The last thing I want is to put anyone in danger. I'll go home."

"Of course you won't!" David, deeply perturbed for her, spoke more crisply than he intended. It was obvious Sonya was in a highly emotional state. He couldn't have her rushing off on her own. It was out of the question. On the other hand, he felt he could no longer leave her with Rowena. Rowena wasn't a young woman. The safest possible place for Sonya was at his parent's.

Sonya didn't take kindly to that. He knew she wouldn't. "No, thank you, David," she said, with a positive shake of her head. "I can't think your mother is as sympathetic towards me as you say. Besides, I have nothing to fear. This man will not hurt me. The Madonna will protect me."

It seemed more than his life was worth to tell her not to count on it. "Okay, so I have the house watched 24/7." That should be easy enough, using their security people.

"You think that's necessary, David?" Rowena asked. "There's an excellent security system in place here."

Sonya turned her green eyes on Rowena. "You would feel a whole lot better if I were away from here, Lady Palmerston, wouldn't you?"

"Nonsense, dear," Rowena said firmly. "Our aim is to protect you."

"Let's slow down a minute." David held up an authoritative hand. "Dad has spoken to the commissioner. We should leave it to the police to come up with a plan. That's their job. That's what they're trained for."

"I don't need their help, David," Sonya said, starting to get nervous at the talk of police intervention.

"You *do*," he flatly contradicted, intensely concerned for her safety.

Her white skin flushed. "You're angry with me?"

He exhaled a long breath. "I'm *worried*, Sonya, as I should be. This man must have given you quite a fright coming up behind you, for all you're trying to hide it."

"Worse things have happened to me," she said. "It can be simple, David," she appealed to him. "I wait to get the money. I give it away. It's mine anyway and plenty more besides. I am the rightful heir. I will tell this man I will not lay claim to the Andrassy-Von Neumann estate. He can have *it*. Monster that he is, I know he will take care of it. He has a son. Probably grandchildren. Maybe they are not monsters?"

"We'll soon know if they are," David said wryly. "No one is ever going to hurt you while I'm around, Sonya. When the police come up with a plan I won't be very far from your side."

He stood up purposefully. He had many things to do. Sonya stood too. He put his arm around her. She closed her eyes, nestling against his shoulder.

"You're my world, David," she said, very softly.

He hugged her slender body to him, resting his chin on the top of her head.

They presented quite a tableau. Rowena, looking on, fell back against her armchair. Her face, so concerned, broke into a smile of pure delight.

My goodness me! So that's how the land lies!

She couldn't have been more pleased. Brave Sonya nursing a dangerous secret for far too long would come through all her pain and loss with Rowena's splendid nephew beside her. In his own way, dear Marcus had begun the healing process. Only destiny had its own plan for Sonya and David. It had reached out and touched them with a magic wand.

Could there be anything more satisfying than a happy ending? Rowena thought. But first there was business to attend to…

CHAPTER TEN

A SHAGGY-HAIRED young man, with a mobile glued to his ear, paid little attention to him as he walked through the security door as the young man was walking out, still talking into his phone. How foolish these young people were to assume he had legitimate business in the building. The fact that he dressed smartly must have confirmed he was an all-right guy.

He had no problem either with the lock on the countess's door. Routine, performed without even trying. Within seconds he was in. He knew where Wainwright had taken her. He knew he had time to make a thorough search of the apartment. From long experience he would leave no sign he had been there. He could have told the count the icon was not in the apartment, but the count listened to no one.

Twenty minutes later. No icon. He wasn't a man who was easily unnerved, but he was wary of the fact the countess now had powerful people on side. And this was *their* country. That gave them a big advantage. The Countess Sonya was like no one he had ever known. He admired her, her illustrious name. He came from an impoverished family. He had left an abusive home as soon as he could, living on the streets, surviving by using his wits and his physical strength. Ten years before Count Laszlo Andrassy-

Von Neumann had recruited him, hearing of his "talents". The count was a man with no conscience who thought nothing of monstrous deeds as long as he didn't have to carry them out himself. A couple more jobs would set him up. He would quietly disappear to where even the count wouldn't be able to find him. The count was a disgrace to his ancient name.

They were having a quiet dinner together; a small out-of-the-way restaurant, but the food and the service were good. The entrée had just been taken away when Sonya's mobile rang.

She stared across at David, her eyes gone wide. "It must be him."

"Answer it," he said, knowing there was a trace on her mobile.

She sucked in her breath. "Hello," she said with enviable calm. A second later, she indicated to David with her hand it was the call they had been expecting.

David listened to Sonya as she spoke, his eyes not leaving her face. She looked and sounded perfectly in control. That told him so much about the dangers she'd had to endure. He couldn't understand a word of it. She was speaking Hungarian, as the voice at the other end must be. Was the same nationality a bond? He had to hope so.

The count's emissary delivered his message in a quiet, respectful voice. "You will know now, Countess, your cousin has kept his part of the bargain." That was true. The money had arrived in her bank, very probably to their great shock with more shocks to come. "Now we arrange the transfer of the icon, Countess." He kept up the homage. "You have it?"

"Of course." Sonya's eyes remained fixed on David's

striking face the whole time she spoke. His presence steadied her, made her feel near invincible.

"I need to have it in hand tomorrow," the man said.

"Then I suggest we meet at the Archibald Fountain in Hyde Park."

"The time, Countess?"

"Make it lunchtime." The timing had been pre-arranged. "Say, one fifteen p.m. People about, enjoying their lunchtime break."

"You come alone."

It wasn't a question. "Of course." She spoke haughtily, as if insulted he would doubt her word.

"No back up people, Countess. No Mr Wainwright. I play fair with you. You play fair with me. We both know the count isn't the man to cross."

"We both know he's a murderer," Sonya returned, stung into speaking passionately. "Even if he paid some criminal to do it. *You*, do not be late. I very much dislike being kept waiting."

"That will not happen, Countess." He broke the connection.

Her hands were shaking as she put her mobile away.

"Sonya," he exclaimed, hating what was happening to her.

"It's all right. I know this because you are with me."

His dark eyes glittered. "It's where I intend to stay," he assured her. "I got the Archibald Fountain bit, the rest was, well—Hungarian." He gave her a half-smile.

"David, I don't want this man to be arrested." There was appeal in her sparkling green eyes.

He couldn't answer for a minute, he felt so angry. "Sonya, why not?'

She watched as his expression turned tense. "I don't

want to cause him trouble. I do not have a bad feeling about his man. He has been most respectful. I know he hates Laszlo."

"He *works* for him, Sonya." David packed a whole lot of warning into his words. "Don't get carried away here. You can be certain this man had done some pretty terrible things. You cannot trust someone like that."

She inhaled a shaky breath. "Perhaps. I don't know." She shook her head. "People get forced into living bad lives, David. You have had a life of peace and privilege."

"You think I don't know that?" He pinned her gaze. "But I don't believe I could have been corrupted into a life of crime."

She offered her hand across the table. "Sorry, sorry. I stupidly offend you. All I'm saying is I do not believe he wants to hurt *me*."

He caught her fingers, with a groan. "Sonya, he will do what he has to. That's why there's a plan in place. The immigration department would like to have a little chat with your Mr Metzger. We have the name now. Or one of his names."

"Like *me*," she said, with a strange little smile. "Sonya Erickson, Sonya Von Neumann. A few in between. Once I changed my appearance with brown contact lenses. I could hardly see through them."

He looked back at her very gravely. She was wearing a short dress of silvery lace, very feminine, very seductive. No jewellery except for a silver bracelet and crystal drop earrings, high heels on her feet. She looked incredibly beautiful, the light shimmering off her radiant skin and hair. "Let's go," he said abruptly, holding up his hand to signal for the bill. "I'm desperate to make love to you."

Her emerald eyes suddenly held a tantalizing female taunt. “So, your place?”

“Where else? The truth is I can’t bear to have you out of my sight.”

Once inside his apartment they succumbed to the driving need that was in them. The *thrill* of it!

“I could die for this,” Sonya moaned. They were helping each other undress, throwing clothes about without thought or care. The frustrations of being apart, the inherent dangers of the situation Sonya had found herself in, provided an ever more passionate coming together. The tempo of their kissing, the frantic embraces mounting to a symphonic pitch. Nothing had ever felt so *right*!

She was stretched out on his bed, her long, slender legs falling gently outwards like the petals of a flower. “Do you love me?”

His answer came in an instant against her open mouth. “Really, you don’t know it already?” In a strange way this level of ecstasy was a form of torture, but both of them were meeting their feelings head-on.

“Perhaps I need more convincing?” She was gasping with pleasure.

“I’ve never known a woman remotely like you. You like to torment me, don’t you?”

“You mean like *now*?” She reached down to lightly stroke him with her hand. His skin was like velvet.

He drew in a deep shuddering breath in response. “Marry me, Sonya,” he said through shivery, ever-mounting waves of pleasure. “One thing though, my love. I’ll never allow you to do the disappearing act.”

She rolled atop him. “So you think I would ever *want* to? Are you *crazy*?”

He held her hips, staring up into her highly charged face. "You want the truth? It's *yes*! I'm crazy about you. Marry me, Sonya Von Neumann. I want all the world to see how much I love you."

She lowered her upper body into his, feeling the wild thud of his heart knock into hers. "You honour me," she said, pressing her mouth to his cheek. Then she lifted her blonde head about to make her important announcement. "I will take on the job of being Mrs David Wainwright."

"For how long?" He laughed in triumph. "You won't escape me, Contessa."

"For ever," she proclaimed. "I *love* you."

"I love you too. If I lost everything I possess, I'd still be the richest man in the world."

"So, *I* look after you," she said.

Afterwards they sat in his huge bath together, his tanned feet hooked around her white hips. The peaks of her breasts showed dusky pink through the foaming, *chypre*-scented water. David had the softest white towelling wash cloth in hand. He turned her this way and that, marvelling at the softness and the white perfection of her skin. He worked the washer over her face, her throat, her shoulders, her breasts, tipping her head forward onto his shoulder so he could rub her back. Then he made her stand up very slowly in the white foaming water.

"Aphrodite rising out of the sea foam!" he crooned. "All you need is a scallop shell." Naked, her long hair pulled into a careless knot, she looked dazzlingly beautiful.

Afterwards, she lifted her arms as he wrapped her in one of his big bath towels, and then he carried her back to his bed. There was a marvellous range of ways to make love. They could try them all.

* * *

A perfect cloudless blue, the sky was reflected in the waters of the fountain. People strolled through the leafy park, admiring the splendid playing fountain, others sat on benches or spread themselves out on the plush green grass enjoying a packed lunch. A few like him were out jogging the paths. Police in everyday clothes were stationed in the area. He couldn't pick them and he had tried. He hoped Metzger couldn't either. He thought his own disguise wasn't all that bad. Navy vest, navy jogging shorts, a wide navy band with a green and white logo worn Indian-style around his forehead. At least it kept the sweat from running into his eyes. He had refused to be left out of this. Sonya was too precious to him. He had made that very clear.

He was slowing up beside a big blazing flower bed when he saw a tall, powerfully built man approaching Sonya. The man was wearing a trendy straw hat pulled down low on his head.

Metzger. An internal alarm went off.

Immediately he leaned down and yanked at a strap on his joggers. Nothing wrong with the strap of course. The police would have been following his movements around the park as well, probably having a laugh. All of them knew who he was. It had been agreed he could join in the action but only if something went very wrong. It was not anticipated anything would. Sonya and the target would be surrounded.

Metzger raised his straw hat to her. "Good afternoon, Countess. Well met. You have the icon?"

She shook her head. "Did you seriously imagine I would hand it over to my cousin?"

Metzger, for a career criminal, looked positively astounded. "But, Countess, you have the *money.* Why would you do this? It's madness."

"Why? Why should *you* ask me such a thing?" Her

green eyes flashed. "The icon is a family treasure. It has been in *my* family for hundreds of years. *I* am the rightful heir, not Laszlo."

It was obvious Metzger was poleaxed and he didn't try to hide it. "I understand what has happened to you, Countess, but you could be in great danger. *I* will most certainly be in danger."

Sonya was acutely aware of that. "What do you need to disappear, Mr Metzger?" she asked. Against all the odds, she felt compassion for this stranger. Probably he had led a terrible life, but she felt there was some good in him.

"A lot of money, Countess." Fear had crept into his voice. "Your cousin would consider I had committed treason. In his own way he is *mad*. He would have me followed for the rest of my life. I must *go*!" He thrust out a hand to her and that was when several things happened at once.

David put on such a burst of speed he was onto Metzger within seconds, taking him down headlong onto the grass. The country's greatest footballer couldn't have executed a better tackle. Brawny as he was, Metzger found himself groaning in pain. To have been overpowered so easily was devastating to a man like him. Someone very strong had a hard foot rammed into the middle of his back. His mouth was filled with grass clippings, making him splutter.

Four plain-clothes policemen tore across the park, converging on the scene with ear-splitting shouts of, "Police!"

They took over from David while a crowd of bystanders stared in astonishment at the drama in progress. It was first thought to be a scene from a cop show, but there were no television cameras in sight. This was real life. But nothing sensational was happening apart from that spectacular tackle. Gradually they dispersed with the sensation of a let-down, going back to finish off their lunch.

The irony was, Metzger had only been planning on saying farewell to the countess he had found he couldn't harm. It was fast established he was unarmed. Regardless he was taken away, if not cuffed. He was informed he was not being arrested. He was simply being taken in for questioning. The investigation into Count Laszlo Andrassy-Von Neumann and his activities was already under way. Metzger, along with his numerous aliases, was Andrassy's known henchman.

Left alone David gathered Sonya in so tight an embrace, he might have decided not to let go of her at all. "Promise me, promise me you won't do this sort of thing again," he implored with a shudder.

She spoke in a soft, appeasing tone. "I knew he wouldn't hurt me, David. But *you* hurt him." A laugh escaped her.

"We did hit the ground rather hard," he said wryly. "How was I supposed to know he was just trying to say goodbye?" His arm around her waist, he began to walk her out of the park up towards High Street.

She gave him a teasing little smile, feeling such ease, such peace, such a new certainty in life she was luminous with it. "You look very sexy in your little jogging shorts," she commented. "Such an outfit displays your superb body."

"Well, *you* would know all about that." He hugged her to his side. "When we get our lives sorted—very soon, I hope—you can come jogging with me."

"Don't think you would have to give me a start. Well, not much of a one. I am very fit too."

"Top of the class!" He had witnessed how much courage she had. There had been no evidence Metzger would have wished a target safe.

They walked on, both feeling immense relief this part of proceedings was over. "What is going to happen to

Metzger, do you suppose?" Sonya asked at length. "I don't want Laszlo to be able to get to him."

He stared down at her. "*You*, wicked girl, are the one who refused to hand him over the icon," he scoffed. He was, in fact, rather in awe of her stand.

"I know, I take the money," she admitted, without regret. "But it's *my* money. Money Laszlo stole. We will give it away. Maybe I will give some to Metzger so he can go hide in some place Laszlo can't find him. Brazil, somewhere like that."

"Antarctica might be better," David said, very dryly. "You can't give the guy money, Sonya. He fell for you. Simple as that. Had you been plain with buck teeth he might have acted differently."

"No one has buck teeth in Australia," she said, taking him seriously. "All the orthodontists, the health care, the parents making sure their children grow up beautiful."

"Be that as it may, it's as I've told you before—beautiful women have a lot of power. You only have to consider what you've done to *me*."

"So I prepared a spell!" For so long she had thought true love would elude her. Only it had been waiting for her all along. "I intend to keep the recipe to hand for the rest of our lives," she told him, with her lovely smile.

David slowed their progress to a halt, feeling humbled by the strength of her commitment. They were standing beneath a magnificent shade tree. Dappled sunlight flowed over her in a stream; birds sang, love lapped them around. "*Eternity* would be better," he said in a voice that thrilled her.

"You don't care what some people might say about me?" She searched his dark eyes.

There was an incredulous lift to his brows. "Say *what* about you?" He held up her chin, bent his dark head to kiss her lovely upturned mouth. "All they can say is David Wainwright is madly in love with Sonya Von Neumann and they're going to be married early in the coming year. Does that suit?"

She could have cheered aloud. Never more to have to *hide*. "More than you can *ever* imagine! I love you, David. God has been very good to me."

He caught up her fingers, kissed them. "He's been very good to *me* too. I might even consider turning religious."

"*I* am," she told him quietly.

"I know, my darling!" Tenderly he drew her into his strong protective arms. "I think we might take in Hungary on our honeymoon. What do you think? Word is your cousin could be spending his future behind bars."

"Amen to that!" Sonya said fervently, laying her radiant head against his chest. The steady beat of his heart resounded in her ear. This was the heart that beat for *her*. "He deserves punishment. He is a destructive man."

"Well, it appears very much like he's going to get what's coming to him," David said with grim satisfaction.

"I do feel sorry for his family." Sonya, so happy herself, could find some forgiveness in her heart.

"Not your problem, darling." He kissed the top of her head. "You have *me*."

"That is the *greatest* thing!" she said, truly believing it was. "I have absolute faith in you."

Arm in arm they walked out of the golden green shade, into the bright sunlight. The dazzling prospect of an even brighter future awaited them, David thought. His heart was overflowing with love and a wonderful renewed sense of purpose. There is only one way to handle life, he thought. Take it firmly in hand. Focus all one's energies on accomplishing *good*. He loved Sonya as he'd never thought he would be lucky enough to love a woman. He had a huge job ahead of him as his father's heir. It wasn't all a life of privilege. It was hard work with the extra burden of responsibility. Many hundreds of lives were dependent on Wainwright Enterprises. The drive forward mightn't be easy at times, but his love for Sonya and hers for him made all the difference in the world. He felt himself a man truly blessed.

EPILOGUE

THREE months later Sonya was enjoying morning tea with Sharron, her mother-in-law, and Rowena when Robert Wainwright rang to give them some stunning news just to hand. Count Laszlo Andrassy-Von Neumann, who had been deeply embroiled in investigations into his affairs in the United States, Europe and Hungary, had been killed when his car had crashed into a tree on the Andrassy-Von Neumann estate in Hungary. Investigations were ongoing but suicide was a strong theory. The count had been known to have been deeply depressed and outraged by the multiple attacks against him; especially from people within his ranks who had come forward. The count was survived by his son, Miklos, and his four grandchildren, all of whom lived happily in the United States.

It wasn't until David and Sonya were almost a year into their idyllic marriage that the whole matter of the rightful heir to the Hungarian estate was at last resolved by the courts. Sonya's American cousins didn't want any part of it. They had all suffered from the ruinous stories that came out about their father and grandfather. Judgment was handed down. Sonya Von Neumann-Wainwright, the claimant, was the rightful heir.

It was Sonya and David who decided the palace and

the beautiful grounds of the estate would be opened to the public like many other stately homes. Permission was given for the palace to be used for grand functions. Laszlo had begun the reconstruction. It would take five more years for the palace and the grounds to be restored to their pre-war glory. In this way, tradesmen and craftsmen were to enjoy years of steady, well-paid work. Everyone from the government down took great pride in the restoration of one of Hungary's grandest national treasures.

During this time Sonya and David, his parents, and Lady Palmerston made frequent visits. They had become a closely knit family; even closer when Sonya conceived her and David's first child in the splendour of the master suite. Robert and Sharron now had their first grandchild. It was an occasion for great rejoicing. The child was named Stefan, after Sonya's father.

The man, Metzger, who hadn't been detained long by the police, mysteriously disappeared, never to be heard of again. Obviously someone had given him help and very likely an injection of money to get away.

Who?

HER LITTLE SECRET

CAROL MARINELLI

CHAPTER ONE

'AFTER you.'

Alison Carter gave brief thanks as someone stepped aside and she shuffled onto the bus, coffee in hand, and took a seat in her usual spot, halfway down, to the left of the bus and next to the window.

Morning was just peeking in and the sky was full of purples and oranges as the doors hissed closed and the bus made its slow way up the hill. Even though she'd bought a newspaper, till the bus turned the corner Alison did as she always did and stared out at the glorious view—to the energetic joggers on the foreshore, the walkers on the beach, the swimmers in the ocean and out beyond, to where the patient surfers bobbed quietly, waiting for the next good wave.

It was a slice of heaven.

A view that reminded Alison, because sometimes she needed reminding, that she lived in surely the most beautiful part of the world, that she had absolutely nothing to complain about. It was an internal pep talk that she delivered to herself quite often when the travel bug stung—yes, there were other beaches, other worlds to explore, but here was where she belonged and, if you had to be stuck somewhere, then Coogee was a very nice place to be…

Stuck.

Alison closed her eyes for just a second, leant her temple against the window and told herself to stop using that word.

Having recently read an article on positive thinking and the harm of negative self-talk and thoughts, she was resolutely reframing and rephrasing, but she was finding it to be an almost full-time job.

It was a very nice place to *be*, Alison told herself.

To just be!

As the bus took on its next load of passengers, then commenced its slow turn into the hilly street that would take them from Coogee to Eastern Beaches Hospital where she worked, Alison turned away to concentrate on her newspaper.

Then she saw him.

Craning his neck for a final glimpse of the beach too, it was, Alison was sure, the man who had let her on the bus before himself. The flash of blond hair and pale shirt that she'd glimpsed as she'd turned and briefly thanked him actually belonged to a man more beautiful than any she had ever seen and only then did she recall his English accent, and she was sure, quite sure, that the man she was looking at was *the* Nick Roberts.

Despite having been on days off from her job as an

accident and emergency nurse, Alison had heard all about him from her friends and colleagues. Ellie had told her all about the gorgeous, *completely* gorgeous new locum registrar, who was filling in in Emergency while the senior registrar, Cort Mason, took some long overdue extended leave. Even Moira had sent her two texts worth of information about the nice surprise she'd found on her late shift one afternoon, warning her that he had to be seen to be believed.

Presuming that it was him, thanks to the hospital grapevine, and because nurses loved to gossip, Alison knew rather a lot about the handsome stranger on her bus. He had been travelling for six months and was doing a two-month stint in Sydney, getting some money together to spend on his prolonged journey home, first to New Zealand and then home to the UK via Asia, and, Ellie had said droolingly, while he was in Sydney, he was staying in Coogee.

It probably wasn't him, Alison told herself. Coogee was hardly the outback, there were loads of gorgeous men, loads of travellers, yet she was quite sure that it was him, because this man *had* to be seen to be believed.

Taller than most, he was sitting on a side seat, doing the crossword in the newspaper, and he kept forgetting to tuck his legs in, having to move them every time someone got on or got off. He had on dark grey, linen trousers and a paler grey shirt. And, yes, there were loads of Englishmen staying in Coogee—he could be anyone, but holidaymakers and travellers weren't usually on the two-minutes-past-six bus. It was, Alison knew, after nearly three years of taking this very route, a fairly regular lot she joined on the bus each morning.

Of course he caught her looking and he gave her a very nice smile, an open, possibly even flirting smile, and all it served to do was annoy Alison as she pulled her eyes away and back to her newspaper. In fact, she wanted to tell him that she'd been looking, not because he was drop dead gorgeous but because she thought she knew who he was.

And if she was right, then he'd be the last person she'd be interested in.

She'd heard all about him from her friends—the string of broken hearts he had left behind on his travels and daredevil attitude in his quest for adventure.

So, instead of thinking about him, Alison, as always, read her horoscope, which was too cryptic for such an early hour, so she turned, as she always did on a Friday, to the travel section, only the sting she so regularly felt became just a touch more inflamed as she read that airfares had come down dramatically. Even if it was too early for cryptic horoscopes the arithmetic was easy—her meticulous savings, combined with the money her father had left her, were enough for a tiny deposit on an even tinier flat or a round-the-world trip and a year or two spent following her heart.

Alison knew what her father would have chosen.

But she knew too what it would do to her mother.

She glanced up again to the man she thought was

Nick Roberts. He had given up on his crossword and sat dozing now, and Alison stared, annoyed with a stranger who had been nothing but polite, jealous of a man she had never even met—because if this was Nick Roberts, then he was living her dream.

Maybe he felt her watching, because green eyes suddenly opened and met hers. He had caught her looking again and smiled. Embarrassed, Alison stood as her bus stop approached, and it was either be extremely rude or return his smile as she walked past.

'Morning,' Alison said, and then to show him she said morning and smiled at *everyone*, she said it to someone else who caught her eye as she moved down the bus.

And it *had* to be him because he was standing up too and this was the hospital bus stop and there certainly couldn't be two people as lovely as him working there.

They probably weren't, but Alison felt as if his eyes were on her as she walked through the car park and towards Emergency, and she was rather relieved when her friend and colleague Ellie caught up with her.

'Nice days off?' Ellie asked. 'Any luck with the flat-hunt?'

'None,' Alison admitted. 'Well, there was one flat that I could just about afford but it needs a kitchen.'

'You could live without a nice kitchen for a while,' Ellie pointed out.

'There's a hole in the side wall where the kitchen burnt down.' Alison managed a wry laugh as she recalled the viewing, the initial optimism as she'd walked through the small but liveable lounge, and then the sheer frustration as the renovator's delight that she'd thought she had found had turned out to be uninhabitable. 'It's impossible…' Alison carried on, but she'd lost her audience because Dr Long Legs had caught up, and Ellie, who never missed an opportunity to flirt, called over to him and he fell in step beside them.

'This is Alison. Alison, this is Nick,' Ellie said, and none-too-discreetly gave her friend a nudge that said he was *the* Nick. 'He's with us for a couple of months.'

'Hi, Nick,' Alison said, and then to salvage herself, she gave him a smile. 'We met on the bus.'

'We did.'

'Anyone new tends to stand out—it's a pretty regular lot on the six a.m.,' Alison added, just to make it clear why she'd noticed him!

'Alison's flat-hunting,' Ellie said.

'Shoebox-hunting,' Alison corrected.

At twenty-four it was high past the time when she should have left home. Yes, most of her friends still lived at home and had no intention of leaving in a rush, but her friends didn't have Rose as a mother, who insisted on a text if she was going to be ten minutes late, and as for staying out for the night—well, for the stress it caused her mother it was easier just to go home.

Alison had moved out at eighteen to share a house with some other nursing students but at the end of her training, just as she'd been about to set off for a year of travel that her mother had pleaded she didn't take, her brother and father had died in an accident. Of course, she had moved straight back home, but though it had seemed right and necessary at the time, three years on Alison was beginning to wonder if her being there was actually hindering her mother from moving on. House-sharing no longer appealed and so the rather fruitless search for her own place had commenced.

'There are a couple of places I've seen that are nice and in my price range,' Alison sighed, 'but they're miles from the beach.'

'You're a nurse…' Ellie laughed. 'You can't afford bay views.'

'I don't need a view,' Alison grumbled, 'but walking distance to the beach at least…' She was being ridiculous, she knew, but she was so used to having the beach a five-minute walk away that it was going to be harder to give up than coffee.

'I'm on Alison's side.' Nick joined right in with the conversation. 'I'm flat-sitting for a couple I know while they're back in the UK.' He told her the location and Alison let out a low whistle because anything in that street was stunning. 'It's pretty spectacular. I've never been a beach person, but I'm walking there every morning or evening—and sitting on the balcony at night…'

'It's not just the view, though,' Alison said. They were walking through Emergency now. 'It's just…' She didn't really know how to explain it. It wasn't just the beach either—it was her walks on the cliffs, her coffee from the same kiosk in the morning, her cherry and ricotta strudel at her favourite café. She didn't want to leave it, her mother certainly didn't want her to leave either, but, unless she was going to live at home for ever, unless she was going to be home by midnight every night or constantly account for her movements, she wanted somewhere close enough to home but far enough to live her own life.

'I'm going to get a drink before…' He gave her a smile as they reached the female change rooms. 'I look forward to working with you.'

'Told you!' Ellie breathed as they closed the doors. 'I told you, didn't I?'

'You did,' Alison agreed, tying up her long brown hair and pulling on her lanyard. 'Have you got my stethoscope?'

'That's all that you've got to say?'

'Ellie, yes, you did tell me and, yes, for once you haven't exaggerated. He's completely stunning, but right now I need my stethoscope back.' She certainly didn't need to be dwelling on the gorgeous Nick Roberts who was there for just a few weeks and already had every woman completely under his spell.

'Here.' Ellie handed back the stethoscope she had yet again borrowed. 'Have a look at him on Facebook—there's one of him bungee-jumping and he's upside down and his T-shirt's round his neck…' Ellie grinned as Alison rolled her eyes. 'There's no harm in looking.'

Ellie raced off to the staffroom, ready to catch up on

all the gossip, and for a moment Alison paused, catching sight of her reflection—brown hair, serious brown eyes, neat figure, smart navy pants and white top. Her image just screamed sensible. Too sensible by far for the likes of Nick. Yes, he was a fine specimen and all that, but he also knew it and Alison was determined not to give him the satisfaction of joining his rather large throng of admirers.

He was sitting in the staffroom as he had on the bus, with his long legs sprawled out, drinking a large mug of tea and leading the conversation as if he'd been there for years instead of one week, regaling them all with his exploits—the highlight a motorbike ride through the outback—which did nothing to impress Alison. In fact, the very thought made her shudder and prompted a question.

'How is that guy from last week?' Alison turned to Ellie. 'Did you follow him up?'

'What one?'

'Just as I went off last Sunday—the young guy on the motorbike?' And then she stopped, realising it sounded rude, perhaps a touch inappropriate given Nick's subject matter, though she hadn't meant it to. Nick had just reminded her to ask.

'We didn't have any ICU beds,' one of the other staff answered, 'so he was transferred.'

'Thanks,' Alison said, looking up at the clock, and so did everyone else, all heading out for handover.

She really didn't want to like him.

He unsettled her for reasons she didn't want to examine and she hoped he was horrible to work with—arrogant, or dismissive with the patients. Unfortunately, he was lovely.

'I'm here for a good time, not a long time,' she heard him say to some young surfer who had cut his arm on the rocks. Nick was stitching as Alison came in to give the young man his tetanus shot. 'I want to cram in as much as I can while I'm here.'

'Come down in the morning,' surfer boy said. 'I'll give you some tips.'

'Didn't I just tell you to keep the wound clean and dry?' Nick admonished, and then grinned. 'I guess salt water's good for it, though. I'll look forward to it.'

'You're going surfing with him?' Alison blinked.

'He lives near me and who better to teach me than a local?' Nick said. 'Do you?'

'Do I what?'

'Surf.'

Alison rolled her eyes. 'Because I'm Australian?'

'No,' he said slowly, those green eyes meeting hers. 'Because you want to.' And she stood there for a moment, felt her cheeks darken, felt for just a moment as if he was looking at her, not staid, sensible Alison but the woman she had once been, or rather the woman she had almost become, the woman who was in there, hiding.

'If I wanted to, I would,' Alison replied, and somehow, despite the wobble in her soul, her voice was even. 'I've got a beach on my doorstep after all.'

'I guess,' Nick said, but she could almost hear his tongue in his cheek. 'I'll let you know what it's like.'

His assumption irritated her, perhaps more than it should have, but she wasn't going to dwell on it. She'd save a suitable come-back for later—perhaps this time tomorrow morning when she was stitching his forehead after his board hit him, Alison thought, taking the next patient card from the pile.

'Louise Haversham?' Alison called out to the waiting room, and when there was no answer she called the name again.

'Two minutes!' came the answer, a pretty blonde holding up her hand at Alison's interruption and carrying on her conversation on her phone, but perhaps realising that Alison was about to call the next name on the list she concluded her call and walked with Alison to a cubicle.

'How long have you had toothache for?' Alison asked, checking Louise's temperature and noting it on her card.

'Well, it's been niggling for a couple of weeks but it woke me up at four and I couldn't get back to sleep.'

'Have you seen your dentist?' Alison asked, and Louise shook her head.

'I've been too busy—I'm working two jobs.' She glanced up at the clock. 'How long will the doctor be? I'm supposed to be at work at nine.'

Then Alison had better hurry the doctor along!

'Who's next?' Nick asked cheerfully. 'A nice motorbike crash, perhaps?' He winked, just to show her he'd heard her in the staffroom.

'I'm saving the good stuff for later,' Alison said. 'I've got a toothache.'

'I'm sorry to hear it.'

She rolled her eyes at the very old joke, but it did make her smile just a little bit and he *was* so easy to talk to, because somewhere between the work station and Cubicle Five she'd told him that she was going to the dentist herself next week. He opened the curtain where the very pretty blonde with a sore tooth that couldn't possibly wait till nine a.m. for a dentist was no longer chatting on her phone but cupping her jaw in her hand and looking an absolute picture of misery.

'Good morning.' He introduced himself and Louise introduced herself and managed, Alison noted, despite her agony, to perk up just a touch and give him a very brave smile.

'I'm so sorry.' She was far nicer to Nick than she had been to Alison. 'I just couldn't stand it any longer. I haven't slept all night…'

'Not at all. Dental pain's awful,' Nick said. Warning her he wasn't a dentist, he first had a feel of her jaw before he looked in her mouth, then long brown fingers examined her jaw again and felt around her neck. 'What was her temperature?' Nick asked, and Alison told him it was normal. 'There's no swelling. Still, I think we should give you something for the pain and a poultice for the tooth, but you really do need to see your dentist.' He turned round. 'Alison, do we have any oil of cloves?'

Right at the back of the treatment cupboard.

'Busy?' her friend Moira asked minutes later as she watched Alison curiously.

'Frantic!' She rolled her eyes to show that she wasn't in the least. 'I'm making an oil-of-cloves poultice,' Alison said, her own teeth slightly gritted.

'A what?' Moira frowned. 'What's that?'

'Some old English treatment. Actually, I remember my mum giving this to me once. I've never been asked for it.'

'Nick?' Moira checked and gave a little sigh. 'He asked me for some gentian violet yesterday.' She held up her palms to show the evidence. 'He dishes out the TLC, wish he'd dish some out in my direction!' Moira was Irish, just passing through Coogee too as she nursed and travelled her way around the world. She was fun and flirty and just…fun!

'Is he always so nice to everyone? It's like a social club in Section B.'

'Always,' Moira said cheerfully.

Returning to Cubicle Five, Alison wondered if he'd still be so nice when the place *was* frantic, but for now he was taking his time with his patient.

'Okay, Louise, I've given you a note for the dentist—you need to get that seen to this morning.'

Louise, once she'd bitten down on her cotton bud

soaked in oil of cloves, managed to rally enough to tell him the name of the bar she worked at in the city, and that she was on at the weekend if he wanted to stop by for a drink on the house.

'I'm working...' Nick grinned '...but that's terribly kind of you.'

'He's worth getting toothache for,' Louise commented as he swept out and only the fresh scent of him lingered. They shared a little smile. 'If I suddenly come over all dizzy, will you call him back for me?'

'I'll get Amy, the other registrar.' Alison winked. 'She's good with dizzy females.'

'Shame.'

Nick changed the atmosphere of the place—he seemed delighted to be there, nothing was too trivial and nothing major unnerved him, as Alison found out when the husband of a swollen-ankle case suddenly complained of chest pain and started to pass out. Still Nick remained unruffled, breaking the gentleman's fall as Alison quickly wheeled out his wife, pressing the emergency bell and collecting the crash trolley.

By the time she returned, about twenty seconds later, the man had gone into full arrest and between them they had him clipped to the portable monitor, with Alison commencing cardiac massage even before help had arrived.

'Let's get him down to Resus.' Amy, the emergency registrar, called for a trolley, but Nick thought otherwise.

'Let's just keep going here.' It was a tiny override, or just a difference of opinion—nothing really—but when Amy, who easily took offence, simply nodded and they all just carried on working on the man on the cubicle floor, Alison realised the respect he had garnered in the short while he had been here.

Pads on, Nick shocked him, and before the crash team had arrived, the poor man was back in sinus rhythm and starting to come round.

'It's okay, sir...' Nick's was absolutely the voice you wanted to come round to. He didn't talk down to the man and he didn't scare him as he lay there groaning. 'You're doing fine—your heart went into an irregular rhythm but it's beating normally now.' He smiled up to Amy. 'Okay, let's get him on a trolley and down to you guys. I'll go and speak with his wife.'

'What was he in for?' Amy asked.

'He's here with his wife, Doreen,' Nick explained. 'She's got an ankle injury.'

Having seen what was going on, Libby, the receptionist, had taken Doreen to an interview room and taken the husband's details from the shaken woman. After quickly writing his notes and checking the new patient's name, Nick walked down to the interview room with Alison.

He was very thorough, first checking her husband's details and assuming nothing—that Ernest was, in fact, her husband and finding out if she had contacted anyone. Then Nick got to the point, explaining that it would appear Ernest had had a heart attack.

'It probably doesn't feel it now, but your husband is an extremely lucky man—he could not have been in a better place when this happened.'

'Will he be okay?'

'We certainly hope so. He's conscious, the cardiologists will be running some tests now, but certainly the next twenty-four hours will be critical. I'm going to go and speak with my colleagues now and find out some more for you. I suggest you ring your son and get some family here to support you.' He stood and shook her hand. 'And I'll be back soon to take a good look at your ankle.'

He was a complete and utter pleasure to work with, to be around, so much so that when Alison ducked into the staffroom for a ten-minute break later that morning, she wanted to turn tail and run, because it was just him in there and to be alone in his rather dazzling company rather terrified her.

'What about this…?'

She frowned as he handed her the local newspaper with an advertisement circled—a one-bedroom flat, two streets from the beach, and it wasn't that expensive. 'I've already seen it,' Alison admitted. 'It's above a pub that has live music six nights a week.' She sat down next to him. 'I did seriously think about it, though. Thanks,' she added. 'You didn't have to do that.'

'Can't help myself,' Nick admitted. 'I love looking at real estate—I've chosen the one I want…' And he showed her the stunning apartment he'd circled, with bay views and a balcony as big as the staffroom they were sitting in. 'Nice to dream.'

And it was, because Alison had circled the very same one in her own local newspaper, had looked it up on the net and taken a virtual tour of the place.

'You can't have it because it's already mine.'

'It's a great spot,' Nick said. 'I can absolutely see why you don't want to move away.'

And they got to talking, about she was on late shift tomorrow and she had to squeeze in two flat inspections beforehand, and there was a mixture of both relief and disappointment when he told her he was off for the weekend. Relief that he'd told a little white lie to Louise and the stab of disappointment Alison did her very best to ignore. Instead she told him how she loved to walk on the cliffs on her days off and, strange as it sounded, there was the most beautiful cemetery that he just had to explore, then about the coffee bar that did the ricotta cheese and cherry strudel which she rewarded herself with now and then. Then the intercom buzzed—someone searching for Nick—and Alison realised that her fifteen-minute break had turned into twenty-five.

'Told you.' Ellie smirked when she came round that evening on her way out for the night.

'Told me what?' Alison said, letting her in. There was no way she'd give Ellie so much as a hint that he'd won her over too, but Ellie was having none of it. Once she'd said hi to Rose, and chatted for a few minutes about an engagement present for a friend's party the following week, she asked to go on the computer.

'There!' Ellie was already a friend of his on Facebook—along with four hundred and thirty-seven others—and, yes, hanging upside down on a rope, his stomach looked lovely with his T-shirt around his neck. Alison did note that his status was single, and held her breath as she read about his crazy adventures—white-water rafting, rock-climbing, swimming in waterholes. And she didn't care if there were only freshwater crocodiles there, he was dangerous and reckless and everything she didn't want.

Great day at work—I love this place, Nick suddenly updated his status, and Alison blinked.

She thought of the toothaches and grumbles and moans down in section B and the drama with Ernest, which was pretty much routine in Emergency—it had been an okay day, even a good day perhaps, but hardly great.

Except, somehow he'd made it so.

Out to sample local delights, he added, and Alison rather hoped it wasn't Louise.

Ellie happily scrolled through what was just loads of chatter and comments from friends, and about a thousand photos.

'He broke off his engagement before he came here,' Ellie said knowledgeably.

'How do you know?'

'You can find out anything on this. Well, I'm not sure

he broke it off, but I think so, and look…' Ellie was a machine and in no time at all had located photos of the once happy couple, but Alison had better things to do than fill her head with Nick.

'Come out with us,' Ellie pushed. 'Get some dinner… listen to a band.'

And Alison was about to again say no, she had to be up early for flat inspections and then work a late shift tomorrow, as Rose pointed out.

'There are a few of us meeting up.' Ellie smiled. 'You never know who'll be there.'

Which was a very good reason to decline, a very good reason to stay away, but instead of declining Alison gave her mum a smile.

'I'll be fine for tomorrow.' She tried not to notice her mother's pursed lips as she left Ellie on the computer and headed to her room, straightening her already straight hair till it looked a little more *done* and pulling through some hair gloss, then putting on make-up as she changed from her shorts and T-shirt into something a little more dressy, but not too much. She checked her reflection in the mirror and tried to tone down the blusher on her cheeks before realising it was her own complexion.

'If you're going to be out late…' Rose came to her door.

'I'm not going to be late,' Alison said and then, unusually, she qualified a touch. 'But if I am, I'll give you a call.'

'You can't really stay out too long…' Rose didn't add the unspoken *You've got work…*

Alison didn't want to argue, she didn't want to point out again that she was twenty-four, that Ellie was on an early shift tomorrow and was still going out—that she had a life, that she wanted to live it…

Instead she crammed her ATM card, her mobile, some cash and her keys into a tiny bag and only when she had bitten back a smart retort did she look up.

'I'll let you know if I'm going to be late.' She gave her mum a kiss on the cheek and said goodnight then headed out to the cool, dark street and along to the bar, trying to join in with Ellie's easy chatter, but it was hard to be light-hearted when her mother made it such an effort to just go out. As she stepped into the bar, however, it wasn't her mother's veiled warning or an excess of blusher that had her cheeks pinking up again.

There was Moira and a few others, even Amy the registrar was sitting at the heavy wooden table. Making room for Ellie and Alison to join them, they ordered pizza. It wasn't at all unusual for the emergency crew to go out on a Friday night and, yes, Coogee was lovely and this bar was one hospital staff often frequented. It was just a rather good turnout from Emergency and Alison knew why—because coming back from the bar, balancing a jug of beer and some glasses with a bottle of water tucked under his arm, was the reason.

'Hey!' Nick gave her a smile and gave Ellie one too. This was her local, Alison told herself as she took a seat and glanced through the menu. She didn't just work nearby, she lived here, so more than anyone she had good reason to be there.

Except, Alison silently admitted, he was the real one.

CHAPTER TWO

EMERGENCY staff the world over knew how to have a good time when they were out, as Nick pointed out. Even the rather aloof Amy was letting her hair down and had had a dance, when she wasn't monopolising Nick.

'It's like a home from home!' Nick said to Alison as the table got louder and louder. 'Not that I regularly joined the Friday night out.'

'Too senior?' Alison asked.

'Too sombre,' Nick said, at least that was what she thought he said, because the music was really loud. 'Do you come here often?'

Alison grinned as, tongue in cheek, he delivered the cheesy line with a smile. 'I live five minutes away, but, no, not that often,' she admitted, because, well, it was true. 'I like the cafés and restaurants.' She didn't get to finish as Moira tottered over, a little the worse for wear, and tugged at Nick to go and dance. Alison didn't await his response, instead she disappeared through the beer garden and to the loo, where she stood for an inordinately long time, fiddling with her hair. Not that it made any difference but, ridiculously, she felt safer in there.

She could hear the thud-thud-thud of the band through the wall and it matched the thud-thud-thud of her heart, because she'd never, not once, found someone so instantly attractive. Oh, she knew she wasn't the only one, yet he was the only one—the only one who just on sight triggered something, just on voice confirmed it, just on scent…

'Moira…' Nick peeled the nurse's arm from around his neck with a smile. He was actually very good at letting a girl down gently, he'd had plenty of practice and though he'd enjoyed his holiday to date, the fun stopped when he started work—that sort of fun anyway. He took his work seriously, commanded respect and that was rather hard to come by the morning after a reckless night before. 'I don't dance.'

He didn't flee to the toilets like Alison had, but he made his way there, a little annoyed that he had come, but Amy had suggested it and it had seemed a bit rude to say no. He had sensed things were getting a little out of hand and had been about to head off, but had got talking to Alison and somehow forgotten that he was supposed to be heading for home.

And there she was, walking toward him right now, and here too was the very reason he hadn't headed for home when he should have.

'Hey.' He smiled down at her and she stopped walking. They stood in the beer garden amidst the noise and the chatter.

'I thought you were dancing.'

'Not for me.' He gave her a smile, but it was a wry one, a lying one, a strained one, because as the music tipped into something a little slower, he would at that very moment have danced, would have loved to do just that, because somehow she exceeded his limits, somehow he knew she could break his self-imposed rule, because all of a sudden work didn't matter.

'I'm just about to head off,' Alison admitted, because even if her stilettos seemed glued to the floor her heart was telling her to run.

'Do you want to go somewhere?' Nick's mouth said the words, though his brain insisted he shouldn't. 'Just us.' And Alison's eyes jerked down instead of up. Down to his forearm, to the blond hairs on it, to long-fingered hands that she wanted to wrap around hers. And maybe it was the overhead gas heaters in the beer garden, but the air was hot and her mind wasn't clear because with the pulse of the music and the laughter from beyond, it would, at that moment, have been so very easy to just be twenty-four.

To just be.

And, of course, just a moment later she recalled why she couldn't just be.

Alison looked up then to green eyes that awaited her response, that could never guess the inner turmoil inside her, who assumed, that for Alison, it was as easy as making a decision and grabbing her bag.

She shook her head and with good reason. Coogee was teeming with holidaymakers, with good-looking, testosterone-laden, 'here for a good time not a long time' males, and even if he was gorgeous, Nick could never be any different.

'No, thanks.'

'Hey, Nick!' Moira's radar located them and rather unsteadily she teetered towards them. 'We're heading into town…'

Alison didn't wait to see if Nick was joining them. Instead she said goodnight, gathered her bag and walked, not along the street but along a beach that was dotted with small groups and some couples, and it was a relief to be out of there and a relief to be alone.

He *was* dangerous.

At least, he was to someone like her.

He had been flirting—oh, not anything major, but his glorious attention had homed in on her, more than a touch. She was quite sure that Nick did want to get to know her a little better—which, to Alison, just seemed pointless. He'd be gone in a few weeks, he was just there for some fun, which Alison didn't readily do.

Why, she asked herself as she walked along the beach she knew and loved, couldn't she be like Ellie, or Moira—just out there having fun, without worrying about tomorrow?

Her phone buzzed in her bag and she didn't need to

check it to know it was from her mother. It was fifteen minutes after midnight after all.

'I just texted you!' Rose said as she walked in the door. 'I just wanted to know if you were going to be late.'

'I said I'd call if I was.'

'Well, it is after midnight.'

'Well, it is after midnight.' For a shadow of a second, she could almost hear Tim's voice, could almost picture her brother standing right where she was in the kitchen, good-naturedly teasing Rose when he came in late at night and Rose complained.

Except there had been Dad then to argue his case for him and, anyway, Tim had a way to him that always won their mum around.

God, but she missed him.

And her father too.

Missed, not just the people but the family they had been then, the security the others had provided, unnoticed at the time, the certainty they were there for each other, which had all been ripped away. So instead of a smart retort Alison looked instead at the fear in her mother's eyes and apologised for not texting and had a cup of tea and a chat with her mum, till Rose headed off for bed.

Then later, alone, when surely all her friends were still out, she went on the computer and checked her social network profile. She had one friend request and, yes, it was from Nick. He must befriend everyone,

Alison decided, but she did click on his name, hoping for another little peek at his profile, except that, apart from his photo, all the rest of the photos and information were private.

She went to accept his friend request and for a moment her finger hovered, then she chose to ignore it.

Very deliberately she ignored it, even if they did have eighteen mutual friends between them.

It was one a.m. on a Saturday after all.

A girl had some pride.

CHAPTER THREE

'ARE you okay?'

They were waiting for a multi-trauma at eight a.m. on Monday morning. The sky was black with a storm and the roads like ice after a long dry spell. Alison was in Resus this morning and so too was Nick. She'd said good morning at the bus stop, then moved to her regular seat. Ignored him in the staffroom that morning, her head buried in the crossword, but now they stood on opposite sides of the trauma bed, all set up and gowned up, waiting for the patients to arrive, though they were taking longer to get there than anticipated and Alison was quiet.

'I'm fine.'

'Look, about the other night…'

'What about the other night?' She frowned over her mask to him.

'I got waylaid by Moira and then you'd gone.'

'I'm not even thinking about that—I just hate getting kids in.'

Yes, it happened day in and day out, but some days

you just hated it so and Nick, cool, confident Nick, actually coloured up a little bit, because for once, with a woman, it wasn't about him. He'd awoken slightly disconcerted on Saturday, and had spent the rest of the day trying ignore a niggle. He'd swum, walked for a while, but had ended up at a cemetery that was, strange as it might sound, both fascinating and beautiful, and then back to the flat, where that niggle had developed a name as he'd checked his social network profile and, no, she hadn't responded to that request either.

'ETA five minutes!' Sheila called, and he watched as Alison blinked twice.

'They're taking ages.'

'Rush-hour.'

'It's still ages.'

'It might not be that bad,' Nick said. 'We're set up for everything; we'll worry, if we need to, when they get here.'

It was actually very good advice and Alison gave a thin smile. 'Is that what you do?'

'I try to,' Nick replied. 'Right now I'm trying to work out seven down—begins with L, ends in E, recurring.'

'Life,' Alison said, and he grinned. 'I'm stuck on it too.'

'How's the flat-hunting?' he asked. 'Any luck?'

And she was about to shrug, to get back to worrying about the family that was coming in, but Nick was right. Until they arrived there was no point, so instead she followed his lead.

'Actually, yes!' She'd sworn not to get her hopes up, not to say a word, but she was so delighted she couldn't help herself. 'I got a phone call from a real estate agent about a flat, and though it's not officially on the market yet, he's arranging an inspection. It's within my price range and they want a quick sale… It all sounds a bit too good to be true.'

'It might be your time for some good luck.'

'How was the rest of your weekend?' Alison asked, because, well, she was interested and she wanted to get back to normal with him and he *was* so easy to talk to. 'Any surfing?'

'Well, I wouldn't quite call it surfing, but I did manage to get up and stay up for about half a second. It was great…' He stopped in mid-sentence as a siren blared the first ambulance's arrival. 'Okay,' Nick said, 'now we can get back to worrying.'

Her name was Polly and she was seven and petrified and on a trauma board, her head strapped down. She was so scared that she wasn't even crying.

'Hi, there, Polly.' Nick smiled down at her. 'I'm Nick, I'm a doctor. You're having a rotten morning, aren't you?' He spoke reassuringly to her as he rapidly examined her while Alison transferred the oxygen tubes. The paramedics had started an IV and were feeding information as they worked on. Alison was cutting off Polly's school uniform, attaching her to monitors and getting her observations.

'Where's my mum?' Her little teeth were chattering, just one thing on her mind, and Alison glanced over at Todd, the paramedic, who nodded his head towards the door and Alison went over.

'She's being cut out of the car,' Todd explained. 'She's conscious, but she's got some nasty cuts and is really agitated. She should be in soon. The police are trying to get hold of Dad.'

'Thanks,' Alison said, but nothing else, and headed back to Polly. 'Mum will be coming in soon, and we're getting hold of Dad, but right now we need to make sure you're okay.'

Amazingly she appeared to be.

There were some minor cuts and bruises, but she was neurologically sound and her abdomen was soft and non-tender. After a thorough examination and some cervical spine films, they peeled off the board and beneath it was a little girl who was a bit calmer, but still shaky, asking after her mum and very worried about her dad.

'He's got an interview.' Now Polly did start crying.

'Hey,' Nick said, 'don't worry about that. Your dad will be so relieved that you're okay.' Except the little girl could not be consoled.

'Can I move her over to a cubicle?' Alison checked with Nick, and then spoke away from Polly. 'Mum's about to arrive…'

'Sure, just…' He didn't finish, and Alison didn't wait to find out or to be told—yes, she would keep a very close eye on Polly.

She could see Todd hanging around, taking ages to sort out the blankets, and she deliberately ignored him. Alison didn't like him. He was good at his job and everything but he had asked her out a few times and didn't know how to take no for an answer. He'd also been out with half the department, and expected Alison to follow suit.

'Hey, Alison.' Todd came over. 'How is she?'

'Fine,' Alison answered. 'We're just about to move her out of Resus.'

'How are you?'

'Fine,' came her reply, but she didn't elaborate, actually refusing to speak to him about anything other than work.

She was glad she had moved Polly out, though her mum's sobs still reached the cubicle and after rechecking the little girl's obs, Alison didn't try to placate her. 'I'll go and find out how she is.'

The police were outside in the corridor and they brought Alison up to speed on things before she went in. Ellie and Sheila, the unit manager, were helping Nick and Alison observed for a moment before asking how she was doing.

'She's got a nasty arm laceration that needs to go straight to Theatre,' Ellie said. 'She's hysterical. Nick's told her that her little girl's okay.'

'This is the nurse looking after Polly,' Nick told his patient, and Alison went over to the distraught woman. 'Rebecca,' he added, and Alison nodded.

'I'm looking after Polly,' Alison said. 'She's doing really well. As soon as you're more settled you can see her.'

'David?'

'Your husband?' Alison checked. 'I've just spoken to the police and he's on his way in.'

'He'll be so worried.'

'I'll look out for him,' Alison promised. 'I'll speak to him the second he arrives and I'll bring him in to Polly and to you just as soon as I can.'

'He'll be—'

'I'll look after him,' Alison said gently. 'Try not to worry.'

'Where are they?' The man, who was chalk-white and looked as if he might pass out any second, needed no introduction. Alison knew this must be the father. A security man was running in behind him, about to tell him to move his car, but Alison dealt with practicalities, got the keys from him and asked for permission for Security to move it. David was really in no state to drive.

'They're going to be okay,' Alison said, and guided him straight to a side room. 'Let me just talk to you for a moment and then I'll take you in to see Polly.' She knew he needed to see his daughter, but in the state he was in, he would just upset Polly more.

'Polly's escaped lightly,' Alison explained. 'She's got some cuts and a few bruises across her chest and to her shoulder from the seat belt, but she's talking and she's fine.'

'Rebecca?'

'She's got a nasty arm laceration and they're talking about taking her straight to Theatre. There might be some concussion and they're going to arrange for a head CT. She's very distressed, they had to cut her out of the car, but she knows where she is and what's happened, and she's very worried about Polly and about you.'

'Oh, God.' He bunched his hands by his head and took in some deep breaths. 'I thought the worst…'

'Of course you did,' Alison said gently. 'We were prepared for the worst too, but they do seem to be relatively okay. I'll get the doctor to speak to you just as soon as he can.'

'I don't think I even said goodbye this morning. I've got a job interview today…' Alison frowned, because she'd heard Polly going on about it. 'I was so worked up about it, I can't even remember if I said goodbye…' And he broke down then and Alison listened and found out that he had lost his job nine months ago, that he had, in fact, had a nervous breakdown and was still struggling to deal with things, but was slowly picking up. And because she listened she heard too that today was a vital day, so much hope had been pinned on it, that this job had meant everything, right up till this point. She could understand now how upset Rebecca would be, not about the job but about her husband's reaction.

'Let me take you in to Polly,' Alison said when he had

calmed down. 'And I'll let your wife know that you're here.'

He did really well, he smiled and said all the right things to Polly—that the interview didn't matter a scrap, just as long as she and her mother were okay, that they would be fine, that they were all going to be fine. Rarely for Alison, she felt a sting of tears at the backs of her eyes and left them to it to go and speak with the wife.

'Hi, Rebecca.' Alison came in as Nick and the trauma surgeons looked at the patient's arm, and though Nick was concentrating, he still heard her speak. 'Polly's fine, her dad's with her—and he's fine. He really is okay.' Rebecca started crying and bizarrely for a second it sounded to Nick as if it was the husband who was hurt. 'I've told him that when the surgeons have finished looking at your arm I'll bring him in to see you. Rebecca, he's holding up really well.' And the arm Nick was holding down for the surgeons to assess relaxed just a little bit beneath his fingers.

'David's told me all that's been going on,' Alison continued, 'and, honestly, now that he knows you two are going to be okay, he really is fine.'

'He can't cope with things,' Rebecca said, and it was the first proper conversation she'd managed since her arrival.

'Not the little things perhaps,' Alison said, and stroked the poor woman's cheek. 'But he's dealing well with this. Maybe he's finding out he's stronger than he thinks.'

'So much hinges on today...'

'I know.' She glanced up at Nick. 'David had an important job interview today,' Alison explained, then looked back at the patient. 'When things are more settled we could ring the company and explain what's happened.' She paused and hoped, not wanting to presume but grateful when he stepped in.

'I'm happy to do that,' Nick said.

'That's good,' Alison said to Rebecca. 'It will sound better coming from a doctor.' And Nick looked down at his patient and saw her close her eyes in relief, felt her body relax and he realised that head CT wasn't quite so urgent.

'There's a lot of stress going on for them,' Alison murmured to Nick. 'They really didn't need this.'

'Thanks,' Nick said. He realised he'd learned something, and whatever it was he decided he would process it later.

As Ellie prepared Rebecca for Theatre, knowing what would put his patient's mind at rest more than any medication, Nick made the phone call Alison had suggested, then returned to tell the couple how it had gone. 'They were really grateful for you letting them know,' Nick told David. 'Especially with all that's going on. They've asked you to ring later in the day or tomorrow if you get a chance to arrange another time. They sound pretty keen,' he added, then glanced up as Alison came in with a nervous Polly.

'Here's Mum,' Alison said, and Rebecca and Polly

had a kiss and a cuddle before Rebecca was taken to Theatre, because only seeing her mum would truly reassure the anxious child.

'I'm going to take her up to the children's ward soon,' Alison told Rebecca. 'Just for observation. They'll make a fuss of her. You can ring her this evening when you're back from Theatre and feeling better—or one of the staff might bring her up for a little visit.'

'She's nice…' Rebecca said when Alison had left. Nick agreed, saying that Polly was being well looked after by her, then told his patient to put her oxygen mask back on because he didn't want to think about how nice Alison was—there was more to Alison than there was time to know, more to her than there was scope to explore. No, he really didn't need this.

Heading into the staffroom for a quick lunch break later, when Ellie asked if he was going to the social club that night, it would have been far more sensible to answer that gleam in her eye with a smile and a 'Yes', or take Moira up on that offer to go to that Irish pub, because instinct told him that they knew the rules—that he was on holiday and not here for a long time, just a good one, but instead all he *really* noticed was that Alison had glasses on today while doing the crossword and didn't look up to hear his response, though her cheeks burnt red and her ears were pink as she pretended to concentrate on the puzzle in front of her. Because the seat next to her was the only one left, he chose it, peered over her shoulder and, yes, she was stuck on the same word as he'd been. He was about to nudge her, to tease her, because 'leitmotif' was a word it had taken him a full morning to get, but he deliberately stopped himself.

'Leitmotif!' He heard the triumph in her voice and ignored it, felt the haste of her pen beside him, and it took every bit of effort not to turn round and join her in that moment.

No, *this* Nick really didn't need.

CHAPTER FOUR

'ALISON doesn't want to be my friend.'

He lasted two days.

Two days trying not to notice how her neck went a little bit pink when he spoke to her. Two days ignoring the fragrance of her hair when their heads occasionally met over a patient, or that now and then she'd rub her forehead and on would come her glasses. Two days of just talking, just keeping it as it was, then, as happened at times, but had to happen on this day, Alison came off the worse for wear with an inebriated patient. Showered and changed into the most threadbare, faded scrubs, Nick got the most astonishing view of what appeared to be a purple bra and panties, before Sheila pointed the problem out and Alison put on a theatre gown. Like a dressing gown over pyjamas, Nick thought, and then tried not to think, and then just stopped thinking for a dangerous moment as she sat next to him writing up his notes, her ponytail wet and heavy, and he forgot, just simply forgot not to flirt.

'Why don't you want to be my friend, Alison?' He

nudged her as if they were sitting in a classroom and Alison, who wasn't having the greatest day, annoyed with herself for not replacing her spare uniform, found herself trying not to smile, yet she did carry on the joke and put her arm over the notes she was writing as if he was trying to copy her.

'I am your friend, Nick.'

'Not on Facebook…'

'I haven't got time to *play* online…' Alison said. 'Some of us live and work in the real world—I'm studying to get on this trauma course.'

'You're friends with Ellie.' He grinned and then stopped, and so too did Alison. There was this charge in the air; it would be far safer to carry on writing, or just get up and go, but she didn't, she just sat. 'Are you going to have to get the bus wearing that? Only I can—'

'I washed my uniform and begged them on the rehab ward to use their tumbledryer…' She didn't get to finish because screams filled the department and Nick jumped up as a man was stretchered in, sucking on the gas, in sheer agony at the prospect of being moved from the stretcher to the gurney.

'Can I have a quick look before you move him?'

His jeans had already been cut off and it was a rather horrible sight, his dislocated patella causing the whole leg to look deformed. It was an excruciating injury and Alison blinked as, without X-ray, without delay, Nick told the man to suck on the gas and with one flick popped it back.

A shriek filled the department and then a sob and then the sound of relieved silence.

'Let's get him on the gurney and then we'll need X-rays.' He chatted for a moment to his extremely grateful patient, then chatted a bit more to the rather impressed paramedics, then he walked over to where Alison was now on the computer, checking some blood results, and she could feel the heat whoosh up her neck as he came over.

'God, I'm good.' He grinned and, yes, it was arrogant, but it was funny too, and Alison couldn't help but smile as she rolled her eyes.

'Yeah, but you know it.'

He looked at her and he wanted to look away, to walk away, to remember he was there for reasons other than this, except there was something about Alison that was hard to resist. Something about her that meant stern warnings could so easily be ignored.

'Hey…' Moira dashed past '…are you coming to the beach later, Alison?' She gave a hopeful glance at Nick. 'There are a few of us going—Amy…'

'Not for me,' Alison said.

'Or me!' Nick said. Moira shrugged and moved on. It was like sugar to artificial sweetener, Nick decided, because sugar was something he was trying to give up too. Yes, sweeteners tasted okay, once you got used to them, and for a while there they sufficed, but sooner rather than later you went back for the real thing…. And maybe he should just go to the beach, or a bar, or just home and have that takeaway that Amy had offered. Instead he found himself asking Alison if she wanted to go for a coffee.

'I've got a dentist appointment.'

'Ouch.' He pulled a sympathetic face. 'Hope it's not too painful.'

'Oh, it's just my six-monthly check-up.' And she smiled, but it sort of faded as she turned back to the computer, because it just about summed her up.

She *had* six-monthly check-ups, and when this one was done, no doubt, she'd do as she always did and while she was there make an appointment for the next one and write it in her diary, and she'd be there—she never missed.

Same as her eight-weekly trim at the hairdresser's.

Same as she booked in the dog to be shampooed and clipped.

She bet Nick hadn't spent ages on the computer, researching dentists to ensure he didn't miss his six-monthly check-up.

The most gorgeous, sexy man was asking her for coffee and she'd turned him down for a dental appointment!

'We could meet up afterwards, but not for long, I've got to look at that flat.' She could hear her own words and inwardly reeled at them, and even as she mistyped the patient's UR number she sounded almost blasé as she dipped in her toe and felt only warmth. 'So long as I don't end up getting a filling or something.'

'Let's just hope you've been flossing.'

She had been.

Alison lay in the chair with her mouth open as the dentist tapped each tooth in turn.

Not a single filling.

Again.

He cleaned them, polished them and they felt like glass as she ran her tongue over them. As she paid and headed out, she didn't get why she was so nervous.

Why she wanted to just not show up.

Because it might just be coffee and strudel and then she'd be disappointed, Alison thought as she stepped out onto the street with her sparkly clean teeth. Or, worse, it might be more than coffee and strudel…

Maybe that was what he did—pick someone wherever he went, dazzle her with the full glare of his spotlight.

And he really could dazzle.

Since two minutes past six on Friday morning, he'd been on her mind.

She rang her mum, told her she was having coffee with friends before she went to look at the flat, and as she turned the corner he was there already and looked up and smiled as she made her way over and took her seat at the pavement café.

'How was the dentist?'

'Fine,' Alison said, 'I've earned my strudel.'

He ordered, and her nerves disappeared because, absolutely, he was still easy to talk to and easy to listen to, too. Not working for a few months, Nick said, was the single best thing he had ever done. 'Because,' he continued, spooning *four* sugars into his coffee as Alison tapped in a sweetener, 'I actually missed it.'

'Well, you love your job,' Alison said. 'That's obvious.'

'But I didn't,' Nick said, and Alison blinked at his admission. 'That's one of the reasons I took a year off. I wasn't even sure if I wanted to do medicine any more, let alone work in Emergency.'

'But you seem to enjoy it.'

'I'm starting to.' He was in no rush, just sat and drank his coffee as if he'd be happy to sit there all evening and told her a little about himself. 'There was never any question that I'd be a doctor—preferably a surgeon. My dad's one, my grandfather was one, my elder brother is, as is my sister…' He rolled his eyes. 'Can you imagine what we talk about over dinner?'

'What about your mum?'

'Homework monitor,' Nick said, and Alison laughed. 'There was no question and, really, I accepted that, right up till the last year of medical school—which I enjoyed, but…' He shrugged. 'I don't know, I wanted to take a year off to travel, but I ended up taking an internship.'

'I was the same,' Alison interrupted, which was rare for her. Normally she sat quietly and listened. 'I wanted a year off when I finished school, but Mum and Dad said I should finish my studies.'

'I had the same conversation with mine.' Nick

groaned. 'So I did my internship, decided I liked emergency work, met Gillian and it was all…'

'Nice,' Alison offered.

And they could hardly hear the other's story for telling their own, or hardly tell their own for hearing the other person's.

'Work was okay about it—they gave me a year's unpaid leave, but they made it pretty clear that there'd be no extension. I've no idea how bad divorce must be,' Nick said, 'because breaking up after four years was hard enough. I mean, there was no real reason—it was just the talk of mortgages and babies and if we'd hyphenate our names…' He called the waiter and ordered another coffee and Alison ordered a hot chocolate. 'I was having a midlife crisis apparently!' Nick said. 'At thirty!'

'I had one too,' Alison said, 'and I'm only twenty-four.' And she laughed, for the first time she laughed about the sorry situation she had found herself in a year ago. She told him a little about Paul, her one serious relationship—how well he'd got on with her mother, how hard it had been to end it—but there was something she wanted to know about him. 'So…' Alison was cautious, but terribly, terribly curious. 'Are you two having a break…?'

'No,' Nick said. 'I ended it and it wasn't nice, but it was necessary. I just hope one day she can see that—four weeks later I'd got a round-the-world ticket and was flying to New York.'

And she sat outside a pavement café with a man who came from the other side of the world, but who felt somehow the same, and there was a fizz in her veins she'd never felt before, a glow inside as they chatted on, and she could have stayed and spoken to him for hours, except she had her real estate appointment at seven.

'Do you want me to come?' Nick asked. 'I love looking at houses.'

'It's an apartment.'

'It's someone else's!' Nick grinned. 'I love being nosy.'

And Alison smiled back because, even if flat-hunting was hell, yes, she liked that aspect of it too, loved that peek into others' lives, the solace that wardrobes the length and breadth of Coogee were filled fit to bursting, that some people didn't even make their beds when they had people coming round to view. And she told him so and told him some more. 'One couple were rowing on Saturday,' Alison said.

'The owners?' Nick asked, and she loved how his eyes widened in glee.

'I think they were breaking up.' Alison nodded. 'They stood on the balcony and had this screaming match during the open inspection.'

'God, I wish I'd been there,' Nick said, and she kind of wished he'd been there too—liked that he liked the same things as her, that odd little things pleased.

'Come on, then.' She went to fish out her purse, but Nick waved her away and it would have been embarrassing really to protest—and even there he was different. Paul had decided on their first date that equality meant you split the bill—and she told him so as they walked down the hill and turned at the chemist's.

'He lived in constant terror that he might end up paying for a round of garlic bread when he hadn't eaten a slice,' Alison said, and then wondered if she should have said that, if it was bitchy to talk about your ex like that. 'He was a great guy, just toward the end…' She trailed off and Nick got it, he just completely got it.

'Gillian and I ended up the same,' he said as they walked up the hill to meet the real estate agent. 'At first I used to love it that she did my crossword, but near the end I was setting my alarm early and nearly breaking my neck to get down the stairs and to the newspaper first.' He glanced over to check that she got it too and Alison smiled. 'It's not the crossword, or the garlic bread, is it?'

'He was great,' Alison said. 'It was more…' And she told him a bit about herself, not enough to have him running in the opposite direction, just a little. 'It was too nice,' Alison said. 'Too easy, almost. Mum's a bit overprotective and he didn't seem to mind… In fact, Paul suggested he move in.' She still burnt at the memory. 'Mum was delighted, it felt like they had it all worked out.'

'They just forgot to ask you,' Nick said, and for the first time in her life, she felt as if someone got her.

CHAPTER FIVE

ALISON had very few expectations as the real estate agent opened the front door and she stepped inside. There had been so many disappointments, so many let-downs, that, in the name of self-preservation, she kept her hopes determinedly down.

Even as they looked at the surprisingly spacious lounge, even that this apartment actually had a kitchen, though even the real estate agent managed a wry smile at the supposed glimpse of the bay. Nick could see it because he was a full foot taller, but apparently, there at the top right hand side of the kitchen window was her beloved beach.

'There is a second bedroom.' Alison peered into a cupboard. 'Well,' the real estate agent attempted, 'it would make a nice nursery.'

'Or study,' Nick offered when Alison laughed, and then they moved along the hall.

'This is the main bedroom.'

It was larger than expected too, and, really, all

Alison's wishes had been answered. The owners were off to London, the husband leaving the next day apparently, and the wife following in a month's time. 'Really, he'd like to know it was all taken care of before he leaves,' the real estate agent explained. 'They want a thirty-day settlement...'

And she listened to the wah-wah white noise as the agent did his spiel, but it wasn't the large airy bedroom Alison could see but the suitcase beside the bed, and it truly dawned that if she bought this flat, she was, without doubt, saying goodbye to her dream of travelling, and even though she'd thought it through, even though she'd gone over it a hundred million times, when it came to it, she stalled at the final hurdle.

'Can I have till the morning?' Alison saw the agent's eyebrows rise in surprise. For weeks he had seen her at open inspections at places far less nice than this and now he was almost handing her this opportunity on a plate and at the last minute the *genuine buyer* he'd ensured the vendors he had was faltering.

'The vendors want to save on advertising, that's why I agreed to bring you through, but the photographer is booked for midday and it will go on the market then, unless I hear otherwise.'

'Sure,' Alison said. 'I'll ring tomorrow.'

'I'm impressed,' Nick said as they walked down the street.

'Why?'

'I thought you'd snatch his hand off to get it—you certainly know how to play it cool.'

'It's not that,' Alison started, and then halted herself. She was hardly going to tell a virtual stranger, albeit a very nice virtual stranger, her dilemma—and then, in that moment she realised the stark truth, it wasn't even a dilemma. She really had no choice in the matter. 'I just want to speak to Mum first.'

'It's a big decision,' Nick said, and Alison stopped walking.

'I turn off here.' She gave him a nice smile. 'Thanks for the coffee.'

'Thanks for the company.'

It was a strange moment. The light-heartedness of earlier had gone—Alison heavy with indecision and Nick no doubt not understanding why.

'I'll see you at work tomorrow.'

She turned up the street and bizarrely felt like crying. She knew, was positive in fact, that he was watching her and that made her walk faster. She wanted to turn, wanted to run back to him, to go to a club or a bar, to ask him about his adventures, she wanted to sit and listen to music, to be late, to not go home. Instead she turned the key in the door.

'Hi, Mum.'

'I was just starting to get worried.'

'It's not even eight!' Alison pointed out.

'You said you were out for coffee,' Rose said. 'A quick phone call would have been nice...'

There was a retort on Alison's tongue, an urge to yet again point out her age, another beginning to a row that had never taken place but one they were steadily building towards. Then Alison caught sight of her father and brother's photo on the shrine that used to be a mantelpiece, and swallowed down her bitter response, knew this was the small price she paid for living, knew she would do her best to avoid arguing and knew for certain that she had to move out.

'I went to look at that flat.' She saw her mother's rapid blink. 'I think I've finally found one.' She spoke quickly into the ensuing silence. 'It's a ten-minute walk away, it's got everything—two bedrooms, even a little balcony...' And she waited for her mother to fill in the gap, to point out that she could live here for nothing, that it was stupid, pointless, but for once Rose didn't speak, and not for the first time Alison tried to be honest. 'I don't know if I should take it. I mean, I'll have a mortgage, there's no way I'd be able...' She glanced up and saw Rose swallow. 'You know I always wanted to travel...'

And Rose in that moment had a choice between the lesser of two evils. She must have, because for once she didn't jump in with all the reasons Alison would be stupid to leave home; for the first time ever she bordered on enthusiastic about her daughter moving out.

'It sounds a nice flat.' There was a wobble to Rose's voice. 'Two bedrooms, you say?'

'Well, only one that's actually big enough for a bed, but the other could be a nice study.'

'You'll need a study if you do your trauma course.'

'The thing is, Mum—'

'I know you want to travel…' Rose broke in. 'I've been thinking. I've given it a lot of thought, actually. We deserve a treat.' As Alison opened her mouth to protest, Rose overrode her. 'I know you've always wanted to go to Bali. I wouldn't mind seeing it too… My treat,' she said loudly as Alison tried to interrupt.

And as she lay in her single bed later on, Alison tried not to cry. She felt horribly selfish actually, because in the space of a few hours she'd found a flat and been offered a fortnight's trip to Bali. It was just…

The first year after the accident she'd taken her mum for weekends away, she and Paul had taken her for a holiday once too, with Alison sharing a room with her mum. Then last year they'd been to Queensland for a week—her mum saying all the time how much her father and brother would have liked it.

She ripped back the sheet, and almost ran to the window.

There were no bay views from her bedroom but there was the distant roar of the ocean as she pushed the window open and gulped in the cool night air. And there were the sounds of the bars and the backpackers and youth and fun, and she was tempted to run down in her nightdress, tempted to find what ever bar Nick was in, to rush up to him and kiss his face off, to take him by the hand and dance and dance, to come back at dawn *without* sending her mother a text.

To be free.

CHAPTER SIX

'YAY!' The whole staffroom cheered when a beaming Alison revealed her news as she walked into her late shift.

She'd soon got over herself—a brisk walk on the beach at the crack of dawn and a stern talk with herself had turned things round in her head. Then, at nine a.m. she'd rung the real estate agent, at nine-forty she'd been at the bank, at nine fifty-five she'd handed the deposit over and signed a mountain of forms, and now, at midday, she almost had a mortgage.

'Congratulations.' Nick pulled her aside the first chance he got. It had been a busy afternoon and Alison had been working the paediatric cots while Nick had been in Resus, but as she came back from her coffee break, he was just heading off for his.

'Thanks!' Alison said. 'It's pretty exciting.'

'How about dinner,' Nick offered, 'to celebrate?' And when she paused, when she didn't just jump in and say yes, Nick upped the offer. 'With lots of garlic bread.'

'Why?' He didn't understand the hurt in her eyes, he

didn't really understand the question. 'Why would we go out for dinner?'

'Because you want to?' Nick said, because he was sure that she did. 'Because I want to?'

'I don't…' Her voice trailed off, and her words hung in the air, the wrong words because she did want to, very much. She had been about to say that she didn't see the point in pursuing this, except when he was around she did see the point—he was nice and funny and whatever attraction was, it was there, for both of them.

'I'm not sure.' She changed tack, headed for safer ground, used a method far safer than exposing her heart. 'What with work and everything.'

Nick could have pointed out that it was just dinner, that, given they'd been out on Friday, clearly work colleagues did meet up outside the walls of Emergency. Except it wasn't just dinner and it wasn't the emergency crew he wanted to see more of out of hours—it was her. And, yes, he was bending his own rules, but it was, after all, just for a short while and even if it was work, it was still a holiday. He wasn't asking for for ever, he wasn't threatening to run away with her heart, he just wanted more of the smile that sometimes brightened her serious face, wanted more of the woman he was getting to know.

'We could keep it quiet.' He ran a hand through his hair as he renegotiated his own boundaries.

'Sounds good.'

And those words were the bravest she'd uttered.

'About ten?' Nick said, and her smile disappeared when she realised he meant tonight, that his impulsive world was invading hers. 'Ten-thirty?' he said, and named a nice bar. 'I'll pick you up.' And she thought of her mother and shook her head at the image.

'Ten-thirty's great.' She forced a smile. 'I'll meet you there.'

Thankfully, she was kept almost busy enough not to be nervous. It wasn't a date, she kept telling herself, it was just friends going out for a couple hours. She managed not to think about it, especially when dealing with a very restless baby and an extremely anxious mum.

'She's putting on weight.' Lucia, the paediatric intern, was thorough and nice and doing her best to reassure Shelly, the mother of an eight-week-old. 'I know reflux babies are hard, but you are doing everything right.' And she went through all the medications and thickeners that little Casey was on, and checked that she was being positioned properly.

'She won't settle, though,' Shelly said. 'She hardly goes two hours.'

'That's why my registrar suggested you look at the mother and baby day clinic,' Lucia said. 'She's well, though.' Despite everything, the baby was well. There were no signs of dehydration, her nappies were wet, her obs were normal—she was just a very fussy baby. 'You've got an appointment coming up with the paediatrician…' Her pager was going off, her registrar had already looked over the baby and deemed little Casey well enough to go home, and there was only one paediatric bed left to last the night. Lucia was only checking her over again because the mother was still concerned, and despite Lucia's reassurances, as she said goodbye Alison knew Shelly wasn't reassured. Neither was she, though her concern wasn't just for the baby. She could see Shelly's shaking hands as she did up the poppers on her baby's little outfit, saw that despite the baby screaming, Shelly said nothing to soothe her, just wrapped her up and put her in her little car seat, without a word, without a cuddle. There was no malice in her actions. She was just a mother very close to the edge.

'Amy saw this baby and handed her over to Paeds.' She handed Nick the notes. 'Amy's gone home and Paeds have seen the baby and they're happy to discharge. I'm just concerned…' She waited as he read through the notes, waited for him to roll his eyes, or sigh, or say 'I'll get to it,' but instead he listened as Alison voiced her concerns and he read easily between the lines. 'Lucia did suggest the day clinic to sort out her sleeping pattern.'

'What did Mum say to that?'

'She agreed to it, but there's normally a two-week wait.'

'Do you think she's depressed?'

'I'm sure she is,' Alison said, 'just not enough for an urgent admission. And frankly I'd be feeling depressed. I tried feeding her and it was hard work.'

'Okay.' He slid off his stool and went over and introduced himself. He chatted to Shelly about her babe, taking her out of her little seat and examining the infant himself. 'When is she due for a feed?'

'She's constantly due!' Shelly said through gritted teeth. 'She never finishes a bottle, she screams as if I'm pouring acid down her throat instead of milk...' The young mother bit back angry tears as her baby lay on the mattress, screaming. 'I know she's got reflux, I know it will get better...'

'Okay,' Nick said, and when Shelly didn't, Alison started to dress the baby again. She waited for him to suggest she get a bottle, that he observe the babe feed, or a little bit more of what had taken place on and off for the last four hours, but he did none of that. He gave a brief smile and nodded and said he'd be back in a moment as Shelly blew out a long breath.

'What's happening?'

'I'm not sure,' Alison said, as the baby's screams quadrupled. 'Here,' she said, when Shelly sat down beside the cot and put her head in her hands, 'would you like me to take Casey for a little walk? I'll see if I can find out what's happening.'

Casey did stop crying, the motion, the bright lights, the activity all distracting her enough as Alison walked through the department and found Nick perched back on his stool.

'What's happening?'

'She'll be admitted,' Nice said. 'I've just paged the paed reg.'

'He's happy for her to go home and be seen in Outpatients…'

'Well, I'm not,' Nick said. 'Which means that she's going to be admitted.'

And he told the paediatric reg the same when he picked up the phone. Yes, he was friendly and perfectly reasonable at first, and then Alison got her first glimpse of a different Nick, an extremely assertive Nick who, despite the smile and the easygoing banter, took his job very seriously and would not be argued with.

A Nick who was going to go far.

'It's not even an option,' Nick said, turning his pen over and over between the desk and his fingers, clearly in no rush. 'She can be transferred to another hospital if there are no beds here, but I'm not happy to send her home, so either ring your intern and tell her to come and do the paperwork, or I can ring your consultant to discuss it further. But whatever comes of it, this baby isn't going home.'

'That told them,' Alison said.

'I don't see why everything has to be an argument—it's the same everywhere,' Nick added. 'I know there are hardly any beds, I know she's not acute, but…' He glanced down towards the bay. 'I'm going to have a word with Mum.'

He was nice and practical and explained that Casey should be monitored and was upfront about Shelly's tension. 'We need to be really sure we haven't overlooked anything and if everything checks out, we need to make sure you get the support you need with Casey.'

He just dealt with things, without fuss or drama, and he didn't moan as he did so.

'He's nice, that doctor,' Shelly commented as Alison took her up to the ward, the porter wheeling the mother and baby in a chair.

'He is,' Alison agreed, and then she remembered.

She was having dinner with that nice doctor tonight.

Taking the bus simply wasn't an option. By the time she had taken Shelly up to the ward *and* dashed back, it was already well after nine and she'd missed her bus, and as much as Nick might be expecting her to change quickly and dash back out, and as much as Alison wanted to look as if she'd changed quickly and dashed back out, there was no girl facing such a prospect who would. Which was why, despite now being a responsible, soon-to-be homeowner, Alison splurged on a taxi, though she made sure that it dropped her off at the end of the street to avoid even more questions from her mum.

'Out?' Rose frowned as Alison flew in the door.

'For dinner,' Alison said. 'To celebrate getting the flat.'

'Who with?'

'Friends from work,' Alison said, and it wasn't a lie, she consoled herself as she dashed up the stairs. It was just a slight exaggeration, or rather playing the situation down, because friends from work was safe, a friend from work a bit different.

A male friend from work.

A gorgeous, blond, funny, sexy, 'here for a good time, not a long time' male friend from work.

Getting ready for Nick was rather like getting a patient quickly prepared for Theatre. Alison went through a rapid mental checklist, cleaning her teeth, shaving her legs, even cleaning her ears, body lotion, perfume, subtle make-up, hair gloss, nice underwear, really, really nice underwear—not that he'd be seeing it, but just because, because, because…

She was simply meeting a friend from work, Alison told herself over and over as she trawled through her wardrobe till the contents lay on a heap on her bed, wondering how she could have nothing to wear when her entire bed was covered. She settled for a pale grey tube skirt that she'd had for ever and a cheap but cheerful top she'd bought the previous week, pulled on some bracelets as she dashed downstairs, wished her mum goodnight and flew down the street, rather surprised to find Nick waiting for her at the end.

'Don't want you walking on your own.'

'I do it all the time,' Alison said.

'You look nice.' His eyes told her that he meant it.

'Oh.' She gave a casual shrug, one that said it had been no effort at all! 'Thanks.'

He was just a friend, Alison told herself as he went to kiss her on the cheek.

Or maybe not, because very deliberately he avoided her cheek and met her mouth, and it was slow and deliberate and its meaning was clear, crystal clear, that this was more than just friendship.

And for Nick it was confirmation too.

He felt first her hesitancy, her guardedness and then he felt what he knew, or rather had guessed at. Felt this gathering of passion on full lips and despite self-issued warnings he wanted to unleash it.

'Just so we don't spend the whole night wondering,' Nick said, and pulled back, even though he wanted more. And she smiled because now, instead of wondering, she knew.

So she kissed him, just to confirm it, and despite Nick's best-laid plans, now they would spend the whole night not just wondering but wanting too, because one taste of his tongue and Pandora's box opened and it was passion that slithered out. Alison could feel the press of brick wall on her back, feel the silk of his hair on her fingers, and ten doors from prison he turned the key and she flew, her body just flew to his, met his, wanted his, and she'd never kissed or been kissed like this, his hands on her hips and his mouth drinking hers. And it was absolutely right that he stop, that he look into her eyes, pupils so dilated he might have put in atropine drops, and she watched him taste his own lips, taste her again and try to get his breath.

'Let's eat,' Nick said.

Let's not, Alison wanted to reply as his forehead met

hers as they rested just a moment to regroup, because, as Alison had just found out, kisses changed things.

Good ones especially.

Their restaurant was chosen by the delicious herby scent that wafted onto the street, and it was Italian. Alison chose giant ravioli in a creamy mushroom sauce and Nick didn't skimp on the garlic bread either.

It was different from any other date she'd been on because there was neither awkwardness nor ease, or rather there was, just not in the usual rhythm.

There was ease to the conversation, it was the table between them that made things awkward—just watching each other's mouths as they ate, that made them tense.

'Is everything okay?' The waiter checked when, plates quickly cleared, Nick asked for the bill.

'I'll get dinner next time,' Alison said when he paid, and it was as assured as that, for both of them, that there would be a next time.

'Your wine.' The waiter handed them their half-bottle and Nick smiled at the little differences around the world, because till a few minutes ago they could have been anywhere. Walking out of the restaurant with wine in hand, they saw the show of the ocean endlessly unfolding, the night warm, the sky thick with stars. Yes, it was late, but too early to end their evening, and a walk on the beach was cleansing after the noise in the restaurant. 'Do you want to come back for coffee?' Nick said, and then he winced a bit. 'I do mean coffee.'

Alison would have loved to because she wanted

more of him and a coffee would be nice too, except she couldn't.

'I really have to get back soon.' She hadn't dared check her phone. 'I've got loads on tomorrow.'

So instead they sat and Nick had a mouthful from the bottle and so too did Alison and, yes, she was home, but it felt like paradise.

She stared out at the stars and there were millions of them. The more she looked the more she could see, and she wished she could read them, wished she could point to a constellation, and she told him that. 'I'm going to do an astronomy course one day.'

'Never interested me,' Nick admitted, 'till I came to Australia. I've never seen stars like it.'

And they lay back on the sand and just stared, and she could have lain there for ever, but she really did have to get back and she told him, well, not quite the truth but a little bit more than she had previously—that her mum would be starting to worry.

'Why don't you ring her if she'll be worrying?' came Nick's practical suggestion, because for most twenty-four-year-olds a phone call would suffice.

'And tell her what?' Alison dodged the issue. 'That I'm lying on a beach and I'm worried that he's going to kiss me, because I really don't think I'll be able to stop?'

'I'm worried this time too,' Nick said, and her heart twisted as they spoke their own shorthand, that he remembered her words as she remembered his.

'I have visions,' Alison admitted, turning from the stars to his lovely, lovely face, and for some reason she felt free to be just a little more honest. 'Of me at forty, or fifty, and I'm a lot larger than I am now, I've got a big shiny red face and I'm a virgin, and it's Tuesday and Mum's serving me dinner at the table—beef stroganoff…'

And he didn't leap from the beach and run. He just smiled and rolled over on his side and his hand moved and toyed without thinking with the bottom of her skirt, because her admission brought only one question.

'And are you a virgin?'

'No,' Alison said, 'but in this vision I've lied for so long, I think I've turned into one.'

That unthinking hand was at the side of her knee. She could taste his breath and they were still talking and not going anywhere.

'Why would you lie?'

'It's just easier to with my mum.' And it was impossible to explain, so she didn't try to—impossible to tell this gorgeous, free man about the tentacles that were tightening ever more firmly around her, impossible to admit what he could never understand.

'Do you get them?' She broke the silence.

'What?'

'Visions of a possible future.'

'No.' His mouth found her cheek and then slid to her ear and she was terribly glad she'd cleaned them.

'Never?' Alison checked, trying to talk, trying to

breathe, trying very hard not to kiss him. 'Don't you see scenarios, like if you don't do this, then that might happen?'

He nibbled at her neck while he thought about it. 'At work.' Nick stopped in mid-nibble with his answer. 'Sometimes when I'm looking at an injury I know if we don't do that or prescribe that, then this might happen.'

He got it.

'And in your life?' Alison asked, rolling into him, feeling his jean-clad sandy legs in between her bare ones, feeling his long, tanned fingers circling her nipples through her T-shirt, and she wanted to rest her breast in his palm, just kissing and lying and talking, and her body was the most alive it had ever been.

'No.' But Nick did think about it as he played with her breasts and what she loved the most was that he *did* think about it. 'Actually, I did have one.' His hands moved from her breasts and made lovely strokes through the cotton on her skirt down her stomach as he spoke. 'When I was having my supposed premature midlife crisis.' He could see her teeth as she smiled. 'I was on call and the baby was screaming, the nanny had the night off and we were rowing because Gillian was working the next day...' He blinked at his own admission. 'I get it.'

'What was the nanny's name, then?' Alison asked.

'My visions aren't that detailed,' Nick said. 'Helga?' he offered, but she shook her head. 'Svetlana?'

'Better,' Alison said.

And he got it and that came with reward—her lips, unworried, met his and he kissed her mouth and pressed her into the sand. She felt the damp salt of the ocean on his shirt and she tasted it on his mouth.

She felt the press of his leg and the roam of his hands, the sand in her hair and the slide of his tongue, and the dangerous beckoning of his loaned flat, and the pull of her home, all tightening in her stomach as his mouth pursued.

It was a kiss that struck at midnight, and she turned, but only in his arms, a kiss that had her hips rise into his groin, and it could never be enough.

A kiss that had her breast slip out of her bra and though encased in fabric still fall into his palm.

A kiss where you didn't have to go further to enjoy it, but for Alison it was already too late to stay, though it was Nick who pulled away, because if he kissed her for a moment longer, he would forget they were on a beach!

'I ought to go,' Alison said.

'Yes, you ought to,' Nick said, and she let him help her up, and then he did the nicest of things—he dusted her down.

It was *the* nicest thing.

The stroke of his hand on her body, the attention to detail, the warmth of his palm stroking her bottom and then dusting damp sand from her calves. It was so seemingly innocent but it was like sex with clothes on—actually far better than any sex Alison had ever had—and she stood, compliant, but she wanted to run with him, back to his flat, and never mind the coffee. And she nearly said 'Your turn', nearly put her hands out to deal with his sandy jeans, but he took her hand instead because it would have been far too dangerous, and they walked up the beach, tossed the bottle in the bin and then headed for her street. They walked in silence to her turn-off and this time when she went to say goodbye, Nick insisted on walking her to her door.

With their kiss she was a little more his, even if just for a little while, which meant he walked with her. She just wished he wouldn't, but couldn't say so.

'We're both off at the weekend.' Nick knew because he'd looked. 'I was thinking of getting a bike, going for a ride in the mountains…' He sensed her reluctance and misinterpreted it. 'I'll book two rooms.'

'I don't know, Nick.' So badly she wanted to go, but it wasn't just the weekend and sleeping arrangements that had her in knots, but getting on a bike, the recklessness of it—all of it. 'Actually, I've got some things I need to do and then I've got a week of nights…' And the evening ended there, and she gave him just a little kiss on the cheek, because she knew her mother was watching, and she knew too that he was watching her as she walked to her door.

He was.

And he must be getting good at her vision game, because as Nick walked home he was having one of his own and there wasn't a crying baby or Svetlana in sight, more an Alison uncut vision.

Alison let loose, Nick thought with a smile, pulling up in surprise at just how much he wanted to share his vision with her…

'Oh, you're back.' Rose stood by the kettle, as if she hadn't been at the window. 'I was just making a cup of tea to take back to bed. Do you want one?'

'No, thanks, Mum.'

'Nice night.'

'Really nice.'

'How was your friend?'

'Great,' Alison said, hearing the singular, and she turned to go to bed, but then relented. 'We just had some pasta, and then walked.'

'You're covered in sand.'

'We walked on the beach.'

Rose humphed, and no doubt there was half the beach in her hair and why did she feel guilty? Why was her mother sulking when she had done absolutely nothing wrong? 'Am I allowed to ask his name?'

Alison hesitated. It was all too new and too soon to be naming him, she wanted to pull apart her own thoughts and feelings without sharing things first, but her mum wanted conversation, inclusion, and at every turn Alison did try.

'Nick,' Alison said, and her mum just waited. 'He's a friend from work. So what did you do tonight?'

'Not much—I looked through some photos.' She gave a wan smile. 'I'll have to find something to do once you're gone.'

'I'll be ten minutes away, Mum.'

'Oh.' Rose suddenly changed the subject. 'Your uncle Ken rang. They're having a barbecue at the weekend, so don't go making any plans—they're looking forward to seeing you.'

'What day?' Alison asked, sure, quite sure what was coming next.

'I'm not sure…' Rose's forehead crinkled as she tried to recall. 'Memory like a sieve—I'll ring tomorrow.'

To arrange a sudden barbecue, Alison thought, but didn't say. ''Night, Mum.' She kissed her mother on the cheek and went upstairs, headed for her room and wished, wished, wished she'd met Nick in a couple of months' time, when she had her own flat.

But as Alison climbed into bed, she knew it wasn't that simple.

In thirty days' time, twenty-eight, in fact, she'd have been in more of a position to let him into her life.

To climb on a bike and head into the hills and, yes, maybe not tonight, but the way her body had thrummed to his kiss, soon, very soon, the night would have had a very different conclusion. Her own reaction tonight, though so natural at the time, startled her now as she lay there. She wanted to ring him, right now this minute, to explain that this was out of character for her. That wine and kisses on the beach… She burnt at the memory, but it was in embarrassment now. She wasn't like that—well, she was, but only with him.

He'd hardly appreciate the admission, Alison realised. Nick had wanted fun, so too had she.

Maybe it was better this way, Alison decided, turning to the wall and willing sleep to come.

Maybe caution was merited here, even if she resisted it, because, as a little voice in her head grew louder, Nick would be around for a couple of months only and two weeks of that had already gone.

Yes, if she had the flat, if she had some freedom, she could let him more into her life.

But how much harder would it be then to have him leave?

CHAPTER SEVEN

'ALISON, could I have a word?' Nick caught her right at the end of her shift on Friday when all week she'd done her absolute best to avoid him.

Of course they'd talked, but about patients and things, and Alison had been very careful to take her break only when Nick was busy with a patient, but just as she thought she'd got through the working week he caught her at three-twenty p.m. as she and Ellie headed for the bus stop.

'I'm rushing for the bus.'

'We've already missed it, the next one isn't due for twenty minutes.' Ellie, dear Ellie, beamed. 'I'll wait for you at the stop.'

'Sorry,' he started, 'I haven't been avoiding you, and there just hasn't been a chance to talk to you.'

'I know.' Alison smiled, even though she'd engineered it that way. 'It's been a crazy week.'

'Look, about this weekend,' Nick said. 'I thought we could go out.'

'You're going away.'

'I'd rather…' There was a rare awkwardness to him. 'I'm happy to give it a miss. I'd rather spend some time with you.'

'I've got a family thing tonight…' Alison said, which was now true. 'My dad's brother's having a barbecue, it's always a bit awkward…' She saw him frown. 'My dad's dead, we get together and it always ends up a bit of a reminisce…'

'What about the rest of the weekend?' Nick was direct. It was a barbecue she was going to after all, so she struggled for an answer, one that let her off the hook.

'I really have to go to the home furnishings store.' It was the most pathetic of excuses. 'I need some stuff for the flat.'

Somehow, and she really didn't know how and certainly not why, but for reasons of his own, a shopping trip and dinner at his place afterwards was more appealing to Nick than a bike ride in the mountains and somehow, and she did know why, he was still so very easy to talk to, still so very hard not to want to like. 'I need to give the car a run,' Nick explained when he offered to pick her up, 'or the battery will go flat.'

'I'll see.' She gave him a thin smile. 'I just need to…' She didn't bother to explain, in fact she didn't have to explain, Alison realised, didn't have to tell him about every beat of her heart. 'I'll let you know.'

She caught up with Ellie at the bus stop. 'Thanks a

lot.' Alison gave her friend a wry smile. 'I was actually trying to get away back there!'

'Then you're mad!' Ellie said. 'He's gorgeous, he's nice and from the way he's always looking at you or, oh, so casually asks "Who's on a late today?" or "Who's on in the morning?" and loses interest after it gets to your name, I think we can all safely assume he likes you. Lucky thing.'

'Hardly—he's only here for a few weeks.'

'So?' Ellie gave her an odd look.

'There's just no point.'

'Well, I suppose there's no point if you're looking for a husband.' Ellie let out a laugh. 'I don't get you, Alison. He's gorgeous. You were saying the other week you wanted some fun and adventure, and now it's handed to you on a plate…'

She wished, how she wished she could be more like Ellie, could see only the positives, but all Alison could see was a sure-fire recipe for hurt and she told Ellie so.

'I like him,' she admitted. 'I could see myself *really* liking him.'

'So go for it.'

'You know what Mum's like,' Alison said. 'Once I've got my own place…'

Ellie just laughed. 'How did you survive your teens? I mean, before…' Yes, Ellie laughed at most things, but her voice did trail off then. She genuinely liked Rose and knew all Alison had been through.

'Tim was the one who was always in trouble.' Alison could smile at the memory now. 'I used to just say I was staying at a friend's if I wanted to go out.'

'Do that, then.' Ellie shrugged. 'Till you get your own place, say you're staying at mine. Anyway, by then you might find out that he's the most crushing bore, or walk in to find him dressed in your underwear and stilettos. Go out and have some fun, for God's sake…he doesn't have to be "the one" to enjoy him.'

Ellie was right.

Alison stepped off the bus and instead of heading for home she walked on the beach, sensible shoes in hand. She felt the sand between her toes, and the sun warming her back, tasted the salt on her lips and felt the wind in her hair, and for the first time in years she tasted adventure, for the first time in so long Alison felt just a little bit free.

She'd yearned for adventure, escape, and Nick was just that.

Nick didn't need to know all of her—Nick didn't need to know that the nights out and kisses on the beach were rarities.

She could do this, Alison told herself, walking past the very spot where they had lain. She could throw caution to the wind, could be the woman her body was begging her to be, could close her mind to the pitfalls and problems and for once just enjoy.

But how? the sensible part of her mind asked. When even staying out after midnight required the stealth and ability to lie like a teenager to her mum. Surely the last thing Nick needed from a holiday romance was the crush of her problems landing in his lap.

Why should she put herself through it?

Because you want to.

Nick's voice seemed to carry on the wind, echoing her own thoughts, and she *did* want to.

And surely she could handle it?

She was far too serious about things, Alison conceded. It didn't have to be for ever to be worthwhile.

Around 10:30 if you can still make it.

She held her breath and sent the text and then held it again till he replied: *Great.*

And Ellie was right again.

She didn't want to lie to her mum, she didn't want to *have* to lie to her mum, but she did enjoy having him in her life.

And he could never be boring. As for Ellie's other suggestion, well, the thought made her laugh.

Right there at the barbecue that evening, as she cut herself a slice of pavlova, she let out a little laugh so, yes, she did enjoy having him in her life, even when he wasn't there.

As she stood, chatting to her uncles and aunts, there was an inner glow in knowing that she would see him tomorrow, just this extra smile as she described the flat to her uncle Ken, because she'd seen it with Nick.

'I'm going to look at furniture tomorrow,' Alison said as her mum came over. 'I want to look at desks.'

'I might come along,' Rose replied. 'I was thinking of getting some bar stools for the kitchen bench. Are you taking Tim's car?'

It was one of the reasons she rarely drove; the car would always be Tim's. Her mother wouldn't part with it, insisted Alison use it, then got teary when she did.

'Actually, Nick's taking me.'

'Nick?' Ken smiled, pleased to see his favourite niece not just with a sparkle in her eyes but gently standing up to his sister-in-law.

'A friend from work,' Alison said, smiling back at her uncle.

And friends dropped around and friends were asked in.

'Mum, this is Nick.'

Alison tried very hard to treat him as if it were Ellie or Moira or just any friend coming in on Saturday morning before they headed out for a shopping expedition. Rose did the same as Alison finished getting ready, offering him a cup of tea, which Nick accepted, and chatting to him about the hospital and about England and how she and her late husband had wanted to take a trip around Europe when they retired.

'So you're just here for a couple of months, then?' Alison heard her mum saying as she walked into the kitchen.

'That's the plan.' Nick nodded. 'I've got a cousin in New Zealand who's getting married.' Nick was pleasant and polite, and from the way he chatted he was in no rush to head out—in fact, he even accepted Rose's offer of some toast and ginger marmalade.

'Alison can't stand it,' Rose said as Alison rolled her eyes. 'It was Tim's favourite.'

'Tim?' Nick said as the air in Alison's chest stopped moving.

'My son,' Rose said, and thankfully Nick didn't push. But his eyes swept past her a couple of times to the endless photos on the mantelpiece and when Alison went to her bedroom to find a missing shoe, it came as no surprise when Rose followed her.

'What time will you be back from the shops?'

'Actually…' Alison swallowed. 'There's a party on tonight. Vicky, one of the A and E nurses, is getting engaged.' She saw her mother's rapid blink. 'I told you last week.' Which she had, and it was true, except Vicky was actually Ellie's friend and Alison's was more a casual invitation than an expected guest, and she could have sworn she felt her nose grow a touch as she continued. 'She's down the road from Ellie—Ellie said I could stay at hers.' She gave her mum a hurried kiss on the cheek. 'I'll text and let you know what's happening.'

And then finally, *finally*, they were in the car and heading off, and following blue lines to a parking spot.

'You'd rather this than a bike ride in the mountains?' Alison commented as she grabbed a pencil and tape measure.

'We can do that another time,' Nick replied, and Alison walked on in silence. 'I've missed this.' He nudged her as they walked through. 'I'm not joking. I want to do something *normal*.'

He was actually very helpful. The fact he had seen the flat, combined with a male brain, meant he could remember strange details like there was a window where she wanted *that* large bookshelf, and that there was no way on earth that desk was going to fit where Alison intended.

'It's the same the world over.' Nick grinned as they sat in the canteen with their meatballs and chips and red berry jam amidst frazzled couples, yet maybe because they weren't a couple and it wasn't *their* bed or their sofa they were buying, they could just sit there and enjoy. Nick even bought her a little bottle of wine with a glass that screwed to the bottle.

'I'm going to keep this.' Alison was delighted.

'Emergency supplies for your bedroom!' Nick said, and went up to get one for himself too. It was just a tiny reference that he'd picked up on the tension at home, though he said nothing else about it.

Not until later, much later when they were sitting on the balcony, having eaten a mountain of prawns. Nick had cooked and Alison had tossed a salad—a ten-minute meal that would stay in her memory for ever. They were looking out at the ocean and the view was somehow nicer than the one from the bus and from the one walking on the beach. The sun was setting behind them, the colours reflecting on the water, and the waves were very active that evening. She had pinched one of his jumpers and it was worrying how nice his company was, how thrilling it felt to just be with him—for normal things to be so invigorating. He made no suggestion that they go out, or head off to Vicky's party, gave no indication the day had been less exciting than what he was used to.

In fact, for Nick, silence, mutual silence, was lovely.

For months now he'd been a guest—in another country, or at a friend's, or a hotel or hostel, or a hospital—with strangers who were about to become friends. Yes, it was fun and exhilarating, but it was also exhausting—perpetual new faces at breakfast, having to dress for bed in case you needed to get up in the night to go to the loo. It had been a welcome relief to have, after all this time, a flat to himself and a glimmer of a routine, but he shared that precious space with surprising ease now.

And looking over at Alison, who was staring out to the ocean she loved, there was no need to regale, just a deeper need to know, to go that bit further, to find out a little more, and so he asked her.

'What happened to Tim?'

She'd sort of known that the question would come all day, and in some way she'd been waiting for it.

'He was with my dad,' Alison said. 'They were fishing.' He didn't say anything and she was glad of that. 'The weather wasn't that bad, probably a day like this. They got into trouble, ended up too close to the rocks…'

'When?'

'Two, nearly three years ago. I'd finished my training—I was doing some shifts in emergency before I headed off overseas.'

'They weren't, I mean, you weren't there when they…?' She could hear the dread in his voice and immediately she shook her head.

'No. I wasn't at work or anything. I was sharing a flat with friends. I got a call from Mum to come straight home and the police were at the house when I got there. It was all over by then.'

'Doesn't it kill you,' Nick said, after a very long silence, 'working in Emergency?'

Again Alison shook her head.

'I like it. Dad and Tim never even got to Emergency—at least the people who get there have some chance. It's nice to see that there are some happy endings, despite the most terrible odds.'

'It's not just the kids that upset you, is it?' He remembered that morning how he had learnt something, he just wasn't sure what.

'It's the family.' Alison nodded. 'All that's taken away, and the chaos that they're thrown into…not just the ones who are killed. Like with David. That interview was so important to him—and it all just fell apart. I know in the greater scheme of things his wife and daughter were far more important, but I can remember when Tim and Dad had their accident—I was supposed to be flying out at the weekend and I knew it didn't matter, but it did.' She closed her eyes as she tried to explain it. 'I felt selfish even thinking about me, but I did and I wanted someone to step in, to cancel the tickets, to deal with the airline, to deal with the details, to help look after Mum.'

'How's your mum now?'

Alison shrugged. 'Stuck in a time warp, really. I moved home when it happened, but…' She looked over into his kind green eyes and even though she'd sworn not to land it on him, somehow, under his gaze, she could. 'She's petrified of anything happening to me. I'm petrified of it too,' Alison admitted. 'Not for me, though, but for her. I mean, how would she cope if something happened to me?'

'You can't live like that.'

'I know,' Alison said. 'Which is why in a few weeks' time I'll have my own place, and won't have to account for my every move.' She gave him a smile, tried to move the conversation away, because he didn't belong in that space. 'It's complicated.' She gave a small shrug. 'It doesn't matter.'

Except it did.

It did matter, because when they were lying on his sofa and revisiting that kiss on the beach, only this time without Alison having her top on, when she should be able to close her eyes and just sink into him, she was all too aware that she was five minutes away from a call that needed to be made—a lie that she was willing to tell.

His back was against the sofa, his long legs holding her from falling, and there was a film coming to end of which they'd only seen the opening credits, and there was the bliss of privacy for them both. His mouth was on her ear and his hand was stroking her breast. Her hands, which had traced his chest, were stealing downwards now. They had left the balcony door open but neither the roar of the ocean nor his kiss in her ear could dull the call of duty. She wriggled back just a little, breathless and moist from his kiss. Yes, hell yes, she would lie for him.

'I've just got to make a phone call.' His mouth was in her neck and her body was in his arms and it was almost torture to pull just a little further away. She didn't know whether to pull on her top and hamper an easy return to his arms, but neither did she want to shiver half-naked in his bathroom.

'And tell her what?' His question came as a surprise, not to Alison but to Nick. He shouldn't ask, he told himself, because it was no business of his, and he shouldn't really care.

He just did.

'Nick?' She shook her head, would not elaborate—was a little cross even as he thwarted her attempts to stop reality invading. 'I won't be a moment.'

'Alison.' He caught her wrist and even though she'd been half-naked in his arms, she felt stupid standing there with her top half exposed, could feel the blush creeping down over her chest as he asked questions a man like Nick shouldn't have to. 'You don't have to lie for me.'

'Who said I'm lying?'

'They did.' He pointed to her rosy breasts and somehow she almost managed a smile.

'My mum's…' Alison swallowed, she truly didn't want to land him with all of it; even Ellie, who had seen it all, struggled to fathom how rigid her mother could be. 'She's difficult.'

'They often are,' Nick said, and he handed her her top. 'And with all she's been through.'

'She was the same before,' Alison admitted, 'though when Dad and Tim were there…' She couldn't really explain, but without further explanation Nick seemed to understand.

'You weren't in the full spotlight?' When she nodded he continued, 'So where are you tonight?'

'Don't worry about it.' She tried blasé, tried casual, but Nick could tell otherwise and she knew it. 'You really picked the wrong girl to have your torrid Sydney fling with.'

And he looked up at her and was silent for a moment because, yes, he had. He could see stains of hurt in her serious brown eyes and he didn't want to add to them, except inevitably he already had. Already this was turning into something else, something bigger, something he hadn't come to Australia for.

'It doesn't feel like a fling,' Nick admitted.

'It's all it can be.' Alison was practical, even if she was shaking inside.

'Come on.' He stood and looked around for his keys. 'I'll walk you home.'

'It's five minutes away.'

And he should say goodnight here, Nick knew.

End it here.

But Nick never went for the easy option, so he reached for his keys.

'You're not walking on your own.'

They walked back to Alison's home in pensive silence, and he didn't kiss her on the doorstep, because he knew she didn't want him to, but as she let herself in her mouth still tingled from his and her body held the scent and memory of him. Her eyes must have glittered with stirred passion because Rose's face screamed of martyrdom as she offered Alison a cup of tea. Even though she didn't want tea, even though she wanted to go to bed and think of Nick and read the text he'd just sent because she could feel the vibration of her phone in her bag, that this time made her feel giddy with wanting to read it, she said, 'That would be nice,' and curled up on the sofa and took the mug from her mum.

'I thought you were at a party.'

And instead of saying she had been, or offering the usual half-truth, Alison was honest.

'We gave it a miss,' she admitted. 'We went back to Nick's for dinner.'

'He seems nice,' Rose said, because after all he'd brought her baby home.

'He is nice.'

'How long did he say he was here for?' Skilfully, so skilfully, Rose took the pin and deflated the bubble Alison was floating on. Carefully, lovingly, perhaps, she warned her daughter that this could never, ever be. 'Nice-looking man,' Rose said. 'He must have broken a few hearts on his travels,' she added, just to make sure her daughter got it.

'I'm going to bed.' Alison tried to keep her voice light.

She peeled off her clothes and read her text, which was hardly torrid, hardly from a man hell bent on getting in her knickers and promptly breaking her heart. It just thanked her for a nice day and a really nice night, that he'd enjoyed it.

She should stop this now, common sense said.

Just turn her back on his charm, because there really was no point.

She swam between the flags, certainly wasn't into casual relationships, and that was really all it could be with Nick. In a few weeks he'd be off and she'd be left, and if she wasn't extremely careful, Alison knew she'd be nursing a broken heart.

Actually, she already knew she would be.

He'd arrived in her life as blonde and as dazzling as summer. He just lit everything up and enhanced it all some more.

She didn't get him, but she wanted to.

She wanted the little bit of him that was possible, because there was something about Nick that got her, something that was…just a little bit like the single word she sent back to him.

Same. x

CHAPTER EIGHT

'I'M NOT stalking you!'

She grinned as she walked across the foyer to Emergency on Monday night and Nick joined her. 'Amy asked yesterday if I could cover her week of nights.'

'Oh.'

'I got called in yesterday,' Nick explained.

'I didn't see you on the bus.'

'I drove. It was a last-minute thing. I didn't know whether to ring and offer a lift…' He admitted only a quarter of it—if the truth were told, he hadn't known what to do, full stop.

Despite her kisses, despite the thrum between them, there was more to Alison, of that he was sure. He didn't want to hurt anyone, didn't want to get involved.

Or that was what he had told himself.

Sunday had been spent turning down offers to go out, and not just from colleagues. He'd been called in for a multi-trauma late afternoon and had found a rather blatant card from a Louise H., reminding him where she worked and that she'd love to see him there.

It would actually have been the safer option.

Instead he'd accepted Amy's suggestion they ring out for takeaways, which they'd eaten in her office. The conversation had been easy and before he'd known it, the clock had been edging towards midnight and he'd agreed to take over her week of nights.

But Alison was on nights too.

He headed straight for the staffroom, Alison to her locker, and if she hurried there was time for a drink before she started.

'God!' Moira was tying back her hair. 'I'm tired before we've even started. Try sharing a house with eight travellers and doing a week of night shift!' She gave her dazzling smile. 'All worth it, though.' They walked through to the staffroom and Moira gave a delighted whoop as she saw Nick. 'Are you on nights too?'

''Fraid so.'

'Now, that *does* cheer me up,' Moira said, and she was just so light and uninhibited with her banter, Alison would have killed for a little of the same. 'There's not a spare room at that fancy house of yours, is there?' Moira rattled on. 'For a fellow travelling night worker?'

'It's a one-bedroomed flat.' Nick grinned.

'Move over in the bed, then!' Moira winked. Of course, she had no idea about Alison and Nick, she was just having fun…

Sort of.

'Alison.' Sheila popped her head around the staffroom door. 'We've had a lot of staff ring in sick tonight. Mary will be in charge, but apart from that it's agency.' She gave a brief smile to Moira and a couple of the others. 'Luckily it's been quiet. The wards all have beds, so you shouldn't have too many problems. Can you make sure the restocking and drug orders get done, and make sure the trolleys are all wiped down. Oh, and there's a list up on the notice-board—you need to do a refresher lifting course. Make sure you tick off what session you're attending.'

So Alison did, and tried not listen to Moira's chatter and Nick's easy replies—tried not to feel as if he was surely thinking he'd set his sights on the wrong girl. After all, he and Moira were both here on holiday.

This was her life.

It showed in so many little ways through out the night, perhaps because it was a particularly quiet one.

Moira and the other nurses sat chatting when it was quiet.

Alison did the stock ordering. Working around them, she climbed up on footstools to count packets of gauze, and to everyone else Nick appeared not to notice her. He did notice, she knew, because she could feel his lingering eyes at times, or a smile that was there waiting every now and then when she looked up and turned round.

He was brilliant with each and every patient that came through the doors, but during the many, many lulls that filled this quiet night Nick scrolled through his social networking site—there was no registrar's office bulging with a backlog of work for him…probably because there was no backlog when you were just passing through.

'Moira,' Alison asked, 'can you put these boxes away?'

'Sure.' Moira jumped off her stool. 'Where do they go?'

'In the second storage room.'

And she *was* willing, but by the time Alison had shown her where it was, and when for the third time she had to borrow Alison's ID to gain access, it was just far easier to do it herself. There was just a touch of a martyred air to Alison as an hour later she took a gulp of cold tea in the nurses' station and found out all the biscuits she'd brought in were gone.

'I've bought earplugs,' Moira chatted on happily, 'but hopefully everyone will be so hungover, no one will be up before midday and I can get some peace and quiet. I'm a shocking sleeper on nights. What about you, Nick?'

'Sorry?'

'How do you sleep on nights?'

'Like a log,' Nick said, without looking up from the computer, and Alison realised that despite being pleasant, despite the good-natured bantering, there was no flirting from Nick, that he gave nothing back to Moira, as he hadn't to Louise. It was aimed all at her, Alison realised as now he did look up from the computer and gave her a very nice smile, those green eyes turning her pink as she gave a small smile back.

'Is there anything you need me to do?'

'Nothing,' Alison said. It was five a.m., the board was clear and as Nick checked an X-ray with the resident he stretched and yawned. 'I'm going to lie down—call if you need me.'

'Lucky,' Alison grumbled, hauling out the trolleys to be cleaned, and for just a moment their eyes met and Nick felt as if he was back in far North Queensland, standing on a platform with a piece of elastic around his ankle, wanting to jump, knowing it was reckless, ridiculous, that there was no rhyme nor reason to it, yet wanting to all the same.

'What time do you finish?'

'By the time we've given handover—about seven-thirty.'

'I'm here till eight, if you want to hang around—I'll be quicker than the bus.'

He would be, there wasn't one till ten minutes to.

'Thanks,' Alison said.

She cleaned and polished the trolleys, and tried not to think about it as she dealt with the occasional patient, who was seen by the resident and didn't require Nick.

In the morning, when Moira was still teasing for a loan of his bed and he was skilfully deflecting her thinly disguised offer, the rest of the night team, apart from Mary, sped off on the dot of seven-thirty. Alison hung around for a quick chat with Ellie, put her name on the list for the lifting refresher course and then, when Sheila asked if she had five more minutes to go over some annual leave requests, she nodded. When there was nothing else to linger for, except Nick, he walked down the corridor, blonde, tired, offering a lift. Alison smiled and said thanks.

When with him, when it was just them, the doubts that plagued her when they were apart were silenced as always.

'Better than the bus?' Nick asked as she sank back into the passenger seat.

'This morning—yes,' Alison admitted.

'Do you drive?' He glanced over.

'Sometimes—I just prefer the bus for work. The traffic getting in and the staff car-park is impossible sometimes so it's nice just to sit and read the paper.'

'It's been nice *not* driving,' Nick admitted, 'but I can't stand the thought of a bus ride after being on all night—I'd fall asleep.'

'It's always happening to me,' Alison said. 'I end up being woken by the driver.'

He was so easy to talk to—about the complicated, about the mundane—but even though they chatted easily, there was a definite charge in the air, which had a sleepy Alison on the alert. He must have shaved yesterday morning, rather than before coming to work, because he was clearly unshaven now, she noticed. Just as she noticed when he pulled on dark glasses against the glare of the morning sun. Just as she noticed his long tanned fingers tapping on the steering-wheel as they sat in heavy traffic.

'Do you sleep well?' Nick asked, because he had heard about the whole nursing crew's habits and he wanted to find out about hers.

'Depends,' Alison said. 'Mum's at work so the house is quiet…' And her voice trailed off, because somehow that charge in the air intensified, and there was this pause, this silent pondering, a false night that stretched ahead and a shining window of opportunity.

'Do you want to go somewhere for breakfast?' Nick asked as the bay came into view.

'No, thanks,' Alison said, because she wasn't thinking about breakfast.

Just bed.

Bed.

And though they were both tired and sleepy and longing for bed, as he pulled up outside her door, there was no denying it—they were longing for each other too—and as naturally as breathing she turned to him. There was no awkwardness, no will he, won't he, just the bliss of a night spent looking and thinking and pretending you didn't want to, all melting away now that no one else was around. It was a really nice kiss, a slow, morning kiss that could tip easily to more, but there was no way she was asking him in because Alison knew where his kiss could lead and probably there was no chance of her mum coming home, but she just couldn't put herself or her mother in that situation.

'Have a good sleep.' She pulled her mouth away, but she wanted to dive back in.

'I doubt it,' Nick said, and Alison doubted she would either.

She was a kiss away from his bed, Nick knew that, and for the first time in his quest for freedom Nick felt as if he needed to spell out the rules, needed to be very sure that she knew, and so he said it.

He made himself say it.

'I can't stay…'

And she smiled and was very brave, even managed a little joke. 'I didn't ask you in.'

But he wasn't talking about that—she knew he wasn't talking about that as she climbed out of his car.

He watched her walk up the garden path and for the first time in a long time, at least where women were concerned, Nick was confused—Nick the one almost willing her not to turn round—because of how much he wanted her, and for the foreseeable future, this wasn't how it was supposed to be.

Except this was how it was.

She was exhausted, utterly and completely exhausted, but though her body ached for bed as she walked up her garden path, she ached for him too. It was just criminal that a few streets apart he'd be in bed and she'd be in bed and they had a whole day, a whole wonderful day, if only she would take it. She had her key in the front door, and she opened it, turned round to give him a wave, and he just sat there, looking at her, and she stood there, looking at him, and wished he'd drive off, would just go, except he didn't.

Then she panicked that he would drive off, that he'd pull off the handbrake and she'd miss her chance.

Her one lovely chance to be wild and brave and sexy and impulsive.

Alison slammed the door closed again and turned round. She could see his smile even from the garden, see the want in his eyes as she made the one reckless decision of her life and sped down the garden path. He had the passenger door open before Alison got there. She jumped in like an eager puppy, and he was an equally eager master because he was pulling her in and kissing her, this smothering kiss that sighed and groaned with mutual consent of what was to come. There was just a flicker of sanity, of what would the neighbours think because it was eight a.m. and they were necking like teenagers. Then he pulled back and gave her the most fantastic smile and Alison, who had craved wild, craved passion and adventure, took a breath, took the plunge, and what she said was from her wildest dreams, because she said what Alison Carter would never have—looked into eyes that looked into hers, and in the mirror of them she saw herself, found herself, was finally herself. 'I want breakfast in bed.'

CHAPTER NINE

HE KISSED her even as the front door closed and for a moment, just a moment, she did wonder what the hell she was doing and tried not to worry that she'd been working all night and must smell of hospitals, consoling herself, that so too must he, but then his kiss did its magic, produced an Alison that only he could.

'You taste fantastic.' She said her thoughts out loud, because with him she could, and his hands roamed her body, as they had been longing to all night, and she leant against the hall wall and he kissed her some more.

It was a relief to get to the bedroom.

Yes, it had the most stunning view from the bedroom, except they didn't want to see it. It was an exercise in frustration as they tried to quickly close the blinds and for the first time she heard him swear as it stuck halfway down, but then, yippee, they were closed and he was kissing her again.

'God, Alison…' He made light work of the buttons on her blouse because he'd been undoing them in his head all night. He stripped her—it was such a brilliant word, Alison thought. He stripped her blouse, her navy three-quarter-length Capri pants, he stripped her mind of doubt because his hands and mouth adored her, he stripped her of care and worry till all that was left was her bra and panties and a mind that was free. Now it was her turn and she would, Alison decided as she took off the grey shirt he had been wearing that first day, remember this for ever and ever, because she'd been guessing and peeking and driving herself insane with imagination. Now the big day was here and, unlike Nick, she didn't tear open the wrappers on her parcels. No, she had a nice feel of his chest through the material, tried one more image of what might be inside and slowly, very slowly, tongue on her bottom lip, she peeled one button open, and then another, and he was telling her to hurry but she refused to be rushed.

One more button and she could see a flat brown nipple. She ran her hand over it then bent her head and kissed it, and she could feel his hands undoing her bra, feel the drop of aching breasts as he freed her. Yet still she would not be rushed. She had his shirt open a little more now, down to that lovely flat stomach, and all his online pictures combined couldn't capture how nice it was in real life, taut and smooth. She ran her hands over him and he was pulling off her bra and she slid down his shirt and then she went back for another taste of his nipple, heard him moan, felt his hands in her hair and then he moved them, because Nick wanted his pants down.

'Don't spoil my fun.' She pushed his hands away and she was cruel and she wasn't kind. She fiddled with the button and refused to let him help her. He was breathing so hard, his hands toying with her bottom, laid-back Nick, just brimming now with urgency, but she was in no rush.

Well, maybe a little bit, because beneath linen pants that he almost fell over to step out of were the sexiest hipsters and she felt him again, gave her present a little squeeze to gauge it and she couldn't tease any more, because she wanted to see, she wanted to feel, wanted what was hers. And he was completely spectacular, and hers for now and she held it, over and over she held it, till her breathing was doing strange things now, because he had his hands on the cheeks of her bottom and was pressing her into him, and his mouth was on hers and then he wanted more, more of her than he should sensibly want, because when he should be diving in he was diving down, pushing her on the bed and running his mouth up her thighs, and it was Nick in no rush now.

He kissed and he teased and he relished her throb in his mouth, but there was this strange moment, a warning almost, because though it felt like sex and tasted of it too, it was teetering into something more. A place where he had to *remember* to stop, to put on a condom, not just slide up and slide in as he so badly wanted to. A different place, because as he drove deep within her, why was he saying her name over and over?

And this was what he did, Alison reminded herself

as she tried to hold back, tried and failed to cling onto that last bit of restraint.

This was what that smile promised, Alison told herself, except her body didn't want to register dire warnings, it wanted to be free, and trapped beneath him, finally she was.

'It's the quiet ones you have to worry about.' She lay next to Nick and smiled at his voice as she came back to earth and when half an hour later, still neither were sleeping, she said yes when he offered to make a drink and lay there, just a little awkward as to what he was thinking as she heard him walk out to the kitchen.

What *was* he thinking?

Nick wasn't sure as he filled a glass with water and emptied it in one and then, rather than think, he flicked on the television as he waited for the kettle to boil. But there was no solace there, an armchair psychologist was telling him to face up to feelings, to be honest with himself—only Nick didn't want to.

'How many sugars?' he called down the hall, because *that* was how it should be, except he remembered before she even answered.

'Have you got any sweeteners?'

He didn't, so she settled for sugar then grumbled that it tasted different as he climbed in bed beside her, then admitted, as Nick lay there, that she actually preferred the real thing.

'It's bad for you, though,' Nick said, and he'd forgotten

to turn the television off, so he padded back out and aimed the remote like a loaded gun, because honesty was not the best policy here.

It wasn't just Alison he was worried about hurting here.

It was himself.

CHAPTER TEN

SHE could tell it was Tuesday the second she stepped inside. The slow cooker was on and the scent of beef stroganoff filled the house. Her heart was in her mouth as she waited for her mum to appear and say she'd been off sick and where the hell had she been all day, but the house was still and silent. Alison checked her mobile and the house phone and there were no messages, and *starving* Alison had some stroganoff between two slices of bread and butter then showered and headed straight to bed, to cram in a couple more hours' sleep, which she managed amazingly well. She was woken at six-thirty by her mum's knock on the door.

'Did you sleep well?'

'Really well,' Alison said, hiding her guilty blush.

'Good. I tried not to wake you when I came in. Dinner's almost ready.'

'How was work?' Alison asked as they sat and ate dinner. It was a nice dinner and a nice conversation and they even had a laugh. Alison would miss this and did love her so, it was just the little things that added up, like Nick wanting the crossword and Paul's garlic bread, that built and built until they became big things and change really was needed, because a row with her mother, hurting her mother, Alison would avoid at all costs.

Little things like Rose insisting she take leftovers for her meal break.

'I can put some in a container and you can have it on your break,' Rose offered.

'Put it in the freezer,' Alison said. 'I think I'll get something from the canteen.'

'From the vending machine?' Rose said.

'They do sandwiches and things and there are nice vol-au-vents.'

'Why would you pay for something when you can take it in?' Rose said, pulling out a container and filling it with Tuesday's beef stroganoff.

'I just fancy—'

'You need to be more careful—you've got a mortgage to think of now.'

She took the stroganoff.

Still, it *was* appreciated.

By Nick, who was sick of canteen sandwiches and mushroom vol-au-vents.

To describe a busy week of night shifts as the best week of her life would have once been laughable, but for the first time since the tragedy Alison actually glimpsed normality in upside-down week.

A gorgeous normality where work was busy, a happy

normality where she ate dinner with her mum each night and packed leftover dinner for her evening break.

An easy normality, where she didn't have to lie, well, not outright, and she didn't have to race home at midnight. All she had to do was be.

Nick would drive her home. More often than not she'd see her mum at the bus stop or pop in just to check that she had gone, and, just to be sure, Alison would leave a little note on the kitchen bench that read something like, *Gone shopping*, or *At dentist*, which she'd tear up when she got home at four. Then she'd grab some clothes and race down the street to Nick's car, to him, to a gorgeous normality, where they shut the blinds on the world and lay in bed and talked and laughed, and made lovely love, or rather, she corrected herself, had torrid, wild sex and slept.

She knew from the start, though, that it couldn't last.

'Can I borrow you before you go, Nick?' Amy clipped in for her day shift at the end of the week, all scented, suited and gorgeous, as an exhausted Alison subtly hung back for her lift.

'I shouldn't be long,' Nick managed as he disappeared into his colleague's office, but no matter how many times Alison checked the staff roster, and no matter how chatty her colleagues were, by eight-fifteen she was starting to look as if she had no home to go to.

'Where is Amy?' Sheila barked from a cubicle, then marched out to the intercom. 'It's all very well swapping her shifts, but the occasional appearance on the shop floor would be nice.' Her voice was a lot sweeter when she pressed the button. 'Amy, we need you out here.'

'Is it urgent?' came Nick's voice, and Sheila rolled her eyes.

'Pressing, not urgent.'

'Let us know if that changes,' came Nick's firm reply.

'Good luck!' Alison smiled to Sheila as she heaved up her bag and headed for the bus stop, but despite a rapid run she missed it and despite the sun she shivered at the stop, tired and, as Nick's car pulled up a full twenty minutes later, just a little fed up.

'Sorry about that.'

It would have been childish not to get in.

'I was thinking…' Nick negotiated the early-morning traffic easily, even laughed when she grumbled about rush-hour, telling her she should try driving where he lived in England if she wanted a *real* rush-hour, and then he got back to thinking. 'How about we do the Sydney Harbour Bridge climb this weekend?'

'I can't even think about bridges and climbing at this hour.'

'It will be fun.'

Alison could think of other words to describe it and her eyes flicked to the clock on the dashboard—had she left on time and taken the bus, she'd already be in bed. 'What did Amy want?' It was a childish question to ask perhaps, or perhaps it was the edge to her voice, because Nick glanced over.

'There was something she needed to discuss.'

Which gave her no answer and the silence wasn't comfortable as he stopped at the traffic lights and again he looked over at her.

'Don't ask me to betray a confidence, Alison, just because we're…' His eyes shuttered for a moment, perhaps ruing his near choice of words. 'Work's separate,' Nick said. 'We both agreed.'

It wasn't a row, it wasn't anything she could pin down, yet stupidly she felt like crying, relieved almost when Nick stopped at a corner shop and got out. 'I need milk.'

And it was a tiny time out, a welcome time out, because by the time he came out of the shop, all gorgeous and yawning, Alison had convinced herself she was tired, that was all, not questioning and jealous, just ratty, premenstrual and coming off a full week of sex and nights.

'Here.' He handed her one of two newspapers he had bought, gave her a kiss and then smiled. 'There's always a simple solution.'

There just wasn't to this.

And even if they were talking, even if there hadn't been a row, things felt different this morning.

Nick had a call from his boss in the UK then another from his mum, both reminding Alison there was a world that was waiting for him to rejoin it, and she was all too aware that next week she'd be back on days, which meant home by midnight, that the slice of freedom she'd carved for them was drawing to a close and it was either lie there and cry or just pretend to be asleep when a long hour later, damp from the shower, his tired body slipped into bed.

'Alison?' She heard his voice and didn't answer, lay with her eyes closed till she didn't have to pretend any more, didn't have to pretend that she could do this, but it was a fitful sleep, an uneasy sleep. She woke at two, and looked over at him and he really was exquisite.

Alison didn't generally prefer blonds—she just preferred Nick.

He must have felt her wake, because he stirred a bit beside her, rolled a little toward her and his legs trapped hers and pulled her in a bit so her face was closer to his chest. She'd been enjoying looking, but now she was enjoying feeling the sleepy body beside hers as she lay awake, exploring the sensation of his long limbs loosely wrapped around hers and the scent of him. There was more than just thought there, because it woke him, this energy, this want that hauled him from slumber, because he slid her up a little till their faces met.

'Morning.'

'Morning,' Alison answered, even if it was mid-afternoon and, better than a kiss, he answered what was still on her mind.

'Amy was offering me more work.'

'Overtime?'

'Extra time,' Nick said. 'She was just sounding me out, there's nothing definite...'

'Isn't Cort coming back?' Alison blinked, curious for other reasons. Cort had taken leave suddenly three months ago, and all the senior staff had been tight-lipped as to why—as Nick was being now.

'It's not that.' He closed his eyes. 'You can't say anything.'

'I wouldn't.' But Nick wouldn't reveal any more. Still, that he was considering staying was what she wanted to hear, but she knew his struggle, because hers was the same. 'What about Asia?'

'I can't do both.'

'Could you, though?' Alison asked. 'Could you take more time off?'

'They very reluctantly gave me this year.' It was too much to think about, too much to consider, so he pulled her closer instead and there were forty-seven minutes, give or take, till she had to up and leave, and they both smiled at that pleasurable thought.

Both awake, and even if their minds were racing with new possibilities, their bodies were still pliant and just a little lazy, because they moved in just a little closer, and his legs wrapped around hers a little tighter. The bed was so warm and it felt so nice, and Alison gladly kissed him back, which was so much better than thinking about Asia and careers and sky-high bridges, except the thoughts were in the bed with them too, because it wasn't fair, Alison thought, as his kiss deepened. It wasn't bloody fair, his mouth agreed as he pulled her in tighter. A little lazy, a little bit angry, a little bit reckless, or just greedy for a little bit more. When he pulled her even closer, Alison didn't move back, or away. She could feel his warm, heavy length between her legs, and she wanted him there, and he wanted to be there, because there he stayed a while.

She felt a low tremble in her body as he ran his tip over her moist place, she could feel his kiss deepen even more, feel the tightening of her throat and the flood of desire that bade him on, not consciously, more naturally, just a deepening kiss at both ends of their bodies, and he was just a little way in and her body willed him to go further, beat for him to join her. But sense hauled them back from that dangerous place, Nick rolling over and sheathing himself, Alison dizzy at what they had almost done but grateful for common sense prevailing. Then he was back and, yes, they were both angry, not with the other but at time that wouldn't pause. With every thrust she counted the days and her hips rose, defiant at the injustice.

She *was* angry.

And he let her be.

He let her be selfish and taste his mouth and his chest for as long as she wanted, he let her tension rise till she thought she might push him off, because she didn't know how to feel like this, she didn't know how far she could go. So he showed her, he pushed her, he waited for her, till she stopped counting the days and berating the past, stopped chasing the future till she was in an empty, silent space that was theirs alone to fill—with her scream and his release, with new sensations, deeper sensations than either had felt before.

And something shifted, something definitely shifted, because a little while later, when the alarm bleeped its warning, for the first time Nick grumbled, pulled her back when she said she had to go.

'Stay a bit longer,' Nick said.

And she did.

Alison reset the alarm and climbed back in, wondering if in a few weeks he'd do the same for her.

CHAPTER ELEVEN

LIKE Louise Haversham's toothache, sometimes the agony woke her, but for a while, if she didn't push or probe, Nick's nearing departure was kept at a niggle, a gnawing in the background. Two months had never seemed long enough. In fact, by the time she'd met him, a week of that had already passed, by the time she'd decided to just go for it, another week, and since then she'd seen Sydney thorough the eyes of a tourist, had been on whale-watching trips and a jet-board ride, though she'd declined his suggestion for a tandem sky dive! With the keys to the flat soon to be hers, they were in the final countdown and it wasn't just her feeling it, at every turn she was reminded of the fact. But the hint that Cort's return might be delayed was her ray of hope on the horizon and Alison was determined to let it shine.

'These are for you!' David said. 'For all of you.' But he smiled especially at Alison as he handed over a large tin of chocolates and he was a different man indeed from the one she had met just a month ago. 'Rebecca's here for her outpatient appointment. We just wanted to stop by and thank everyone.'

'You're more than welcome.' Alison jumped down from her stool and accepted the chocolates. It rarely happened, but when patients came back, it was a treat indeed.

'How's the arm?' Alison asked, and she was thrilled to see Rebecca wiggle all her fingers.

'I'm doing loads of physio, but I'm getting there.' She smiled as Nick and Amy came over and she showed them her moving fingers again.

'I'm glad you're here,' David said to Nick. 'We thought you might be back on your travels.'

'A couple more weeks yet,' Nick said, and Amy rolled her eyes.

'What will we do without you?'

And that niggle was flaring. It was a line Alison was starting to hear far too often when she was around Nick, and it shot an arrow into her heart each and every time she heard it.

'We really are grateful,' David said, and Alison looked at his suit and his smile and the new-found confidence in this family and knew what was coming. 'I got that job, by the way.'

'Fantastic.' She could not have been more pleased. 'That's marvellous.' She was delighted for them all.

'Hello, there!' Ellie joined them and chatted for a moment. 'Has it really been a month?'

And it had been and it was, because just a couple of days later Alison had a mortgage and a set of keys.

'I don't remember the carpet being *this* green.' She walked around with Nick and wondered if she'd bought the same place. 'Were the walls really brown?'

'It will look great with furniture.' Nick was optimistic and then realistic. 'And a coat of paint.' He saw her glance up at the grey ceiling and then blow her fringe skywards at the job ahead. 'I'll help you. We can go and look at paint this evening and get it done over the next few days.'

'You've got better things to do than paint a flat,' Alison pointed out.

'No.' He pulled her towards him. 'I like spending time with you—here.' He pulled out a present from the bag he had been carrying that had had Alison wondering, and she opened it and it was a plant in a bright red pot that he put on the tiny balcony table. 'That's the garden sorted.'

Then he pulled out champagne and, of course, he'd forgotten glasses, but as they had that night on the beach they sat on the floor and drank from the bottle. Though it was cool and fizzy, Alison just had a mouthful because, yes, the flat was hers and Nick was here and it was a great day, but somehow she was finding it hard to feel like celebrating, especially when Nick pointed out she should hold off getting her furniture delivered till the flat had been painted. It was practical, sensible of course, but she wanted to move in so badly.

'We'll get it done in a week,' Nick said. 'Then we've still got...' His voice trailed off, because then all they would have was a week.

And it just got ever closer—the future was fast approaching and it caught up at six p.m. on the Friday. Alison was trying to wrestle damp legs into her stockings as her mum chatted to Nick in the lounge.

There was a seafood restaurant at the Quay Nick wanted to try and even if it was supposed to be gorgeous and the views and food to die for, Alison was exhausted and, frankly, a box of noodles and a DVD would have sufficed.

She peered at her slightly pale reflection and added a dash more blusher. She could hear the laughter from the living room, because even Rose seemed to have loosened up and was getting on with Nick. Everyone did. It just made it harder, that was all.

'Ready!' She was wearing high heels and a black dress with a sheer black blouse over it, and her hair was behaving. Nick's eyes lit up in pleasure as she walked in and Alison's did the same.

He was in dark trousers and a dark shirt, which accentuated his blondness. She wished her flat was ready and he had picked her up from there!

'What time's the table booked for?' Rose asked.

'Seven,' Nick said, 'so we'd better get a move on.' He kissed Alison on the cheek and he was clearly thinking along the same lines as she was because as Rose turned her attention to the television, he whispered the real time in her ear. 'Eight,' he said, and that made her smile. They were just about to dash off for their supposed seven p.m. booking, but really his flat, when his phone rang. He glanced at it, about to ignore it, then frowned. 'I'd better get this.'

Alison sorted out her bag and checked for lipstick and things as Nick went out to the little garden, and she could hear the restrained delight in his voice, hear him laugh, hear him talk. 'It's a huge surprise!' she heard him say. 'Thanks so much for considering me.' She glanced over at her mum and forced a smile, then poured herself a glass of water as Nick spoke for a little while longer and then came in.

'Work,' Nick said, and Alison gave a tiny frown.

'In England.'

'Oh.'

Rose suddenly remembered she had the iron on in the laundry and Nick must have remembered that he oughtn't to smile quite so widely, because he contained his delight just a touch. 'They've asked me to cut short my trip. Not this bit,' he added hastily, 'just get back from Asia a month early.' As she listened she found out that one of his seniors was leaving and there was a fast track to consultant, and she did absolutely everything right. Alison smiled and kissed him and offered congratulations, but it was the strangest feeling, because she was wishing him well for a time that didn't involve her.

'I haven't said yes,' Nick pointed out.

'It's still something to celebrate—so it's my turn to get the champagne!' Alison said, and she kissed him. She really tried, she did everything right, but Nick couldn't help but compare it to the more genuinely happy response she'd had to David's news, and it didn't irk him.

He got it.

Somehow they didn't dash back to his place for some alone time. Instead, by unvoiced mutual consent, they headed straight to Darling Harbour, walked around for half an hour and then shared a meal that should have been sumptuous, but there was just this sadness in the air and it was Nick who broached it.

'It's not looking hopeful for Asia.'

Alison forced a tight smile. 'You've got offers all round. What's happening with Cort?'

'Cort?' Nick frowned.

'Amy said there might be a spot…'

'That's still up in the air.

'It's going to be harder than I thought.' He took her hand, but it stayed in a ball beneath his. 'Saying goodbye.'

'It's going to be exactly as hard as I thought,' Alison said, and her eyes flashed with tears for the very first time.

'It doesn't have to end just because—'

'Oh, please…' She was almost accusing. 'I'll accept your friendship on Facebook.' Then she shook her head, because she wouldn't.

Because she could not stand the thought of following him, reading about him, and not having him. That at some point she'd have to block him, because he was taking with him her heart.

'We can still keep things going…' But he didn't push it, he paid the bill and though there was conversation, both were hurting.

'Alison,' Nick said as he pulled up at her house, neither having even suggested they go to his place for a while. 'I never intended… I mean…'

'Why couldn't you have been boring?' Alison turned to him. 'Why couldn't I have found you in high heels and my underwear?' And she started to laugh, but it was squeezed out with tears and Nick pulled her into him and held her for a moment.

'I'll pick you up tomorrow, we'll talk, we'll try and work something out.' His mind raced for solutions, and there was but one he could think of and that required deeper thought. 'Tomorrow,' Nick said, 'I'll pick you up.'

'I don't want to paint.'

'We're not going to paint,' Nick said. 'We're going to work something out. You just be ready at ten.'

'For what?'

'Eight letters,' Nick smiled. 'Starts with S, ends with E.'

'I hate surprises.'

He cupped her face with his hand and looked over to

her, as if reading her for the very first time. 'You really do, don't you?'

And she pulled away, stepped out of the car and headed into her house—just a touch shaken by what he'd said, a touch unsure what he'd meant.

A touch worried that he'd stepped on a truth.

CHAPTER TWELVE

'HI, MUM.' She was tired and confused and all Alison wanted was bed, but Rose seemed determined to chat.

'How was it?'

'Lovely,' Alison said.

'You're early.'

'I'm just tired.'

'You didn't go for a walk afterwards?' Rose asked. 'Or back to his place for coffee?'

'I told you…' Alison frowned, unsure what Rose was getting at, but she found out a split second later when her mother's hand slapped her cheek, and furious words erupted from her.

'You tell me nothing!' Rose snarled, and then she tossed a handful of little packages at Alison, like confetti to a bride. 'Strawberry flavoured…' Rose sneered. 'Banana flavoured—you tart!'

'Mum, please…' Shamed, embarrassed, shocked, still she tried to calm things down, but Rose would not let her speak.

'How could you, Alison?'

'I'm twenty-four!' She spelt it out, repeated it, said it again, but Rose would not relent.

'How could you?'

She was seventeen again, only there wasn't her dad or Tim to deflect her mother. It was ridiculous and they both knew it—and for the first time Alison told her mother so.

'You turned a blind eye with Paul.'

'Paul was serious about you!' came Rose's savage reply.

'So's Nick. He's not using me.' Alison's voice was rising, but she wasn't just arguing with Rose, she was arguing with herself. 'It's not some fling…'

'It's exactly what it is,' Rose responded. 'What? Do you think he's going to give it all up? You heard him tonight. He's got a promotion. It couldn't possibly work. And you're *sleeping* with him.' It was all too close to the bone for Alison and she sat there and tried to take it, but Rose would not stop. 'You were always trouble, always the one we worried about, always wild, and yet it was poor…' She stopped, but not in time. The words might just as well have been said—Alison had lived, Tim had died. It stung and it burnt and tears shot from her eyes, not just at her mother's thoughts but what she had done to her brother's memory.

'Tim was fun, Tim knew how to laugh. You've canonised him, Mum, you've turned him into some sort of saint. No matter what I do, I can never live up to him.'

'Alison…' Rose maybe realised she had gone too far. 'This isn't about Tim, it's about this man.'

'This man,' Alison said, 'is called Nick, and he makes me laugh and he makes me happy. And…' she threw the condoms on the floor '…you have no right to go through my things. I can't wait to move out!' In fact, she didn't have to wait now. 'I'm going.'

'With him?'

And Rose broke down then, just melted onto the chair. And Alison wanted to storm out, to go to bed, to curl up in a ball, but instead she sat with her arms around her mum, her own tears not helping her stinging cheek. Yes, it was a row that had needed to be had, but Alison knew what it was really all about.

'I was talking about the flat. I'm not going to England, Mum.' She stroked her mum's shoulders. 'He's not going to ask, and if by some miracle he did, I wouldn't go.'

She wouldn't.

She couldn't.

She'd had it confirmed now.

It wasn't about Nick, it wasn't about England. It could be Thailand, or a bungee jump, or a car, or a wave, and the row would have been the same. Even if cruel words had been spoken, she knew she was loved—it just stifled her.

'I'm not going to England,' Alison repeated. 'I may be moving into a flat, but I'm not going to leave you—I never would, Mum. But—' she was firm, really firm with her mum for the first time '—I do have to live.'

CHAPTER THIRTEEN

It was horribly awkward the next morning.

'Yes, please' to tea, and 'No, thanks' to toast.

And 'You should eat something.'

'I'm honestly not hungry.' Alison wasn't—she felt sick when she thought of the condoms, and just all churned up from their row. She had no idea what was happening today either. She had a bikini on beneath her denim skirt and halter neck and something a little more dressy laid out on her bed, in case...well, just in case Nick's plans were upmarket.

'Mum,' Alison tried, 'about last night...'

'Let's forget about that,' Rose said. 'It's sorted now.'

Except it wasn't, Alison knew that. She looked at her mum's strained face, at the panic that was always in her eyes, and it was more than Alison could deal with, more than she could help with, and she broached what she had once or twice before.

'Have you thought about talking to someone?' Alison swallowed. 'That grief counsellor you saw...'

'Can they bring them back?' Rose shook her head. 'Anyway, I'm fine. I am sorry about last night, I had no right to go through your things.'

'Mum,' Alison attempted, but the conversation was closed.

'What are you up to today?'

'I've no idea,' Alison admitted. 'Nick's planning something.'

And to Rose's credit she gave a bright smile. 'That sounds exciting.' But her smile faded as there was a low rumble in the street and as Rose went to the window she glanced anxiously at her daughter.

'Nick's here,' Rose said. 'On a bike.'

And, worse, he had two helmets.

'Hi, Rose.' Nick grinned. 'I'm taking Alison to Palm Beach—where they film that soap…'

'Nick…' She could see her mother's bleached face and knew she had to do something. 'I haven't been on a bike.'

'I'm the one riding it,' Nick said. 'All you have to do is hold on. Come on, Alison, I've got everything planned.'

The sun was in his eyes, so maybe he couldn't see her expression. Part of her knew she was being ridiculous, he was hardly going to go roaring off. It *should* have been the perfect surprise; it almost was. She wanted to grab the helmet he was offering, to climb on, to be the young woman she once had been, to spend a precious day with the man she adored.

So she tried.

'See you, Mum.'

'Alison, be ca—' And Rose tried too because she smothered down her warning. 'Have a good day.'

'I'll call you,' Alison promised, before her mum asked, and there was fear and trepidation but a certain exhilaration too as she took the helmet and did as he asked and just held on.

She held onto his back and felt the machine thrum into life, her lips tightly closed, breathing through her nose, utterly rigid as they made their way through the city and over the vast bridge. She wanted so many times to tell him to stop, to let her off, and yet there was a thrill, a thrill that felt almost like pure joy as they left the city behind. The bay glistened ever more beautiful with every turn, every incline, and Alison found out what it meant to leave her worries behind.

'Amazing, isn't it?' He paused the bike and they sat for a moment just admiring, and Alison waited for him to take a photo, but he didn't, he just sat and gazed out and drank it all in.

'We used to come here for a drive on Sundays,' Alison said. 'When we were kids,' she explained. 'If we go back a couple of kilometres, there's a nice picnic spot.'

'I've got it all worked out,' Nick said, turning the engine back on, and instead of going back they went on, further than she had been, and it felt faster too, but a faster that didn't unsettle her. She had her cheek pressed into his back, could feel the heat from his body and the blue of the water before her eyes and the wind on her legs and her hair whipping her mouth, and she wanted the road to last for ever.

Nick really had worked it out. He took the bike off the beaten path and he really had found the perfect spot. It was cool and mossy and a thick curtain of trees allowed no glimpse of the ocean, but you could hear the rumble of it in the background as they spread out the blanket and opened up the food.

'I couldn't sleep last night,' Nick admitted, opening up some wine as she scooped out rice onto plastic plates and shared out prawns. 'How about you?'

'It wasn't a great night…' Alison admitted, but she was reluctant to tell him about her mum, to bog him down with the endless problems, but *then* he surprised her.

'I couldn't sleep without you.'

And she tried not to let her heart leap, because then it would have to fall.

'I don't want this to end, Alison.' His eyes never moved, but his fingers found the knot of her bikini, his long slim fingers at the back of her neck, and she wanted to arch into them, but she just knelt there, felt the slight drop of her breasts as he unravelled the knot.

'Bet you say that to all your gals…' She tried to make a joke of it, but it petered out at the end. 'Here.' She pushed towards him a plate.

'I'm not hungry.'

Neither, suddenly, was she.

'Did you like the bike ride?'

'No,' Alison said.

'Liar.' Nick smiled, and it had all gone as planned, because that was supposed to be his lead in, something about bikes, he reminded himself, except his fingers had freed another knot now, and his train of thought was diverted as he peeled down her halter like the skin of a grape and saw the lovely plump flesh within, and maybe he was a little hungry after all.

'I couldn't sleep last night,' he repeated, but this time with different intent. And to others it might be tame, but to Alison it felt wild—she could feel the cool breeze on her breasts and she liked it, liked it more with each hot kiss he trailed because the breeze cooled her again. There was the hum of flies around neglected food and he kissed her off the blanket and away from them. She liked too the pillow of moss on her bottom as he slid her skirt up and in this, with him, there was no inhibition, and sometimes she wanted to explain, to tell him that this wasn't her, except in his arms it felt as if it was.

She slid down his zipper, slipped her hands inside and freed him, and such was her want she gave a sob of frustration as his hand slid to his trouser pocket, gritting her teeth and willing him to hurry it on, but it tore, and he cursed in frustration and dug in his pocket again. And she hated them so, with him, she hated them so, especially when they were in his wallet on the blanket, and there was a moment, not even a moment, where she looked in his eyes and there was a *Will we?* Only they never found out—a screech of brakes filled the warm air and a thud that had them both leaping up.

They were pulling at their clothes and Nick leapt on the bike and Alison did the same. 'It was that way,' Alison said, pointing left, and they headed along the cliff. She felt the slight wobble of the bike as his attention was diverted and her heart was already pumping faster before she saw it for herself—the front of a car crumpled into a tree and a man talking into his phone and waving frantically. Nick slowed down, pulling to a halt, and they both jumped off.

'I missed the bend,' the guy was shouting as they took off their helmets. 'I was going too fast, trying to get to the hospital, she suddenly wanted to push…'

It was so far better than it could have been, except Alison's heart wouldn't slow down.

'What's your name?' Nick asked as they ran to the car.

'Richard.' His wife's name was Carly and there was already an ambulance on the way, Richard told them.

Nick was assessing the passenger for injuries and apart from being in advanced labour, there appeared to be none.

'I'm only thirty-five weeks.'

'That's okay…' He was incredibly calm, unlike Alison. 'Thirty-five weeks is just fine. Alison, there's a first-aid box on the bike.' There was, the hire company had made sure of that, but her hands were shaking so much she could hardly open the clip, and in the end it was Nick who came over and waded through it. There wasn't much, but there were gloves and Nick pulled them on and told her to do the same then he headed back to the car and gave instructions.

'Alison.' She was aware he'd repeated it. 'Can you help me get Carly into the back?'

She helped the pregnant woman, rolled up a beach towel she found into a pillow and made her a bit more comfortable so she was semi-prone and though Richard was clearly beyond relieved there was a doctor present there was actually very little they needed to do, because nature was taking good care of both patients. All that was required from Nick were a few words of encouragement as he held the baby's head and guided the new life into the world.

'The head's out.' His voice was calm and Alison looked over his shoulder. She was holding Richard's T-shirt ready to wrap the babe, and it was all under control, except her heart was still thudding, she could feel the sun beating on her head and hear the distant blare of sirens. But the baby wasn't waiting for them—with just one final push the body was delivered and there was a bellow of rage from a rather small baby as Nick delivered it onto Carly's stomach.

'She's okay?' Carly checked, and Nick grinned.

'He's great.'

'I'm having a girl,' Carly insisted, pulling up her baby boy, but it was a happy mistake and from Richard's shout of joy, he wasn't complaining.

The arrival of the ambulance brought comfort rather than relief. Todd and his partner were wonderful with the new parents and baby. Richard cut the cord and then the paramedics transferred Carly to a stretcher.

Nick was on a high. There was a euphoria to him, and he stood with his arm around Alison as the stretcher was loaded into the ambulance.

'How good was that?' Nick grinned, with all the joy of someone who finally, absolutely, definitely loved their job. 'How good was that?'

Only Alison didn't answer, uncomfortable suddenly as Todd climbed out from the back and closed the ambulance door and she wriggled out of Nick's arm, remembering they were keeping things away from work.

She could feel Todd's eyes roam her body, feel her breasts loose without a bra, and as, embarrassed, she ran a hand through her hair she felt leaves and knew, *knew* how she looked, knew what Todd was thinking.

'Nice work!' Todd winked at Nick when he'd closed the ambulance and Alison stood with her cheeks flaming. 'Good to get an easy one.'

'Thanks very much.' Nick shook his hand and all she could see as the ambulance drove away was the car against a tree and all she felt was reckless, and Alison loathed it. All she felt was a tart Nick had taken to the hills—so very easily, as Todd had pointed out.

'Thanks very much!' she hurled at him. 'Did you not hear what he was insinuating?'

'What?' Nick frowned.

'"Good to get an easy one"!'

'Alison.' Nick shook his head. 'He was talking about the birth.'

'No!' She felt sick, she actually felt sick. 'He was talking about me.'

And coming down from the high of the birth Nick started to see it, but Alison didn't want to hear his apology.

'I want to go home.'

'You're going to let what he said ruin—'

'It's already ruined,' Alison said. 'And even if we do patch it up, it will be ruined next week…'

'That's what I brought you here to talk about.' He hadn't meant to say it like this, hadn't meant to just blurt it out, but she left him with no choice. 'I'm going to ring work and tell them I'm not coming back early.' For Alison hope flared, but it was fleeting, so fleeting it was gone before it was recognised. 'I want to do Asia.'

She could have slapped him.

'With you,' Nick said quickly. 'I do have to go to this wedding in New Zealand but, look, I've been thinking about it…' All night he'd been thinking about it. He saw the flash of tears in her eyes, but he hadn't finished yet. 'Why don't you come—just for a few weeks, however much annual leave you've got…' He was finding this awkward, he knew she was proud. 'I know you must be stretched with the mortgage and everything, I'll sort out the tickets and things…' Alison screwed her eyes closed. 'We can have a couple of weeks away, just us.' And it sounded perfect, almost.

But then she'd have to come back.

'It's not that easy.'

'None of this is easy,' Nick said. 'Alison, surely you can have a holiday, a few weeks of fun.' And that word jolted, because that was what this was to him, she reminded herself, fun and a holiday that he wanted to extend—take the good sex with him, and slowly dismantle her heart. She wanted to nod, to say yes, to carry on the crazy ride, but she was scared to.

'I can't.' She shook her head in fury. 'I can't just up and leave.'

'Won't,' Nick said, and the pounding pulse in her head stopped for a second and he said it again. 'You won't come.'

'You don't know what you're talking about.' How dared he? Except Nick did.

'You didn't even consider it before you said no.'

'You don't know how hard things are for me. I had a massive row with my mother last night…' Stunned, she watched as he pulled out an imaginary violin. 'You bastard.'

'You've had me pegged as one from the start.' Yes, he was being mean, but finally he was angry. 'I'm asking you to come with me, or at least to just think about coming with me.'

'And I'm telling you I can't.'

'You can't, can you?' Finally he got it. 'It's not your mum holding you back, Alison.'

'Just leave it.'

'No.' He couldn't and he wouldn't. 'It's not just your mum.'

'Let's just finish it.' If she was being unreasonable, well, she felt unreasonable. 'Let's just finish it here.'

And she did.

When the police arrived and summoned a tow truck, and a couple pulled over in their car and asked if there was anything they could do—actually, there was something.

'Could you give me a lift, please?'

CHAPTER FOURTEEN

IT HAD to be better this way, Alison told herself as she ignored Nick's texts over the next few days and tried to get used to lugging around a broken heart.

The dazzling blond doctor was a just a little less so over the coming week.

Tired, a bit distracted and to the rest of the team just a little less fun, but he was thorough and kind to the patients and sometimes, quite a lot actually, she felt his eyes follow hers, and sometimes they frowned just a touch when their eyes met, because the Alison he had known simply wasn't there any more.

He was kicking himself, angry with himself about how he had handled it. But he was angry with her too—at how readily she could let them go, at how she just retreated back into her quiet, serious shell. Though she was polite and smiled and spoke when she had to, the Alison he knew was in there seemed to have gone.

'I'm getting nowhere.' Amy was unusually tense as she handed over her night to Nick. 'This poor man came in at three—he's an oncology patient with a brain tumour, but he's got acute abdomen. He had a scan last week in Outpatients that was apparently all clear, the surgeons don't want him to have anything till they've seen him, but they're doing an aneurism repair we had in—'

'So he's had nothing for pain?' Nick checked sharply.

'Five of morphine,' Amy said. 'I couldn't ask him to wait any longer, but it hasn't touched sides, and the second-on surgeons are in Theatre as well.' It was a regular scenario—the surgeons couldn't asses an acute abdomen if the patient was pain free, but the surgeons were stuck in Theatre. 'I can't get his notes, he was seen in Outpatients last week...'

Amy really was frazzled—and from the nursing handover it made sense. It had been an extremely busy night, but nothing usually fazed Amy. Still, Alison remembered she had swapped her nights with Nick for a family thing a few weeks ago and guessed that maybe it had something to do with things.

'If they're in Theatre it's not going to be this team that takes him.' Nick was completely reasonable. He looked up at the medical roster. 'I'll ring Howard's team—he's on take today and I'll get one of them to come down before they start rounds. I'll go and have a quick look at him now.

'Alison,' he added, because she was cleaning up the night staff's chaos, because she was the only one around, because he had to, 'can you come with me?'

'His daughter, Vivienne, is getting upset,' Amy added.

'I'll sort it,' Nick replied. 'Go home,' he ordered.

'Thanks,' Amy said. 'What will we do without you?'

Nick could have sworn he felt the roll of Alison's eyes, but chose to ignore it, heading for the cubicle instead. 'Hi, I'm Nick. I'm an emergency registrar...'

'So was the other one!' A woman, presumably Vivienne, snapped. 'Where are the surgeons?'

'I'm going to speak with today's team,' Nick said, 'but first I need to take a quick look for myself at your father.'

Jim was frail, thin and clearly in pain, and Nick didn't prod and poke him unnecessarily, but he agreed with Amy's finding that the problem was acute—because even if Jim's condition was terminal, an operation might be needed to relieve his pain.

'I need those old notes,' Nick said once they were outside the cubicle.

'The day receptionist is here,' Alison said, 'and Outpatients will be opening. I'll ask her to track them down.'

'Thanks.' He hesitated. 'Alison?'

'Yes?'

'Are you okay?'

'I'm fine,' Alison said.

'Can we talk?'

'About work?' she checked, and when he pushed his

tongue into his cheek, she shrugged. 'Then sorry, no,' Alison said, and headed for Reception.

'How's the flat?' Another line she was getting used to. Libby, the receptionist, asked the question as Alison popped in to check on the location of Jim's notes.

'Shabbier than I remember it,' Alison admitted. 'I'm painting before I move in and I don't remember a pea-green carpet when I bought it, but it must have been there.'

'Are you replacing it?' They stood making idle chit-chat as Libby tapped away on the computer and did her best to locate the notes Nick wanted.

'I was going to learn to live with it,' Alison said, 'but the more I paint, the greener it gets.'

'You'll get there,' Libby said, and then she shook her head. 'Those notes can't have come back from Outpatients.'

'They really need them,' Alison said. 'He's been seen by Gastro and the surgeons and they're all passing him on. He needs to be sorted. The family's getting really frustrated and frankly I don't blame them. Can you ring them again?'

'For all the good it will do.' Libby rolled her eyes. 'I'll go over now and have a look myself,' she offered. 'Could you just take these through for me?' She handed Alison a couple of rosters but as Alison walked through, the family caught her.

'Did you get his notes?'

'The receptionist is going to go over to Outpatients

now—' She didn't get to finish. Jim's daughter let out several hours of frustration in a few caustic sentences, and Alison stood there, shaking her head a touch as a security man started to walk over.

'I know how hard this must be—'

'You know nothing,' Vivienne retorted. 'That's my father suffering in there, not that you care. Did you enjoy your coffee break? He hasn't had a drink since he arrived, he's sobbing for some water—'

'Vivienne.' Nick came over, gave Alison a tight, grim smile. 'Let's take this to an interview room.' He'd cut right in and Alison was grateful for it, annoyed with herself for not suggesting the same thing but glad that someone else was dealing with it. Alison glanced down at them as she popped the medical rosters on the bench. They were nothing to do with her, just the doctors rosters for the next four weeks, and normally she wouldn't have given them thought. Except today, she scanned the sheet and saw the absence of Nick's name, saw that Cort Mason was, in fact, coming back, and it just rammed home the truth. There it was, in black and white, as if she needed reminding, that in just a few days Nick Roberts would be gone.

'She apologises.' Nick came over to make a phone call. 'She's going to say it herself—'

'There's no need.'

She was close to tears all of a sudden but was determined not to let him see. 'Libby's gone over to

Outpatients to try and find them—he was there last week.'

'He should have been admitted last week,' Nick said, and then, a little more tactfully, he told the voice on the end of the phone the same thing, and as Alison went to go he caught her wrist, which was the most physical he had ever been at work and the only contact in days. And she couldn't bear it, yet she took it, waited as he concluded his call, Nick doodling on the hateful rosters as he spoke on the phone.

'They're going to admit him.' He gave her the details and then there was just a slight frown as he looked her over and she didn't like his scrutiny.

'Are you really okay?'

'I'll get over you, Nick, don't worry.' She didn't turn round, because for the first time since his arrival, the first time in years in fact, there were tears, not just in her eyes but trickling down her cheeks, and Alison fled to the toilets, blew her nose and told herself she was being stupid, told herself she'd warned herself that this would happen.

'Alison?' Ellie was just dashing in before the start of her late shift, the surprise evident in her voice at catching her friend less than strong, because over the years she'd never seen her cry. 'Are you okay?'

'I'm tired,' she admitted, because suddenly she was. 'And there's this poor man, he's been shoved from pillar to post. He's been here since two this morning and we've only just found him a bed, his daughter just went off at me—'

'I know,' Ellie said, because anyone who worked in Emergency did know that families sometimes took out their frustration on the closest target, and even if Vivienne hadn't been that bad, some days it just hurt.

'All okay?' Sheila, the NUM, came in then and Alison even managed a wry smile that her *escape* to the loos had become so public and made a little note to herself not to go into meltdown till she was safely in a cubicle.

'A relative upset her,' Ellie explained.

'It's not just that,' Alison admitted. 'I don't feel so great.'

'You don't look so great,' Sheila said, and because it was Alison, who was always stoic, she knew it wasn't an excuse. 'Why don't you take a half-day? What are you on tomorrow?'

'An early.'

'Go home.' Sheila was firm and fair and knew how hard her staff worked. 'If you don't feel any better this evening, give us a call so we can arrange cover tomorrow.'

Alison felt more than a little guilty as she collected her bag, because even if she was tired and teary, there was another reason for it. The bus took for ever, it just crawled along and stopped at every stop. Maybe she was more than tired, she decided, trudging up the street to her house. Maybe she was getting the flu or something.

It was Tuesday, because the house smelt like beef stroganoff as she entered, though it smelt stronger today. Alison headed for her room, but the smell was in there too, permeating the whole house. She opened a window, swallowing a couple of times, and then fled to the loo, which was thankfully a lot quieter than the one at work.

'No.'

She actually said it out loud as she headed back to the bedroom, climbed into bed and very deliberately blocked that thought, and blocked it again when her mum came home and Alison had to fly back to the bathroom again.

'I think I've got gastro,' Alison said, and there were benefits to living at home, because she got some water, then tea and toast all brought to her, and her mum rang up Sheila to say that she wasn't well and wouldn't be in tomorrow.

You okay? I heard you were sick.

She read his text at ten p.m. and didn't reply.

Just turned on her side and tried to get to sleep.

She truly didn't know what to say.

CHAPTER FIFTEEN

'YOU look terrible.' Ellie breezed into her bedroom on her way to a late shift. 'Or are you just not wearing mascara?'

'Both.' Alison tried to smile.

'Alison…' Ellie was tentative for once. 'I can see that you and Nick…well, you both look pretty miserable.' As quiet as they'd kept it, of course Ellie knew. 'I'm assuming it's over?'

'It was always going to be.'

'I'm sorry,' Ellie said. 'I feel like I pushed you into it…'

'I pushed myself into it,' Alison admitted.

'You can talk to me.'

'I know,' Alison said. 'Just not yet.'

'It's his leaving do on Friday. I just thought I should warn you…'

'I'm on days off Thursday and Friday,' Alison said, 'and I'm off sick today. I won't be seeing him again.'

And that was hard to say, let alone admit, and she couldn't really talk about it with Ellie—they were just different personalities, Ellie so light and breezy, she herself so serious. She'd been a fool to think she could do a relationship any other way. Surprisingly it was Rose who bought comfort, bringing her in some lunch and sitting on the bed for a while.

'I went and saw Anna,' Rose said, 'that grief counsellor…' The bite of scrambled egg stilled in her mouth as Rose spoke on. 'I was shocked by what happened, that I could hit you…' She started to cry a bit and Alison held her hand. 'I already had Tim by the time I was your age—and despite what I told your father, what I've told myself enough over the years, he wasn't actually my first.'

Alison was shocked, especially when Rose continued.

'Or my second.'

'Enough information!' Alison smiled.

'I've been holding you back for my own selfish reasons and you've been a wonderful daughter, Alison… but you need your life too.' And she told her what Nick had. 'You're holding back too.'

'No.' Alison shook her head and Rose, as she often did, rammed home her point. 'What's happening with Nick?'

'He leaves on Sunday,' Alison said. 'We had a bit of a row.' She took a deep breath. 'He offered to fly me out to Asia—do some travelling with him, just for a few weeks. It's not that simple, though.'

'Can you afford it?' Rose asked, and Alison was so

proud of how she was trying—so relieved to have such a long-awaited *real* conversation with her mum.

'He offered to pay,' Alison said. 'It should be cheap—he's going right off the beaten track...'

'You'd need some immunisations...'

Alison shook her head. 'It's not the money, Mum. I don't want to feel like this again in a few weeks. I just want it over with, I just want him gone.' And she couldn't even cry because she wanted to be sick, which she was, dashing across the hall and just making it to the loo as Rose stood outside, fretting.

'Maybe just stick with toast.'

And Alison didn't answer, just leant over the loo and closed her eyes, because it wasn't scrambled egg making her sick, and it wasn't her mother or money stopping her from following her heart now, it wasn't even her.

She was in no position to be getting immunisations and going off the beaten track.

No position at all.

Of that, she was almost certain.

CHAPTER SIXTEEN

SHE'D bought several pregnancy tests from this chemist without giving it a thought. Ellie panicked on regular occasions, but now that the test was for herself, she felt as if she knew half the shop and was sure the girl serving was the daughter of one of her mum's friends, though hopefully she didn't recognise her.

They'd been careful, Alison told herself as she took her little parcel home.

But not quite careful enough, Alison realised as she stared at the little blue cross. And maybe it was coincidence, but as her mind drifted to Nick, his must have drifted to her, because she felt the buzz of her phone.

Can I see you before I go?

Still sick, Alison replied.

I can come over. Do you need anything?

She was tempted to text back *Pram, cot, nappies,* but instead she wrapped all the evidence back up in a paper bag, put that inside a carrier bag and then in another one and then put it in the outside bin before she texted him back the absolute truth.

I need space.

CHAPTER SEVENTEEN

'YOU missed a great night!' Moira was at her most bubbly, so too was everyone else as Alison dragged herself into work. 'Nick knows how to have a good time.'

It was all she heard all morning.

How great the party had been, how much everyone would miss him, and Alison couldn't face the staffroom on her lunch break, so instead she slipped outside to the little patch of grass behind Emergency, sat in the sun and tried not to think that this time tomorrow he would be on a plane.

There was no question that she must tell him.

The baby was his, he had a right to know, and their child had a right to know about its father too.

And, yes, Alison thought as she closed her eyes and the sun warmed her skin, it would be more sensible by far to have this difficult conversation face to face, but it would be so much easier another way.

She could plan what she said better, Alison told herself, tried to convince herself.

He needed to know that there would be no pressure on him.

It was her choice to keep the baby.

It would be better by email, Alison decided, then wavered. The truth was she couldn't stand to see his reaction as she crushed all his dreams.

'Am I disturbing you?' Amy sat on the bench beside her.

'Not at all,' Alison said.

'I just wanted a bit of peace.' Amy gave a tired smile. 'I've got so much going on at the moment and they're all…' Her voice trailed off for a moment. 'I'm going to miss Nick,' she said, and Alison looked, really looked, and saw a flash of tears in the registrar's eyes. Then Amy's phone bleeped and she looked down and smiled as she read the text.

'Speak of the devil.'

This time Alison made sure she was actually *in* the toilet cubicle when she had her little meltdown.

She was overreacting, she told herself, and yet…and yet… Amy had been acting differently lately and she and Nick did get on.

What? her angry brain demanded. When she had gone home to her mum's, had Amy come round?

Had Nick told Amy to keep things quiet too?

Oh, God!

Up came her coffee and half a slice of toast and down came the tears.

She needed her head straight, needed to *really* think this through before she told him.

Somehow she got through the rest of the day. Amy shut herself in her office, no doubt to cry over him, Alison thought savagely.

By the time she was on the bus-ride home she had visions of Amy and herself stuck together in the same maternity ward.

Hell, maybe Moira would be there too.

'Alison!' She nearly jumped out of skin as she stepped off the bus and Nick was waiting for her. 'I was hoping we could talk. I don't want to leave with things as they are,' Nick said, as she walked along silently beside him. 'I don't want it to end on this note…'

It wasn't going to!

They walked down the road and he suggested something to eat, which was the last thing she wanted. 'Can we just sit?'

So they sat on a bench and watched the world go by for a moment.

'Alison, I don't know what happened,' Nick admitted. 'I know you think the paramedic insinuated something—I didn't see it as that. Alison, if I had thought for a moment… Do you really think I'd let someone speak about you like that?'

'How will you speak of me?' Her eyes glittered with challenge. 'When you're showing your photos, how are you going to describe me?'

'Confusing,' Nick said, 'because sometimes I feel

closer to you than I ever have to anyone and other times…'

Nick was very easy to talk to, it was she that wasn't. She was concentrating so hard on not crying, on not challenging him, on just getting through, she hardly said a word.

'Will you please at least think about Asia?' Nick said to her silence.

'I can't go to Asia.'

'Alison, if it's the money…'

'It's not the money,' Alison gulped, 'it's…' And she bit down on her lips, because she needed to know how she felt before she shared it with him, needed just a moment's pause before everything in her life suddenly changed.

'Just go, Nick.'

'Just like that?' he challenged.

'Just like that,' she confirmed.

And because it had just been a few weeks, because there was no baggage, because he was just moving on, he took her at her word and stood, and so did Alison.

'Do you want to keep in touch?' Nick offered, because the poor man had no idea what was coming, no idea just how in touch they'd need to be.

And she didn't say a word, just nodded, and because she had to, it was Alison who walked away.

'You okay, darling?'

'Yes. Sorry I was late, I went to the flat.'

'You're not at work, Alison,' the new Rose said. 'You don't have to apologise for being late. How's the flat looking?'

'Orchid white.' Alison gave a wry smile. 'I've finished the lounge, I'm going back tomorrow to do a couple of other rooms, but it looks like an indoor tennis centre with that carpet.'

'It will be fine once it's got the furniture in,' Rose said, and then sat down. 'You know, I've been looking at some brochures…' She handed one to Alison and for just a second Alison wondered if she knew, because there were pictures of London and her mind jumped for a moment, then swung back as Rose faltered on. 'Your father and I always spoke about doing a trip to Europe, taking a couple of months…' And then Alison looked at the brochure, really looked, and, as she seemed to be doing rather a lot lately, tried to keep the tears from coming. 'It's for over-fifties, for widows, divorcees… It's not a meeting thing,' Rose said primly. 'They just sort out the accommodation, it's company…'

'It sounds wonderful,' Alison said.

'I want my life back too.' Rose was the one crying now. 'I want to do the things that I always said I would.'

'And you should.'

'There's a cancellation,' Rose said, and Alison realised then that her mother wasn't just thinking about it, she really was going to do it. 'But I'd have to go in three weeks. I've got enough annual leave stored up.'

'Go for it,' Alison said, and kissed her mum.

'You might need help with the flat and—'

'Mum!' Alison kept her voice light but firm. 'You have to go.'

And they spent an hour looking on the computer at all the places Rose would visit, all the things she would finally do, and Alison was pleased, more than pleased for her mother, but there was a hollow sadness there too. The conversation, the row that she had staved off for so long—now, she wished she could have had it sooner, because now everyone was moving on and *she* was the one who was…

Stuck.

She tried to reframe it, tried to rephrase it.

Pregnant, with a mortgage.

She tried and she tried and she tried once again, but no matter how she tried, as she walked into her new home the next day, there was only one other word she could think of—*trapped*.

Was it wrong to feel trapped?

Was *trapped* even the right word?

There was another word there, an emotion there that she didn't want to examine, so instead Alison slapped orchid-white paint on the walls and felt like the worst person in the world, because this wasn't how it was supposed to be, this wasn't how she was supposed to feel.

Except she did.

She stared at what was going to be her study, and even

that had been a concession, a trauma course instead of a journey, but now even that was looking impossible.

A nursery.

She'd laughed when the real estate agent had said it, he had been so completely off track, yet just a few weeks later that was exactly what it was about to become.

And she stood in the little room and tried hard to picture it.

Staggering in for two a.m. feeds.

She actually could, she could see herself all dishevelled and exhausted and stressed, just like Shelly, could see a pink, screaming baby and a lonely flat and a fridge stuck with postcards from Daddy.

Or worse, far worse for Alison, would be the sight of Nick in the doorway, unshaved and annoyed, and trying to snatch some sleep because he was on call, and just so removed from his own dream…

She slapped the paint onto the wall.

She'd rather, far rather, far, far rather, do it alone.

Which she did.

She got the main bedroom done, and the kitchen and all the lights were blazing until late in the night. And despite what she'd said, a part of her hoped for a knock at the door, for the space she'd insisted on to be suddenly filled, but Nick had clearly taken her at her word.

The smell of paint made her sick, so late in the evening she walked the short walk home, along the foreshore, and she couldn't help what she did next. Maybe she was a stalker, but she took a little diversion past where Nick was staying and the lights were off and, yes, he could be out, but there was something about an empty home, and Alison knew then he had gone. She took a deep breath and thought about the little bean-sized thing in her womb, the baby he had unwittingly left behind.

'Can you do me a favour?' Her voice was a bit shaky and she should perhaps have apologised to Ellie for ringing her so late, but she was frantic.

'Sure.'

'Can you tell me your Facebook password?'

'It says never to reveal your password to anyone.' Ellie laughed and then promptly revealed it. 'Don't you want him to know you're watching?'

'You know me too well.'

There was a pause, a tiny pause. 'You know that he's…' Her voice trailed off and Ellie sat in silence on the phone as Alison, with a few short clicks, found out Nick was in New Zealand.

'Are you okay, Alison?'

'I'm fine,' Alison said, then relented, admitting a little of her truth. 'It just hurts more than it should. I mean, I knew it wasn't for ever, I knew it could only be short term…' She couldn't believe he'd gone. Okay, she'd asked him to, but he really was, grinning from the top of a rock in his profile picture, like that cat that had got the cream, and here she was, feeling as if she was on the top of a rock, but without the safety harness.

She waited till her mum went to bed then sat with a

big mug of tea, and it felt different clicking on his profile without Ellie over her shoulder, peering into his life and scrolling through to find out more about the man she loved.

He was more social than her by far.

There were school friends, friends from med school and not just cyber friends. They were in his life, joking with him to get a job, asking when he'd be back, missing him at football and concerts and nights out, and that was aside from family.

And there was Moira.

Missing him already *and* she'd added a kiss.

And she hoped to catch up with him in Asia.

And there was Gillian, who still messaged him—pretty, funny and patient.

His status was single.

And that hurt.

So too was the fact he never mentioned her—that their ride to Palm Beach, their one massive row was just described as 'an interesting day'.

There was a life and a family and friends and a whole world waiting for him on the other side of the world, and on this side there was Alison and the little bean-sized thing growing inside that she was trying to get used to.

And maybe she really was a stalker, because she scrolled through Ellie's friends and then Nick's and there was no sign of Amy.

And then he updated.

Back from sampling local delights. Great to meet cousins—loving it here.

This probably wasn't the best place to announce a pregnancy, so she contained herself and clicked off and then she went up to bed and lay with her flat stomach and tried to be nice to it.

'We'll be okay,' Alison said, in a voice that didn't sound entirely convinced.

CHAPTER EIGHTEEN

ALISON *was* sensible.

The world should have been back where it had been two months ago, except a blond English doctor had upended her life and now she somehow had to put it back.

She chose not to tell her mum, because she didn't want Rose not to take her trip.

But she took folate and saw her GP and then later an obstetrician, who scanned her and told her she was ten weeks pregnant, and she was about to correct him, because Nick had only been gone for two weeks, then remembered that it was dated from the start of her cycle.

And she had to tell him; she'd tried to tell him.

There were about fifty attempts in the draft box of her email and she'd rung three times but hung up before it could connect.

Tonight.

Alison decided as she put on her lanyard and checked

all her pens. Tonight she would ring him, before he headed for Asia.

Or maybe, a little voice said as she smiled at Ellie, who was on her way home from night shift, she should wait till he's there.

'God, I hate nights,' Ellie said, and then she looked at her friend. 'You look awful.'

'I shifted my stuff yesterday and I'm trying to help Mum pack for her trip—sleep is a distant memory.'

'Here.' Ellie handed over her make-up bag. 'You'll scare the patients.'

She so could not be bothered with make-up, but Ellie was right—she did look terrible—so Alison retied her hair and put on some mascara and a bit of lip gloss, and when Ellie doused herself in perfume she squirted some at her friend.

'Still missing him?' Ellie asked, but Alison just gave a noncommittal shrug.

'The best way to get over a man is to get under another.' Ellie grinned. 'And you've no hope looking like that.'

'Thanks for the sage advice.'

'You *will* thank me.' Ellie beamed. 'Come on, you're late and I'm skiving off early.'

They walked out together, talking much about nothing, and then the world stopped because there at the nurses' station was Nick, smiling as she walked over. Her heart was in her mouth and her face must have paled but thank God for Ellie, who had ensured she was at least wearing mascara!

'Hi, there,' he said as she stood waiting for hand-over.

'Hi.' Alison could hardly get the word out, her throat was squeezed closed so tightly. 'How was New Zealand?'

'Great.'

And he just stood and she just looked and he just waited—and there were so many things that she wanted to say, to ask, and so much she wanted to avoid, so awkwardly she just stood.

'Nick!' Sheila was far more effusive. 'What on earth? It is so good to see you—we've had to battle through with the most miserable locum in the southern hemisphere.' She glanced over her shoulder just in case he was around, then shrugged. 'How long till you disappear?'

'Not sure,' Nick said. 'I've got a few things I need to sort out.'

He *did* change the energy of the place.

Moira squealed in delight when she came on at midday and though he was holed up an awful lot in Amy's office, Alison tried not to be jealous, or get ahead of herself and believe that it was *them* he had come to sort out. And yet, as she showed around a new group of student nurses, she was reminded of a certain matter that needed discussing.

'X-ray.' The familiar call came from Resus, and Alison moved the group back.

'Just be careful,' Alison warned. 'They do call out, but just be aware that there are a lot of portable X-rays taken here.'

'Is Resus lead lined?' a student asked, and Alison shook her head.

'You just need to keep your distance when they're shooting, and wear a gown.' She knew it was safe, had pored over all the information, knew that the safest place to stand was behind the radiographer, and that, really, the level of exposure was tiny, and yet, and yet… 'If you're pregnant, or think there's a chance you might be, it's best to let us know if you're not happy to be in there when they're taking films.' And then Alison realised just how futile those words were and offered the next best thing. 'Or just slip away…'

Which she tried to do when her shift ended, but Nick caught her as she slunk off.

'I want a word with you.' He was waiting outside the changing room. 'Several, in fact. If you want to, that is.' And she didn't know what she wanted so he spoke into the silence. 'I know a nice café that does ricotta cheese and cherry strudel—I'll be there at five.'

He was there before her again.

Only her teeth didn't feel like glass. Instead her mouth felt like it was filled with sand as she made her way over.

'I've already ordered,' Nick said as a waitress came over.

'I might not have come.'

'I'm always hungry.' They sat in silence as two lattés and two strudels were placed before them and Alison took a sip of her drink.

'What happened, Alison?'

And she had to tell him, except the words wouldn't come out.

So she toyed with her strudel, and went to take a bite, then remembered that soft cheese was on the list of forbidden foods her obstetrician had given her, and as she put the pastry down she saw him frown, almost saw the thought process in his eyes. And then two words were said, presumably by her, because it sounded like her voice and Nick's lips weren't moving.

And then she closed her eyes, because she didn't want to see all his dreams evaporating, didn't want to witness him realise that his twelve months of freedom had just delivered him every last thing he'd been trying to avoid.

'When did you find out?' His voice sounded normal.

'A few days ago.' Alison swallowed. 'When I was sick.'

'That was more than a few days ago, that was a few *weeks* ago, Alison.'

'I'm sorry.' Only Nick wasn't cross with her for not telling him.

'You shouldn't have been holding this in on your own.' He dragged a hand through his hair. 'I knew there was something wrong. I thought it was the promotion, me leaving...'

It was.

And it was a whole lot more too.

'You *could* have told me,' Nick said.

Not *should*, for which she was grateful. 'I was trying to sort out what I want.'

'And what do you want?'

'I don't know,' Alison admitted. 'I won't have an abortion so I guess it's not really about that...' She wasn't making much sense, but she didn't care. 'If you're feeling trapped, believe me, you're not alone.'

'I never said I was feeling trapped.'

'Oh, please.' She was angry, not at him but at the world. 'Well, I do. I haven't even left home and guess what—now I probably won't be able to. I'll end up renting the flat out. Mum can babysit while I work.' She could feel the walls closing in, she absolutely could see the walls closing in as she envisaged the future.

'You don't think I'd support you.'

That just made her crosser.

'Oh, yes, that's right, you're so Mr PC that you'll send a lovely cheque for his schooling and we'll fly over to you once year or you'll come here and we'll be all civil—'

'Alison,' he interrupted, 'did it never enter your head that I'd stay, that we could do this together?' And that just made her crosser still because, yes, of course it had entered her head, and now he was suggesting it, it just made it harder because she didn't want it to be that way, didn't want to force his hand, didn't want the man who had come here for fun and to find himself, a man who so clearly didn't want to settle down, to be forced to.

'You'll resent me,' she said, shuddered it out, the most horrible of all her horrible thoughts. 'You might never say it, you might never show it, but I'll know. I'll always know that if it wasn't for the baby…'

'Alison—'

She didn't let him finish. 'Please, do us both a favour, go on your adventure, have your trip, have your fun, and if you have an epiphany somewhere in Nepal—'

'Nepal?' For the first time he bordered on sounding cross. 'Are we talking about your dream holiday or mine? Alison, I'm not going to just get on a plane—'

'Please do!' She struggled not to shout. 'And if fatherhood and babies and maternity bras and nappies suddenly appeal, I'll still be here, getting bigger and fatter, and we can sort something out. Or you can head back to London and we can sort something out from there, but right now I want space, I want time, I want to work out my future, so please go and live yours.'

'You really want space.'

'Yes.' Could she make it any clearer? 'I want to get my head around this myself, and I can't do that with you.'

CHAPTER NINETEEN

HE GAVE her space and she loathed him for it.

He spoke politely at work, and he didn't text, or ring, or email.

There was one room left to do in the flat and she couldn't face it.

Could not go in and again picture a cot, so she opened up her laptop on the disgusting green carpet and logged in as Ellie again and tortured herself with his latest postings.

He was back to earn more money, apparently.

And one of the many that jarred was a response to a question from Gillian.

Bangkok here I come!

'It's me and you,' she said to the slight curve on her stomach—and she slapped paint on her baby's wall and refused to wait for Nick's epiphany to come. She would keep on keeping on.

But when she had her first ever ring on her own doorbell, she didn't feel so sure.

He was blond and unshaven and looking just a bit fed up with his lot.

'Just how much space do you need, Alison?' he asked. 'Because this is driving me crazy. You can't just ignore it.'

'I'm not ignoring it.'

'No one knows—I saw you lifting a patient, all the X-rays in Resus…'

'I go out,' Alison said. 'I wear a lead gown.'

'Does your mum know?'

'Not yet. I'm not keeping it from her,' Alison said. 'Well, I am, but she's going on holiday, I don't want to ruin it.' And she burst into tears. 'Like I ruined yours.'

'You haven't ruined anything,' Nick said, and she couldn't even begin to believe him. 'I'm crazy about you. I have been since that bus ride.'

'Oh, please…' And out it came then, all the pent-up insecurity, all the doubts, all the things she'd stored up and tried to pretend didn't matter.

'You're single online,' she flung it at him. 'Off out, having *fun*—' she tossed that word up at him '—delivering babies up mountains, climbing bridges, and not a single mention of me…'

'Alison…' He was trying not to smile, and it incensed her. 'You're single, I can see that in the small part of the profile you allow to be visible, and you won't even be my friend…' He nudged her, tried to pull her from her tears as if they were in the school playground.

'No!' She was furious, close, dangerously close, to painting a gloss ochre strip on his suit with the paint-brush she pointed at him. 'I don't go on there.' Well, she did, all the time lately, but she wasn't actively on there was what she would say if challenged, but she was on a roll now. 'You say you're crazy about me, that you can't stop thinking about me, but you're on there every night, and I seem to slip your mind every time.' And then she burst into hears as she recited his latest posting. 'Bangkok here I come!'

He laughed.

He had the audacity to laugh, but not at her, Alison realised, because in the middle of hell she actually laughed too, a laugh that was laced with tears but a laugh anyway. 'You're such a bastard.'

'But I'm not.' He shook his head. He rued his words and the pain he had caused her, but he knew at least that he could put that bit right. 'I'm not a bastard, Alison, I'm not even a good backpacker, I'm the worst back-packer. That person you're reading about…' And she watched him struggle to explain it. 'Do you know how hard it was to justify taking a year off? Do you know how hard it was to end a very good relationship, for no good reason?'

And she did, she did.

'It seemed incredibly important to…' He raked his hand through his hair. 'To cram everything in, to have a ball, to validate…' Then he was completely serious. 'And I've loved doing all those things, but the bit I've loved most is the photos, is the afterwards, is sitting on the balcony with you. I can't tell her I'm no longer single on a computer, that's a face to face, or a difficult phone call at the very least, and I wouldn't do that to Gillian. I honestly didn't know you were looking, or I'd have explained…' She shook her head, sick of his smooth talk, not wanting to be a woman who just believed because it was safer. It annoyed him, she could tell, so much so that he opened his laptop and she ignored him, carried on painting the wall as he logged on.

Not sure about Bangkok. Alison is pregnant, but she hasn't told her mum yet and we're not sure what to do. That bloody ride to Palm Beach was awful. I had meant to tell her I was serious and we spend some time overseas to get to know each other more. She got all stroppy and hitchhiked a lift home, she was completely mental…

'Do you want me to post it?'

She just stood there and read over his shoulder.

'Do you see that the person you've read about isn't all of me?'

She could.

'That there are other sides?' She nodded. 'I rang Gillian.' Alison felt her world still. 'I told her about you, because even though we're over, even though it ended more than six months ago—' and she got what he was saying '—she didn't need to read about it first.'

'I know.'

'And there's something else you should know,' Nick

said, 'which you might not like and you might not understand. But I told her about the baby too. I know there are other people we need to tell…'

And she didn't like it, because it confirmed her darkest fears.

'It gives you the reason to stay.'

'I've already got a reason,' Nick said. 'I already had a reason.' He pulled her close. 'You.' Then he ran a hand over her stomach. 'This one just speeds up the decision-making process.'

'It's not what you wanted.'

'Not with Gillian,' Nick said. 'Alison, I don't believe in accidents.'

'So I meant it to happen.'

'I don't mean that.'

'You work in Accident and Emergency, you're going to be consultant when you get back…' Her voice was rising. 'And you're standing here telling me that you don't believe in accidents.' She was incensed now. 'What? Do you think my father and brother secretly wanted to die, that they deliberately—?'

'I mean *this* sort of accident…' He closed his eyes. 'I'm not saying this very well.'

'No, Nick, you're not.' She couldn't believe what she was hearing. 'You really think I set out to—'

'No.' He interrupted. 'No.' He said it again.

'Then what?'

'We knew,' Nick said. 'We, more than anyone, knew. And, yes, we were careful, but not *that* careful.'

And she opened her mouth to argue, but nothing came out, because she'd been over and over and over their oh, so careful love-making, except sometimes it hadn't been. Sometimes passion had overruled common sense and she was very cross with herself for that. With Paul she'd been contracepted to the neck, if there was such a word. With Paul she could have raged at the sky, at the gods, at the injustice, because she had been so very, very careful, but with Nick… She screwed her eyes closed, because the only person she was raging at was herself.

'I knew the risks too.' He caught her racing brain and sent it on a different track. 'Oh, I wasn't actively thinking…' The words weren't coming easily for Nick, but he was at least trying, this conversation incredibly honest, dangerously honest perhaps. 'I'm responsible, Alison, I've *never* not been careful except with you.' And it was raw and honest and the truth. 'And, yes, I should have taken more care, you can throw that at me too if you want to, but I guess for the first time passion won. There was someone, you, that I was willing not to be so practical and sensible with…' And he looked at her then and stated a fact. 'That's how babies are made, have been since the beginning of time. The chance was worth it at the time.'

'Is it worth it now?'

'Of course it is.' He sounded very sure.

'You want to travel.'

'The world will still be there, waiting.' And then

he grinned. 'To tell you the truth, I'm sick of throwing myself off cliffs. You've saved me another bungee-jump, yet another sodding extreme sport to show I'm having a good time.'

'What will your parents say?' Alison asked.

'Trapped by a colonial!' He rolled his eyes. 'They'll come round. I know you can't leave her, Alison, and I completely see why.'

'What about your job?'

'I've got a job! I've been offered a year's work when Amy goes on maternity leave next week.' And he gave a little grimace. 'Keep that quiet—I mean it. She's adopting a baby from overseas and she's beside herself—doesn't want to tell anyone till he's actually here.'

And someone *was* looking after her, because Nick would never need to know how little she had trusted him, how this gorgeous blonde sexy doctor somehow really was just that.

'What about your mum?'

'She'll be completely and utterly delighted.' And there was a wobble in her voice, a strange fizz of excitement that had, till now, when she thought of the baby been absent, a vision, a glimpse of a future, only now she could see Nick and herself and a beach and a baby…

And then she admitted something, something she hadn't dared admit, not even to herself.

'I'm scared.'

'I know.'

'No, you don't,' Alison said. 'It's not trapped that I feel, it's…'

'Scared,' he offered, and she nodded, sure he didn't really get it, except it would seem he did. 'Scared you might love it too much?' he said, and she nodded. 'Scared you might lose it?'

And he shouldn't say that, Alison thought frantically, because if he said it, then maybe it would happen.

'I think being a parent means you're scared for the rest of your life.'

'I can't stand what my mum went through.'

'Then you've got a choice,' Nick said. 'You can hold back, never fully live, never fully love, just in case…' Which was what she had been doing. 'But that doesn't work, because sooner or later living wins. Look at your mum,' Nick went on. 'Look at you.' He put his hand on her stomach, the result of taking a chance, and he was right because, cautious or not, life threw in surprises whether you liked them or not.

'I got you a present.'

And out of his laptop bag he produced not a ring but a rather tatty airplane magazine folded on one page. And it was nicer than a ring, nicer than anything actually, because it was a flight map showing all the destinations that airline went to, and Nick pointed a couple of them out.

'There's Sydney,' he said, 'and there's London, and there's an awful lot of world in between. You choose the stopovers.'

'Sorry?'

'Well, even if they are a pain, even if they are miserable and controlling, I guess I do love my family, and I'm going to be going home once a year, hopefully with you, or we can drop you off somewhere and pick you up on the way back. Me and the baby, I mean. It might take a while to complete your gap year...' he grinned '...but you can do it in stages.'

And it was the nicest picture. It would be the first on her wall, one she would take to the shop tomorrow and have properly framed, because it wasn't the red dots, or the destinations, but the generosity that came with it—the acceptance, the space, the future they would create.

And she could do this, Alison realised.

She could love and she could live, and, yes, it might be scarier than safe, but it was nicer than safe, better than safe, and anyway Nick made her feel safe.

'Choose the honeymoon.'

'You don't have to marry me.'

'Actually, I do,' Nick said. 'Makes me feel more secure.' And then he grinned, and grinned even wider as a delicious thought struck. 'Oh, God,' said Nick, 'you know what this means...' He was grinning and sounding delighted. 'No condoms. Monogamy, here I come.'

They had to undress in the dark because there were no curtains and would have to be up at the crack of dawn if they didn't want to be on public display.

'I don't like the look of this,' he warned as he pushed at the inflatable bed. 'I think it needs more air.'

'It's been filling for ages,' Alison said. 'You go first.' Because she'd rather topple onto him than have him topple onto her.

'It's comfortable.' Nick sounded surprised and he took her hand as she climbed in beside him and lay a moment adjusting to floating on air—her first night in her flat and Nick was beside her, and she lay there for a moment, trying to fathom how in so little time her life had changed, was changing, and would keep on doing so.

He rolled towards her and she lay in silence, could feel him watching.

'Are you happy, Alison?'

'I think…' She thought and paused as she examined her heart. 'That I'm going to have to get used to being happy.'

'Hey!' Nick said. 'We could move in with your mum, save a bit of money—rent this place out…' She kicked him, which wasn't a great idea in that bed because he almost fell out, and he held on like he was climbing up onto a life raft.

'It's a bit awkward,' Nick said, and he was right. It was awkward, less then two months in and suddenly here they were, except, she realised, Nick was talking about the bed, because he toppled onto her with a touch more gusto than intended, his lips meeting hers. They were warm and firm as she had so often remembered and his tongue was smooth and warm and tasted of Nick. And he was here, and that was going to take some getting used to, that this gorgeous, stunning man was here, not for baby, not for duty, but for her.

'I'm scared,' Nick said, and she was about to admit again that she was too—scared of telling everyone, scared of the future, scared that what they had found was too good to last—except as he came up for air, again Alison realised that he was talking about the bed. 'That we're going to topple over.'

There was the difference. Nick was in the now, living in the present, and for Alison grief and tragedy meant she lived with every scenario, every vision, knew how easily it all could change. And she wanted his faith and his presence in each moment, and she stepped into it as he moved deep within her, she let her mind still, concentrated on nothing more than the pleasure he gave her, focused on the now and all that they were.

And it was a precarious position, a shift to the left or the right and the passion that was building would crumble, but he locked his arms under her, cocooned her middle, trapped her where she wanted to be.

'I've got you.'

And she knew that he wasn't talking about the bed, that she was safe, and that they didn't need cartwheels. Just a dodgy bed and the other's body was enough for them.

EPILOGUE

'WHAT are you doing?'

Nick woke up and found her standing in the dark kitchen on tiptoe. 'Looking at our ocean view.' It was the only room in the house you could see it from. Right there between a couple of buildings there was their glimpse of the ocean, and even if it was tiny and she had to stand on tiptoe to see it, every day Alison did so, and tonight she had to see it too.

Her mum had been absolutely delighted, of course. She'd be delighted to babysit so that Alison could work, but only a couple of evenings if Alison was on a late shift, because Rose was busy getting her own life back.

And, of course, Nick's parents hadn't taken it so well—this Australian hussy who had dragged their son screaming from his lovely structured life—but she and Nick had spent a couple of months in the UK and his parents had been over for a visit and were coming in three weeks when their grandchild was due.

'Come back to bed,' Nick said, because he'd worked

the previous night and had been up all day, trying to turn what was surely a cupboard into a nursery. But more importantly he was loving this last trimester. Who would have thought pregnancy could be so sexy?

'My waters broke.' Just like that, Alison said it. 'Half an hour ago.'

'And you didn't wake me?'

'I just wanted…' Alison gave a little shrug '…a bit of time before everything happens.' And he heard the wobble in her voice and she was such a deep little thing, and he could see, even in the darkness, the sparkle of tears in her eyes, which meant she was scared. And though he never wanted her to be, he accepted that sometimes she was.

'You've got time,' he said, even when she bent over with a contraction. 'How far apart?'

'Ages,' Alison said.

'Come on,' Nick said, and he took her back to their bed, and he understood exactly where she was coming from because part of him didn't want the rest of the world right now, didn't want to ring the hospital or the excited, expectant families. He wanted just a little bit more time that was just for them.

And always he surprised her. Every morning, every night, every day he surprised her, because he was hers, because he got her, because he made her more of herself, and they surprised each other too.

Like this morning.

She had never trusted in them more completely, in him, in herself.

She had thought about labour, as to how it should be, would be, might be, and had prepared, she thought, for every eventuality, was open to drugs and epidurals and a Caesar if it had to be. She had scared herself senseless while never imagining this.

To lie in their bed, with him beside her, with no rush and no haste.

To be held and kissed for that first couple of hours, because that wasn't in any of the books, and they certainly weren't sexy kisses, just confirmation, and then later, just to be held and stroked as the pains deepened.

And then later, to be locked so deep in pain and know he was there at the other end, to close her eyes and go with it and to hear his lovely silence. She didn't want to move, didn't want to leave their little nest.

And he thought about it.

Dr Nick, who had been, till that moment, had anyone bothered to ask, against home births, for all the obvious reasons, found himself outside the obvious and so deep in the moment that, yes, he thought about breaking the rules and having his babe at home.

'We need to go to the hospital.' He was reluctantly practical. 'We really need to go now.' He climbed out of bed and wanted to climb back in, but he went and got the car out of the garage and rang the hospital, and helped her down the stairs.

She could feel the salty air on her lips and the cool

of the morning, and she knew they'd left it a bit late, because the sun was peeking up and she was so, so ready to bear down.

The first bus of the morning was idling, passengers climbing in, and she hoped they all looked around to their fellow passengers and maybe met the person that bettered them, that every one of them could be as lucky as her.

'We're going to get told off,' Nick said as they pulled in at Maternity a little later.

'You'll get told off,' Alison said, really trying not to push. 'You're the doctor!'

But they didn't get told off, because everybody loved Nick.

And, yes, they'd spoken briefly about it once, but Alison had quickly declined. There was no way she'd let him deliver their baby, no way on earth, except the birthing suite was all dark and lovely, and if she closed her eyes she could almost be at home. The midwife was just glorious, just so calm and non-invasive, but Alison was glad she was there, and just very glad to hear Nick's voice.

'Come on, Alison, one more and the head will be out.'

It was the midwife holding her leg and Nick holding their baby's head, and it had all happened so naturally, far, far nicer than she could ever have envisaged. And she pushed as hard as she could till he told her to stop and, yes, it hurt, but in a moment her baby was there and it was Nick who had delivered her.

Her, because he couldn't help himself from saying it.

'She's perfect.'

She was.

Blonde and long limbed and completely her father's daughter, because with one look Alison's heart was taken, and like it or not there could be no holding back—she already loved her.

'Some souvenir!' Nick smiled a little while later, when holding his daughter for the first time.

'More than you bargained for?' Alison asked, but Nick shook his head.

'More than I could ever have envisioned.' He tore his eyes away from his daughter and towards Alison. 'And I did.'

'And in these visions,' Alison checked, 'did your daughter have a name?'

'Martha.'

'Martha?' Alison went to shake her head, but stopped because, as she was starting to trust, this was his dream too.

Here was their biggest adventure.

THE BRIDESMAID'S BABY BUMP

KANDY SHEPHERD

To my wonderful editor, Laura McCallen, whose insight and encouragement help me make my books the best they can be. Thank you, Laura!

CHAPTER ONE

ELIZA DUNNE FELT she had fallen into a fairytale as Jake Marlowe waltzed her around the vast, glittering ballroom of a medieval European castle. Hundreds of other guests whirled around them to the elegant strains of a chamber orchestra. The chatter rising and falling over the music was in a mix of languages from all around the world. Light from massive crystal chandeliers picked up the gleam of a king's ransom in jewellery and the sheen of silk in every colour of the rainbow.

Eliza didn't own any expensive jewellery. But she felt she held her own in a glamorous midnight-blue retro-style gown with a beaded bodice, nipped-in waist and full skirt, her dark hair twisted up with diamante combs, sparkling stilettos on her feet. Jake was in a tuxedo that spoke of the finest Italian tailoring.

The excitement that bubbled through her like the bubbles from expensive champagne was not from her fairytale surroundings but from her proximity to Jake. Tall, imposing, and even more handsome than the Prince whose wedding they had just witnessed, he was a man who had intrigued her from the moment she'd first met him.

Their dance was as intimate as a kiss. Eliza was intensely aware of where her body touched Jake's—his arm around her waist held her close, her hand rested on his broad shoulder, his cheek felt pleasantly rough against the smoothness of her own. She felt his warmth, breathed in his scent—spicy and fresh and utterly male—with her eyes closed, the better to savour the intoxicating effect it had on her senses. Other couples danced around them but she was scarcely aware of their presence—too lost in the rhythm of her private dance with him.

She'd first met Jake nearly two years ago, at the surprise wedding of her friend and business partner Andie Newman to *his* friend and business partner Dominic Hunt. They'd been best man and bridesmaid and had made an instant connection in an easy, friends of friends way.

She'd only seen him once since, at a business function, and they'd chatted for half the night. Eliza had relived every moment many times, unable to forget him. He'd been so unsettlingly *different*. Now they were once more best man and bridesmaid at the wedding of mutual friends.

Her other business partner, Gemma Harper, had just married Tristan, Crown Prince of Montovia. That afternoon she and Jake, as members of the bridal party, had walked slowly down the aisle of a centuries-old cathedral and watched their friends make their vows in a ceremony of almost unimaginable splendour. Now they were celebrating at a lavish reception.

She'd danced a duty dance with Tristan, then with Dominic. Jake had made his impatience obvious, then had immediately claimed her as his dance partner. The room was full of royalty and aristocrats, and Gemma had breathlessly informed her which of the men was single, but Eliza only wanted to dance with Jake. This was the first chance she'd had to spend any real time with the man who had made such a lasting impression on her.

She sighed a happy sigh, scarcely realising she'd done so.

Jake pulled away slightly and looked down at her. Her breath caught in her throat at the slow-to-ignite smile that lit his green eyes as he looked into hers. With his rumpled blond hair, strong jaw and marvellous white teeth he was as handsome as any actor or model—yet he seemed unaware of the scrutiny he got from every woman who danced by them.

'Having fun?' he asked.

Even his voice, deep and assured, sent shivers of awareness through her.

'I don't know that *fun* is quite the right word for something so spectacular. I want to rub my eyes to make sure I'm not dreaming.' She had to raise her voice over the music to be heard.

'It's extraordinary, isn't it? The over-the-top opulence of a royal wedding… It isn't something an everyday Australian guy usually gets to experience.'

Not quite an everyday guy. Eliza had to bite down on the words. At thirty-two, Jake headed his own technology solutions company and had become a billionaire while he was still in his twenties. He could probably fund an event like this with barely a blip in his bank balance. But on the two previous occasions when she'd met him, for all his wealth and brilliance and striking good looks, he had presented as notably unpretentious.

'I grew up on a sheep ranch, way out in the west

of New South Wales,' she said. 'Weddings were more often than not celebrated with a barn dance. This is the stuff of fairytales for a country girl. I've only ever seen rooms like this in a museum.'

'You seem like a sophisticated city girl to me. Boss of the best party-planning business in Sydney.' Jake's green eyes narrowed as he searched her face. 'The loveliest of the Party Queens.' His voice deepened in tone.

'Thank you,' she said, preening a little at his praise, fighting a blush because he'd called her lovely. 'I'm not the boss, though. Andie, Gemma and I are equal partners in Party Queens.'

Eliza was Business Director, Andie looked after design and Gemma the food.

'The other two are savvy, but you're the business brains,' he said. 'There can be no doubt about that.'

'I guess I am,' she said.

She was not being boastful in believing that the success of Party Queens owed a lot to her sound financial management. The business was everything to her and she'd given her life to it since it had launched three years ago.

'Tristan told me Gemma organised the wedding herself,' Jake said. 'With some long-distance help from you and Andie.'

'True,' said Eliza.

Jake—the 'everyday Aussie guy'—was good friends with the Prince. They'd met, he'd told her, on the Montovian ski-fields years ago.

'Apparently the courtiers were aghast at her audacity in breaking with tradition.'

'Yet look how brilliantly it turned out—another success for Party Queens. My friend the Crown Princess.'

Eliza shook her head in proud wonderment. 'One day she'll be a real queen. But for Gemma it isn't about the royal trappings, you know. It's all about being with Tristan—she's so happy, so in love.'

Eliza couldn't help the wistful note that crept into her voice. That kind of happiness wasn't for her. Of course she'd started out wanting the happy-ever-after love her friends had found. But it had proved elusive. So heartbreakingly elusive that, at twenty-nine, she had given up on hoping it would ever happen. She had a broken marriage behind her, and nothing but dating disasters since her divorce. No way would she get married again. She would not risk being trapped with a domineering male like her ex-husband, like her father. Being single was a state that suited her, even if she did get lonely sometimes.

'Tristan is happy too,' said Jake. 'He credits me for introducing him to his bride.'

Jake had recommended Party Queens to his friend the Crown Prince when Tristan had had to organise an official function in Sydney. Tristan had been incognito when Gemma had met him and they'd fallen in love. The resulting publicity had been off the charts for Party Queens, and Eliza would always be grateful to Jake for putting the job their way.

Jake looked down into her face. 'But you're worried about what Gemma's new status means for your business, aren't you?'

'How did you know that?' she asked, a frown pleating her forehead.

'One business person gets to read the signs in another,' he said. 'It was the way you frowned when I mentioned Gemma's name.'

'I didn't think I was so transparent,' she said, and realised she'd frowned again. 'Yes, I admit I *am* concerned. Gemma wants to stay involved with the business, but I don't know how that can work with her fifteen thousand kilometres away from our headquarters.' She looked around her. 'She's moved into a different world and has a whole set of new royal duties to master.'

Eliza knew it would be up to her to solve the problem. Andie and Gemma were the creatives; she was the worrier, the plotter, the planner. The other two teased her that she was a control freak, let her know when she got too bossy, but the three Party Queens complemented each other perfectly.

Jake's arm tightened around her waist. 'Don't let your concern ruin the evening for you. I certainly don't want to let it ruin mine.'

His voice was deep and strong and sent a thrill of awareness coursing through her.

'You're right. I just want to enjoy every moment of this,' she said.

Every moment with him. She closed her eyes in bliss when he tightened his arms around her as they danced. He was the type of man she had never dreamed existed.

The Strauss waltz came to an end. 'More champagne?' Jake asked. 'We could drink it out on the terrace.'

'Excellent idea,' she said, her heart pounding a little harder at the prospect of being alone with him.

The enclosed terrace ran the length of the ballroom, with vast arched windows looking out on the view across the lit-up castle gardens to the lake, where a huge pale moon rode high in the sky. Beyond the lake were snow-capped mountains, only a ghostly hint of their peaks to be seen under the dim light from the moon.

There was a distinct October chill to the Montovian air. It seemed quite natural for Jake to put his arm around her as Eliza gazed out at the view. She welcomed his warmth, still hyper-aware of his touch as she leaned close to his hard strength. There must be a lot of honed muscle beneath that tuxedo.

'This place hardly seems real,' she said, keeping her voice low in a kind of reverence.

'Awesome in the true sense of the word,' he said.

Eliza sipped slowly from the flute of champagne. Wine was somewhat of a hobby for her, and she knew this particular vintage was the most expensive on the planet, its cost per bubble astronomical. She had consulted with Gemma on the wedding wine list. But she was too entranced with Jake to be really aware of what she was drinking. It might have been lemon soda for all the attention she paid it.

He took the glass from her hand and placed it on an antique table nearby. Then he slid her around so she faced him. He was tall—six foot four, she guessed—and she was glad she was wearing stratospheric heels. She didn't like to feel at a disadvantage with a man—even this man.

'I've waited all day for us to be alone,' he said.

'Me too,' she said, forcing the tremor out of her voice.

How alone? She had a luxurious guest apartment in the castle all to herself, where they could truly be by themselves. No doubt Jake had one the same.

He looked into her face for a long moment, so close

she could feel his breath stir her hair. His eyes seemed to go a deeper shade of green. *He was going to kiss her.* She found her lips parting in anticipation of his touch as she swayed towards him. There was nothing she wanted more at this moment than to be kissed by Jake Marlowe.

Yet she hesitated. Whether she called it the elephant in the room, or the poisoned apple waiting to be offered as in the fairytale, there was something they had not talked about all day in the rare moments when they had been alone. Something that had to be said.

With a huge effort of will she stepped back, folded her arms in front of her chest, took a deep breath. 'Jake, has anything changed since we last spoke at Tristan's party in Sydney? Is your divorce through?'

He didn't immediately reply, and her heart sank to the level of her sparkling shoes. 'Yes, to your first question. Divorce proceedings are well under way. But to answer your second question: it's not final yet. I'm still waiting on the decree nisi, let alone the decree absolute.'

'Oh.' It was all she could manage as disappointment speared through her. 'I thought—'

'You thought I'd be free by now?' he said gruffly.

She chewed her lip and nodded. There was so much neither of them dared say. Undercurrents pulled them in the direction of possibilities best left unspoken. Such as what might happen between them if he wasn't still legally married…

It was his turn to frown. 'So did I. But it didn't work out like that. The legalities… The property settlements…'

'Of course,' she said.

So when will *you be free?* She swallowed the words before she could give impatient voice to them.

He set his jaw. 'I'm frustrated about it, but it's complex.'

Millions of dollars and a life together to be dismantled. Eliza knew all about the legal logistics of that, but on a much smaller scale. There were joint assets to be divided. Then there were emotions, all twisted and tangled throughout a marriage of any duration, that had to be untangled—and sometimes torn. Wounds. Scars. All intensely personal. She didn't feel she could ask him any more.

During their first meeting Jake had told her his wife of seven years wanted a divorce but he didn't. At their second meeting he'd said the divorce was underway. Eliza had sensed he was ambivalent about it, so had declined his suggestion that they keep in touch. Her attraction to him was too strong for her ever to pretend she could be 'just friends' with him. She'd want every chance to act on that attraction.

But she would not date a married man. She wouldn't kiss a married man. Even when he was nearly divorced. Even when he was Jake Marlowe. No way did she want to be caught up in any media speculation about being 'the other woman' in his divorce. And then there was the fact that her ex had cheated on her towards the end of their marriage. She didn't know Jake's wife. But she wouldn't want to cause her the same kind of pain.

Suffocating with disappointment, Eliza stepped back from him. She didn't have expectations of any kind of relationship with him—just wanted a chance to explore the surprising connection between them. Starting with a kiss. Then…? Who knew?

She cleared her throat. 'I wish—' she started to say.

But then an alarm started beeping, shrill and intrusive. Startled, she jumped.

Jake glanced down at his watch, swore under his breath. 'Midnight,' he said. 'I usually call Australia now, for a business catch-up.' He switched off the alarm. 'But not tonight.'

It seemed suddenly very quiet on the terrace, with only faint strains of music coming from the ballroom, distant laughter from a couple at the other end of the terrace. Eliza was aware of her own breathing and the frantic pounding of her heart.

'No. Make your call. It's late. I have to go.'

She doubted he'd guessed the intensity of her disappointment, how much she'd had pinned on this meeting—and she didn't want him to see it on her face. She turned, picked up her long, full skirts and prepared to run.

Then Jake took hold of her arm and pulled her back to face him. 'Don't go, Eliza. Please.'

Jake watched as Eliza struggled to contain her disappointment. She seemed to pride herself on having a poker face. But her feelings were only too apparent to him. And her disappointment had nothing on his.

'But I have to go,' she said as she tried to pull away from him. 'You're still married. We can't—'

'Act on the attraction that's been there since the get go?'

Mutely, she nodded.

Their first meeting had been electric—an instant *something* between them. For him it had been a revelation. A possibility of something new and exciting beyond the dead marriage he had been struggling to revive. Eliza had been so beautiful, so smart, so interesting—yet so unattainable. The second time they'd met he'd realised the attraction was mutual. And tonight he'd sensed in her the same longing for more that he felt.

But it was still not their time to explore it. She'd made it very clear the last time they'd met that she could not be friends with a married man—and certainly not more than friends. He'd respected her stance. As a wealthy man he'd met more than a few women with dollar signs flashing in their eyes who had held no regard for a man's wedding vows—or indeed their own.

When Tristan had asked him to be best man at his wedding he'd said yes straight away. The bonus had been a chance to see Eliza again. In her modest lavender dress she'd been the loveliest of the bridesmaids, eclipsing—at least in his admittedly biased eyes—even the bride. Tonight, in a formal gown that showed off her tiny waist and feminine curves, she rivalled any of the royalty in the ballroom.

'This is not what I'd hoped for this evening,' he said.

'Me neither.' Her voice was barely louder than a whisper as she looked up to him.

He caught his breath at how beautiful she was. Her eyes were a brilliant blue that had him struggling to describe them—like sapphires was the closest he could come. They were framed by brows and lashes as black as her hair, in striking contrast to her creamy skin. Irish colouring, he suspected. He knew nothing about her heritage, very little about her.

Jake thirsted to know more.

He—a man who had thought he could never be interested in another woman. Who had truly thought he had married for life. He'd been so set on hanging on to his marriage to a woman who didn't want to be married any more—who had long outgrown him and he her—that he hadn't let himself think of any other. Until he'd met Eliza. And seen hope for the future.

He cursed the fact that the divorce process was taking so long. At first he'd delayed it because he'd hoped he could work things out with his soon-to-be ex-wife. Even though she'd had become virtually a stranger to him. Then he'd discovered how she'd betrayed him. Now he was impatient to have it settled, all ties severed.

'A few months and I'll be free. It's so close, Eliza. In fact it's debatable that I'm not single again already. It's just a matter of a document. Couldn't we—?'

He could see her internal debate, the emotions flitting across her face. Was pleased to see that anticipation was one of them. But he was not surprised when she shook her head.

'No,' she said, in a voice that wasn't quite steady. 'Not until you're legally free. Not until we can see each other with total honesty.'

How could he fault her argument? He admired her integrity. Although he groaned his frustration. Not with her, but with the situation.

He pulled her close in a hug. It was difficult not to turn it into something more, not to tilt her face up to his and kiss her. A campaign of sensual kisses and subtle caresses might change her mind—he suspected she wanted him as much as he wanted her. But she was right. He wasn't ready—in more ways than one.

'As soon as the divorce is through I'll get in touch,

come see you in Sydney.' He lived in Brisbane, the capital city of Queensland, about an hour's flight north.

Scarcely realising he was doing so, he stroked the smooth skin of her bare shoulders, her exposed back. It was a gesture more of reassurance than anything overtly sexual. He couldn't let himself think about Eliza and sex. Not now. Not yet. Or he'd go crazy.

Her head was nestled against his shoulder and he felt her nod. 'I'd like that,' she said, her voice muffled.

He held her close for a long, silent moment. Filled his senses with her sweet floral scent, her warmth. Wished he didn't have to let her go. Then she pulled away. Looked up at him. Her cheeks were flushed pink, which intensified the blue of her eyes.

'I've been in Montovia for a week. I fly out to Sydney tomorrow morning. I won't see you again,' she said.

'I have meetings in Zurich,' he said. 'I'll be gone very early.'

'So…so this is goodbye,' she said.

He put his fingers to the soft lushness of her mouth. 'Until next time,' he said.

For a long moment she looked up at him, searching his face with those remarkable eyes. Then she nodded. 'Until next time.'

Without another word Eliza turned away from him and walked away down the long enclosed terrace that ran along the outside of the ballroom. She did not turn back.

Jake watched her. Her back was held erect, the full skirts of her deep blue dress with its elaborately beaded bodice nipped into her tiny waist swishing around her at each step. He watched her until she turned to the right through an archway. Still she didn't look back, although he had his hand ready to wave farewell to her. Then she disappeared out of sight.

She left behind her just the lingering trace of her scent. He breathed it in to capture its essence. Took a step to go after her, then halted himself. He had no right to call her back a second time. He groaned and slammed his hand against the ancient stone wall.

For a long time he looked out through the window to the still lake beyond. Then he looked back to the ballroom. Without Eliza to dance with there was no point in returning. Besides, he felt like an impostor among the glittering throng. His role as best man, as friend to the Prince, gave him an entrée to their world. His multi-million-dollar houses and string of prestige European cars made him look the part.

Would they welcome him so readily into their elite company if they knew the truth about his past? Would Eliza find him so appealing if she knew his secrets?

He took out his phone and made his business call, in desperate need of distraction.

CHAPTER TWO

Six months later

ELIZA NOTICED JAKE MARLOWE the instant he strode into the business class lounge at Sydney's Kingsford Smith Airport. Tall, broad-shouldered, with a surfer's blond hair and tan, his good looks alone would attract attention. The fact that he was a billionaire whose handsome face was often in the media guaranteed it. Heads turned discreetly as he made his way with his easy, athletic stride towards the coffee station.

He was half a room away from her, but awareness tingled down Eliza's spine. A flush of humiliation warmed her cheeks. She hadn't seen him or heard from him since the wedding in Montovia, despite his promise to get in touch when his divorce was through. And here he was—on his way out of Sydney.

Jake had been in her hometown for heaven knew how long and hadn't cared to get in touch. She thought of a few choice names for him but wouldn't let herself mutter them, even under her breath. Losing her dignity over him was not worth it.

Over the last months she'd gone past disappointed, through angry, to just plain embarrassed that she'd believed him. That she'd allowed herself to spin hopes and dreams around seeing him again—finally being able to act on that flare of attraction between them. An attraction that, despite her best efforts to talk herself out of it, had flamed right back to life at the sight of him. She'd failed dismally in her efforts to extinguish it. He looked just as good in faded jeans and black T-shirt as he looked in a tuxedo. Better, perhaps. Every hot hunk sensor in her body alerted her to that.

But good looks weren't everything. She'd kidded herself that Jake was something he wasn't. Sure, they'd shared some interesting conversations, come close to a kiss. But when it boiled down to it, it appeared he was a slick tycoon who'd known how to spin the words he'd thought would please her. And she'd been sucker enough to fall for it. Had there been *anything* genuine about him?

Jake had put her through agony by not getting in touch when he'd said he would. She never wanted that kind of emotional turmoil in her life again. Especially not now, when Party Queens was in possible peril. She needed all her wits about her to ensure the future of the company that had become her life.

Perhaps back then she'd been convenient for Jake—the bridesmaid paired with the best man. An instant temporary couple. Now he was single and oh-so-eligible he must have women flinging themselves at him from all sides. Even now, as she sneaked surreptitious glances at him, a well-dressed woman edged up close to him, smiling up into his face.

Jake laughed at something she said. Eliza's senses jolted into hyper mode. *He looked so handsome when he laughed.* Heck, he looked so handsome whatever he did.

Darn her pesky libido. Her brain could analyse exactly what she didn't want in a man, but then her body argued an opposing message. She'd let her libido take over at Gemma's wedding, when she'd danced with Jake and let herself indulge in a fantasy that there could be something between them one day. But she prided herself on her self-control. Eliza allowed herself a moment to let her eyes feast on him, in the same way she would a mouthwatering treat she craved but was forbidden to have. Then she ducked her head and hid behind the pale pink pages of her favourite financial newspaper.

Perhaps she hadn't ducked fast enough—perhaps she hadn't masked the hunger in her gaze as successfully as she'd thought. Or perhaps Jake had noticed her when he came in as readily as she had noticed him.

Just moments later she was aware of him standing in front of her, legs braced in a way that suggested he wasn't going anywhere. Her heart started to thud at a million miles an hour. As she lowered the newspaper and looked up at him she feigned surprise. But the expression in his green eyes told her she hadn't fooled him one little bit.

She gathered all her resolve to school her face into a mask of polite indifference. He could not know how much he'd hurt her. Not *hurt.* That gave him too much power. *Offended.* His divorce had been splashed all over the media for the last three months. Yet there'd been no phone call from him. What a fool she'd been to have expected one. She'd obviously read way too much into that memorable 'next time' farewell.

Eliza went to get up but he sat down in the vacant seat next to her and angled his body towards her. In doing so he brushed his knee against her thigh, and she tried desperately not to gasp at his touch. Her famed self-control seemed to wobble every which way when she found herself within touching distance of Jake Marlowe.

He rested his hands on his thighs, which brought them too close for comfort. She refused to let herself think about how good they'd felt on her body in that close embrace of their dance. She could not let herself be blinded by physical attraction to the reality of this man.

'Eliza,' he said.

'Jake,' she said coolly, with a nod of acknowledgment.

She crossed her legs to break contact with his. Made a show of folding her newspaper, its rustle satisfyingly loud in the silence between them.

There was a long, awkward pause. She had no intention of helping him out by being the first one to dive into conversation. Not when he'd treated her with such indifference. Surely the thread of friendship they'd established had entitled her to better.

She could see he was looking for the right words, and at any other time she might have felt sorry for this intelligent, successful man who appeared to be struggling to make conversation. Would have fed him words to make it easier for him. But she knew how articulate Jake could be. How he had charmed her. This sudden shyness must be all part of his game. It seemed he felt stymied at seeing her by accident when he'd so obviously not wanted to see her by intent.

She really should hold her tongue and let him stumble through whatever he had to say. But she knew there wasn't much time before her flight would be called. And this might be her only chance to call him on the way he had broken his promise.

Of course it hadn't been a *promise* as such. But, spellbound by the magic of that royal wedding in Montovia, she had believed every word about there being a 'next time', when he was free. She'd never believed in fairytales—but she'd believed in *him.*

Even though the lounge chairs were spaced for privacy in the business class lounge—not crammed on top of each other like at the airport gate, where she was accustomed to waiting for a flight—she was aware that she and Jake were being observed and might possibly be overheard. She would have to be discreet.

She leaned closer to him and spoke in an undertone. 'So whatever happened to getting in touch? I see from the media that your divorce is well and truly done and delivered. You're now considered to be the most eligible bachelor in the country. You must be enjoying that.'

Jake shifted in his seat. Which brought his thigh back in touch with her knee. She pointedly crossed her legs again to break the contact. It was way too distracting.

'You couldn't be more wrong.' He cleared his throat. 'I want to explain.'

Eliza didn't want to hear his half-hearted apologies. She glanced at her watch. 'I don't think so. My flight is about to be called.'

'So is mine. Where are you headed?'

It would be childish to spit, *None of your business*, so she refrained. 'Port Douglas.'

She'd been counting the days until she could get

up to the resort in far north-east tropical Queensland. From Sydney she was flying to Cairns, the nearest airport. She needed to relax—to get away from everyday distractions so she could get her head around what she needed to do to ensure Party Queens' ongoing success.

Jake's expression, which had bordered on glum, brightened perceptibly. 'Are you on Flight 321 to Cairns? So am I.'

Eliza felt the colour drain from her face. It couldn't be. It just *couldn't* be. Australia was an enormous country. Yet she happened to be flying to the same destination as Jake Marlowe. What kind of cruel coincidence was that?

'Yes,' she said through gritted teeth.

Port Douglas was a reasonably sized town. The resort she was booked into was pretty much self-contained. She would make darn sure she didn't bump into him.

Just then they called the flight. She went to rise from her seat. Jake put his hand on her arm to detain her. She flinched.

He spoke in a fierce undertone. 'Please, Eliza. I know it was wrong of me not to have got in touch as I said I would. But I had good reason.'

She stared at him, uncertain whether or not to give him the benefit of the doubt. He seemed so sincere. But then he'd seemed so sincere at the wedding. Out there on the terrace, in a place and at a time that hardly seemed real any more. As if it *had* been a fairytale. How could she believe a word he said?

'A phone call to explain would have sufficed. Even a text.'

'That wouldn't have worked. I want you to hear me out.'

There was something about his request that was difficult to resist. She wanted to hear what he had to say. Out of curiosity, if nothing else. Huh! Who was she kidding? How could she *not* want to hear what he had to say? After six months of wondering why the deafening silence?

She relented. 'Perhaps we could meet for a coffee in Port Douglas.' At a café. Not her room. Or his. For just enough time to hear his explanation. Then she could put Jake Marlowe behind her.

'How are you getting to Port Douglas from Cairns?' he asked.

'I booked a shuttle bus from the airport to the resort.'

His eyebrows rose in such disbelief it forced from her a reluctant smile.

'Yes, a shuttle bus. It's quite comfortable—and so much cheaper than a taxi for an hour-long trip. That's how we non-billionaires travel. I'm flying economy class, too.'

When she'd first started studying in Sydney, cut off from any family support because she'd refused to toc her father's line, she'd had to budget for every cent. It was a habit she'd kept. Why waste money on a business class seat for a flight of less than three hours?

'Then why…?' He gestured around him at the exclusive waiting area.

'I met a friend going through Security. She invited me in here on her guest pass. She went out on an earlier flight.'

'Lucky for me—otherwise I might have missed you.'

She made a *humph* kind of sound at that, which drew a half-smile from him.

'Contrary to what you might think, I'm very glad to see you,' he said, in that deep, strong voice she found so very appealing.

'That's good to hear,' she said, somewhat mollified. Of course she was glad to see him too—in spite of her better judgement. How could she deny even to herself that her every sense was zinging with awareness of him? She would have to be very careful not to be taken in by him again.

'Are you going to Port Douglas on business or pleasure?'

'Pleasure,' she said, without thinking. Then regretted her response as a flush reddened on her cheeks.

She had fantasised over pleasure with *him*. When it came to Jake Marlowe it wasn't so easy to switch off the attraction that had been ignited at their very first meeting. She would have to fight very hard against it.

It had taken some time to get her life to a steady state after her divorce, and she didn't want it tipping over again. When she'd seen the media reports of Jake's divorce, but hadn't heard from him, she'd been flung back to a kind of angst she didn't welcome. She cringed when she thought about how often she'd checked her phone for a call that had never come. It wasn't a situation where she might have called *him*. And she hated not being in control—of her life, her emotions. Never did she want to give a man that kind of power over her.

'I mean relaxation,' she added hastily. 'Yes, relaxation.'

'Party Queens keeping you busy?'

'Party Queens always keeps me busy. Too busy right

now. That's why I'm grabbing the chance for a break. I desperately need some time away from the office.'

'Have you solved the Gemma problem?'

'No. I need to give it more thought. Gemma will always be a director of Party Queens, for as long as the company exists. It's just that—'

'Can passengers Dunne and Marlowe please make their way to Gate Eleven, where their flight is ready for departure?'

The voice boomed over the intercom.

Eliza sat up abruptly, her newspaper falling in a flurry of pages to the floor. Hissed a swearword under her breath. 'We've got to get going. I don't want to miss that plane.'

'How about I meet you at the other end and drive you to Port Douglas?'

Eliza hated being late. For anything. Flustered, she hardly heard him. 'Uh…okay,' she said, not fully aware of what she might be letting herself in for. 'Let's go!'

She grabbed her wheel-on cabin bag—her only luggage—and half-walked, half-ran towards the exit of the lounge.

Jake quickly caught up and led the way to the gate. Eliza had to make a real effort to keep up with his long stride. They made the flight with only seconds to spare. There was no time to say anything else as she breathlessly boarded the plane through the cattle class entrance while Jake headed to the pointy end up front.

Jake had a suspicion that Eliza might try to avoid him at Cairns airport. As soon as the flight landed he called through to the garage where he kept his car to have it brought round. Having had the advantage of being the first to disembark, he was there at the gate to head Eliza off.

She soon appeared, head down, intent, so didn't see him as he waited for her. The last time he'd seen her she'd been resplendent in a ballgown. Now she looked just as good, in cut-off skinny pants that showed off her pert rear end and slim legs, topped with a form-fitting jacket. Deep blue again. She must like that colour. Her dark hair was pulled back in a high ponytail. She might travel Economy but she would look right at home in First Class.

For a moment he regretted the decision he'd made to keep her out of his life. Three months wasted in an Eliza-free zone. But the aftermath of his divorce had made him unfit for female company. Unfit for *any* company, if truth be told.

He'd been thrown so badly by the first big failure of his life that he'd gone completely out of kilter. Drunk too much. Made bad business decisions that had had serious repercussions to his bottom line. Mistakes he'd had to do everything in his power to fix. He had wealth, but it would never be enough to blot out the poverty of his childhood, to assuage the hunger for more that had got him into such trouble. He had buried himself in his work, determined to reverse the wrong turns he'd made. But he hadn't been able to forget Eliza.

'Eliza!' he called now.

She started, looked up, was unable to mask a quick flash of guilt.

'Jake. Hi.'

Her voice was higher than usual. Just as sweet, but strained. She was not a good liar. He stored that information up for later, as he did in his assessments of clients. He'd learned young that knowledge of people's weaknesses was a useful tool. Back then it had been for survival. Now it was to give him a competitive advantage and keep him at the top. He could not let himself slide again.

'I suspected you might try and avoid me, so I decided to head you off at the pass,' he said.

Eliza frowned unconvincingly. 'Why would you do that?'

'Because you obviously think I'm a jerk for not calling you after the divorce. I'm determined to change your mind.' He didn't want to leave things the way they were. Not when thoughts of her had intruded, despite his best efforts to forget her.

'Oh,' she said, after a long pause. 'You could do that over coffee. Not during an hour's drive to Port Douglas.'

So she'd been mulling over the enforced intimacy of a journey in his car. So had he. But to different effect.

'How do you know I won't need an hour with you?'

She shrugged slender shoulders. 'I guess I don't. But I've booked the shuttle bus. The driver is expecting me.'

'Call them and cancel.' He didn't want to appear too high-handed. But no way was she going to get on that shuttle bus. 'Come on, Eliza. It will be much more comfortable in my car.'

'Your rental car?'

'I have a house in Port Douglas. And a car.'

'I thought you lived in Brisbane?'

'I do. The house in Port Douglas is an escape house.'

He took hold of her wheeled bag. 'Do you need to pick up more luggage?'

She shook her head. 'This is all I have. A few bikinis and sundresses is all I need for four days.'

Jake forced himself not to think how Eliza would look in a bikini. She was wearing flat shoes and he realised how petite she was. Petite, slim, but with curves in all the right places. She would look sensational in a bikini.

'My car is out front. Let's go.'

Still she hesitated. 'So you'll drop me at my resort hotel?'

Did she think he was about to abduct her? It wasn't such a bad idea, if that was what it took to get her to listen to him. 'Your private driver—at your service,' he said with a mock bow.

She smiled that curving smile he found so delightful. The combination of astute businesswoman and quick-to-laughter Party Queen was part of her appeal.

'Okay, I accept the offer,' she said.

The warm midday air hit him as they left the air-conditioning of the terminal. Eliza shrugged off her jacket to reveal a simple white top that emphasised the curves of her breasts. She stretched out her slim, toned arms in a movement he found incredibly sensual, as if she were welcoming the sun to her in an embrace.

'Nice and hot,' she said with a sigh of pleasure. 'Just what I want. Four days of relaxing and swimming and eating great food.'

'April is a good time of year here,' he said. 'Less chance of cyclone and perfect conditions for diving on the Great Barrier Reef.'

The garage attendant had brought Jake's new-model four-by-four to the front of the airport. It was a luxury to keep a car for infrequent use. Just as it was to keep a house up here that was rarely used. But he liked being able to come and go whenever he wanted. It had been his bolthole through the unhappiest times of his marriage.

'Nice car,' Eliza said.

Jake remembered they'd talked about cars at their first meeting. He'd been impressed by how knowledgeable she was. Face it—he'd been impressed by *her*. Period. No wonder she'd been such a difficult woman to forget.

He put her bag into the back, went to help her up into the passenger's seat, but she had already swung herself effortlessly up. He noticed the sleek muscles in her arms and legs. Exercise was a non-negotiable part of her day, he suspected. Everything about her spoke of discipline and control. He wondered how it would be to see her come to pieces with pleasure in his arms.

Jake settled himself into the driver's seat. 'Have you been to Port Douglas before?' he asked.

'Yes, but not for some time,' she said. 'I loved it and always wanted to come back. But there's been no time for vacations. As you know, Party Queens took off quickly. It's an intense, people-driven business. I can't be away from it for long. But I need to free my head to think about how we can make it work with Gemma not on the ground.'

Can't or *didn't want to* be away from her job? Jake had recognised a fellow workaholic when he'd first met her.

'So you're familiar with the drive from Cairns to Port Douglas?'

With rainforest on one side and the sea on the other,

it was considered one of the most scenic drives in Australia.

'I planned the timing of my flight to make sure I saw it in daylight.'

'I get the feeling very little is left to chance with you, Eliza.'

'You've got it,' she said with a click of her fingers. 'I plan, schedule, timetable and organise my life to the minute.'

She was the total opposite of his ex-wife. In looks, in personality, in attitude. The two women could not be more different.

'You don't like surprises?' he asked.

'Surprises have a habit of derailing one's life.'

She stilled, almost imperceptibly, and there was a slight hitch to her voice that made him wonder about the kind of surprises that had hit her.

'I like things to be on track. For me to be at the wheel.'

'So by hijacking you I've ruined your plans for today?'

His unwilling passenger shrugged slender shoulders.

'Just a deviation. I'm still heading for my resort. It will take the same amount of time. Just a different mode of transportation.' She turned her head to face him. 'Besides. I'm on vacation. From schedules and routine as much as from anything else.'

Eliza reached back and undid the tie from her ponytail, shook out her hair so it fell in a silky mass to her shoulders. With her hair down she looked even lovelier. Younger than her twenty-nine years. More relaxed. He'd like to run his hands through that hair, bunch it back from her face to kiss her. Instead he tightened his hands on the steering wheel as she settled back in her seat.

'When you're ready to tell me why I had to read about your divorce in the gossip columns rather than hear it from you,' she said, 'I'm all ears.'

CHAPTER THREE

JAKE WAS VERY good at speaking the language of computers and coding. At talking the talk when it came to commercial success. While still at university he had come up with a concept for ground-breaking software tools to streamline the digital workflow of large businesses. His friend Dominic Hunt had backed him. The resulting success had made a great deal of money for both young men. And Jake had continued on a winning streak that had made him a billionaire.

But for all his formidable skills Jake wasn't great at talking about emotions. At admitting that he had fears and doubts. Or conceding to any kind of failure. It was one of the reasons he'd got into such trouble when he was younger. Why he'd fallen apart after the divorce. No matter how much he worked on it, he still considered it a character flaw.

He hoped he'd be able to make a good fist of explaining to Eliza why he hadn't got in touch until now.

He put the four-by-four into gear and headed for the Captain Cook Highway to Port Douglas. Why they called it a highway, he'd never know—it was a narrow two-lane road in most places. To the left was dense vegetation, right back to the distant hills. To the right was the vastness of the Pacific Ocean, its turquoise sea bounded by narrow, deserted beaches, broken by small islands. In places the road ran almost next to the sand. He'd driven along this road many times, but never failed to be impressed by the grandeur of the view.

He didn't look at Eliza but kept his eyes on the road. 'I'll cut straight to it,' he said. 'I want to apologise for not getting in touch when I said I would. I owe you an explanation.'

'Fire away,' Eliza said.

Her voice was cool. The implication? *This had better be good.*

He swallowed hard. 'The divorce eventually came through three months ago.'

'I heard. Congratulations.'

He couldn't keep the cynical note from his voice. 'You *congratulate* me. Lots of people congratulated me. A divorce party was even suggested. To celebrate my freedom from the ball and chain.'

'Party Queens has organised a few divorce parties. They're quite a thing these days.'

'Not *my* thing,' he said vehemently. 'I didn't want congratulations. Or parties to celebrate what I saw as a failure. The end of something that didn't work.'

'Was that because you were still…still in love with your wife?'

A quick glance showed Eliza had a tight grip on the red handbag she held on her lap. He hated talking about stuff like this. Even after all he'd worked on in the last months.

'No. There hadn't been any love there for a long

time. It ended with no anger or animosity. Just indifference. Which was almost worse.'

He'd met his ex when they were both teenagers. They'd dated on and off over the early years. Marriage had felt inevitable. He'd changed a lot; she hadn't wanted change. Then she'd betrayed him. He'd loved her. It had hurt.

'That must have been traumatic in its own way.' Eliza's reply sounded studiously neutral.

'More traumatic than I could have imagined. The process dragged on for too long.'

'It must have been a relief when it was all settled.'

Again he read the subtext to her sentence: *All settled, but you didn't call me.* It hinted at a hurt she couldn't mask. Hurt caused by *him*. He had to make amends.

'I didn't feel relief. I felt like I'd been turned upside down and wasn't sure where I'd landed. Couldn't find my feet. My ex and I had been together off and on for years, married for seven. Then I was on my own. It wasn't just her I'd lost. It was a way of life.'

'I understand that,' she said.

The shadow that passed across her face hinted at unspoken pain. She'd gone through divorce too. Though she hadn't talked much about it on the previous occasions when they had met.

He dragged in a deep breath. *Spit it out. Get this over and done with.* 'It took a few wipe-out weeks at work for me to realise going out and drinking wasn't the way to deal with it.'

'It usually isn't,' she said.

He was a guy. A tough, successful guy. To him, being

unable to cope with loss was a sign of weakness. Weakness he wasn't genetically programmed to admit to. But the way he'd fallen to pieces had lost him money. That couldn't be allowed to happen again.

'Surely you had counselling?' she said. 'I did after my divorce. It helped.'

'Guys like me don't do counselling.'

'You bottle it all up inside you instead?'

'Something like that.'

'That's not healthy—it festers,' she said. 'Not that it's any of my business.'

The definitive turning point in his life had not been his divorce. That had come much earlier, when he'd been aged fifteen, angry and rebellious. He'd been forced to face up to the way his life was going, the choices he would have to make. To take one path or another.

Jake didn't know how much Eliza knew about Dominic's charity—The Underground Help Centre in Brisbane for homeless young people—or Jake's involvement in it. A social worker with whom both Dominic and Jake had crossed paths headed the charity. Jim Hill had helped Jake at a time when he'd most needed it. He had become a friend. Without poking or prying, he had noticed Jake's unexpected devastation after his marriage break-up, and pointed him in the right direction for confidential help.

'Someone told me about a support group for divorced guys,' Jake said, with a quick, sideways glance to Eliza and in a tone that did not invite further questions.

'That's good,' she said with an affirmative nod.

He appreciated that she didn't push it. He still choked at the thought he'd had to seek help.

The support group had been exclusive, secret, limited to a small number of elite men rich enough to pay the stratospheric fees. Men who wanted to protect their wealth in the event of remarriage, who needed strategies to avoid the pitfalls of dating after divorce. Jake had wanted to know how to barricade his heart as well as his bank balance.

The men and the counsellors had gone into lockdown for a weekend at a luxury retreat deep in the rainforest. It had been on a first-name-only basis, but Jake had immediately recognised some of the high-profile men. No doubt they had recognised him too. But they had proved to be discreet.

'Men don't seem to seek help as readily as women,' Eliza said.

'It was about dealing with change more than anything,' he said.

'Was that why you didn't get in touch?' she said, with an edge to her voice. 'You changed your mind?'

Jake looked straight ahead at the road. 'I wasn't ready for another relationship. I needed to learn to live alone. That meant no dating. In particular not dating *you*.'

Her gasp told him how much he'd shocked her.

'*Me?* Why?'

'From the first time we met you sparked something that told me there could be life after divorce. I could see myself getting serious about you. I don't want serious. But I couldn't get you out of my head. I had to see you again.'

To be sure she was real and not some fantasy that had built up in his mind.

* * *

Eliza didn't even notice the awesome view of the ocean that stretched as far as the eye could see. Or the sign indicating the turn-off to a crocodile farm that would normally make her shudder. All she was aware of was Jake. She stared at him.

'*Serious?* But we hardly knew each other. Did you think I had my life on hold until you were free so I could bolt straight into a full-on relationship?'

Jake took his eyes off the road for a second to glance at her. 'Come on, Eliza. There was something there between us. Something more than a surface attraction. Something we both wanted to act on.'

'Maybe,' she said.

Of course there had been something there. But she wasn't sure she wanted to admit to it. Not when she'd spent all that time trying to suppress it. Not when it had the potential to hurt her. Those three months of seeing his divorce splashed over the media, of speculation on who might hook up with the billionaire bachelor had hurt. He had said he'd get in touch. Then he hadn't. How could she trust his word again? She couldn't afford to be distracted from Party Queens by heartbreak at such a crucial time in the growth of her business.

The set of his jaw made him seem very serious. 'I didn't want to waste your time when I had nothing to offer you. But ultimately I had to see you.'

'Six months later? Maybe you should have let *me* be the one to decide whether I wanted to waste my time or not?' She willed any hint of a wobble from her voice.

'I needed that time on my own. Possibly it was a mistake not to communicate that with you. I was married a long time. Now I'm single again at thirty-two. I haven't had a lot of practice at this.'

Eliza stared in disbelief at the gorgeous man beside her in the driver's seat. At his handsome profile with the slightly crooked nose and strong jaw. His shoulders so broad they took up more than his share of the car. His tanned arms, strong and muscular, dusted with hair that glinted gold in the sunlight coming through the window of the car. His hands— Best she did not think about those hands and how they'd felt on her bare skin back in magical Montovia.

'I find that difficult to buy,' she said. 'You're a really good-looking guy. There must be women stampeding to date you.'

He shrugged dismissively. 'All that eligible billionaire stuff the media likes to bang on about brings a certain level of attention. Even before the divorce was through I had women hounding me with dollar signs blazing in their eyes.'

'I guess that kind of attention comes with the territory. But surely not *everyone* would be a gold-digger. You must have dated *some* genuine women.'

She hated the thought of him with another woman. Not his ex-wife. That had been long before she'd met him. But Eliza had no claim on him—no right to be jealous. For all his fine talk about how he hadn't been able to forget her, the fact remained she was only here with him by accident.

Jake slowly shook his head. 'I haven't dated anyone since the divorce.' He paused for a long moment, the silence only broken by the swish of the tyres on the road, the air blowing from the air-conditioning unit.

Jake gave her another quick, sideward glance. 'Don't you get it, Eliza? There's only one woman who interests me. And she's sitting here, right beside me.'

Eliza suddenly understood the old expression about having all the wind blown out of her sails. A stunned, 'Oh…' was all she could manage through her suddenly accelerated breath.

Jake looked straight ahead as he spoke, as if he was finding the words difficult to get out. 'The support group covered dating after divorce. It suggested six months before starting to date. Three months was long enough. The urge to see you again became overwhelming. I didn't get where I am in the world by following the rules. All that dating-after-divorce advice flew out the window.'

Eliza frowned. 'How can you *say* that? You left our seeing each other again purely to chance. If we hadn't met at the airport—'

'I didn't leave anything to chance. After six months of radio silence I doubted you'd welcome a call from me. Any communication needed to be face to face. I flew down to Sydney to see you. Then met with Dominic to suss out how the land lay.'

'You *what*? Andie didn't say anything to me.'

'Because I asked Dominic not to tell her. He found out you were flying to Port Douglas this morning. I couldn't believe you were heading for a town where I had a house. Straight away I booked onto the same flight.'

Eliza took a few moments to absorb this revelation. 'That was very cloak and dagger. What would have happened if you hadn't found me at the airport?'

He shrugged those broad shoulders. 'I would have abducted you.' At her gasp he added, 'Just kidding. But I *would* have found a way for us to reconnect in Port Douglas. Even if I'd had to call every resort and hotel I would have tracked you down. I just had to see you, Eliza. To see if that attraction I'd felt was real.'

'I… I don't know what to say. Except I'm flattered.'

There was a long beat before he spoke. 'And pleased?'

The tinge of uncertainty to his voice surprised her.

'Very pleased.'

In fact her heart was doing cartwheels of exultation. She was so dizzy that the warning from her brain was having trouble getting through. Jake tracking her down sounded very romantic. So did his talk of abduction. But she'd learned to be wary of the type of man who would ride roughshod over her wishes and needs. Like her domineering father. Like her controlling ex. She didn't know Jake very well. It must take a certain kind of ruthlessness to become a billionaire. She couldn't let her guard down.

'So, about that coffee we talked about…?' he said. 'Do you want to make it lunch?'

'Are you asking me on a *date*, Jake?' Her tone was deliberately flirtatious.

His reply was very serious. 'I realise I've surprised you with this. But be assured I've released the baggage of my marriage. I've accepted my authentic self. And if you—'

She couldn't help a smile. 'You sound like you've swallowed the "dating after divorce" handbook.'

His brows rose. 'I told you I was out of practice. What else should I say?'

Eliza started to laugh. 'This is getting a little crazy.

Pull over, will you, please?' she said. She indicated a layby ahead with a wave of her hand.

Jake did so with a sudden swerve and squealing of tyres that had her clutching onto the dashboard of the car. He skidded to a halt under the shade of some palm trees.

Still laughing, Eliza unbuckled her seatbelt and turned to face him. 'Can I give you a dating after divorce tip? Don't worry so much about whether it's going to lead to something serious before you've even gone on a first date.'

'Was that what I did?'

She found his frown endearing. How could a guy who was one of the most successful entrepreneurs in the country be having this kind of trouble?

'You're over-thinking all this,' she said. 'So am I. We're making it so much harder than it should be. In truth, it's simple. There's an attraction here. You're divorced. I'm divorced. We don't answer to anyone except ourselves. There's nothing to stop us enjoying each other's company in any way we want to.'

He grinned in that lazy way she found so attractive. 'Nothing at all.'

'Shall we agree not to worry about tomorrow when we haven't even had a today yet?'

Eliza had been going to add *not even a morning*. But that conjured up an image of waking up next to Jake, in a twist of tangled sheets. Better not think about mornings. Or nights.

Jake's grin widened. 'You've got four days of vacation. I've got nothing to do except decide whether or not to offload my house in Port Douglas.'

'No expectations. No promises. No apologies.'

'Agreed,' he said. He held out his hand to shake and seal the deal.

She edged closer to him. 'Forget the handshake. Why don't we start with a kiss?'

CHAPTER FOUR

JAKE KNEW THERE was a dating after divorce guideline regarding the first physical encounter, but he'd be damned if he could think about that right now. Any thoughts other than of Eliza had been blown away in a blaze of anticipation and excitement at the invitation in her eyes—a heady mix of sensuality, impatience and mischief.

It seemed she had forgiven him for his broken promise. He had a second chance with her. It was so much more than he could have hoped for—or probably deserved after his neglect.

He hadn't told her the whole truth about why he hadn't been in touch. It was true he hadn't been able to forget her, had felt compelled to see her again. He was a man who liked to be in the company of one special woman and he'd hungered for her. But not necessarily to commit to anything serious. Not now. Maybe not ever again. Not with her. Not with any woman. However it seemed she wasn't looking for anything serious either. Four days without strings? That sounded like a great idea.

She slid a little closer to him from her side of the car. Reached down and unbuckled his seat belt with a low, sweet laugh that sent his awareness levels soaring. When her fingers inadvertently trailed over his thigh he shuddered and pulled her kissing distance close.

He focused with intense anticipation on her sweet mouth. Her lips were beautifully defined, yet lush and soft and welcoming. She tilted her face to him, making her impatience obvious. Jake needed no urging. He pressed his mouth against hers in a tender kiss, claiming her at last. She tasted of salt—peanuts on the plane, perhaps?—and something sweet. Chocolate? Sweet and sharp at the same time. Like Eliza herself—an intriguing combination.

She was beautiful, but his attraction had never been just to her looks. He liked her independence, her intelligence, her laughter.

The kiss felt both familiar and very different. Within seconds it was as if *her* kiss was all he'd ever known. Her lips parted under his as she gave a soft sigh of contentment.

'At last,' she murmured against his mouth.

Kissing Eliza for the first time in the front seat of a four-by-four was hardly ideal. Jake had forgotten how awkward it was to make out in a car. But having Eliza in his arms was way too exciting to be worrying about the discomfort of bumping into the steering wheel or handbrake. She held his face between her hands as she returned his kiss, her tongue sliding between his lips to meet his, teasing and exploring. He was oblivious to the car, their surroundings, the fact that they were parked in a public layby. He just wanted to keep kissing Eliza.

Was it seconds or minutes before Eliza broke away from him? That kind of excitement wasn't easily measured. Her cheeks were flushed, her eyes shades brighter, her lips swollen and pouting. She was panting, so it took her some effort to control her voice. 'Kissing you was all I could think about that night in the castle.'

'Me too,' he said.

Only his thoughts had marched much further than kissing. That last night he hadn't been able to sleep, taunted by the knowledge she was in the apartment next to his at the castle, overwhelmed by how much he wanted her. Back then his married state had been an obstacle. Now there was nothing stopping them from acting on the attraction between them.

He claimed her mouth again, deeper, more demanding. There'd been enough talking. He was seized with a sense of urgency to be with her while he could. He wasn't going to 'over-think' about where this might lead. Six months of pent-up longing for this woman erupted into passion, fierce and hungry.

As their kiss escalated in urgency Jake pulled her onto his lap, one hand around her waist, the other resting against the side of the car to support her. He bunched her hair in his hand and tugged to tilt her face upward, so he could deepen the kiss, hungry for her, aching for more. The little murmurs of pleasure she made deep in her throat drove him crazy with want.

His hands slid down her bare arms, brushed the side curves of her breasts, the silkiness of her top. She gasped, placed both hands on his chest and pushed away. She started to laugh—that delightful, chiming laughter he found so enchanting.

'We're steaming up the windows here like a coupled of hormone-crazed adolescents,' she said, her voice broken with laughter.

'What's wrong with being hormone-crazed *adults,*' he said, his own voice hoarse and unsteady.

'Making out in a car is seriously sexy. I don't want to stop,' she said, moaning when he nuzzled against the delicious softness of her throat, kissing and tasting.

The confined area of the car was filled with her scent, heady and intoxicating. 'Me neither,' he said.

Eliza was so relaxed and responsive she took away any thought of awkwardness. He glanced over to the back seat. There was more room there. It was wider and roomier.

'The back seat would be more comfortable,' he said.

He kissed her again, manoeuvring her towards the door. They would have to get out and transfer to the back, though it might be a laugh to try and clamber through the gap between the front seats. Why not?

Just then another car pulled into the layby and parked parallel to the four-by-four. Eliza froze in his arms. Their mouths were still pressed together. Her eyes communicated her alarm.

'That puts paid to the back seat plan,' he said, pulling away from her with a groan of regret.

'Just as well, really,' Eliza said breathlessly.

She smoothed her hair back from her face with her fingers and tucked it behind her ears. Even her ears were lovely—small and shell-like.

'The media would love to catch their most eligible bachelor being indiscreet in public.'

He scowled. 'I hate the way they call me a *bachelor.* Surely that's a term for someone who has never been married?'

'*Most eligible divorcé* doesn't quite have the same headline potential, does it?' she said.

'I'd rather not feature in *any* headlines,' he growled.

'You might just have to hit yourself with the ugly stick, then,' she said. 'Handsome and rich makes you a magnet for headlines. You're almost too good to be true.' She laughed. 'Though if you scowl like that they might forget about calling you the most eligible guy in the country.'

Jake exaggerated the scowl. He liked making her laugh. 'Too good to be true, huh?'

'Now you look cute,' she said.

'*Cute?* I do *not* want to be called cute,' he protested.

'Handsome, good-looking, hot, smokin', babelicious—'

'Stop right there,' he said, unable to suppress a grin. 'You don't call a guy *babelicious*. That's a girl word. Let me try it on you.'

'No need,' she protested. 'I'm not the babelicious type.'

'I think you are—if I understand it to mean sexy and desirable and—' Her mock glare made him stop. 'How about lovely, beautiful, sweet, elegant—?'

'That's more than enough,' she said. 'I'll take elegant. Audrey Hepburn's style is my icon. Not that I'm really tall enough to own *elegant*. But I try.'

'You succeed, let me assure you,' he said.

'Thank you. I like *smokin'* for you,' she said, her eyes narrowing as she looked him over.

Her flattering descriptive words left him with a warm feeling. No matter how he'd tried to put a brave face on it, the continued rejection by his ex had hurt. She'd found someone else, of course. He should have realised earlier, before he'd let his ego get so bruised.

The admiration in Eliza's eyes was like balm to those bruises. He intended to take everything she offered.

'I'd rather kiss than talk, wouldn't you?' he said.

He'd rather do so much more than kiss.

'If you say so,' she said with a seductive smile.

They kissed for a long time, until just kissing was not enough. It was getting steamy in the car—and not in an exciting way. It was too hot without the air-conditioning, but they couldn't sit there with the engine on.

The windows really were getting fogged up now. Visibility was practically zero. Eliza swiped her finger across the windscreen. Then spelled out the word KISSING. 'It's very obvious what's going on in here.'

He found her wicked giggle enchanting.

'More so now you've done that,' he said.

Spontaneity wasn't something he'd expected from cool and controlled Eliza. He ached to discover what other surprises she had in store for him.

'We really should go,' she said breathlessly. 'How long will it take to get to Port Douglas?'

'Thirty minutes to my place,' he said.

She wiggled in her seat in a show of impatience. 'Then put your foot to the floor and get us there ASAP, will you?'

Jake couldn't get his foot on the accelerator fast enough.

Eliza had a sense she was leaving everything that was everyday behind her as the four-by-four effortlessly climbed the steep driveway which led from the street in Port Douglas to Jake's getaway house. His retreat, he'd called it. As she slid out of the high-set car she gaped at the magnificence of the architectural award-winning house nestled among palm trees and vivid tropical gardens. Large glossy leaves in every shade of green contrasted with riotous blooms in orange, red and yellow. She breathed in air tinged with salt, ginger and the honey-scented white flowers that grew around the pathway.

This was his second house. No, his third. He'd told her he had a penthouse apartment in one of the most fashionable waterfront developments in Sydney, where his neighbours were celebrities and millionaires. His riverfront mansion in Brisbane was his home base. There were probably other houses too, but she'd realised early on that Jake wasn't the kind of billionaire to boast about his wealth.

Then Jake was kissing her again, and she didn't think about houses or bank balances or anything other than him and the way he was making her feel. He didn't break the kiss as he used his fingerprints on a sensor to get into the house—nothing so mundane as a key—and pushed open the door. They stumbled into the house, still kissing, laughing at their awkward progress but refusing to let go of each other.

Once inside, Eliza registered open-plan luxury and an awesome view. Usually she was a sucker for a water view. But nothing could distract her from Jake. She'd never wanted a man more than she wanted him. Many times since the wedding in Montovia she'd wondered if she had been foolish in holding off from him. There would be no regrets this time—no 'if only'. She didn't want him to stop…didn't want second thoughts to sneak into her consciousness.

In the privacy of the house their kisses got deeper, more demanding. Caresses—she of him and he of her—got progressively more intimate. Desire, warm and urgent, thrilled through her body.

She remembered when she'd first met Jake. He'd flown down to Sydney to be best man for Dominic at the surprise wedding Dominic had organised for Andie. Eliza had been expecting a geek. The athletic, handsome best man had been the furthest from her image of a geek as he could possibly have been. She'd been instantly smitten—then plunged into intense disappointment to find he was married.

Now she had the green light to touch him, kiss him, undress him. *No holds barred.*

'Bedroom?' he murmured.

He didn't really have to ask. There had been no need for words for her to come to her decision of where to take this mutually explosive passion. Their kisses, their caresses, their sighs had communicated everything he needed to know.

She had always enjoyed those scenes in movies where a kissing couple left a trail of discarded clothing behind them as they staggered together towards the bedroom. To be taking part in such a scene with Jake was like a fantasy fulfilled. A fantasy that had commenced in the ballroom of a fairytale castle in Europe and culminated in an ultra-modern house overlooking a tropical beach in far north Australia.

They reached his bedroom, the bed set in front of a panoramic view that stretched out over the pool to the sea. Then she was on the bed with Jake, rejoicing in the intimacy, the closeness, the confidence—the wonderful new entity that was *them.*

Eliza and Jake.

CHAPTER FIVE

ELIZA DIDN'T KNOW where she was when she woke up some time later. In a super-sized bed and not alone. She blinked against the late-afternoon sunlight streaming through floor-to-ceiling windows with a view of palm trees, impossibly blue sky, the turquoise sea beyond.

Jake's bedroom.

She smiled to herself with satisfaction. Remembered the trail of discarded clothes that had led to this bed. The passion. The fun. The ultimate pleasure. Again and again.

He lay beside her on his back, long muscular limbs sprawled across the bed and taking up much of the space. The sheets were tangled around his thighs. He seemed to be in a deep sleep, his broad chest rhythmically rising and falling.

She gazed at him for a long moment and caught her breath when she remembered what a skilled, passionate lover he'd proved to be. Her body ached in a thoroughly satisfied way.

Beautiful wasn't a word she would normally choose to describe a man. But he *was* beautiful—in an intensely masculine way. The tawny hair, green eyes—shut tight at the moment—the sculpted face, smooth tanned skin, slightly crooked nose. His beard had started to shadow his jaw, dark in contrast to the tawny blond of his hair.

There were some things in life she would never, ever forget or regret. Making love with Jake was one of them. Heaven knew where they went from here, but even if this was all she ever had of him she would cherish the memory for the rest of her days. In her experience it was rare to want someone so intensely and then not be disappointed. Nothing about making love with Jake disappointed her.

Eliza breathed in the spicy warm scent of him; her own classic French scent that was her personal indulgence mingled with it so that it became the scent of *them.* Unique, memorable, intensely personal.

She tentatively stretched out a leg. It was starting to cramp under his much larger, heavier leg. Rolling cautiously away, so her back faced him, she wondered where the bathroom was, realised it was en suite and so not far.

She started to edge cautiously away. Then felt a kiss on her shoulder. She went still, her head thrown back in pleasure as Jake planted a series of kisses along her shoulder to land a final one in her most sensitive spot at the top of her jaw, below her ear. She gasped. They had so quickly learned what pleased each other.

Then a strong arm was around her, restraining her. 'You're not going anywhere,' he said as he pulled her to him.

She turned around to find Jake lying on his side. His body was so perfect she gasped her admiration. The sculptured pecs, the flat belly and defined six-pack, the muscular arms and legs… He was without a doubt the hottest billionaire on the planet.

Eliza trailed her hand over the smooth skin of his chest. *'Smokin',* she murmured.

He propped himself up on his other elbow. Smiled that slow smile. 'Okay?' he asked.

'Very okay,' she said, returning his smile and stretching like one of her cats with remembered pleasure. 'It was very sudden. Unexpected. So soon, I mean. But it was good we just let it happen. We didn't get a chance to over-think things. Over-analyse how we felt, what it would mean.'

'Something so spontaneous wasn't in my dating after divorce guidebook,' he said with that endearing grin.

His face was handsome, but strong-jawed and tough. That smile lightened it, took away the edge of ruthlessness she sensed was not far from the surface. He couldn't have got where he had by being Mr Nice Guy. That edge excited her.

'Lucky you threw it out the window, then,' she said. 'I seriously wonder about the advice in that thing.'

'Best thing I ever did was ignore it,' he said.

He kissed her lightly on the shoulder, the growth of his beard pleasantly rough. She felt a rush of intense triumph that she was here with him—finally. With her finger she traced around his face, exploring its contours, the feel of his skin, smooth in parts, rough with bristle in others. Yes, she could call this man *beautiful.*

He picked up a strand of her hair and idly twisted it between his fingers. 'What did you do to get over *your* divorce?'

The question surprised her. It wasn't something she

really wanted to remember. 'Became a hermit for a while. Like you, I felt an incredible sense of failure. I'm not used to failing at things. There was relief though, too. We got married when I was twenty-four. I'd only known him six months when he marched me down the aisle. Not actually an aisle. He'd been married before so we got hitched in the registry office.'

'Why the hurry?'

'He was seven years older than me. He wanted to start a family. I should have known better than to be rushed into it. Big mistake. Turned out I didn't know him at all. He showed himself to be quite the bully.'

She had ended up both fearing and hating him.

'Sounds like you had a lucky escape.'

'I did. But it wasn't pleasant at the time. No break-up ever is, is it? No matter the circumstances.'

Jake nodded assent. 'Mine dragged on too long.'

'I know. I was waiting, remember.'

'It got so delayed at the end because her new guy inserted himself into the picture. He introduced an element of ugliness and greed.'

Ugliness. Eliza didn't want to admit to Jake how scary *her* marriage had become. There hadn't been physical abuse, but she had endured some serious mental abuse. When she'd found herself getting used to it, even making excuses for Craig because she'd hated to admit she'd made a mistake in marrying him, she'd known it was time to get out. The experience had wounded her and toughened her. She'd vowed never again to risk getting tied up in something as difficult to extricate herself from as marriage.

'It took me a while to date again,' she said. 'I'd lost faith in my judgement of men. Man, did I date a few duds. And I turned off a few guys who were probably quite decent because of my interrogation technique. I found myself trying to discover anything potentially wrong about them before I even agreed to go out for a drink.'

Jake used her hair to tug her gently towards him for a quick kiss on her nose before he released her. 'You didn't interrogate me,' he said.

'I didn't need to. You weren't a potential date. When we first met at Andie and Dominic's wedding you were married. I could chat to you without expectation or agenda. You were an attractive, interesting man but off-limits.'

He picked up her hand, began idly stroking first her palm and then her fingers. Tingles of pleasure shot through her body right down to her toes. Nothing was off-limits now.

'You were so lovely, so smart—and so accepting of me,' he said. 'It was a revelation. You actually seemed interested in what I had to say.'

As his ex hadn't been? Eliza began to see how unhappy Jake had been. Trapped in a past-its-use-by-date marriage. Bound by what seemed to have been misplaced duty and honour.

'Are you kidding me?' she said. 'You're such a success story and only a few years older than me. I found you fascinating. And a surprise. All three Party Queens had been expecting a stereotype geek—not a guy who looked like an athlete. You weren't arrogant either, which was another surprise.'

'That was a social situation. I can be arrogant when it comes to my work and impatient with people who don't get it.'

His expression hardened and she saw again that underlying toughness. She imagined he would be a demanding boss.

'I guess you have to be tough to have got where you are—a self-made man. Your fortune wasn't handed to you.'

'I see you've done your research?'

'Of course.' She'd spent hours on the internet, looking him up—not that'd she'd admit to the extent of her 'research'. 'There's a lot to be found on Jake Marlowe. The media loves a rags-to-riches story.'

'There were never rags. Clothes from charity shops, yes, but not rags.' The tense lines of his mouth belied his attempt at a joke. 'My mother did her best to make life as good for me as she could. But it wasn't easy. Struggle Street is not where I ever wanted to stay. Or go back to. My ex never really got that.'

'You married young. Why?' There hadn't been a lot in the online information about his early years.

He replied without hesitation. 'Fern was pregnant. It was the right thing to do.'

'I thought you didn't have kids?'

'I don't. She lost the baby quite early.'

'That's sad…' Her voice trailed away. *Very* sad. She would not—could not—reveal how very sad the thought made her. How her heart shrank a little every time she thought about having kids.

'The pregnancy was an accident.'

'Not a ploy to force your hand in marriage?' She had always found the 'oldest trick in the book' to be despicable.

'No. We'd been together off and on since my last year of high school. Marriage was the next step. The pregnancy just hurried things along. Looking back on it, though, I can see if she hadn't got pregnant we might not have ended up married. It was right on the cusp, when everything was changing. Things were starting to take off in a big way for the company Dominic and I had started.'

'You didn't try for a baby again?'

'Fern didn't want kids. Felt the planet was already over-populated. That it was irresponsible to have children.'

'And you?' She held her breath for his answer.

During her infrequent forays into dating she'd found the children issue became urgent for thirty-somethings. For women there was the very real fact of declining fertility. And men like her ex thought they had biological clocks too. Craig had worried about being an old dad. He'd been obsessed with being able to play active sports with his kids. Boys, of course, in particular. Having come from a farming family, where boys had been valued more than girls, that had always rankled with her.

Jake's jaw had set and she could see the hard-headed businessman under the charming exterior.

'I've never wanted to have children. My ex and I were in agreement about not wanting kids.'

'What about in the future?'

He shook his head. 'I won't change my mind. I don't want to be a father. *Ever.*'

'I see,' she said, absorbing what he meant. What it meant to her. It was something she didn't want to share with him at this stage. She might be out of here this afternoon and never see him again.

'My support group devoted a lot of time to warnings

about women who might try and trap a wealthy, newly single guy into marriage by getting pregnant,' he said.

'Doesn't it take two to get a woman pregnant?'

'The odds can be unfairly stacked when one half of the equation lies about using contraception.'

Eliza pulled a face. 'Those poor old gold-diggers again. I don't know *any* woman I could label as a gold-digger, and we do parties through all echelons of Sydney society. Are there really legions of women ready to trap men into marriage by getting pregnant?'

'I don't know about legions, but they definitely exist. The other guys in that group were proof of that. It can be a real problem for rich men. A baby means lifetime child support—that's a guaranteed income for a certain type of woman.'

'But surely—'

Jake put up a hand at her protest. 'Hear me out. Some of those men were targeted when they were most vulnerable. It's good to be forewarned. I certainly wouldn't want to find myself caught in a trap like that.'

'Well, you don't have to worry about me,' she said. In light of this conversation, she *had* to tell him. 'I can't—'

He put a finger over her mouth. She took it between her teeth and gently nipped it.

'Be assured I don't think of you like that,' he said. 'Your fierce independence is one of the things I like about you.'

'Seriously, Jake. Listen to me. I wouldn't be able to hold you to ransom with a pregnancy because…because…' How she hated admitting to her failure to be able to fulfil a woman's deepest biological purpose. 'I… I can't have children.'

He stilled. 'Eliza, I'm sorry. I didn't know.'

'Of course you didn't know. It's not something I blurt out too often.' She hated to be defined by her infertility. Hated to be pitied. *Poor Eliza—you know she can't have kids?*

'How? Why?'

'I had a ruptured appendix when I was twelve years old. No one took it too seriously at first. They put my tummy pains down to something I ate. Or puberty. But the pain got worse. By the time they got me to hospital—remember we lived a long way from the nearest town—the appendix had burst and septicaemia had set in.'

Jake took her hand, gripped it tight. 'Eliza, I'm so sorry. Couldn't the doctors have done something?'

'I don't know. I was twelve and very ill. Turned out I was lucky to be alive. Unfortunately no one told me, or my parents, what damage it had done to my reproductive system—the potential for scar tissue on the fallopian tubes. I wasn't aware of the problem until I tried to have a baby and couldn't fall pregnant. Only then was I told that infertility is a not uncommon side effect of a burst appendix.'

He frowned. 'I really don't know what to say.'

'What *can* you say? Don't try. You can see why I don't like to talk about it.'

'You said your ex wanted to start a family? Is that why you split?'

'In part, yes. He was already over thirty and he really wanted to have kids. His *own* kids. Adoption wasn't an option for him. I wanted children too, though probably later rather than sooner. I never thought I wouldn't be able to have a baby. I always believed I would be a mother. And one day a grandmother. Even a great-grandmother. I'll miss out on all of that.'

'I'm sorry, Eliza,' he said again.

She couldn't admit to him—to anyone—her deep, underlying sense of failure as a woman. How she grieved the loss of her dream of being a mother, which had died when the truth of her infertility had been forced into her face with the results of scans and X-rays.

'They don't test you until after a year of unsuccessfully trying to get pregnant,' she said. 'Then the tests take a while. My ex couldn't deal with it. By that stage he thought he'd invested enough time in me.'

Jake spat out a number of choice names for her ex. Eliza didn't contradict him.

'By that stage he'd proved what a dreadful, controlling man he was and I was glad to be rid of him. Still, my sense of failure was multiplied by his reaction. He actually used the word "barren" at one stage. How old-fashioned was that?'

'I'd call it worse than that. I'd call it cruel.'

'I guess it was.' One of a long list of casual cruelties he'd inflicted on her.

Eliza hadn't wanted to introduce such a heavy subject into her time with Jake, those memories were best left buried.

'Where did you meet this jerk—your ex, I mean—and not know what he was really like? Online?'

'At work. I told you when I first met you how I started my working life as an accountant at a magazine publishing company. I loved the industry, and jumped at the chance to move into the sales side when it came up. My success there and my finance background gave me a good shot at a publisher's role with another company. He was my boss at the new company.'

'You married the boss?'

'The classic cliché,' she said. 'But what made him a good publisher made him a terrible husband. Now, I don't want to waste another second talking about him. He's in my past and staying there. I moved to a different publishing company—and a promotion—and never looked back. Then when the next magazine I worked on folded—as happens in publishing—Andie, Gemma and I started Party Queens.'

'And became the most in-demand party-planners in Sydney,' he said.

Sometimes it seemed to Eliza as if her brief marriage had never happened. But the wounds Craig had left behind him were still there. She'd been devastated at the doctor's prognosis of infertility caused by damaged fallopian tubes. Craig had only thought about what it meant to *him*. Eliza had realised she couldn't live with his mental abuse. But she still struggled with doubt and distrust when it came to men.

Thank heaven she'd had the sense to insist they signed a pre-nup. He'd had no claim on her pre-marriage apartment, and she'd emerged from the marriage financially unscathed.

'I suppose your "dating after divorce" advice included getting a watertight pre-nup before any future nuptials?' she said. 'I'm here to suggest it's a good idea. To add to all his faults, my ex proved to be an appalling money-manager.'

'Absolutely,' he said. 'That was all tied up with the gold-digger advice.'

Eliza laughed, but she was aware of a bitter edge to

her laughter. 'I interrogated all my potential dates to try and gauge if they were controlling bullies like my ex. You're on the lookout for gold-diggers. Are we too wounded by our past experiences just to accept people for what they appear to be?'

Jake's laugh added some welcome levity to the conversation. 'You mean the way you and I have done?' he said.

Eliza thought about that for a long moment. Of course. That was exactly what they'd done. They'd met with no expectation or anticipation.

'Good point,' she conceded with an answering smile. 'We just discovered we liked each other, didn't we? In the old-fashioned boy-meets-girl way. The best man and the bridesmaid.'

'But then had to wait it out until we could pursue the attraction,' he said.

She reached out and placed her hand on his cheek, reassuring herself that he really was there and not one of the dreams she'd had of him after she'd got home from Montovia. 'And here we are.'

When it came to a man, Eliza had never shut down her good sense to this extent. She wasn't looking any further ahead than right here, right now. She'd put caution on the back burner and let her libido rule and she intended to enjoy the unexpected gift of time with this man she'd wanted since she'd first met him.

Jake went to pull her closer. Mmm, they could start all over again... Just then her stomach gave a loud, embarrassing rumble. Eliza wished she could crawl under the sheets and disappear.

But Jake smiled. 'I hear you. My stomach's crying out the same way. It's long past lunchtime.'

As he got up from the bed the sheet fell from him. Naked, he walked around the room with a complete lack of inhibition. He was magnificent. Broad shoulders tapered down to a muscled back and the most perfect male butt, his skin there a few shades lighter than his tan elsewhere. He was just gorgeous. The prototype specimen of the human male. She felt a moment's regret for humanity that his genes weren't going to be passed on to a new generation. That combination of awesome body and amazing brain wouldn't happen too often.

She had nothing to be ashamed of about her own body—she worked out and kept fit. But she suddenly felt self-conscious about being naked and tugged the sheets up over her chest. It was only this morning that she'd encountered him at the airport lounge. She wasn't a one-night stand kind of person. Or hadn't been up until now. *Until Jake.*

He slung on a pale linen robe. 'I'll go check what food there is in the kitchen while you get dressed.'

Eliza remembered their frantic dash into the bedroom a few hours before. 'My bag with my stuff in it—it's still in the car.'

'It's in the dressing room,' said Jake, pointing in the direction of the enormous walk-in closet. 'I went out to the car after you fell asleep. Out like a light and snoring within seconds.'

Eliza gasped. 'I do *not* snore!' *Did* she? It was so long since she'd shared a bed with someone she wouldn't know.

'Heavy breathing, then,' Jake teased. 'Anyway, I brought your bag in and put it in there.'

'Thank you,' said Eliza.

The bathroom was as luxurious as the rest of the house. All natural marble and bold, simple fittings like in an upscale hotel. She quickly showered. Then changed into a vintage-inspired white sundress with a full skirt and wedge-heeled white sandals she'd bought just for the vacation.

Standing in front of the mirror, she ran a brush through the tangles of her hair. Then scrutinised her face to wipe the smeared mascara from under her eyes. Thank heavens for waterproof—it hadn't developed into panda eyes. She slicked on a glossy pink lipstick.

Until now she hadn't planned on wearing make-up at all this vacation. But hooking up with Jake had changed all that. Suddenly she felt the need to look her most feminine best. She wanted more than a one-night stand. Four days stretched out ahead of her in Port Douglas and she hoped she'd spend all of them with Jake. After that—who knew?

CHAPTER SIX

JAKE WAITED IMPATIENTLY for Eliza to get dressed and join him in the living area. He couldn't believe she was here in his house with him. It was more than he could have hoped for when he'd intercepted her at the airport.

He welcomed the everyday sounds of running taps, closing doors, footsteps tapping on the polished concrete floors. Already Eliza's laughter and her sweet scent had transformed the atmosphere. He'd like to leave that sexy trail of clothing down the hallway in place as a permanent installation.

This house was a prize in a property portfolio that was filled with magnificent houses. But it seemed he had always been alone and unhappy here. There had been many opportunities for infidelity during the waning months of his marriage but he'd never taken them up. He'd always thought of himself as a one-woman man.

That mindset had made him miserable while he'd refused to accept the demise of his marriage. But meeting Eliza, a woman as utterly different from his ex as it was possible to be, had shown him a different possible path. However he hadn't been ready to set foot on that path. Not so soon after the tumult and turmoil that had driven him off the rails to such detriment to his business.

Extricating himself from a marriage gone bad had made him very wary about risking serious involvement again. He'd stayed away from Eliza for that very reason—she did not appear to be a pick-her-up-and-put-her-down kind of woman, and he didn't want to hurt her. Or have his own heart broken. Ultimately, however, he'd been *compelled* to see her again—despite the advice from his divorce support group and his own hard-headed sense of self-preservation.

She'd told him he'd been over-thinking the situation. Too concerned about what *might* happen before they'd even started anything. Then she'd gifted him with this no-strings interlude. *No expectations or promises, no apologies if it didn't work out.* What more could a man ask for?

Eliza had surprised and enthralled him with her warm sensuality and lack of inhibition. He intended to make the most of her four days in Port Douglas. Starting by ensuring that she spent the entire time of her vacation with him.

He sensed Eliza's tentative entry into the room from the kitchen before he even heard her footsteps. He looked up and his breath caught at the sight of her in a white dress that was tight at her waist and then flared to show off her slim figure and shapely legs.

He gave a wolf whistle of appreciation. 'You're looking very babelicious.'

Her eyes narrowed in sensual appraisal as she slowly looked him up and down. 'You don't look too smokin' bad yourself,' she said.

He'd quickly gone into one of the other bathrooms, showered and changed into shorts and a T-shirt.

'Comfortable is my motto,' he said. He dragged at his neck as if at an imaginary necktie. 'I hate getting trussed up in a suit and tie.'

'I don't blame you. I feel sorry for guys in suits, sweltering in the heat of an Australian summer.'

'It's a suit-free zone at *my* company headquarters.' A tech company didn't need to keep corporate dress rules.

'I enjoy fashion,' she said. 'After a childhood spent in jeans and riding boots—mostly hand-me-downs from my brothers—I can't get enough girly clothes.'

'Your dress looks like something from my grandma's wardrobe,' he said. Then slammed his hand against his forehead 'That didn't come out quite as I meant it to. I meant from when my grandma was young.'

'You mean it has a nice vintage vibe?' she said. 'I take that as a compliment. I love retro-inspired fashion.'

'It suits you,' he said. He thought about saying that he preferred her in nothing at all. Decided it was too soon.

She looked around her. 'So this is your vacation house? It's amazing.'

'Not bad, is it?'

The large open-plan rooms, with soaring ceilings, contemporary designer furniture, bold artworks by local artists, were all designed to showcase the view and keep the house cool in the tropical heat of far north Queensland. As well as to withstand the cyclones that lashed at this area of the coast with frequent violence.

'He says, with the modest understatement of a billionaire…' she said.

Jake liked her attitude towards his wealth. He got irritated by people who treated him with awe because of it. Very few people knew the truth about his past. How closely he'd courted disaster. But a mythology had built up around him and Dominic—two boys from nowhere who had burst unheralded into the business world.

He had worked hard, but he acknowledged there had been a certain element of luck to his meteoric success. People referred to him as a genius, but there were other people as smart as he—smarter, even—who could have identified the same need for ground-breaking software. He'd been in the right place at the right time and had been savvy enough to recognise it and act on it—to his and Dominic's advantage. Then he'd had the smarts to employ skilled programmers to get it right. Come to think of it, maybe there *was* a certain genius to that. Especially as he had replicated his early success over and over again.

'I found some gourmet pizzas in the freezer,' he said. 'I shoved a couple of them in the oven. There's salad too.'

'I wondered what smelled so good,' she said. 'Breakfast seems a long time ago.'

'We can eat out for dinner. There are some excellent restaurants in Port Douglas—as you no doubt know.'

'Yes…' she said. Her brow pleated into a frown. 'But I need to check in at my resort. I haven't even called them. They might give my room to someone else.'

'Wouldn't you rather stay here?' he asked.

Her eyes narrowed. 'Is that a trick question?'

'No tricks,' he said. 'It's taken us a long time—

years—to get the chance to spend time together. Why waste more time to-ing and fro-ing from a resort to here? This is more private. This is—'

'This is fabulous. Better than any resort. Of course I'd like to stay here. But is it too soon to be—?'

'Over-thinking this?'

'You're throwing my own words right back at me,' she said, with her delightful curving smile.

Her eyes seemed to reflect the colour of the sea in the vista visible through the floor-to-ceiling windows that looked out over the beach to the far reaches of the Pacific Ocean. He didn't think he'd ever met anyone with eyes of such an extraordinary blue. Eyes that showed what she was feeling. Right now he saw wariness and uncertainty.

'I would very much like to have you here with me,' he said. 'But of course it's entirely your choice. If you'd rather be at your resort I can drive you there whenever you want.'

'No! I... I want to be with you.'

'Good,' he said, trying to keep his cool and not show how gratified he was that he would have her all to himself. 'Then stay.'

'There's just one thing,' she said hesitantly. 'I feel a little...uncomfortable about staying here in a house you shared with your ex-wife. I notice there aren't any feminine touches in the bathroom and dressing room. But I—'

'She's never visited here,' he said. 'I bought this house as my escape when things started to get untenable in my marriage. That was not long before I met you at Dominic's wedding.'

'Oh,' she said.

'Does that make you feel better?' he asked.

She nodded. 'Lots better.'

He stepped closer, placed his hands on her shoulders, looked into her eyes. 'You're the only woman who has stayed here. Apart from my mother, who doesn't count as a woman.'

'I'm sure she'd be delighted to know that,' Eliza said, strangling a laugh.

'You know what I mean.' Jake felt more at home with numbers and concepts than words. Especially words evoking emotion and tension.

'Yes. I do. And I'm honoured to be the first.'

He took her in his arms for a long, sweet kiss.

The oven alarm went off with a raucous screech. They jumped apart. Laughed at how nervous they'd seemed.

'Lunch is ready,' he said. He was hungry, but he was tempted to ignore the food and keep on kissing Eliza. Different hungers required prioritising.

But Eliza had taken a step back from him. 'After we eat I need to cancel my resort booking,' she said. 'I'll have to pay for today, of course, but hopefully it will be okay for the other days. Not that I care, really. After all I—'

'I'll pay for any expense the cancellation incurs.'

He knew straight away from her change of expression that he'd made a mistake.

'You will *not* pay anything,' she said. 'That's my responsibility.'

Jake backed down straight away, put up his hands as if fending off attack. That was one argument he had no intention of pursuing. He would make it up to her in other ways—make sure she didn't need to spend another cent during her stay. He would organise everything.

'Right. I understand. My credit cards will remain firmly in my wallet unless you give me permission to wield them.'

She pulled a rueful face. 'Sorry if I overreacted. My independence is very important to me. I get a bit prickly when it's threatened. I run my own business and my own life. That's how I like it. And I don't want to ever have to answer to anyone again—for money or anything else.'

'Because of your ex-husband? You described him as controlling.'

'To be honest, he's turned me off the entire concept of marriage. And before him I had a domineering father who thought he had the right to rule my life even after I grew up.'

Jake placed his hand on her arm. 'Hold it right there. Don't take offence—I want to hear more. But right now I need food.' His snack on the plane seemed a long time ago.

She laughed. 'I grew up with three brothers. I know the rules. Number one being never to stand between a hungry man and his lunch.'

Jake grinned his relief at her reply. 'You're right. The pizza will burn, and I'm too hungry to wait to heat up more.'

'There are *more*?'

'The housekeeper has stocked the freezer with my favourite foods. She doesn't live in. I like my privacy too much for that. But she shops for me as well as keeps the house in order.'

'Unlimited pizza? Sounds good to me.'

From the look of her slim body, her toned muscles, he doubted Eliza indulged in pizza too often. But at his height and activity level he needed to eat a lot. There had been times when he was a kid he'd been hungry. Usually the day before his mother's payday, when she'd stretched their food as far as it would go. That would never happen again.

He headed for the oven. 'Over lunch I want to hear about that country upbringing of yours,' he said. 'I grew up here in Queensland, down on the Gold Coast. Inland Australia has always interested me.'

'Trust me, it was *not* idyllic. Farming is tough, hard work. A business like any other. Only with more variables out of the farmer's control.'

She followed him through the kitchen to the dining area, again with a view of the sea. 'I was about to offer to set the table,' she said. 'But I see you've beaten me to it.'

'I'm domesticated. My mother made sure of that. A single mum working long hours to keep a roof over our heads couldn't afford to have me pulling less than my weight,' he said.

That was when he'd chosen to *be* at home, of course. For a moment Jake wondered what Eliza would think of him if he revealed the whole story of his youth. She seemed so moralistic, he wondered if she could handle the truth about him. Not that he had any intention of telling her. There was nothing he'd told her already that couldn't be dug up on an online search—and she'd already admitted to such a search. The single mum. The hard times. His rise to riches in spite of a tough start. The untold story was in a sealed file never to be opened.

'It must have been tough for her. Your mother, I mean.'

'It was,' he said shortly. 'One of the good things about having money is that I can make sure she never has to worry again.' As a teenager he'd been the cause of most of her worries. As an adult he tried to make it up to her.

'So your mother lets you take care of her?'

'I don't give her much of a choice. I owe her so much and I will do everything I can to repay her. I convinced her to let me buy her a house and a business.'

'What kind of business did you buy for her?'

Of course Eliza would be interested in that. She was a hard-headed businesswoman herself.

'She worked as a waitress for years. Always wanted her own restaurant—thought she could do it better. Her café in one of the most fashionable parts of Brisbane is doing very well.' Again, this was nothing an online search wouldn't be able to find.

'There's obviously a family instinct for business,' she said.

He noted she didn't ask about his father, and he didn't volunteer the information.

'There could be something in that,' he said. 'She's on vacation in Tuscany at the moment—doing a residential Italian cooking course and having a ball.'

Eliza smiled. 'Not just a vacation. Sounds like it's work as well.'

'Isn't that the best type of work? Where the line between work and interest isn't drawn too rigidly?'

'Absolutely,' she said. 'I always enjoyed my jobs in publishing. But Party Queens is my passion. I couldn't imagine doing anything else now.'

'From what I hear Party Queens is so successful you never will.'

'Fingers crossed,' she said. 'I never take anything for granted, and I have to be constantly vigilant that we don't slip down from our success.'

She seated herself at the table, facing the view. He swooped the pizza onto the table with an exaggerated flourish, like he'd seen one of his mother's waiters do. 'Lunch is served, *signorina,*' he said.

Eliza laughed. 'You're quite the professional.'

'A professional heater-upper of pizza?'

'It isn't burned, and the cheese is all bubbly and perfect. You can take credit for *that*.'

Jake sat down opposite her. He wolfed down three large slices of pizza in the time it took Eliza to eat one. 'Now, tell me about life on the sheep ranch,' he said. And was surprised when her face stilled and all laughter fled from her expression.

Eliza sighed as she looked across the table at Jake. Her appetite for pizza had suddenly deserted her. 'Are you sure you want to hear about that?'

Did she want to relive it all for a man who might turn out to be just a fling? He'd told her something of the childhood that must have shaped the fascinating man he had become. But it was nothing she didn't already know. She really didn't like revisiting *her* childhood and adolescence. Not that it had been abusive, or anything near it. But she had been desperately unhappy and had escaped from home as soon as she could.

'Yes,' he said. 'I want to know more about you, Eliza.'

His gaze was intense on her face. She didn't know

him well enough to know what was genuine interest and what was part of a cultivated image of charm.

'Can I give you the short, sharp, abbreviated version?' she said.

'Go ahead,' he said, obviously bemused.

She took a deep, steadying breath. 'How about city girl at heart is trapped in a rural backwater where boys are valued more than girls?'

'It's a start.'

'You want more?'

He nodded.

'Okay…smart girl with ambition has hopes ridiculed.'

'Getting there,' he said. 'What's next?'

'Smart girl escapes to city and family never forgives her.'

'Why was that?' He frowned.

She knew there was danger now—of her voice getting wobbly. 'No easy answer. How about massive years-long drought ruins everything?' She took in another deep breath. 'It's actually difficult to make light of such disaster.'

'I can see that,' he said.

She wished he'd say there was no need to go on, but he didn't.

'Have you ever seen those images of previously lush green pastures baked brown and hard and cracked? Where farmers have to shoot their stock because there's no water, no feed? Shoot sheep that have not only been bred on your land so you care about their welfare, but also represent income and investment and your family's daily existence?'

'Yes. I've seen the pictures. Read the stories. It's terrible.'

'That was my family's story. Thankfully my father didn't lose his land or his life, like others did, before the rains eventually came. But he changed. Became harsher. Less forgiving. Impossible to live with. He took it out on my mother. And nothing *I* could do was right.'

Jake's head was tilted in what seemed like real interest. 'In what way?'

'Even at the best of times life in the country tends to be more traditional. Men are outdoors, doing the hard yakka—do you have that expression for hard work in Queensland?'

'Of course,' he said.

'Men are outside and women inside, doing the household chores to support the men. In physical terms it makes a lot of sense. And a lot of country folk like it just the way it's always been.'

'But you didn't?'

'No. School was where I excelled—maths and legal studies were my forte. My domestic skills weren't highly developed. I just wasn't that interested. And I wasn't great at farm work either, though I tried.' She flexed her right arm so her bicep showed, defined and firm. 'I'm strong, but not anywhere near as strong as my brothers. In my father's eyes I was useless. He wouldn't even let me help with the accounts; that was not my business. In a time of drought I was another mouth to feed and I didn't pull my weight.'

She could see she'd shocked Jake.

'Surely your father wouldn't really have thought that?' he said.

She remembered he'd grown up without a father.

'I wanted to be a lawyer. My father thought lawyers were a waste of space. My education was a drain on the farm. Looking back, I can see now how desperate he must have been. If he'd tried to communicate with me I might have understood. But he just walked all over me—as usual.'

'Seems like I've got you to open a can of worms. I'm sorry.'

She shrugged. 'You might as well hear the end of it. I was at boarding school. One day when I was seventeen I was called to the principal's office to find my father there to take me home so I could help my mother. For good. It was my final year of high school. I wasn't to be allowed to sit my end-of-school exams.'

Jake frowned. 'You're right—your dad must have been desperate. If there was no money to feed stock, school fees would have been out of the question.'

'For *me*. Not for my younger brother. My father found the fees for *him*.' She couldn't keep the bitterness from her voice. 'A boy who was never happier than when he was goofing off.'

'So the country girl went home? Is that how the story ended?'

She shook her head. 'Thankfully, no. I was a straight-A student—the school captain.'

'Why does that not surprise me?' said Jake wryly.

'The school got behind me. There was a scholarship fund. My family were able to plead hardship. I got to sit my final exams.'

'And blitzed them, no doubt?'

'Top of the state in three out of five subjects.'

'Your father must have been proud of you then.'

'If he was, he never said so. I'd humiliated him with the scholarship, and by refusing to go home with him.'

'Hardly a humiliation. Half of the eastern states were in one of the most severe droughts in Australia's history. Even *I* knew that at the time.'

'Try telling *him* that. He'd call it pride. I'd call it pig-headed stubbornness. The only thing that brought me and my father together was horses. We both loved them. I was on my first horse before I was two years old. The day our horses had to go was pretty well the end of any real communication between me and my father.'

There was real sympathy in his green eyes. 'You didn't have to shoot—?'

'We were lucky. A wonderful horse rescue charity took them to a different part of the state that wasn't suffering as much. The loss hit my father really hard.'

'And you too?'

She bowed her head. 'Yes.'

Jake was quiet for a long moment before he spoke again. 'You don't have to talk about this any more if you don't want to. I didn't realise how painful it would be for you.'

'S'okay,' she said. 'I might as well gallop to the finish.' She picked up her fork, put it down again, twisted a paper serviette between her fingers. 'Country girl wins scholarship to university in Sydney to study business degree. Leaves home, abandoning mother to her menfolk and a miserable marriage. No one happy about it but country girl…' Her voice trailed away.

Jake got up from the table and came to her side. He leaned down from behind her and wrapped big, strong muscular arms around her. 'Country girl makes good in the big city. That's a happy ending to the story.'

'I guess it is,' she said, leaning back against him, enjoying his strength and warmth, appreciating the way he was comforting her. 'My life now is just the way I want it.'

Except she couldn't have a baby. Underpinning it all was the one area of her life she'd been unable to control, where the body she kept so healthy and strong had let her down so badly.

She twisted around to look up at him. 'And Day One of my vacation is going perfectly.'

'So how about Days Two, Three and Four?' he said. 'If you were by yourself at your resort what would you be doing?'

'Relaxing. Lying by the pool.'

'We can do that here.'

'Swimming?'

'The pool awaits,' he said, gesturing to the amazing wet-edge pool outside the window, its aquamarine water glistening in the afternoon sunlight.

'That water is calling to me,' she said, twisting herself up and out of the chair so she stood in the circle of his arms, looking up at him. She splayed her hands against his chest, still revelling in the fact she could touch him.

For these few days he was hers.

His eyes narrowed. 'I'm just getting to know you, Eliza. But I suspect there's a list you want to check off before you fly home—you might even have scheduled some activities in to your days.'

'List? Schedules?' she said, pretending to look

around her. 'Have you been talking to Andie? She always teases me about the way I order my day.'

'I'm not admitting to anything,' he said. 'So there *is* a list?'

'We-e-ell…' She drew out the word. 'There *are* a few things I'd like to do. But only if you want to do them as well.'

'Fire away,' he said.

'One: go snorkelling on the Great Barrier Reef. Two: play golf on one of the fabulous courses up here. Then—'

Jake put up one large, well-shaped hand in a halt sign. 'Just wait there. Did I hear you say "play golf"?'

'Uh, yes. But you don't have to, of course. I enjoy golf. When I was in magazine advertising sales it was a very useful game to play. I signed a number of lucrative deals after a round with senior decision-makers.'

He lifted her up and swooped her around the room. 'Golf! The girl plays *golf.* One of my favourite sports.'

'You being a senior decision-maker and all,' she said with a smile.

'Me being a guy who likes to swing a club and slam a little white ball,' he said.

'In my case a neon pink ball. I can see it better on the fairway,' she said.

'She plays with a pink ball? Of *course* she does. Are you the perfect woman, Eliza Dunne?' He sounded more amused than mocking. 'I like snorkelling and diving too. Port Douglas is the right place to come for that. All can be arranged. Do you want to start checking off your list with a swim?'

'You bet.'

He looked deep into her face. Eliza thrilled to the message in his green eyes.

'The pool is very private. Swimsuits are optional.'

Eliza smiled—a long, slow smile of anticipation. 'Sounds very good to me.'

CHAPTER SEVEN

ELIZA SOON REALISED that a vacation in the company of a billionaire was very different from the vacation she had planned to spend on her own. Her own schedule of playing tourist and enjoying some quiet treatments in her resort spa had completely gone by the board.

That was okay, but she hadn't had any time to plan her strategy to keep the company thriving without the hands-on involvement of Gemma, Crown Princess of Montovia—and that worried her. Of course Princess Gemma's name on the Party Queens masthead brought kudos by the bucketload—and big-spending clients they might otherwise have struggled to attract. However, Gemma's incredible skills with food were sorely missed. Party Queens was all Eliza had in terms of income and interest. She needed to give the problem her full attention.

But Jake was proving the most enthralling of distractions.

She had stopped insisting on paying for her share of the activities he had scheduled for her. Much as she valued her independence, she simply couldn't afford a vacation Jake-style. Her wish to go snorkelling on the Great Barrier Reef had been granted—just her and

Jake on a privately chartered glass-bottom boat. Their games of golf had been eighteen holes on an exclusive private course with a waiting list for membership. Dinner was at secluded tables in booked-out restaurants.

Not that she was complaining at her sudden elevation in lifestyle, but there was a nagging feeling that she had again allowed herself to be taken over by a man. A charming man, yes, but controlling in his own quietly determined way.

When she'd protested Jake had said he was treating her, and wanted to make her vacation memorable. It would have seemed churlish to disagree. Just being with him was memorable enough—there was no doubt he was fabulous company. But she felt he was only letting her see the Jake he wanted her to see—which was frustrating. It was almost as if there were two different people: pre-divorce Jake and after-divorce Jake. After she'd spilled about her childhood, about her fears for the business, she'd expected some reciprocal confidences. There had been none but the most superficial.

On the afternoon of Day Four, after a long walk along the beach followed by a climb up the steep drive back home, Eliza was glad to dive into Jake's wet-edge pool. He did the same.

After swimming a few laps she rested back against him in the water, his arms around her as they both kicked occasionally to keep afloat. The water was the perfect temperature, and the last sunlight of the day filtered through the palm trees. Tropical birds flew around the trees, squawking among themselves as they settled for the evening. In the distance was the muted sound of the waves breaking on the beach below.

'This is utter bliss,' she said. 'My definition of heaven.'

The joy in her surroundings, in *him*, was bitter-sweet as it was about to end—but she couldn't share that thought with Jake. *This was just a four-day fling.*

'In that case you must be an angel who's flown down to keep me company,' he said.

'That's very poetic of you,' she said, twisting her head to see his face.

He grinned. 'I have my creative moments,' he replied as he dropped a kiss on her forehead.

It was a casual kiss she knew didn't mean anything other than to signify their ease with the very satisfying physical side of this vacation interlude.

'I could see *you* with a magnificent set of angel man wings, sprouting from your shoulder blades,' she said. 'White, tipped with gold.' *And no clothes at all.*

'All the better to fly you away with me,' he said. 'You must have wings too.'

'Blue and silver, I think,' she mused.

She enjoyed their light-hearted banter. After three days with him she didn't expect anything deeper or more meaningful. He was charming, fun, and she enjoyed being with him.

But he wasn't the Jake Marlowe who had so intrigued her with hints of hidden depths when she'd first met him. That Jake Marlowe had been as elusive as the last fleeting strains of the Strauss waltz lilting through the corridor as she had fled that ballroom in Montovia. She wondered if he had really existed outside her imagination. Had she been so smitten with his fallen angel looks that she'd thought there was more there for her than physical attraction?

'We did an angel-themed party a few months ago,' she said. 'That's what made me think about the wings.'

'You feasted on angel food cake, no doubt?'

'A magnificent celestial-themed supper was served,' she said. 'Star-shaped cookies, rainbow cupcakes, cloud-shaped meringues. Gemma planned it all from Montovia and Andie made sure it happened.'

The angel party had worked brilliantly. The next party, when Gemma had been too caught up with her royal duties to participate fully in the planning, hadn't had quite the same edge. Four days of vacation on, and Eliza was still no closer to finding a solution to the lack of Gemma's hands-on presence in the day-to-day running of the company. Party Queens was heading to crisis point.

'Clever Gemma,' said Jake. 'Tristan told me she's shaken up all the stodgy traditional menus served at the castle.'

'I believe she has,' Eliza said. 'She's instigated cooking programmes in schools, too. They're calling her the people's princess, she told me. Gemma's delighted.'

'No more than Tristan is delighted with Gemma.'

Gemma and Tristan had found true love. Whereas *she* had found just a diverting interlude with Jake. After the royal wedding both Gemma and Andie had expressed high hopes for romance between the best man and the bridesmaid. Eliza had denied any interest. But deep in Eliza's most secret heart she'd entertained the thought too. She couldn't help a sense of regret that it so obviously wasn't going to happen.

Idly, Eliza swished her toes around in the water. 'They call these wet-edge pools infinity pools, don't they? Because they stretch out without seeming to end?'

'That's right,' he said.

'In some way these four days of my vacation seemed to have gone on for ever. In another they've flown. Only this evening left.'

'Can you extend your break? By another day, perhaps?'

She shook her head. 'There's still the Gemma problem to solve. And there are some big winter parties lined up for the months ahead. I have back-to-back appointments for the day after I get back. Some of which took me weeks to line up.'

'That's what happens when you run a successful business,' he said.

'As you know only too well,' she said. Party Queens was insignificant on the corporate scale compared to *his* company.

'I'd have trouble squeezing in another day here, too,' Jake said. 'I'm out of the country a lot these days. Next week I fly to Minnesota in the United States, to meet with Walter Burton on a joint venture between him and Dominic in which I'm involved. My clients are all around the world. I'll be in Bangalore in India the following week. Singapore the week after that.'

'Are you ever home?' Her voice rose.

'Not often, these days. My absences were a bone of contention with my ex. She was probably right when she said that I didn't give her enough time.'

Eliza paused. 'It doesn't sound like you have any more time now.'

Jake took a beat to answer. 'Are you any different? Seems to me you're as career-orientated as I am. How much room does Party Queens leave for a man in your life?'

'Not much,' she admitted. She felt bad that she had

fielded so many phone calls while she'd been with him. But being a party planner wasn't a nine-to-five week-day-only enterprise. 'The business comes first, last and in between.'

It could be different! she screamed silently. *For the right man.* But was she being honest with herself? Could Jake be the right man?

'Seems to me we're both wedded to our careers,' he said slowly. 'To the detriment of anything else.'

'That's not true,' she said immediately. Then thought about it. 'Maybe. If neither of us can spare another day to spend here together when it's been so perfect.'

'That tells *me* something,' he said, his voice guarded.

Eliza swallowed hard against the truth of his words. The loss of *what might have been* hurt.

'It could be for the best,' she said, trying to sound matter of fact, but inwardly weeping over a lost opportunity.

She didn't know him any better than on Day One. His body, yes. His heart and soul—no. Disappointment stabbed deep that Jake hadn't turned out to be the man she'd expected him to be when he'd been whirling her around that fairytale ballroom.

Why had she ever hoped for more? When she thought about it, the whole thing with Jake hadn't seemed quite real. From the moonlit terrace in Montovia to the way he'd intercepted her at the airport and whisked her away to this awesome house perched high above the beach, it had all had an element of fantasy.

Jake held her for a long moment without replying. She could feel the thudding of his heart against her back. The water almost stilled around them, with only the occasional slap against the tiled walls of the pool. She had a heart-stopping feeling he was saying goodbye.

Finally he released her, then swam around her so he faced her, with her back to the edge of the pool. His hair was dark with water and slick to his head. Drops of water glistened on the smooth olive of his skin. Her heart contracted painfully at how handsome he looked. At how much she wanted him.

But although they got on so well, both in bed and out of it, it was all on the surface. Sex and fun. Nothing deeper had developed. She needed something more profound. She also needed a man who cared enough to make time to see her—and she him.

'Do you really think so?' he asked.

'Sometimes things are only meant to be for a certain length of time,' she said slowly. 'You can ruin them by wanting more.'

Jake's heart pounded as he looked down into Eliza's face. She'd pushed her wet hair back from her face, showing the perfect structure of her cheekbones, the full impact of her eyes. Water from the pool had dripped down over her shoulders to settle in drops on the swell of her breasts. The reality of Eliza in a bikini had way exceeded his early fantasies.

Eliza was everything he'd hoped she'd be and more. She was an extraordinary woman. They were compatible both in bed and out. They even enjoyed the same sports. But she'd been more damaged by her divorce than he had imagined. Not to mention by the tragedy of her inability to have a baby.

The entire time he'd felt he had to tread carefully around her, keeping the conversation on neutral topics, never digging too deep. For all her warmth and laughter and seeming openness, he sensed a prickly barrier around her. And then there was her insistence on answering her phone at all but their most intimate of moments. Eliza seemed so determined to keep her independence—there appeared little room for compromise. And if there was one lesson he'd learned from his marriage it was that compromise was required when two strong personalities came together as a couple.

She was no more ready for a serious relationship than he was.

Day Four was practically done and dusted—and so, it seemed, was his nascent relationship with Eliza.

And yet… He couldn't tolerate the thought of this being a final goodbye. There was still something about her that made him want to know more.

'We could catch up again some time, when we find ourselves in each other's cities,' he said.

'Absolutely.'

She said it with an obviously forced enthusiasm that speared through him.

'I'd like that.'

She placed her hand on his cheek, cool from the water, looked into his eyes. It felt ominously like a farewell.

'Jake, I'm so glad we did this.'

He had to clear his throat to speak. 'Me too,' he managed to choke out. There was a long pause during which the air seemed heavy with words unsaid before he spoke again. 'We have mutual friends. One day we might get the chance to take up where we left off.'

'Yes,' she said. 'That would be nice.'

Nice? Had all that passion and promise dwindled to *nice?*

Maybe that was what happened in this brave new world of newly single dating. Jake couldn't help a nagging sense of doubt that it should end like this. Had they missed a step somewhere?

'Jake, about our mutual friends…?' she said.

'Yes?' he said.

'I didn't tell them I'd met you here. Can Dominic be discreet?'

'He doesn't know we caught up with each other either.'

'Shall we keep it secret from them?' she asked. 'It would be easier.'

'As far as they're concerned we went our separate ways in Port Douglas,' he said.

He doubted Dominic would be surprised to hear it had turned out that way. He had warned Jake that, fond as he was of Eliza, she could be 'a tough little cookie'. Jake had thought there was so much more to her than that. Perhaps Dominic had been right.

'That's settled, then,' she said. There was an air of finality to her words.

Eliza swam to the wide, shallow steps of the pool, waded halfway up them, then turned back. Her petite body packed a powerfully sexy punch in her black bikini. High, firm breasts, a flat tummy and narrow waist flaring into rounded hips and a perfectly curved behind. Perhaps he'd read too much into this episode. *It was just physical—nothing more.* A fantasy fulfilled.

'I need to finish packing,' she said. 'Then I can enjoy our final dinner without worrying.'

That was it? 'Eliza, don't go just yet. I want to tell you—'

She paused, turned back to face him. Their gazes met for a long moment in the dying light of the day. Time seemed to stand still.

'I've booked a very good restaurant,' he said.

'I'll… I'll look forward to it,' she said. She took the final step out of the pool. 'Don't forget I have an early start in the morning.'

'I'll be ready to drive you to Cairns,' he said.

He dreaded taking that journey in reverse with her, when the journey here from the airport had been so full of promise and simmering sensuality. Tomorrow's journey would no doubt be followed by a stilted farewell at the airport.

'That's so good of you to offer,' she said with excess politeness. 'But I didn't cancel my return shuttle bus trip. It would be easier all round if we said goodbye here tomorrow morning.'

'You're sure, Eliza?' He made a token protest.

'Absolutely sure,' she said, heading towards the house without a backward glance.

Jake watched her, his hands fisted by his sides. He fancied blue angel wings unfurling as she prepared to fly right out of his life.

It was stupid of him ever to have thought things with Eliza could end any other way.

CHAPTER EIGHT

TEN WEEKS LATER Eliza sat alone in her car, parked on a street in an inner western suburb of Sydney, too shaken even to think about driving away from an appointment that had rocked her world. She clutched her keys in her hand, too unsteady to get the key into the ignition.

Eliza hated surprises. She liked to keep her life under control, with schedules and timetables and plans. Surprises had derailed her life on more than one occasion. Most notably the revelation that her burst appendix had left her infertile. But in this case the derailment was one that had charged her with sheer bubbling joy in one way and deep, churning anxiety in the other.

She was pregnant.

'It would take a miracle for you to get pregnant.'

Those had been her doctor's words when Eliza had told her of her list of symptoms. Words that had petered out into shock at the sight of a positive pregnancy test.

That miracle had happened in Port Douglas, with Jake—most likely the one time there had been a slip with their protection. Eliza hadn't worried. After all, she couldn't get pregnant.

Seemed she could.

And she had.

She laid her hand on her tummy, still flat and firm. But there was a tiny new life growing in there. *A baby.* She could hardly believe it was true, still marvelled at the miracle. But she had seen it.

Not *it.*

Him or her.

The doctor had wanted an ultrasound examination to make absolutely sure there wasn't an ectopic pregnancy in the damaged tube.

Active—like me, had been Eliza's first joyous thought when she'd seen the image of her tiny baby, turning cartwheels safe and sound inside her womb. Her second thought had been of loneliness and regret that there was no one there to share the miraculous moment with her. But she wanted this more than she had ever wanted anything in her life.

Her baby.

Eliza realised her cheeks were wet with tears. Fiercely, she scrubbed at her eyes.

Her third thought after the initial disbelief and shock had been to call Jake and tell him. There was absolutely no doubt he was the father.

His baby.

But how could she? He'd made it very clear he didn't *ever* want to be a father.

Dear heaven, she couldn't tell him.

He would think she was one of the dollar signs flashing gold-diggers he so despised. What had he said?

'A baby means lifetime child support—that's a guaranteed income for a certain type of woman.'

She dreaded the scorn in his eyes if she told him.

You know I told you I couldn't have a baby? Turns out I'm pregnant. You're going to be a daddy.

And what if he wanted her not to go forward with the pregnancy? No way—ever—would that be an option for her.

How on earth had this happened?

'Nature can be very persistent,' her doctor had explained. 'The tube we thought was blocked must not have been completely blocked. Or it unblocked itself.'

It really was a miracle—and one she hugged to herself.

She was not daunted by the thought of bringing the baby up by herself. Not that she believed it would be easy. But she owned her own home—a small terraced house in Alexandria, not far from the converted warehouse that housed the Party Queens headquarters. And Party Queens was still doing well financially, thanks to her sound management and the talent and drive of her business partners. And a creative new head chef was working out well. The nature of the business meant her hours could be flexible. Andie had often brought baby Hugo in when he was tiny, and did so even now, when he was a toddler. Eliza could afford childcare when needed—perhaps a nanny. Though she was determined to raise her child herself, with minimal help from nannies and childminders.

Her impossible dream had come true. *She was going to be a mother.* But the situation with her baby's father was more of a nightmare.

Eliza rested her head on her folded arms on top of the steering wheel, slumped with despair. *Pregnant from a four-night stand.* By a man she hadn't heard from since he'd walked her down the steep driveway that led away from his tropical hideaway and waved her goodbye.

Now he'd think she'd tried to trap him.

'I certainly wouldn't want to find myself caught in a trap like that,' he'd said, with a look of horror on his handsome face.

Eliza raised her head up off her folded arms. Took a few deep, steadying breaths. She wouldn't tell Jake. Nor would she tell her best friends about her pregnancy. Not yet. Not when both their husbands were friends with Jake.

If her tummy was this flat now, hopefully she wouldn't show for some time yet. Maybe she could fudge the dates. Or say the baby had been conceived by donor and IVF. The fact that Jake lived in Brisbane would become an advantage once she couldn't hide her pregnancy any longer. He wouldn't have to see her and her burgeoning bump.

But what if the baby looked like Jake? People close to Jake, like Andie and Dominic, would surely twig to the truth. *What if...what if...what if?* She covered her ears with her hands, as if to silence the questions roiling in her brain. But to no effect.

Was it fair *not* to tell him he was going to be a father? If she didn't make any demands on him surely he wouldn't believe she was a gold-digger? Maybe he would want to play some role in the baby's life. She wouldn't fight him if he did. It would be better for the baby. The baby who would become a child, a teenager, a person. A person with the right to know about his or her father.

It was all too much for her to deal with. She put her hand to her forehead, then over her mouth, suddenly feeling clammy and nauseous again.

The sickness had been relentless—so had the bone-deep exhaustion. She hadn't recognised them as symptoms of pregnancy. Why would she when she'd believed herself to be infertile?

Instead she had been worried she might have some terrible disease. Even when her breasts had started to become sensitive she had blamed it on a possible hormonal disturbance. She'd believed she couldn't conceive right up until the doctor's astonished words: *'You're pregnant.'*

But why would Jake—primed by both his own experience with women with flashing dollar signs in their eyes and the warnings of what sounded like a rabid divorce support group—believe her?

She was definitely in this on her own.

Eliza knew she would feel better if she could start making plans for her future as a single mother. Then she would feel more in control. But right now she had to track down the nearest bathroom. No wonder she had actually lost weight rather than put it on, with this morning, noon and night sickness that was plaguing her.

Party Queens was organising a party to be held in two weeks' time—the official launch of a new business venture of Dominic's in which Jake held a stake. No doubt she would see him there. But she would be officially on duty and could make their contact minimal. Though it would be difficult to deal with. And not just because of her pregnancy. She still sometimes woke in the night, realising she had been dreaming about Jake and full of regrets that it hadn't worked out between them.

CHAPTER NINE

THE NEARER JAKE got to Dominic's house in Sydney for the launch party, the drier his mouth and the more clammy his hands on the wheel of the European sports car he kept garaged there. Twelve weeks since he'd seen Eliza and he found himself feeling as edgy as an adolescent. Counting down the minutes until he saw her again.

The traffic lights stayed on red for too long and he drummed his fingers impatiently on the steering wheel.

For most of the time since their four-day fling in Port Douglas he'd been out of the country. *But she'd rarely been out of his mind.* Jake didn't like admitting to failure—but he'd failed dismally at forgetting her. From the get-go he'd had trouble accepting the finality of their fling.

The driveway up to his house in Port Douglas had never seemed so steep as that morning when he had trudged back up it after waving Eliza off on the shuttle bus. He'd pushed open his door to quiet and emptiness and a sudden, piercing regret. Her laughter had seemed to dance still on the air of the house.

No matter how much he'd told himself he was cool about the way his time had gone with her, he hadn't been able to help but think that by protecting himself he had talked himself out of something that might have been special. Cheated himself of the chance to be with a woman who might only come along once in a lifetime.

He'd had no contact with her at all since that morning, even though Party Queens were organising this evening's launch party. Dominic had done all the liaising with the party planners. Of course he had—he was married to the Design Director.

By the time he reached Dominic's house, Jake was decidedly on edge. He sensed Eliza's presence as soon as he was ushered through the door of Dominic's impressive mansion in the waterfront suburb of Vaucluse. Was it her scent? Or was it that his instincts were so attuned to Eliza they homed in on her even within a crowd? He heard the soft chime of her laughter even before he saw her. Excitement and anticipation stirred. Just seeing Eliza from a distance was enough to set his heart racing.

He stood at a distance after he'd found her, deep in conversation with a female journalist he recognised. This particular journalist had been the one to label Dominic—one of the most generous men Jake had ever known—with the title of 'Millionaire Miser'.

Andie and Party Queens had organised a party on Christmas Day two years ago that had dispelled *that* reputation. Planning that party was how Andie had met Dominic. And a week after Christmas Dominic had arranged a surprise wedding for Andie. Jake had flown down from Brisbane to be best man, and that wedding was where he'd met Eliza for the first time.

Jake looked through the wall of French doors that

opened out from the ballroom of Dominic's grand Art Deco house to the lit-up garden and swimming pool beyond. He remembered his first sight of Eliza, exquisite in a flowing pale blue bridesmaid's dress, white flowers twisted through her dark hair. She had laughed up at him as they'd shared in the conspiracy of it all: the bride had had no idea of her own upcoming nuptials.

Jake had been mesmerised by Eliza's extraordinary blue eyes, captivated by her personality. They had chatted the whole way through the reception. He'd been separated from Fern at that stage, but still trying to revive something that had been long dead. Not wanting to admit defeat. Eliza had helped him see how pointless that was—helped him to see hope for a new future just by being Eliza.

Now she wasn't aware that he was there, and he watched her as she chatted to the journalist, her face animated, her smile at the ready. She was so lovely—and not just in looks. He couldn't think of another person whose company he enjoyed more than Eliza's. *Why had he let her go?*

He couldn't bear it if he didn't get some kind of second chance with her. He'd tried to rid himself of the notion that he was a one-woman man. After all, a billionaire bachelor was spoiled for choice. He didn't have to hunt around to find available woman—they found *him*. Theoretically, he could date a string of them—live up to his media reputation. Since Port Douglas he'd gone out with a few women, both in Australia and on his business travels. Not one had captured his interest. None had come anywhere near Eliza.

Tonight she looked every inch the professional, but with a quirky touch to the way she was dressed that was perfectly appropriate to her career as a party planner. She wore a full-skirted black dress, with long, tight, sheer sleeves, and high-heeled black stilettos. Her hair was twisted up behind her head and finished with a flat black velvet bow. What had she called her style? Retro-inspired? He would call the way she dressed 'ladylike'. But she was as smart and as business-savvy as any guy in a suit and necktie.

Did she feel the intensity of his gaze on her? She turned around, caught his eye. Jake smiled and nodded a greeting, not wanting to interrupt her conversation. He was shocked by her reaction. Initially a flash of delight lightened her face, only to be quickly replaced by wariness and then a conscious schooling of her features into polite indifference.

Jake felt as if he had been kicked in the gut. *Why?* They'd parted on good terms. He'd even thought he'd seen a hint of tears glistening in her eyes as she'd boarded the shuttle bus in Port Douglas. They'd both been aware that having mutual friends would mean they'd bump into each other at some stage. She must have known he would be here tonight—he was part of the proceedings.

He strode towards her, determined to find out what was going on. Dismissing him, she turned back to face the journalist. Jake paused mid-stride, astounded at her abruptness. Then it twigged. Eliza didn't want this particular newshound sniffing around for an exclusive featuring the billionaire bachelor and the party planner.

Jake changed direction to head over to the bar.

He kept a subtle eye on Eliza. As soon as she was free he headed towards her, wanting to get her attention before anyone else beat him to it.

'Hello,' he said, for all the world as if they weren't anything other than acquaintances with mutual friends. He dropped a kiss on her cool, politely offered cheek.

'Jake,' Eliza said.

This was Eliza the Business Director of Party Queens speaking. Not Eliza the lover, who had been so wonderfully responsive in his arms. Not Eliza his golfing buddy from Port Douglas, nor Eliza his bikini-clad companion frolicking in the pool.

'So good that you could make it down from Brisbane,' the Business Director said. 'This is a momentous occasion.'

'Indeed,' he said.

Momentous because it was the first time they'd seen each other after their four-day fling? More likely she meant it was momentous because it was to mark the occasion not only of the first major deal of Dominic's joint venture with the American billionaire philanthropist Walter Burton, but also the setting up the Sydney branch of Dominic's charity, The Underground Help Centre, for homeless young people.

'Walter Burton is here from Minnesota,' Eliza said. 'I believe you visited with him recently.'

'He flew in this morning,' he said.

Jake had every right to be talking to Eliza. He was one of the principals of the deal they were celebrating tonight. Party Queens was actually in *his* employ.

However, when that pushy journalist's eyes narrowed with interest and her steps slowed as she walked by him and Eliza, Jake remembered she'd been in Montovia to report on the royal wedding. As best man and bridesmaid, he and Eliza had featured in a number of photo shoots and articles. If it was rumoured they'd had an affair—and that was all it had been—it would be big tabloid news.

He gritted his teeth. There was something odd here. Something else. Eliza's reticence could not be put down just to the journalist's presence.

Jake leaned down to murmur in her ear, breathed in her now familiar scent, sweet and intoxicating. 'It's good to see you. I'd like to catch up while I'm in Sydney.'

Eliza took a step back from him. 'Sorry—not possible,' she said. She gave an ineffectual wave to indicate the room, now starting to fill up with people. The action seemed extraordinarily lacking in Eliza's usual energy. 'This party is one of several that are taking up all my time.'

So what had changed? Work had always seemed to come first with Eliza. Whereas *he* was beginning to see it shouldn't. That there should be a better balance to life.

'I understand,' he said. But he didn't. 'What about after the party? Catch up for coffee at my apartment at the wharf?' He owned a penthouse apartment in a prestigious warehouse conversion right on the harbour in inner eastern Sydney.

Eliza's lashes fluttered and she couldn't meet his eyes. 'I'm sorry,' she said again. 'I… I'm not in the mood for company.'

Jake was too flabbergasted to say anything. He eventually found the words. 'You mean not in the mood for *me*?'

She lifted her chin, looked up at him. For once he couldn't read the expression in those incredible blue eyes. Defiance? Regret? *Fear?* It both puzzled and worried him.

'Jake, we agreed to four days only.'

The sentence sounded disconcertingly well-rehearsed. A shard of pain stabbed him at her tone.

'We left open an option to meet again, did we not?' He asked the question, but he thought he could predict the answer.

She put her hand on her heart and then indicated him in an open-palmed gesture that would normally have indicated togetherness. 'Me. You. We tried it. It…it didn't work.'

The slight stumble on her words alerted him to a shadow of what looked like despair flitting across her face. *What was going on?*

'I don't get it.' Jake was noted for his perseverance. He wouldn't give up on Eliza easily.

A spark of the feisty Eliza he knew—or thought he knew—flashed through.

'Do I have to analyse it? Isn't it enough that I just don't want to be with you again?'

He didn't believe her. Not when he remembered her unguarded expression when she'd first noticed him this evening.

There was something not right here.

Or was he being arrogant in his disbelief that Eliza simply didn't want him in her life? That the four days had proved he wasn't what she wanted? Was he falling back into his old ways? Unable to accept that a woman he wanted no longer wanted *him*? That wanting to persevere with Eliza was the same kind of blind stubbornness that had made him hang on to a marriage in its death throes—to the ultimate misery of both him and his ex-wife? Not to mention the plummeting profit margins of his company—thankfully now restored.

'Is there someone else?' he asked.

A quick flash of something in her eyes made him pay close attention to her answer.

'Someone else? No. Not really.'

'What do you mean "not really"?'

'Bad choice of words. There's no other man.'

He scrutinised her face. Noticed how pale she looked, with dark shadows under her eyes and a new gauntness to her cheekbones. Her lipstick was a red slash against her pallor. More colour seemed to leach from her face as she spoke.

'Jake. There's no point in going over this. It's over between us. Thank you for understanding.' She suddenly snatched her hand to her mouth. 'I'm afraid I have to go.'

Without another word she rushed away, heading out of the ballroom and towards the double arching stairway that was a feature of the house.

Jake was left staring after her. Dumbfounded. Stricken with a sudden aching sense of loss.

He knew he had to pull himself together as he saw Walter Burton heading for him. He pasted a smile on his face. Extended his hand in greeting.

The older man, with his silver hair and perceptive pale eyes, pumped his hand vigorously. 'Good to see you, Jake. I'm having fun here, listening to people complain that it's cold for June. Winter in Sydney is a joke. I'm telling them they don't know what winter is until they visit Minnesota in February.'

'Of course,' Jake said.

He was trying to give Walter his full attention,

but half his mind was on Eliza as he looked over the heads of the people who now surrounded him, nodded vaguely at guests he recognised. *Where had she gone?*

Walter's eyes narrowed. 'Lady trouble?' he observed.

'Not really,' Jake said. He didn't try to deny that Eliza was his lady. Dominic and Andie had had to stage a fake engagement because of this older man's moral stance. He found himself wishing Eliza really was his lady, with an intensity that hurt so much he nearly doubled over.

'Don't worry, son, it'll pass over,' Walter said. 'They get that way in the first months. You know…a bit erratic. It gets better.'

Jake stared at him. 'What do you mean?'

'When a woman's expecting she—'

Jake put up his hand. 'Whoa. I don't know where you're going with this, Walter. Expecting? Not Eliza. She…she can't have children.' And Eliza certainly didn't *look* pregnant in that gorgeous black dress.

'Consider me wrong, then. But I've had six kids and twice as many grandkids.' Walter patted his rather large nose with his index finger. 'I've got an instinct for when a woman's expecting. Sometimes I've known before she was even aware herself. I'd put money on it that your little lady is in the family way. I'm sorry for jumping the gun if she hasn't told you yet.'

Reeling, Jake managed to change the subject. But Walter's words kept dripping through his mind like the most corrosive of acids.

Had she tricked him? His fists clenched by his sides. Eliza? A scheming gold-digger? Trying to trap him with the oldest trick in the book? She had sounded so convincing when she'd told him about the burst appendix and her subsequent infertility. Was it all a lie? If so, what else had she lied about?

He felt as if everything he'd believed in was falling away from him.

Then he was hit by another, equally distressing thought. If she wasn't pregnant, was she ill?

One thing was for sure—she was hiding something from him. And he wouldn't be flying back to Brisbane until he found out what it was.

CHAPTER TEN

JAKE USUALLY NEVER had trouble sleeping. But late on the night of the launch party, back in his waterfront apartment, he tossed and turned. The place was luxurious, but lonely. He'd had high hopes of bringing Eliza back here this evening. To talk, to try and come to some arrangement so he could see more of her. If they'd ended up in bed that would have been good too. He hadn't been with anyone else since her. Had recoiled from kissing the women he'd dated.

Thoughts of his disastrous encounter with her kept him awake for what seemed like most of the night. And then there was Walter's observation to nag at him. Finally, at dawn, he gave up on sleep and went for a run. Vigorous physical activity helped his thought processes, he'd always found.

In the chill of early morning he ran up past the imposing Victorian buildings of the New South Wales Art Gallery and through the public green space of The Domain.

He paused to do some stretches at the end of the peninsula at Mrs Macquarie's Chair—a bench cut into a sandstone slab where it was reputed a homesick early governor's wife had used to sit and watch for sailing ships coming from Great Britain. The peaceful spot gave a panoramic view of Sydney Harbour: the 'coat hanger' bridge and the white sails of the Opera House. Stray clouds drifting around the buildings were tinted pink from the rising sun.

Jake liked Sydney and thought he could happily live in this city. Brisbane seemed all about the past. In fact he was thinking about moving his company's headquarters here. He had wanted to talk to Eliza about that, to put forward the idea that such a move would mean he'd be able to see more of her if they started things up between them again. Not much point now.

The pragmatic businessman side of Jake told him to wipe his hands of her and walk away. Eliza had made it very clear she didn't want him around. A man who had graduated from a dating after divorce workshop would know to take it on the chin, cut his losses and move on. After all, they'd only been together for four days, three months ago.

But the more creative, intuitive side of him, which had guided him through decisions that had made him multiple millions, wouldn't let him off that easily. Even if she'd lied to him, tricked him, deceived him—and that was only a suspicion at this stage—he had a strong feeling that she needed him. And he needed to find out what was going on.

He'd never got a chance to chat with her again at the party—she had evaded him and he'd had official duties to perform. But he'd cancelled his flight back to Brisbane, determined to confront her today.

Jake ran back home, showered, changed, ate breakfast. Predictably, Eliza didn't reply to his text and her phone went to voicemail. He called the Party Queens headquarters to be told Eliza was working at home today. Okay, so he would visit her at home—and soon.

He hadn't been to Eliza's house before, but he knew where it was. Investment-wise, she'd been canny. She'd bought a worker's terraced cottage in an industrial area of the inner city just before a major push to its gentrification. The little house, attached on both sides, looked immaculately restored and maintained. Exactly what he'd expect from Eliza.

It sat on one level, with a dormer window in the roof, indicating that she had probably converted the attic. External walls were painted the colour of natural sandstone, with windows and woodwork picked out in white and shades of grey. The tiny front garden was closed off from the sidewalk by a black wrought-iron fence and a low, perfectly clipped hedge.

Jake pushed open the shiny black gate and followed the black-and-white-tiled path. He smiled at the sight of the front door, painted a bold glossy red to match the large red planter containing a spiky-leaved plant. Using the quaint pewter knocker shaped like a dragonfly, he rapped on the door.

He heard footsteps he recognised as Eliza's approaching the door. They paused while, he assumed, she checked out her visitor through the peephole. Good. He was glad she was cautious about opening her door to strangers.

The pause went on for rather too long. Was she going to ignore him? He would stay here all day if he had to. He went to rap again but, with his hand still on its knocker, the door opened and she was there.

Jake didn't often find himself disconcerted to the

point of speechlessness. But he was too shocked to greet her.

This was an Eliza he hadn't seen before: hair dishevelled, face pale and strained with smudges of last night's make-up under her eyes. But what shocked him most was her body. Dark grey yoga pants and a snug pale grey top did nothing to disguise the small but definite baby bump. Her belly was swollen and rounded.

Eliza's shoulders slumped, and when she looked up at him her eyes seemed weary and dulled by defeat. In colour more denim than sapphire.

She took a deep breath and the rising of her chest showed him that her breasts were larger too. The dress she'd worn the previous night had hidden everything.

'Yes, I'm pregnant. Yes, it's yours. No, I won't be making any claims on you.'

Jake didn't mean to blurt out his doubt so baldly, but out it came. 'I thought you couldn't conceive.'

'So did I. That I'm expecting a baby came as a total surprise.' She gestured for him to follow her. 'Come in. Please. This isn't the kind of conversation I want to have in the street.'

The cottage had been gutted and redesigned into an open usable space, all polished floors and white walls. It opened out through a living area, delineated by carefully placed furniture, to a kitchen and eating area. Two black cats lay curled asleep on a bean bag, oblivious to the fact that Eliza had company. At the back, through a wall of folding glass doors, he saw a small courtyard with paving and greenery. A staircase—more sculpture than steps—led up to another floor. The house was furnished in a simple contemporary style, with carefully placed paintings and ornaments that at another time Jake might have paused to examine.

'I need to sit down,' Eliza said, lowering herself onto the modular sofa, pushing a cushion behind her back, sighing her relief.

'Are you okay?' Jake asked, unable to keep the concern from his voice. A sudden urge to protect her pulsed through him. But it was as if there was an invisible barrier flashing *Don't Touch* around her. The dynamic between them was so different it was as if they were strangers again. He hated the feeling. Somehow he'd lost any connection he'd had with her, without realising how or why.

She gave that same ineffectual wave she'd made the night before. It was as if she were operating at half-speed—like an appliance running low on battery. 'Sit down. Please. You towering over me is making me feel dizzy.'

She placed her hand on her bump in a protective gesture he found both alien and strangely moving.

He sat down on the sofa opposite her. 'Morning sickness?' he asked warily. He wasn't sure how much detail he'd get in reply. And he was squeamish about illness and female things—very squeamish.

'I wish,' she said. 'It's non-stop nausea like I couldn't have imagined. All day. All night.' She closed her eyes for a moment and shook her head before opening them again. 'I feel utterly drained.'

Jake frowned. 'That doesn't sound right. Have you seen your doctor?'

'She says some women suffer more than others and nausea is a normal part of pregnancy. Though it's got much worse since I last saw the doctor.' She grimaced.

'But it's worth it. Anything is worth it. I never thought I could have a baby.'

'So what happened? I mean, how—?'

She linked her hands together on her lap. 'I can see doubt in your eyes, Jake. I didn't lie to you. I genuinely believed I was infertile. Sterile. Barren. All those things my ex called me, as if it was my fault. But I'm not going to pretend I'm anything but thrilled to be having this baby. I… I don't expect you to be.'

Jake had believed in Eliza's honesty and integrity. She had sounded so convincing when she'd told him about her ruptured appendix and the damage it had caused. Her personal tragedy. And yet suddenly she was pregnant. Could a man be blamed for wanting an explanation?

'So what happened to allow—?' He couldn't find a word that didn't sound either clinical or uncomfortably personal.

'My doctor described it as a miracle. Said that a microscopic-sized channel clear in a sea of scar tissue must have enabled it to happen. I can hardly believe it myself.' A hint of a wan smile tilted the corners of her mouth. 'Though the nausea never allows me to forget.'

'Are you sure—?'

She leaned forward. 'Sure I'm pregnant? Absolutely. Up until my tummy popped out it was hard to believe.' She stilled. Pressed her lips together so hard they became colourless. 'You didn't mean that, did you? You meant am I sure the baby is yours.'

Her eyes clouded with hurt. Jake knew he had said inextricably the wrong thing. Though it seemed reasonable for him to want to be sure. He *still* thought it was reasonable to ask. They'd had a four-day fling and he hadn't heard a word from her since.

'I didn't mean—'

Her face crumpled. 'Yes, you did. For the record, I'll tell you there was no one else. There had been no one else for a long time and has been no one since. But feel free to ask for a DNA test if you want proof.'

He moved towards her. 'Eliza, I—'

Abruptly she got up from the sofa. Backed away from him. 'Don't come near me. Don't touch me. Don't quote your dating after divorce handbook that no doubt instructs you about the first question to ask of a scheming gold-digger trying to trap you.'

'Eliza, I'm sorry. I—'

She shrugged with a nonchalance he knew was an absolute sham.

'You didn't know me well at Port Douglas,' she said. 'I could have bedded a hundred guys over the crucial time for conception for all you knew. It's probably a question many men would feel justified in asking under the circumstances. But not *you* of *me*. Not after I'd been straightforward with you. Not when we have close friends in common. A relationship might not have worked for us. But I thought there was mutual respect.'

'There was. There is. Of course you're upset. Let me—'

'I'm not *upset*. I'm *disappointed*, if anything. Disappointed in *you*. Again, for the record, I will not ask anything of you. Not money. Not support. Certainly not your name on the birth certificate. I am quite capable of doing this on my own. *Happy* to do this on my own. I have it all planned and completely under control. You can just walk out that door and forget you ever knew me.'

Jake had no intention of leaving. If indeed this baby was his—and he had no real reason to doubt her—he would not evade his responsibilities. But before he had a chance to say anything further Eliza groaned.

'Oh, no. Not again.'

She slapped her hand over her mouth, pushed past him and ran towards the end of the house and, he assumed, the bathroom.

He waited for what seemed like a long time for her to do what she so obviously had to do. Until it began to seem too long. Worried, he strode through the living room to find her. That nagging sense that she needed him grew until it consumed him.

'Eliza! Answer me!' he called, his voice raw with urgency.

'I… I'm okay.' Her voice, half its usual volume, half its usual clarity, came from behind a door to his left.

The door slowly opened. Eliza put one foot in front of the other in an exaggerated way to walk unsteadily out. She clutched the doorframe for support.

Jake sucked in a breath of shock at how ashen and weak she looked. Beads of perspiration stood out on her forehead. He might not be a doctor, but every instinct told him this was not right. 'Eliza. Let me help you.'

'You…you're still here?' she said. 'I told you to leave.'

'I'm not going anywhere.'

'There…there's blood.' Her voice caught. 'There shouldn't be blood. I… I don't know what to do. Can you call Andie for me, please?'

Jake felt gutted that he was right there and yet not the first person she'd sought to help her.

She wanted him gone.

No way was he leaving her.

He took her elbow to steady her. She leaned into him and he was stunned at how thin she'd become since he'd last held her in his arms. Pregnant women were meant to put *on* weight, not lose it. *Something was very wrong.*

Fear grabbed his gut. He mustn't let her sense it. Panic would make it worse. She felt so fragile, as if she might break if he held her too hard. Gently he lifted her and carried her to a nearby chair. She moaned as he settled her into it.

She cradled her head in her hands. 'Headache. Now I've got a headache.' Her voice broke into a sob.

Jake realised she was as terrified as he was. He pulled out his phone.

'Call Andie…' Her voice trailed away as she slumped into the chair.

He supported her with his body as he started to punch out a number with fingers that shook. 'I'm not calling Andie. I'm calling an ambulance,' he said, his voice rough with fear.

CHAPTER ELEVEN

WHEN ELIZA WOKE up in a hospital bed later that day, the first thing she saw was Jake sprawled in a chair near her bed. He was way too tall for the small chair and his long, blue-jeans-clad legs were flung out in front of him. His head was tilted back, his eyes closed. His hair looked as if he'd combed it through with his hands and his black T-shirt was crumpled.

She gazed at him for a long moment. Had a man ever looked so good? Her heart seemed to skip a beat. Last time she had seen him asleep he had been beside her in his bed at Port Douglas on Day Three. She had awoken him with a trail of hungry little kisses that had delighted him. Now here he was in a visitor's chair in a hospital room. She was pregnant and he had doubts that the baby was his. How had it come to this?

Eliza had only vague memories of the ambulance trip to the hospital. She'd been drifting in and out of consciousness. What she did remember was Jake by her side. Holding her hand the entire time. Murmuring a constant litany of reassurance. *Being there for her.*

She shifted in the bed. A tube had been inserted in the back of her left hand and she was attached to a drip. Automatically her hand went to her tummy. She was still getting used to the new curve where it had always been flat.

Jake opened his eyes, sat forward in his chair. 'You're awake.' His voice was underscored with relief.

'So are you. I thought you were asleep.' Her voice felt croaky, her throat a little sore.

He got up and stood by her bed, looked down to where her hand remained on her tummy. The concern on his face seemed very real.

'I don't know what you remember about this morning,' he said. 'But the baby is okay. *You're* okay.'

'I remember the doctor telling me. Thank heaven. And seeing the ultrasound. I couldn't have borne it if—'

'You'd ruptured a blood vessel. The baby was never at risk.'

She closed her eyes, opened them again. 'I felt so dreadful. I thought I must be dying. And I was so worried for the baby.'

'Severe dehydration was the problem,' he said.

She felt at a disadvantage, with him towering so tall above her. 'I can see how that happened. I hadn't even been able to keep water down. The nausea was so overwhelming. It's still there, but nothing like as bad.'

'Not your everyday morning sickness, according to your doctor here. An extreme form known as *Hyperemesis gravidarum.* Same thing that put the Duchess of Cambridge in hospital with her pregnancies, so a nurse told me.'

He sounded both knowledgeable and concerned. Jake here with her? The billionaire bachelor acting nurse? How had this happened?

'A lot of the day is a blur,' she said. 'But I remember the doctor telling me that. No wonder I felt so bad.'

'You picked up once the doctors got you on intravenous fluids.'

She raised her left wrist and looked up at the clear plastic bag hooked over a stand above. 'I'm still on them, by the looks of it.'

'You have to stay on the drip for twenty-four hours. They said you need vitamins and nutrients as well as fluids.'

Eliza reeled at the thought of Jake conversing with the doctors, discussing her care. It seemed surreal that he should be here, like this. 'How do you know all this? In fact, how come you're in my room?' Eliza didn't want to sound ungrateful. But she had asked him to leave her house. Though it was just as well he hadn't, as it had turned out.

'I admitted you to the hospital. They asked about my relationship to you. I told them I was your partner and the father of the baby. On those terms, it's quite okay for me to be in your room.'

'Oh,' she said. She slumped back on the pillows. Their conversation of this morning came flooding back. How devastated she'd felt when he'd asked if she sure he was the father. 'Even though you don't actually think the baby is yours?' she said dully.

He set his jaw. 'I never said that. I believed you couldn't get pregnant. You brushed me off at the party. Didn't tell me anything—refused to see me. Then I discovered you were pregnant. It's reasonable I would have been confused as to the truth. Would want to be sure.'

'Perhaps,' she conceded.

It hurt that his first reaction had been distrust. But she had no right to feel a sense of betrayal—they'd had a no-strings fling. They'd been lovers with no commitment whatsoever. And he was a man who had made it very clear he never wanted children.

'I believe you when you say the baby is mine, Eliza. It's unexpected. A shock. But I have no reason to doubt you.'

Eliza was so relieved at his words she didn't know what to say and had to think about her response. 'I swear you *are* the father. I would never deceive you about something so important.'

'Even about the hundred other men?' he said, with a hint of a smile for the first time.

She managed a tentative smile in return. 'There was only ever you.'

'I believe you,' he said.

'You don't want DNA testing to be certain? Because I—'

'No,' he said. 'Your word is enough.'

Eliza nodded, too overcome to say anything. She knew how he felt about mercenary gold-diggers. But the sincerity in his eyes assured her that he no longer put her in that category. If, indeed, he ever had. Perhaps she had been over-sensitive. But that didn't change the fact that he didn't want to be a father.

'I don't want to be a father—ever.'

How different this could have been in a different universe—where they were a couple, had planned the child, met the result of her pregnancy test with mutual joy. But that was as much a fantasy as those frozen in time moments of him whirling her around in a waltz, when the future had still been full of possibilities for Eliza and Jake.

Now here he was by her bedside, acting the concerned friend. She shouldn't read anything else into his care of her. Jake had only done for her what he would have done for any other woman he'd found ill and alone.

Eliza felt a physical ache at how much she still wanted him. She wondered—not for the first time—if she would *ever* be able to turn off her attraction to him. But physical attraction wasn't enough—no matter how good the sex. A domineering workaholic, hardly ever in the same country as her, was scarcely the man she would have chosen as the father of her child. Though his genes were good.

'Thank you for calling the ambulance and checking me in to the hospital,' she said. 'And thank you for staying with me. But can I ask you one more thing, please?' *Before we say goodbye.*

'Of course,' he said.

'Can you ask the hospital staff to fix their mistake with my room?' She looked around her. The room was more like a luxurious hotel suite than a hospital room. 'I'm not insured for a private room. They'll need to move me to a shared ward.'

'There's been no mistake,' he said. 'I've taken responsibility for paying your account.'

Eliza stared at him. '*What?* You can't do that,' she said.

'As far as the hospital is concerned I am the baby's father. I pay the bills.'

Eliza gasped. This wasn't right. She needed to keep control over her pregnancy and everything involved with it. 'That was a nice gesture, but I can't possibly accept your offer,' she said.

'You don't have a choice,' he said. 'It's already done.'

Eliza had never felt more helpless, lying in a hospital bed tied up to a drip and monitors. It wasn't a feeling she was used to. 'Jake, please don't make me argue over this.' She was feeling less nauseous, but she'd been told she had to avoid stress and worry as well as keep up fluids and nourishment. 'What happened to you keeping your credit cards in your wallet when it comes to me?'

'You can't have it both ways, Eliza. You want me to acknowledge paternity? That means I take financial responsibility for your care. It's not negotiable.'

This was the controlling side of Jake that had made her wary of him for more than a no-strings fling. 'You don't make decisions for me, Jake. I will not—'

At that moment a nurse came into the room to check on Eliza's drip and to take her temperature and blood pressure. Jake stepped back from the bed and leaned against the wall to let the nurse get on with what she needed to do.

'She's looking so much better now than when you brought her in,' the nurse said.

'Thankfully,' said Jake. 'I was very worried about her.'

Eliza fumed. The nurse was addressing Jake and talking about her as if she was some inanimate object. 'Yes, I *am* feeling much better,' she said pointedly to the nurse. But Jake's smile let her know he knew exactly what was going on—and found it amusing. Which only made Eliza fume more.

'That's what we want to hear,' said the nurse with

a cheerful smile, seemingly oblivious to the undercurrents.

She was no doubt well meaning, but Eliza felt she had to assert herself. It was *her* health. *Her* baby. Under *her* control. 'When can I go home?' Eliza asked.

The nurse checked her chart. 'You have to be on the intravenous drip for a total of twenty-four hours.'

'So I can go home tomorrow morning?'

'If the doctor assesses you as fit to be discharged. Of course you can't leave by yourself, and there has to be someone at home to care for you.'

'That's okay,' said Jake, before Eliza could say anything. 'I'll be taking her home and looking after her.'

The nurse smiled. 'That's settled, then.'

'No, it's not. I—' Eliza protested.

'Thank you,' said Jake to the nurse.

Eliza waited until the nurse had left the room. 'What was that about?' she hissed.

Jake moved back beside her bed. 'I'll be picking you up when you're discharged from hospital tomorrow. We can talk about whether you'd like me to stay with you for a few days or whether I organise a nurse.'

She had to tilt her head back to confront him. 'Or how about I look after myself?' she said.

'That's not an option,' said Jake. 'Unless you want to stay longer in hospital. *Hyperemesis gravidarum* is serious. You have to keep the nausea under control and get enough nourishment for both your health and your baby's sake. You know all this. The doctor has told you that you're still weak.'

'That doesn't mean *you* have to take over, Jake.' Eliza felt she was losing control of the situation and she didn't like it one bit. At the same time she didn't want to do anything to risk harming the baby.

'You have another choice,' he said. 'You could move in with Andie. She's offered to have you to stay with her and Dominic.'

'You've spoken to Andie? But she doesn't know—'

'That you're pregnant? She does now. You asked me to call her this morning. So I did while you were asleep.'

'What did she say?' Andie would not appreciate being left out of the loop.

'She was shocked to find out you and I had had an affair and you'd kept it from her. And more than a little hurt that you didn't take her into your confidence about your pregnancy.'

'I would have, but I didn't want her telling…'

'Telling me?'

'That's right.'

'If I'd flown back to Brisbane this morning instead of coming to see you would you have *ever* told me?' His mouth was set in a grim line.

'I wasn't thinking that far ahead. I just didn't want you to think I was trying to trap you into something you didn't want. You were so vehement about gold-diggers. I… I couldn't bear the thought of seeing disgust in your eyes when you looked at me.'

'You will *never* see disgust in my eyes when it comes to you, Eliza,' he said. 'Disbelief that you would try to hide this from me, but not disgust. We have mutual friends. I would have heard sooner or later.'

'I would rather it had been later. I didn't want you trying to talk me out of it.'

The look of shock on his face told her she might have said the wrong thing.

'I would never have done that,' he said.

She realised how out-of-the-blue her situation had been for him. And how well he was handling it.

'I wasn't to know,' she said. 'After all, we hardly know each other.'

For a long moment Jake looked into her face—searching for what she didn't know.

Finally he spoke. 'That's true. But there should be no antagonism between us. Here isn't the time or the place to discuss how we'll deal with the situation on an ongoing basis.' He glanced down at his watch. 'Andie will be here to visit you soon. I'm going to go. I'll see you in the morning.'

Eliza's feelings were all over the place. She didn't know whether she could blame hormones for the tumult of her emotions. No way did she want Jake—or any other man—controlling her, telling her what to do with her life. But she had felt so safe and comforted with him by her side today. Because while her pregnancy had changed the focus of everything, it didn't change the attraction she'd felt for Jake from the get-go. He had been wonderful to her today. She wished she could beg him to stay.

'Before you leave, let me thank you again for your help today, Jake. I can't tell you how much I appreciate you being with me.'

'You're welcome,' he said. 'I'm just glad you're okay. And so glad I called by to your house this morning.'

She sat up straighter in an attempt to bring him closer. Put out her hand and placed it on his arm. 'I'm sorry,' she said. 'Not sorry about the baby—my miracle baby. But sorry our carefree fling had such consequences and that we've been flung back together again in such an awkward situation.'

'No need to apologise for that,' he said gruffly.

Jake kept up the brave front until he was out of the hospital and on the pavement. He felt totally strung out from the events of the last day. Everything had happened so quickly. He needed time to think it through and process it.

Thank heaven he hadn't encountered Andie on the way out. He'd liked Andie from the moment Dominic had first introduced him to her, on the day of their surprise wedding. Each time he met his friend's wife he liked her more. Not in a romantic way—although she was undoubtedly gorgeous. He liked the way Andie made his best friend so happy after the rotten hand life had dealt Dominic when it came to love. If Jake had had a sister, he would have wanted her to be just like Andie.

But Andie told it how it was. And Eliza was her dearest friend, whom she would defend with every weapon at hand. Jake wouldn't have appreciated a face-to-face confrontation with her on the steps of the hospital. Not when he was feeling so on edge. Not after the conversation he'd already had with her on the phone.

When he'd called to tell her Eliza was in hospital Andie been shocked to hear the reason. Shocked and yet thrilled for Eliza, as she knew how much her friend had wanted to have children but had thought she couldn't conceive.

'This is a miracle for her!' Andie had exclaimed, and had promptly started to sob on the phone. Which had been further proof—not that he'd needed it—that Eliza had not been lying. Then, in true sisterly fashion, Andie had hit Jake with some advice. Advice he hadn't thought he'd needed but he'd shut up and listened.

'Don't you hurt her, Jake,' she'd said, her voice still thick with tears. 'I had no idea you two had had a…a thing. Eliza is Party Queens family. *You're* family. She thinks she's so strong and independent, but this pregnancy will make her vulnerable. She's not some casual hook-up girl. You can't just write a cheque and walk away.'

'It's not like that—' he'd started to protest. But the harsh truth of it, put into words, had hit him like blows to the gut.

Eliza was connected to his life through his best friends, Dominic and Tristan, and their wives. He could argue all he liked that their fling had been a mutually convenient scratching of the itch of their attraction. But that sounded so disrespectful to Eliza. In his heart he knew he'd wanted much more time with her. Which was why he had been considering a move to Sydney. But Eliza's pregnancy had put everything on a very different footing.

Andie had continued. 'Oh, what the heck? This is none of my business. You're a big boy. *You* figure out what Eliza needs. And give it to her in spades.'

Jake was beginning to see what Eliza needed. And also what *he* needed. He'd never been so scared than when she'd passed out on the chair while they were waiting for the ambulance to arrive. In a moment of stricken terror he'd thought he was going to lose her. And it had hit him with the power of a sledgehammer hurtling towards his head how much she had come to mean to him—as a friend as well as a lover. Suddenly a life without Eliza in it in some way had become untenable.

But the phone call with Andie wasn't what had him still staggering, as if that sledgehammer really had connected. It was the baby.

First he'd been hit with the reality of absorbing the fact that Eliza was expecting a baby—and the realisation that it had irrevocably changed things between them. Then he'd been stricken by seeing Eliza so frighteningly ill. But all that had been eclipsed by the events at the hospital.

Once the medical team had stabilised Eliza with fluids—she'd been conscious enough to refuse any anti-nausea medication—they'd wheeled her down, with him in attendance, to have an ultrasound to check that all was well with her developing foetus.

The technician had covered Eliza's bump with a jelly—cold, and it had made her squeal—and then pressed an electronic wand over her bump. The device had emitted high-frequency soundwaves that had formed an image when they'd come into contact with the embryo.

Up until the moment when the screen had come alive with the image, the pregnancy had been an abstract thing to Jake. Even—if he were to be really honest with himself—an *inconvenient* thing. But there on the screen had appeared a *baby*. Only about six centimetres at this stage, the radiographer had explained, but a totally recognisable baby. With hands and feet and a *face*.

To the palpable relief of everyone in the room, a strong and steady amplified heartbeat had been clearly audible. The baby had been moving around and showing no signs of being affected by Eliza's inability to keep down so very little food over the last weeks. It had looked as if it was having a ball, floating in the amniotic fluid, secure in Eliza's womb.

Jake had felt as if his heart had stopped beating, and his lungs had gone into arrest as, mesmerised, he'd watched that image. He was a man who never cried but he'd felt tears of awe and amazement threatening to betray him. He hadn't been able to look at Eliza—the sheer joy shining from her face would have tipped him over. Without seeming to be aware she was doing it, she had reached for his hand and gripped it hard. All he'd been able to do was squeeze it back.

This was a real baby. A child. A *person*. Against all odds he and Eliza had created a new life.

What he had to do had become very clear.

CHAPTER TWELVE

THE NEXT DAY Eliza was surprised at how weak she still felt as Jake helped her up the narrow, steep stairs to her bedroom in the converted attic of her house. She usually bounded up them.

'Just lean on me,' he said.

'I don't want to lean on anyone,' she said, more crossly than she had intended.

Forcing herself to keep her distance from this gorgeous man was stressful. Even feeling weak and fatigued, she still fancied him like crazy. But way back in Port Douglas she'd already decided that wasn't enough. Just because she was pregnant it didn't change things.

'Sometimes you have to, Eliza.'

She knew he wasn't only referring to her taking the physical support his broad shoulders offered.

'You can't get through this on your own.'

There was an edge of impatience to his voice she hadn't heard before. Looking after her the way he'd done yesterday, and now today, wasn't part of their four-day fling agreement. That had been about uncomplicated fun and uninhibited sex. Now he must feel he was stuck with her when she was unwell. He couldn't be more wrong. She didn't need his help.

'I appreciate your concern, truly I do,' she said. 'You've been so good to me. But I'm not on my own. I have friends. My GP is only a block away. I spoke to her yesterday after you left the hospital. Both she and the practice nurse can make home visits if required.'

'You need to be looked after,' he said stubbornly.

Eliza's heart sank as she foresaw them clashing over this. She had been perturbed at how Jake had taken over her vacation—how much more perturbing was the thought that he might take over her life?

Eliza reached the top of the stairs. Took the few steps required to take her to her bed and sat down on the edge with a sigh of relief.

'I'd prefer to look after myself,' she said. 'I'm quite capable of it, you know.'

'It didn't look that way to me yesterday.' He swore under his breath. 'Eliza, what might have happened if I hadn't got here when I did? What if you'd passed out on the bathroom floor? Hit your head on the way down?'

She paused for a long moment. 'It's a very scary thought. I will never be able to thank you enough for being there for me, Jake. Why *did* you come to my house when you did?'

'The obvious. I didn't get why you blanked me at the party and I wanted an explanation.'

Her chin lifted. 'Why did you feel you were owed an explanation? We had a fling. I didn't want to pick up from where we left off. Enough said.'

'Now you're pregnant. That makes it very different. From where I stand, it doesn't seem like you're doing a very good job of looking after yourself.'

Her hackles rose. 'This is all very new to me. It's a steep learning curve.' Eliza took a deep, calming breath. She couldn't let herself get too defensive. Not when Jake had pretty much had to pick her up from the floor.

'There's a lot at stake if you don't learn more quickly,' he said.

She gritted her teeth. 'Don't you think I *know* that? While I was lying there in that hospital bed I kept wondering how I had let myself get into that state.'

'I suspect you thought the sickness was a natural part of pregnancy. That you had to put up with the nausea. Perhaps if you'd told your friends you were pregnant they might have seen what you were going through wasn't normal and that you were headed into a danger zone.'

Eliza wasn't sure whether he was being sympathetic or delivering a reprimand. 'When did you get to know so much?' she said, deciding to err on the side of offered sympathy. The direction of where this conversation was beginning to go scared her. It almost sounded as though it might lead into an accusation that she was an incompetent mother—before she'd even give birth.

'Since yesterday, when the hospital doctor explained it,' he said with a shrug of his broad shoulders. 'I learned more than I ever thought I'd need to know about that particular complication.'

How many men would have just dropped her at the hospital and run? She was grateful to Jake—but she did *not* want him to take over.

'I've learned a lot too,' she said. 'If I keep on top of the nausea, and don't let myself get dehydrated, that shouldn't happen again. I admit this has given me a real shock. I had no reason to think I wouldn't fly through pregnancy with my usual good health. But the doctors have given me strategies to deal with it. Including more time in the hospital on a drip if required. I'll be okay.'

He shook his head. 'I wish I could believe that. But I suspect you'll be back at Party Queens, dragging a drip on its stand along behind you, before you know it.'

That forced a reluctant smile from her. But he wasn't smiling and her smile quickly faded. He was spot-on in his assessment of her workaholic tendencies. Though she didn't appreciate his lack of faith in her ability to look after herself.

'Jake, trust me—I won't over-extend myself. Miracles don't come along too often in a person's life.' She placed her hand protectively on her bump. 'Truth is, this is almost certainly my only chance to have a baby. I won't jeopardise anything by being foolish. Believe me—if I need help, I'll ask for it.'

Asking for help didn't come easily to her. Because with accepting help came loss of control. One of her biggest issues in management training had been learning to delegate. Now it looked as if she might have to learn to give over a degree of control in her private life too. To doctors, nurses, other health professionals. Because she had to consider her baby as well as herself. But she would not give control over to a man.

For a converted attic in a small house, the bedroom was spacious, with an en suite shower room and a study nook as well as sleeping quarters. But Jake was so tall, so broad-shouldered, he made the space seem suddenly cramped.

How she wished things could be different. Despite all that had happened desire shimmered through her when she feasted her eyes on him, impossibly handsome in black jeans and a black T-shirt. Jake, here in her bedroom, was looking totally smokin'.

Then there was her—with lank hair, yesterday's clothes, a big wad of sterile gauze taped to the back of her hand where the drip had been, and a plastic hospital ID band still around her wrist. Oh, and pregnant.

Jake paced the length of the room and back several times, to the point when Eliza started to get nervous without really knowing why. He stood in front of the window for a long moment with his back to her. Then pivoted on his heel to turn back to face her.

'We have to get married,' he said, without preamble.

Eliza's mouth went dry and her heart started to thud. She was so shocked all she could do was stare up at him. '*What?*' she finally managed to choke out. 'Where did *that* come from?' She pulled herself up from the bed to face him, though her shaky knees told her she really should stay seated.

'You're pregnant. It's the right thing to do.'

He looked over her head rather than directly at her. There was no light in his eyes, no anticipation—nothing of the expression she might expect from a man proposing marriage.

'Get married because I'm pregnant?'

She knew she was just repeating his statement but she needed time to think.

'We have to get married,' he'd commanded. There had been no joy, no feeling, certainly no talk of love—and that hurt more than it should have. Not that *love* had ever come into their relationship. Worse, there had been no consultation with her. She'd rank it more as a demand than a proposal. And demands didn't sit well with her.

What would she have done if he had actually proposed? With words of affection and hope? She couldn't think about that. That had never been part of their agreement.

'You being pregnant is reason enough,' he said.

'No, it isn't. You know I don't want to marry again. Even if I did, we don't know each other well enough to consider such a big step.'

The irony of it didn't escape her. They knew each other well enough to make a baby. Not well enough to spend their lives together.

She shook her head. 'I can't do it, Jake.'

The first time she'd married for love—or what she'd thought was love—and it had been a disaster. Why would marrying for less than love be any better? Marrying someone she'd known for such a short time? An even shorter time than she'd known her ex.

'Your pregnancy changes everything,' Jake said. His face was set in severe lines.

'It does. But not in that way.'

'You're having a baby. *My* baby. I want to marry you.'

'Why? For my reputation? Because of the media?'

There was a long pause before he spoke. 'To give the baby a father,' he said. 'The baby deserves to have two parents.'

That was the last reason she would have anticipated from him and it took her aback for a moment. She put her hand to her heart to try and slow its sudden racing. 'Jake, that's honourable of you. But it's not necessary for you to marry me. If you want to be involved with the baby I'm happy—'

'I want the baby to have my name,' he said. 'And a good life.'

'*I* can give him or her a good life. You don't have to do this. We knew marriage wasn't an option for us.'

'It's important to me, Eliza.'

She noticed his fists, clenched by his sides. The tension in his voice. There was something more here—something that belied the straightforwardness of his words.

'You married your ex-wife because she was pregnant,' she said. 'I don't expect that. Really I don't. Please stop pacing the room like a caged lion.'

Her knees felt suddenly too weak to support her. She wanted to collapse back onto the bed. Instead she sat down slowly, controlled, suddenly fearing to show any weakness. Jake was a man used to getting what he wanted. Now it seemed he wanted *her*. Correction. He wanted her for the baby she was carrying. *His baby.*

'Why, Jake? You said you never wanted to be a father. Why this sudden interest?'

Jake sat down on the bed beside her, as far away from her as he could without colliding with the bedhead. He braced both hands on his knees. Overlying Eliza's nervousness was a pang of mingled longing and regret. Back in Port Douglas they wouldn't have been sitting side by side on a bed, being careful not to touch. They would have been making love by now, lost in a breathtaking world of intimacy and mutual pleasure. *Lovemaking that had created a miracle baby.*

'Seeing the baby on the ultrasound affected me yesterday,' he said now. 'The pregnancy which, up until then had been an abstract thing, became very real for me.'

Eliza noticed how weary he looked, with shadows

under his eyes, lines she hadn't noticed before etched by his mouth. She wondered how much sleep he'd had last night. Had he been awake half the night, wrangling with the dilemma she had presented him with by unexpectedly bearing his baby?

'It affected me too.'

She remembered she had been so overcome that she had gripped his hand—so tightly it must have hurt him. Then she had intercepted a smiling glance from the nurse. She and Jake must have looked quite the proud parents-to-be. If only that sweet nurse had known the less than romantic truth.

'You didn't see a scan when your ex—Fern—was pregnant?' she asked Jake.

'She didn't believe in medical intervention of any kind.'

'But an ultrasound isn't like an X-ray. It's safe and—'

'I know that. But that's beside the point. The point is I saw a little person yesterday. A tiny baby who is going to grow up to be a boy, like I was, or a girl like you were. We didn't plan it. We didn't want—'

She put up a hand in a halt sign, noticed her hand wasn't quite steady. 'Stop right there. You mightn't want it—I mean him or her… I hate calling my baby "it"—but I *do* want him or her. Very much.'

'I'm aware of how much you want the baby. Of the tragedy it was for you to discover you couldn't conceive. But the fact is I didn't want children. I would never have chosen to embark on a pregnancy with you. You know that.'

His words stung. Not just because of his rejection of her but because of her baby, unwanted by its father. No way would she have chosen a man she scarcely knew—a man who didn't want kids—as the father of her baby.

'I know we had a deal for four days of no-strings fun,' she said. 'Mother Nature had other ideas. Trust me—I wouldn't have *chosen* to have a child this way either.'

He indicated her bump. 'This is no longer just about me or about you; it's about another person at the start of life. And it's *my* responsibility. This child deserves a better life than you can give it on your own.'

If that wasn't an insult from an arrogant billionaire, she didn't know what was.

She forced herself to sound calm and reasonable. 'Jake, I might not be as wealthy as you, but I can give my child a more than decent life, thank you very much. I'm hardly a pauper.'

'Don't delude yourself, Eliza. You can't give it anything *like* what I have the resources to provide.'

Perspiration beaded on her forehead and she had to clasp her hands to stop them from trembling. It wasn't just that she was still feeling weak. She had a sudden, horrible premonition that she was preparing to do battle for her own child.

So quickly this had turned adversarial. From a proposal to a stand-off. She couldn't help but think how different this would be if she and Jake were together on this. As together and in tune as they had been in bed. Instead they were sitting here, apart on the bed, glaring at each other—she the mother, he the inadvertent sperm donor who wanted to take things further than he had any right to do.

'I can—and will—give this child a good life on

my own,' she said. 'He or she will have everything they need.'

Jake was so wealthy. He could buy anything he wanted. What was he capable of doing if he wanted to take her child from her?

'Except its father's name,' he said.

Eliza was taken aback. She'd expected him to talk about private schooling, a mansion, travel, the best of everything as far as material goods went. Not the one intangible thing she could not provide.

'Is *that* what this is about?' she said. 'Some patriarchal thing?'

'What is that meant to mean?' He stared at her as if she'd suddenly sprouted horns. 'This is about making my child legitimate. Giving it its rightful place in the world.'

My child. How quickly he had claimed her baby as his own.

'Legitimate? What does *that* mean these days?' she asked.

He gave a short, sharp bark of laughter she'd never heard from him before. 'I went through hell as a kid because I was illegitimate. Life for a boy with no father was no fun at all.' His mouth set in a grim line.

'That was thirty years ago, Jake,' she said, trying not to sound combative about an issue that was obviously sensitive for him. 'Attitudes have changed now.'

'Have they really? I wonder… I walked the walk. Not just the bullying from the kids, but the sneering from the adults towards my mother, the insensitivity of the schoolteachers. Father's Day at school was the worst day of the year. The kids all making cards and gifts for their dads… Me with no one. I don't want to risk putting my child through what I went through.'

He traced the slight crookedness of his nose with his index finger. The imperfection only made him more handsome, Eliza had always thought.

'Surely it wasn't such a stigma then?' she asked.

He scowled. 'You have no idea, do you?' he said. 'Born into a family with a father who provided for you. Who gave you his name. His protection.'

Eliza felt this was spiralling away from her. Into something so much deeper than she'd realised. 'No, I don't. Have any idea, I mean.'

One of her first memories was of her father lifting her for the first time up onto a horse's back, with big, gentle hands. How proud he'd been of her fearlessness. No matter what had come afterwards, she had that. Other scenes of her father and her with their beloved horses jostled against the edges of her memory.

Jake's face was set into such grim lines he almost looked ugly. 'Every time I got called the B-word I had to answer the insult with my fists. My mother cried the first time I came home with a broken nose. She soon ran out of tears. Until the day I got big enough to deliver some broken noses of my own.'

Eliza shuddered at the aggression in his voice, but at the same time her heart went out to that little boy. 'I didn't realise how bad it was not to have a dad at home.'

'It's a huge, aching gap.'

His green eyes were clouded with a sadness that tore at her.

'Not one I want my own child to fall into.'

'Why wasn't your father around?'

'Because he was a selfish pig of a man who denied my existence. Is that a good enough answer?'

The bitterness in his voice shocked Eliza. She imagined a dear little boy, with a shock of blond hair and green eyes, suffering a pain more intense than that of any broken nose. She yearned to comfort him but didn't know what she could say about such a deep-seated hurt. At the same time she had to hold back on her feelings of sympathy when it came to Jake. She had to be on top of her game if Jake was going to get tough.

He sighed. Possibly he didn't realise the depth of anguish in that sigh.

She couldn't stop herself from placing her hand over his. 'I'm sorry, Jake. It was his loss.'

He nodded a silent acknowledgment.

Back in Port Douglas she had yearned for Jake to share his deeper side with her. Now she'd been tossed into its dark depths and she felt she was drowning in a sea of hurts and secrets, pulled every which way by conflicting currents. On top of her nausea, and her worries about handling life as a single mother, she wasn't sure she had the emotional fortitude to deal with this.

'Do you know anything about your father?'

About the man who was, she realised with a shock, her unborn child's grandfather. Jake's mother would be his or her grandmother. Through their son or daughter she and Jake would be connected for the rest of their lives—whether they wanted to be or not.

'It's a short, ugly story,' he said, his mouth a grim line. 'My mother was a trainee nurse at a big Brisbane training hospital. She was very pretty and very naïve. He was a brilliant, handsome doctor and she fell for him. She didn't know he was engaged to a girl from a wealthy family. He seduced her. She fell pregnant. He didn't want to know about it. She got booted out of her job in disgrace and slunk home to her parents at the Gold Coast.'

The father handsome, the mother pretty… Both obviously intelligent… For the first time a thought flashed through Eliza's head. Would the baby look like her or like Jake? Be as smart? It wasn't speculation she felt she could share with him.

'That's the end of it?' she said. 'What about child support?'

'Not a cent. He was tricky. My mother's family couldn't afford lawyers. She wanted nothing to do with him. Just to get on with her life. My grandparents helped raise me, though they didn't have much. It was a struggle.'

Poor little Jake. Imagine growing up with *that* as his heritage. Before the drought her parents had loved to tell the story of how they had met at an agricultural show—her dad competing in the Western riding, her mum winning ribbons for her scones and fruitcake. She wondered if they remembered it now. Would her child want to know how she and his or her dad had met? How would she explain why they weren't together?

'You never met him?' she asked.

'As a child, no.' Jake's mouth curled with contempt. 'But when media reports started appearing on the "young genius" who'd become a billionaire, he came sniffing around, looking for his long-lost son.'

'What did you do?'

'Kicked him to the kerb—like he'd sent my mother packing.'

Eliza shuddered at the strength of vengeful satisfaction in his voice. Jake would make a formidable enemy if crossed.

Jake got up from the bed. It was hard to think straight, sitting so close to Eliza She looked so wan and frail, somehow even more beautiful. Her usual sweet, floral scent had a sharp overtone of hospital from the bandage on her hand, which reminded him of what she had been through. He would never forget that terrifying moment when he'd thought she had stopped breathing.

He fought a powerful impulse to fold her in his arms and hold her close. She needed him, and yet he couldn't seem to make her see that. He wanted to look after her. Make sure she and the baby had everything they needed. If his own father had looked after his mother the way he wanted to look after Eliza, how different his life might have been. Yet he sensed a battle on his hands even to get access to his child.

He hadn't intended to confide in her about his father. Next thing he'd be spilling the details of his criminal record. Of his darkest day of despair when he'd thought he couldn't endure another minute of his crappy life. But he'd hoped telling her something of his past might make her more amenable to the idea of getting married to give their child a name.

'I'm asking you again to marry me, Eliza. Before the baby is born. So it—'

'Can you please not call the baby *it*? Try *he* or *she.* This is a little person we're talking about here. I thought you got that?'

He felt safer calling the baby *it.* Calling it *he* or *she* made it seem too real. And the more real it seemed, the more he would get attached. And he couldn't let himself get too attached if Eliza was going to keep the baby from him.

He didn't know a lot about custody arrangements for a child with single parents—though he suspected he was soon to know a whole lot more. But he doubted the courts were much inclined to give custody of a newborn to anyone other than its mother. No matter how much money he threw at the best possible legal representation. Once it got a little older that would be a different matter. His child would not grow up without a father the way he had.

'I want you to marry me before the baby is born so *he* or *she* is legitimate,' he said.

She glared at him. 'Jake, I've told you I don't want to get married. To you or to anyone else. And if I did it would be because I was in love with my husband-to-be.'

Jake gritted his teeth. He had married before for love and look where it had got him. 'That sounds very idealistic, Eliza. But there can be pragmatic reasons to marry, too. There have been throughout history. To secure alliances or fortunes. Or to gain property or close a business deal. Or to legitimise a child.'

Slowly she shook her head. A lock of her hair fell across her eyes. She needed a haircut. She'd obviously been neglecting herself. Why couldn't she see that she needed someone to look after her? *Vulnerable.* That was what Andie had called her. Yet Eliza just didn't seem to see it.

Her eyes narrowed. 'I wish you could hear how you sound, Jake. Cold. Ruthless. This isn't a business deal we're brokering. It's our lives. You. Me. A loveless marriage.'

'A way to ensure our child is legitimate.'

'What about a way to have a woman squirming under a man's thumb? That was *my* experience of marriage. And I have no desire to experience it again.'

'Really?' he said. 'I wouldn't want to see you squirming. Or under my thumb.' Jake held up his fingers in a fist, his thumb to the side. 'See? It's not nearly large enough to hold you down.'

It was a feeble attempt at levity and he knew it. But this was the most difficult conversation he had ever had. The stakes were so much higher than in even the most lucrative of potential business deals.

'I don't know whether to take that as an insult or not. I'm not *that* big.'

'No, you're not. In fact you're not big enough. You've lost weight, Eliza. You need to gain it. I can look after you as well as the baby.'

Her chin lifted in the stubborn way he was beginning to recognise.

'I don't *want* to be looked after. I can look after both myself and my baby on my own. You can see him or her, play a role in their life. But I most certainly don't want to *marry* you.'

'You're making a mistake, Eliza. Are you sure you don't want to reconsider?'

'You can't force me to marry you, Jake.'

'But I can make life so much easier for you if you do,' he said.

'Love is the only reason to marry. But love hasn't entered the equation for us. For that reason alone, I can't marry you.'

'That's your final word?'

She nodded.

He got up. 'Then you'll be hearing from my lawyer.'

Eliza's already pale face drained of every remaining scrap of colour. *'What?'*

She leapt up from the bed, had to steady herself as she seemed to rock on her feet as if she were dizzy. But she pushed aside his steadying hand and glared at him.

'You heard me,' he said. 'I intend to seek custody.'

'You can't have custody over an unborn child.' Her voice was high and strained.

'You're about to see what I can do,' he said.

He turned on his heel, strode to the top of the stairs. Flimsy stairs. Too dangerous. She couldn't bring up a child in this house. He ignored the inner voice that told him this house was a hundred times safer and nicer than the welfare housing apartment he'd grown up in. *Nothing but the best for his child.*

She put up her hand in a feeble attempt to stop him. 'Jake. You can't go.'

'I'm gone, Eliza. I suggest you get back to bed and rest. An agency nurse will be arriving in an hour. I've employed her to look after you for the next three days, as per doctor's orders. I suggest you let her in and allow her to care for you. Otherwise you might end up back in hospital.'

He swung himself on to the top step.

'I'll see you in court.'

CHAPTER THIRTEEN

So it had come to this. Eliza placed her hand protectively on her bump as she rode the elevator up to the twenty-third floor of the prestigious building in the heart of the central business district of Sydney, where the best law firms had their offices. She hadn't heard from Jake for three weeks. All communication had been through their lawyers. Except for one challenging email.

Now she was headed to a meeting with Jake and his lawyers to finalise a legal document that spelled out in detail a custody and support agreement for the unborn Baby Dunne.

She must have paled at the thought of the confrontation to come, because her lawyer gave her arm a squeeze of support. Jake had, of course, engaged the most expensive and well-known family law attorney in Sydney to be on his side of the battle lines.

He'd sent her an email.

Are you sure you can afford not to marry me, Eliza? Just your lawyer's fees alone will stop you in your tracks.

What he didn't realise, high up there in his billionaire world, where the almighty dollar ruled, was that not everybody could be bought. She had an older cousin who was a brilliant family lawyer. And Cousin Maree was so outraged at what Jake was doing that she was representing Eliza *pro bono.* Well, not quite for free. Eliza had agreed that Party Queens would organise the most spectacular twenty-first birthday party possible for Maree's daughter.

Now, Maree squeezed her arm reassuringly. 'Chin up. Just let me do the talking, okay?'

Eliza nodded, rather too numbed at the thought of what she was about to face to do anything else *but* keep quiet.

She saw Jake the moment she entered the large, traditionally furnished meeting room. Her heart gave such a jolt she had to hold on for support to the back of one of the chairs that were ranged around the boardroom table. He was standing tall, in front of floor-to-ceiling windows that looked out on a magnificent mid-morning view of Sydney Harbour. The Bridge loomed so closely she felt she could reach out and touch it.

Jake was wearing a deep charcoal-grey business suit, immaculately tailored to his broad shoulders and tapered to his waist. His hair—darker now, less sun-streaked—crept over his collar. No angel wings in sight—rather the forked tail and dark horns of the demon who had tormented her for the last three weeks with his demands.

At the sound of her entering the room Jake turned. For a split second his gaze met hers. There was a flash of recognition—and something else that was gone so soon she scarcely registered it. But it could have been regret. Then the shutters came down to blank his expression.

'Eliza,' he said curtly, acknowledging her presence with a brief nod in her direction.

'Jake,' she said coolly, despite her inner turmoil.

Her brain, so firmly in charge up until now, had been once more vanquished by her libido—she refused to entertain for even one second the thought that it might be her heart—which flamed into life at the sight of the beautiful man who had been her lover for those four, glorious days. So treacherous her libido, still to clamour for this man. Her lover who had become her enemy—the hero of her personal fairytale transformed into the villain.

Eliza let Jake's lawyer's assistant pull out the chair for her. Before she sat she straightened her shoulders and stood proud. Her tailored navy dress with its large white collar was tucked and pleated to accommodate and show off her growing bump. She hoped her silent message was loud and clear—*she* was in possession of the prize.

But at the same time as she displayed the ace in her hand she felt swept by a wave of inexplicable longing for Jake to be sharing the milestones of her pregnancy with her. She hadn't counted on the loneliness factor of single motherhood. There was a vague bubbling sensation that meant the baby was starting to kick, she thought. At fifteen weeks it was too soon for her to be feeling vigorous activity; she knew that from the 'what to expect' pregnancy books and websites she read obsessively. But she had a sudden vision of Jake, resting his hand on her tummy, a look of expectant joy on his face as he waited to feel the kicking of their baby's tiny feet.

That could only happen in a parallel universe. Jake had no interest in her other than as an incubator.

She wondered, too, if he had really thought ahead to his interaction with their son or daughter? His motivation seemed purely to be making up for the childhood he felt he'd lost because of his own despicable father. To try to right a family wrong and force a certain lifestyle on her whether she liked it or not.

What if their child—who might be equally as smart and stubborn as his or her parents—had other ideas about how he or she wanted to live? He or she might be as fiercely independent as both her, Eliza, and the paternal grandmother—Jake's mother.

Would she ever get to meet his mother? Unlikely. Unless she was there when Eliza handed over their child for Jake's court-prescribed visits.

That was not how it was meant to be. She ached at the utter *wrongness* of this whole arrangement.

Jake settled in to a chair directly opposite her, his lawyer to his right. That was *his* silent statement, she supposed. Confrontation, with the battlefield between them. *Bring it on,* she thought.

It was fortunate that the highly polished dark wooden table was wide enough so there was no chance of his knees nudging hers, her foot brushing against his when she shifted in her seat. Because, despite all the hostility, her darn libido still longed for his touch. It was insane—and must surely be blamed on the up-and-down hormone fluctuations of pregnancy.

Maree cleared her throat. 'Shall we start the proceedings? This is very straightforward.'

Maree had explained all this to her before, but Eliza listened intently as her cousin spoke, at the same time keeping her gaze firmly fixed on Jake's face. He gave nothing away—not the merest flicker of reaction. He ran his finger along his collar and tugged at his tie—obviously uncomfortable at being 'trussed up'. But she guessed he'd wanted to look like an intimidating billionaire businessman in front of the lawyers.

Maree explained how legally there could not be any formal custody proceedings over an unborn child. However, the parties had agreed to prepare a document outlining joint custody to present to a judge after the event of a live birth.

Eliza had known that particular phrase would be coming and bit her lip hard. She caught Jake's eye, and his slight nod indicated his understanding of how difficult it was for her to hear it. Because its implication was that something could go wrong in the meantime. Her greatest fear was that she would lose this miracle baby—although her doctor had assured her the pregnancy was progressing very well.

Jake's hands were gripped so tightly together that his knuckles showed white—perhaps he feared it too. He had been so brilliant that day he'd taken her to hospital.

Eliza was looking for crumbs to indicate that Jake wasn't the enemy, that this was all a big misunderstanding. That brief show of empathy from him might be it. Then she remembered why she was here in the first place. To be coerced into signing an agreement she didn't want to sign.

She was being held to a threat—hinted at rather than spoken out in the open—that if she didn't co-operate Jake would use his influence to steer wealthy clients away from Party Queens. Right at a time when her ongoing intermittent nausea and time away from work, plus the departure of their new head chef to a rival firm, meant her beloved company—and her livelihood—was tipping towards a precipice. What choice did she have?

Maree continued in measured tones, saying that both parties acknowledged Jake Marlowe's paternity, so there would be no need for a court-ordered genetic test once the baby was born. She listed the terms of the proposed custody agreement, starting with limited visits by the father while the child was an infant, progressing to full-on division of weekends and vacations. The baby's legal name would be Baby Dunne-Marlowe—once the sex was known a first name satisfactory to both parents would be agreed upon.

Then Jake's lawyer took over, listing the generous support package to be provided by Mr Marlowe—all medical expenses paid, a house to be gifted in the child's name and held in trust by Mr Marlowe, a trust fund to be set up for—

Eliza half got up from her chair. She couldn't endure this sham a second longer. 'That's enough. I know what's in the document. Just give it to me and I'll sign.'

She subsided in her chair. Bent her head to take Maree's counsel.

'Are you sure?' her cousin asked in a low voice. 'You don't want further clarification of the trust fund provisions? Or the—?'

'No. I just want this to be over.'

The irony of it struck her. Jake had been worried about gold-diggers. Now he was insisting she receive money she didn't want, binding her with ties that were choking all the joyful anticipation of her pregnancy. She tried to focus on the baby. That precious little person growing safe and happy inside her. Her unborn child was all that mattered.

She avoided looking at Jake as she signed everywhere the multiple-paged document indicated her signature was required, stabbing the pen so hard the paper tore.

Jake followed Eliza as she departed the conference room, apparently so eager to get away from him that she'd broken into a half-run. She was almost to the bank of elevators, her low-heeled shoes tapping on the marble floor, before he caught up with her.

'Eliza,' he called.

She didn't turn around, but he was close enough to hear her every word.

'I have nothing to say to you, Jake. You've got what you wanted, so just go away.'

Only she didn't say *go away.* She used far pithier language.

She reached the elevator and jabbed the elevator button. Once, twice, then kept on jabbing it.

'That won't get it here any faster,' he said, and immediately regretted the words. *Why had he said something so condescending?* He cursed his inability to find the right words in moments of high tension and emotion.

She turned on him, blue eyes flashing the brightest he'd seen them. Bright with threatening tears, he realised. Tears of anger—directed at *him.*

'Of course it won't. But I live in hope. Because the sooner I can get away from you, the better. Even a second or two would help.' She went back to jabbing the button.

Her baby bump had grown considerably since he'd last seen her. She looked the picture of an elegant, perfectly groomed businesswoman. The smart, feisty Eliza he had come to— Come to what? Respect? Admire? Something more than that. Something, despite all they'd gone through, he couldn't put a name to.

'You look well,' he said. *She looked more beautiful than ever.*

With a sigh of frustration she dropped her finger from the elevator button. Aimed a light kick at the elevator door. She turned to face him, her eyes narrowed with hostility.

'Don't try and engage me in polite chit-chat. Just because you've forced me to sign a proposed custody agreement it doesn't mean you own me—like you're trying to own my baby.'

You didn't own children—and you couldn't force a woman to marry you. Belatedly he'd come to that realisation.

Jake didn't often admit to feeling ashamed. But shame was what had overwhelmed him during the meeting, as he'd watched the emotions flickering over Eliza's face, so easy to read.

He'd been a teenage troublemaker—the leader of a group of other angry, alienated kids like himself. Taller and more powerful than the others, he'd used his off-the-charts IQ and well-developed street-smarts to control and intimidate the gang—even those older than him.

He'd thought he'd put all that long behind him. Then in that room, sitting opposite Eliza—proud, brave Eliza—it had struck him in the gut like a physical blow. He'd behaved as badly towards her as he had in his worst days as a teenage gang leader. Jim Hill would be ashamed of him—but not as ashamed as he was of himself.

'I'm sorry, Eliza. I didn't mean it to go this far.'

She blinked away the threatening tears. 'You played dirty, Jake. I wouldn't marry you, so you brought in the big guns. I would have played fair with you. Visitation rights. Even the Dunne-Marlowe name. For the sake of our baby. I was *glad* you wanted to play a role in our child's life. But I wasn't in a space for making life-changing decisions right then. I'd just got out of hospital.'

How had he let this get so far? 'I was wrong. I should have—'

'Now the document is signed you think you can placate me? Forget it. Don't you see? You're so concerned about giving this child your name, you're bequeathing to him or her something much worse. A mother who resents her baby's father. Who hates him for the way she's had to fight against him imposing his will on her, riding roughshod over her feelings.'

Now he was on the ground, being kicked from all sides. And the blows were much harder than those Eliza had given the elevator door.

'*Hate?* That's a strong word.'

'Not strong enough for how I feel about you,' she said, tight-lipped. 'I reckon you've let the desire to win overcome all your common sense and feelings of decency.'

Of course. He'd been guilty of *over-thinking* on a grand scale. 'I just want to do the right thing by our child,' he said. 'To look after it and to look after you too, Eliza. You need me.'

She shook her head. 'I don't need you. At one stage I wanted you. And…and I… I could have cared for you. When you danced me around that ballroom in Montovia I thought I was on the brink of something momentous in my life.'

'So did I,' he said slowly.

'Then there was Port Douglas. Leaving you seemed so *wrong.* We had something *real.* Only we were so darn intent on protecting ourselves from hurt we didn't recognise it and we walked away from it. The baby gave us a second chance. To be friends. Maybe more than friends. But we blew that too.'

'There must be such a thing as a third chance,' he said.

She shook her head so vehemently it dislodged the clip that was holding her hair off her face and she had to push it back into place with hands that trembled.

'No more chances. Not after what happened in that room today. You won't break me. I will never forgive you. For the baby's sake, I'll be civil. It would be wrong to pump our child's mind with poison against his or her father. Even if I happen to think he's a…a bullying thug.' Her cheeks were flushed scarlet, her eyes glittered.

Now he'd been kicked to a pulp—bruised black and blue all over. Hadn't the judge used a similar expression when sentencing him to juvenile detention? The words *bully* and *thug* seemed to be familiar. But that had been so long ago. He'd been fifteen years of age. Why had those tendencies he'd thought left well and truly behind him in adolescence surfaced again?

Then it hit him—the one final blow he hadn't seen coming. It came swinging again like that sledgehammer from nowhere to slam him in the head. This wasn't about Eliza needing him—it was about *him* needing *her.* Needing her so desperately he'd gone to crazy lengths to try to secure her.

Just then the elevator arrived.

'At last,' Eliza said as she stepped towards it. She had to wait until a girl clutching a bunch of legal folders to her chest stepped out.

'Eliza.'

Jake went to catch her arm, to stop her leaving. There was so much he had to say to her, to explain. But she shrugged off his hand.

'Please, Jake, no more. I can't take it. I'll let you know when the baby is born. As per our contract.'

She stood facing him as the elevator doors started to slide slowly inward. The last thing he saw of her was a slice of her face, with just one fat, glistening tear sliding down her cheek.

Jake stood for a long time, watching the indicator marking the elevator's progress down the twenty-three floors. He felt frozen to that marble floor, unable to step backwards or forwards.

When the elevator reached the ground floor he turned on his heel and strode back to his meeting. He needed to rethink his strategy. Jake Marlowe was not a man who gave up easily.

CHAPTER FOURTEEN

THE LAST PLACE Eliza expected to be a week after the lawyers' meeting with Jake was on an executive jet flying to Europe. Despite the gravity of the reason for her flight, it was a welcome distraction.

Gemma had called an emergency meeting of the three Party Queens directors. Eliza's unexpected pregnancy had tipped the problem of an absentee director into crisis point. And because Gemma was Crown Princess, as well as their Food Director, she had sent the Montovian royal family's private jet to transport Eliza and Andie from Sydney to Montovia for the meeting.

Just because Gemma *could*, Eliza had mused with a smile when she'd got the summons, along with the instructions for when a limousine would pick her up to take her to the airport where she would meet Andie.

Dominic had decided to come along for the flight, too. He and Andie's little boy Hugo was being looked after by his doting grandma and grandpa—Andie's parents.

Eliza was very fond of Andie's husband. But despite the luxury of the flight—the lounge chair comfort of leather upholstery, the crystal etched with the Montovian royal coat of arms, the restaurant-quality food, the hotel-style bathrooms—she hadn't been able to relax because of the vaguely hostile emanations coming her way from Dominic.

Jake was Dominic's best male friend. The bonds between them went deep. According to the legend of the two young billionaires they went way back, to when they'd been in their first year at university. Together, they had built fortunes. Created a charitable foundation for homeless kids. And cemented that young friendship into something adult and enduring.

In the air, somewhere over Indonesia, Dominic told Eliza in no uncertain terms that Jake was unhappy and miserable. He couldn't understand why Eliza wouldn't just marry Jake and put them *all* out of their misery.

Dominic got a sharp poke in the ribs from his wife's elbow for *that* particular opinion. He was referring to the fact that sympathies had been split down the middle among the other two Party Queens and their respective spouses.

Andie and Gemma were on her side—though they'd been at pains to state that they weren't actually *taking* sides. Neither of her friends saw why Eliza should marry a man she didn't love just to give her baby Jake's name when he or she was born. Nor did they approve of the domineering way Jake had tried to force the issue.

Dominic and Tristan, however, thought differently.

Dominic had an abusive childhood behind him—tough times living on the streets. He'd told Eliza she was both crazy and unwise not to jump straight into the safety net Jake was offering.

Tristan, a hereditary Crown Prince, also couldn't

see the big deal. There was only one way forward. The baby carried Jake's blood. As far as Tristan was concerned, Gemma had told Eliza, Jake was doing the correct and honourable thing in offering Eliza marriage. Eliza must do the right thing and accept. That from a man who had changed the laws of his country regarding marriage so he could marry for love and make Gemma his wife.

Both men had let Eliza know that they saw her stance as stubborn in the extreme, and contributing to an unnecessary rift between very close friends. They stood one hundred per cent by their generous and maligned buddy Jake. The women could not believe how blindly loyal their husbands were to the *bullying thug* that was Jake.

Of course Eliza was well aware that neither Andie nor Gemma had ever called Jake that in front of Dominic or Tristan. They were each way too wise to let problems with their mutual friends interfere with their own blissfully happy marriages to the men they adored. Besides, as Andie told Eliza, they actually still liked Jake a lot. They just didn't like the way he'd treated her.

'Although Jake *is* very generous,' Andie reminded her.

'Of course he is—exceedingly generous,' said Eliza evenly.

Inside she was screaming: *And sexy and kind and even funny when he wants to be.* As if she needed to be reminded of his good points when they were all she seemed to think about these days.

She kept remembering that time in the ambulance, as she'd drifted in and out of consciousness and the man who had never let go of her hand had murmured reassurance and encouragement all the way to the hospital. The man who'd chartered a private boat for her because she'd said she wanted to dive on the Great Barrier Reef. The man who hadn't needed angel wings to send her soaring to heaven when they'd made love.

Eliza wished, not for the first time, that she hadn't actually called Jake a bullying thug—or told Andie she'd called him that. That day she'd got all the way to the bottom of the building on the elevator and seriously considered going all the way back up to apologise. Then realised, as she had just told him she hated him, that it might not be the best of ideas.

'Do you ever regret not marrying him?' Andie asked. 'You would never have to worry about money again.'

'No,' Eliza replied firmly. 'Because I don't think financial security is a good enough reason to marry—not for me, anyway. Not when I'm confident I'll always be able to earn a good living.'

What she couldn't admit—not even to her dearest friend Andie, and certainly not to Dominic—was that these weeks away from Jake had made her realise how much she had grown to care for him. That along with all the other valid reasons for her not to marry Jake there was one overwhelming reason—she couldn't put herself through the torture of a pragmatic arrangement with a man she'd begun to realise she was half in love with but who didn't love her.

By the end of the long-haul flight to Montovia—Australia to Europe being a flight of some twenty-two hours—Eliza was avoiding Dominic as much as she could within the confines of the private jet. Andie was okay. Eliza didn't think she had a clue about how much Eliza was beginning to regret the way she had handled her relationship with Jake. But she didn't want to share those thoughts with anyone.

She hoped she and Dominic would more easily be able to steer clear of each other in the vast expanses of the royal castle. Avoiding Tristan might not be so easy.

The day after she'd landed in Montovia, Eliza sat in Gemma's exquisitely decorated office in the Crown Prince's private apartment at the castle. A 'small' room, it contained Gemma's desk and a French antique table and chairs, around which the three Party Queens were now grouped. Under the window, which looked out onto the palace gardens, there was a beautiful chaise longue that Eliza recognised from her internet video conversations with Gemma.

What a place for three ordinary Aussie girls to have ended up for a meeting, Eliza couldn't help thinking.

The three Party Queens were more subdued than usual, with the future of the company they had started more as a lark than any seriously considered business decision now under threat. It was still considered the best party planning business in Sydney, but it was at a crossroads—Eliza had been pointing that out with increasing urgency over the last months.

'I thought it would be too intimidating for us to meet in the castle boardroom,' auburn-haired Gemma explained once they were all settled. 'Even after we were married it took me a while before I could overcome my nerves enough to make a contribution there.'

Andie laughed. 'This room is so easy on the eye I might find it difficult to concentrate from being too busy admiring all the treasures.'

'Not to mention the distraction of the view out to those beautiful roses,' Eliza said.

It felt surreal to be one day in the late winter of Australia, the next day in the late summer of Europe.

'Okay, down to business,' said Gemma. 'We all know Party Queens is facing some challenges. Not least is the fact that I now live here, while the business is based in Sydney.'

'Which makes it problematical when your awesome skills with food are one of the contributing factors to our success,' said Eliza.

'True,' said Andie. 'Even as Creative Director, there are limitations to what I can do in terms of clever food ideas. Those ideas need to be validated by a food expert to tell me if they can be practical.'

Gemma nodded. 'I can still devise menus from here. And I can still test recipes myself, as I like to do.' The fact that Gemma had been testing a recipe for a white chocolate and citrus mud cake when she had first met Tristan, incognito in Sydney, had been fuel for a flurry of women's magazine articles. More so when the recipe had become the royal wedding cake. 'But the truth is both the time difference between Montovia and Sydney and my royal duties make a hands-on presence from me increasingly difficult.'

Eliza swallowed hard against a dry throat. 'Does that mean you want to resign from the partnership, Gemma?'

'Heavens, no,' said Gemma. 'But maybe I need to look at my role in a different way.'

'And then there's your future as a sole parent to consider, Eliza,' said Andie.

'Don't think I haven't thought of the challenges that will present,' Eliza said.

'Think about those challenges and multiply them a hundred times,' said Andie, and put up her hand to stop the protest Eliza was already formulating. 'Being a parent is tough, Eliza. Even tougher without a pair of loving hands from the other parent to help you out.'

Eliza gritted her teeth. She was sure Andie had meant 'the other parent' in abstract terms. But of course she could only think of Jake in that context.

'I understand that, Andie,' she said. 'And my bouts of extreme nausea showed me that even with the best workaholic will in the world there are times when the baby will have to come before the business.'

Andie raised her hand for attention. 'May I throw into the mix the fact that Dominic and I would like another baby? With two children, perhaps more, I might have to scale down my practical involvement as well.'

'It's good to have everything on the table,' said Eliza. 'No doubt a royal heir might factor into *your* future, Gemma.'

'I hope so,' said Gemma with a smile. 'We're waiting until a year after the wedding to think about that. I need to learn how to be a princess before I tackle motherhood.'

'Now we've heard the problems, I'm sure you've come armed with a plan to solve them, Eliza,' said Andie.

This kind of dilemma was something Eliza was more familiar with than the complications of her relationship with Jake. She felt very confident on this turf.

'Of course,' she said. 'The business is still very healthy, so option one is to sell Party Queens.'

She was gratified at the wails of protest from Gemma and Andie.

'It *is* a viable option,' she continued. 'There are two possible buyers—'

'No,' said Andie.

'No,' echoed Gemma.

'How could the business be the same without us?' said Andie, with an arrogant flick of her blonde-streaked hair. 'We *are* the Party Queens.'

'Good,' said Eliza. 'I feel the same way. The other proposal is to bring in another level of management in Sydney. Gemma would become a non-executive director, acting as ongoing adviser to a newly appointed food manager.'

Gemma nodded. 'Good idea. I have someone in mind. I've worked with her as a consultant and she would be ideal.'

Eliza continued. 'And Andie would train a creative person to bring on board so she can eventually work part-time. I'm thinking Jeremy.'

Freelance stylist Jeremy had been working with them since the beginning—long forgiven for his role in the disastrous Christmas tree incident that had rocked Andie and Dominic's early relationship.

Andie frowned. 'Jeremy is so talented… He's awesome. And he's really organised. But he's not a Party Queen.' She paused. 'Actually, he's a queen of a different stripe. I think he'd love to come on board.'

'Which brings us to *you*, Eliza,' said Gemma.

Eliza heaved a great sigh, reluctant to be letting go.

'I'm thinking I need to appoint a business manager to deal with the day-to-day finances and accounting.'

'Good idea.' Andie reached out a hand to take Eliza's. 'But you, out of all of us, might have a difficult time relinquishing absolute control over the business we started,' she said gently.

'I… I get that,' Eliza said.

Gemma smiled her friendship and understanding. 'Will you be able to give a manager the freedom to make decisions independent of you? Not hover over them and micro-manage them? Like watching a cake rise in the oven?'

Eliza bowed her head. 'I really am a control freak, aren't I?'

Andie squeezed her hand. 'You said it, not me.'

'I reckon your control freak tendencies are a big part of Party Queens's success,' said Gemma. 'You've really kept us on track.'

'But they could also lead to its downfall if I don't loosen the reins,' said Eliza thoughtfully.

'It's a matter of believing someone can do the job as well as you—even if they do it differently,' said Andie.

'Of accepting help because you need it,' said Gemma.

Her friends were talking about Party Queens. But, seen through the filter of her relationship with Jake, Eliza saw how she might have done things very differently. She'd fought so hard not to relinquish control over her life, over her baby—over her heart—she hadn't seen what Jake could bring to her. Not just as a father but as a life partner. Maybe she had driven him to excessive control on his side because she hadn't given an inch on hers.

In hindsight, she realised she might have thought

more about compromise than control. When it came to giving third chances, maybe it should have been *her* begging *him* for a chance to make it right.

CHAPTER FIFTEEN

DINNER AT THE royal castle of Montovia was a very formal affair. Luckily Eliza had been warned by Gemma to pack appropriate clothes. From her experiences of dinners at the castle before the wedding she knew that meant a dress that would be appropriate for a ball in Sydney. Thank heaven she still fitted into her favourite vintage ballgown in an empire style in shimmering blue that was very flattering to her pregnant shape.

Still, when she went down to dinner in the private section of the palace that was never opened to the public, she was astounded to see the level of formality of the other guests. She blinked at the dazzle of jewellery glinting in the lights from the chandeliers. It took her a moment to realise they were all members of Tristan and Gemma's bridal party. Tristan's sister Princess Natalia, his cousin with his doctor fiancée, she and Andie, other close friends of Tristan's. Natalia waved when she caught her eye.

'It's a wedding reunion,' Andie said when Eliza was seated beside her at the ornate antique banqueting table.

'So I see. Did you know about it?' Eliza asked.

'No. Gemma didn't either. Apparently when Tristan knew we were coming to visit he arranged it as a surprise. He invited everyone, and these are the ones who could make it. Obviously we're the only Australians.'

'What a lovely thing for him to do,' Eliza said.

Gemma was glowing with happiness.

'Very romantic,' said Andie. 'Gemma really struck husband gold with Tristan, in more ways than one.'

It was romantic in a very heart-wrenching way for Eliza. Because the most important member of the wedding party was not here—the best man, Jake.

Bittersweet memories of her last visit to the castle came flooding back in a painful rush. During the entire wedding she'd been on the edge of excitement, longing for a moment alone with him. How dismally it had all turned out. Except for the baby. Her miracle baby. Why couldn't it be enough to have the baby she'd yearned for? Why did she ache to have the father too?

What with being in a different time zone, Eliza was being affected by more than a touch of jet-lag. She also had to be careful about what she ate. The worst, most debilitating attacks of nausea seemed to have passed, but she still had to take care. She just picked at course after course of the magnificent feast—in truth she had no appetite. As soon as it was polite to do so she would make her excuses and go back up to her guest suite—the same luxurious set of rooms she'd been given on her last visit.

After dessert had been cleared Tristan asked his guests to move into the adjoining reception room, where coffee was to be served. There were gasps of surprise as the guests trooped in, at the sight of a large screen on one wall, with images of the wedding projected onto it. The guests burst into spontaneous applause.

Eliza stared at the screen. There was Gemma, getting ready with her bridesmaids. And Eliza herself, smiling as she patted a stray lock of Gemma's auburn hair back into place. The images flashed by. Andie. Natalia. The Queen placing a diamond tiara on Gemma's head.

Then there were pictures at the cathedral. The cluster of tiny flower girls. The groomsmen. The best man—Jake—standing at the altar with Tristan. Jake was smiling straight at the first bridesmaid coming up the aisle. *Her.* She was smiling back at him. It must have been so obvious to everyone what was going on between them. And here she was—without him. But pregnant with his baby.

Her hand went to her heart when she saw a close-up of Jake saying something to Tristan. The image was so large he seemed life-size. Jake looked so handsome her mouth went dry and her heart started to thud so hard she had to take deep breaths to try and control it.

She couldn't endure this. It was cruel. No one would realise if she slipped away. They were all too engrossed with the photographs.

She turned, picked up her long skirts.

And came face to face with Jake.

It was as if the image of him that had so engrossed her on the screen had come to life. Was she hallucinating? With a cautious hand, she reached out and connected with warm, solid Jake. He was real all right. She felt the colour drain from her face. He was wearing a similar tuxedo as he was in the photo, but his smile was more reticent. *He was unsure of his welcome from her.*

'Jake…' she breathed, unable to say another thing.

She felt light-headed and swayed a little. *Please. Not now.* She couldn't pass out on him again.

'You need some fresh air,' he said, and took her arm.

She let him look after her. *Liked* that he wanted to look after her. Without protest she let him lead her out of the room and then found her voice—though not any coherent words to say with it.

'What…? How…?'

'I was in London when Tristan called me about the wedding party reunion. I got here as soon as I could when I heard you were in Montovia.'

Eliza realised he was leading her onto the same terrace where they'd parted the last time they'd been in Montovia. Not quite the same view—it must be further down from that grand ballroom—and not a full moon over the lake either. But a new moon—a crescent moon that gave her a surge of hope for a new start.

She took another deep, steadying breath. Looked up at him and hoped he saw in her eyes what she was feeling but was unable to express.

'Jake, I'm asking for a third chance. Will you give it to me?'

Jake prided himself on being able to read Eliza's expressions. But he couldn't put a label on what he saw shining from her eyes. He must be reading into it what he longed to see, not what was really there. But he took hope from even that glimmering of emotion.

'Of course I give you a third chance,' he said hoarsely. He'd give her a million chances if they brought her back to him. 'But only if you'll give *me* a third chance.'

'Third chance granted,' she said, a tremulous edge to her voice.

He pulled her into his arms and held her close, breathed in her sweet scent. She slid her arms around his back and pressed closer with a little sigh. He smiled at the feel of her slender body, with the distinct curve of his baby resting under her heart. *His baby. His woman.* Now he had to convince her—not coerce her—into letting him be her man.

He looked over her head to the dark night sky, illuminated only by a sliver of silver moon, and thanked whatever power it was that had given him this chance to make good the wrongs he'd done her.

'I've missed you,' he said, not sure how to embellish his words any further.

'I've missed you too. Terribly.'

He'd flown back to Brisbane after she'd left him at the lawyer's office. His house had seemed empty—his life empty. He'd longed to be back with Eliza in her little house, with the red front door and the dragonfly doorknocker. Instead he'd tied her down to a contract to ensure his child's presence in his life and in doing so had driven her away from him.

Over and over he'd relived his time with her in Port Douglas. The passion and wonder of making love with her. Thought of the real reason he wanted to spend millions to relocate his company to Sydney. The overwhelming urge to protect her he'd felt as he'd held her hand in the ambulance and soothed her fears she might lose the baby she'd longed for. *His baby.* The incredible gift he'd been able to give her. The baby was a bonus. Eliza was the prize. But he still had to win her.

Eliza pulled away from his arms but stayed very close.

'Jake, I don't hate you—really, I don't.' The words tumbled out of her as if she had been saving them up. 'And I don't think you're a bullying thug. I… I'm really sorry I called you that.'

He'd always known he'd have to tell her the truth about his past some time—sooner rather than later. Her words seemed to be a segue into it. There was a risk that she would despise him and walk away. But he had to take that risk. If only because she was the mother of his child.

He cleared his throat. 'You're not the first person to call me a bully and a thug,' he said.

She frowned. 'What do you mean?'

'When I was fifteen years old I came up in front of the children's court and was charged with a criminal offence. The magistrate used just those words.'

'Jake!'

To his relief, there was disbelief in her voice, in the widening of her eyes, but not disgust.

'I was the leader of a gang of other young thugs. We'd stolen a car late one night and crashed it into a shopfront. I wasn't driving, but I took responsibility. The police thought it was a ram-raid—that we'd driven into the shop on purpose. In fact it was an accident. None of us could drive properly. We didn't have a driver's licence between us—we were too young. With the pumped-up pride of an adolescent male, I thought it was cooler to be charged with a ram-raid than admit to being an idiot. It was my second time before the court so I got sentenced to a spell in juvenile detention.'

Eliza kept close, didn't back away from him in horror. 'You? In a gang? I can't believe it. Why?'

'Things weren't great at home. My grandfather,

who was the only father I'd ever known, had died. My mother had a boyfriend I couldn't stand. I was angry. I was hurting. The gang was a family of sorts, and I was the kingpin.'

'Juvenile detention—that's jail, isn't it?'

'A medium security prison for kids aged from eleven to sixteen.'

She shuddered. 'I still can't believe I'm hearing this. How awful for you.'

He gritted his teeth. 'I won't lie. It *was* awful. There were some really tough kids in there.'

'Thank heaven you survived.' Her voice was warm with compassion.

She placed her hand on his cheek. He covered it with his own.

'My luck turned with the care officer assigned to me. Jim Hill. He saw I was bored witless at school and looking for diversion.'

'The school hadn't realised you were a genius?'

'They saw me as a troublemaker. Jim really helped me with anger management, with confidence-building. He showed me I had choices.' Jake smiled at the memory. 'He knew I hungered for what I didn't have, after growing up poor. Jim told me I had the brains to become a criminal mastermind or to make myself a fortune in the commercial world. The choice was mine. When my detention was over he worked with my mother to get me moved to a different school in a different area, further down the coast. The new school put me into advanced classes that challenged me. I chose to take the second path. You know the rest.'

Eliza's eyes narrowed. 'Jim Hill? The name sounds familiar.'

'He heads up The Underground Help Centre. You must have met him at the launch party.'

'So you introduced him to Dominic?'

'Jim introduced *me* to Dominic. Dominic was under his care too. But that's Dominic's story to tell. Thanks to Jim, Dominic and I already knew each other by the time we started uni. We both credit Jim for getting our lives on track. That's why we got him on board to help other young people in trouble like we were.'

'How have you managed to keep this under wraps?'

'Juvenile records are sealed when a young offender turns eighteen. I was given a fresh start and I took it. Now you know the worst about me, Eliza.'

Jake was such a tall, powerfully built man. And yet at that moment he seemed to Eliza as vulnerable as his fifteen-year-old self must have been, standing before a magistrate, waiting to hear his sentence.

She leaned up and kissed him on his cheek. It wasn't time yet for any other kind of kiss. Not until they knew where this evening might take them. Since they'd last stood on this terrace together they'd accumulated so much more baggage. Not to mention a baby bump.

'That's a story of courage and determination,' she said. 'Can you imagine if someone ever made a movie of your life story?'

'Never going to happen,' he growled.

'Well, it will make a marvellous story to tell your child one day.'

'Heavily censored,' he said, with a hint of the grin she had got so fond of.

She slowly shook her head. 'I wish you'd told me before. It helps me understand you. And I've been struggling to understand you, Jake.'

To think she had thought him superficial. He'd just been good at hiding his wounds.

He took both her hands in his and drew her closer. 'Would it have made a difference if I'd told you?'

'To help me see why you're so determined to give your child a name? Yes. To make me understand why you're so driven? Yes. To make me love you even more, knowing what you went through? Yes. And I—'

'Stop right there, Eliza,' he said, his voice hoarse. 'Did you just say you love me?'

Over the last days she'd gotten so used to thinking how much she loved him, she'd just blurted out the words. She could deny it. But what would be the point?

She looked up into his face, saw not just good looks but also his innate strength and integrity, and answered him with honesty. 'Yes, Jake, I love you. I fell in love with you… I can't think when. Yes, I can. Here. Right here on this terrace. No. Earlier than that. Actually, from the first moment. Only you weren't free. And then there was Port Douglas, and I got all tied up in not wanting to get hurt again, and…'

She realised he hadn't said anything further and began to feel exposed and vulnerable that she'd confessed she'd fallen in love with a man who had never given any indication that he might love *her*.

She tried to pull away but he kept a firm grip on her hands. 'I… I know you don't feel the same, Jake, so I—'

'What makes you say that? Of *course* I love you. I fell in love with you the first time I was best man to your bridesmaid. We must have felt it at the same moment. You in that blue bridesmaid's dress, with white flowers in your hair…'

'At Andie's wedding?' she said, shaking her head in wonder.

'At Dominic's wedding,' he said at the same time.

He drew her closer. This man who wanted to care for her, look after her, miraculously seemed to love her.

'You laughed at something I said and looked up at me with those incredible blue eyes and I fell right into them.'

'I remember that moment,' she said slowly. 'It felt like time suddenly stopped. The wedding was going on all around me, and all I could think of was how smitten I was with you.'

'But I was too damn tied up with protecting myself to let myself recognise it,' he said.

'Just as well, really,' she said. 'I wasn't ready for something so life-changing then. And you certainly weren't.'

'You could look at it that way. Or you could see that we wasted a lot of time.'

'Then the baby complicated things.'

'Yes,' he said.

The spectre of that dreadful contract hovered between them.

'Your pregnancy brought out my old fears,' he said. 'I'd chosen not to be a father because I don't know *how* to be a father. I had no role model. My uncle lived in the Northern Territory and I rarely saw him. My grandfather tried his best to be a male influence in my life but he was quite old, and suffering from the emphysema that eventually killed him.'

She nodded with realisation. 'You were *scared* to be a father.'

'I was *terrified* I'd be a bad father.'

'Do you still think that way?'

'Not so much.'

'Why?'

'Because of you,' he said. 'I know you're going to be a brilliant mother, Eliza. That will help me to be the best father I can be to our child.'

'Thank you for the vote of confidence,' she said a little shakily. 'But I'll have to *learn* to be a mother. We'll *both* have to learn to be parents. And I know our daughter will have the most wonderful daddy who—'

'Our *daughter*?'

Eliza snatched her hand to her mouth. 'I haven't had a chance to tell you. I had another ultrasound last week.'

For the first time Jake placed his hand reverently on her bump. 'A little girl…' he said, his voice edged with awe. 'My daughter.'

For a long moment Eliza looked up at Jake, taking in the wonder and anticipation on his face.

'So…so where does that leave us?' she asked finally.

'I'm withdrawing my offer of marriage,' he said.

'*What?*'

Jake looked very serious. 'It was more a command than a proposal. I want to do it properly.'

'Do *what* properly?'

But she thought she might know what. Hope flew into her mind like a tiny bird and flew frantically around, trilling to be heard.

'Propose,' he said.

Jake cradled her face in his big, strong hands. His green eyes looked intently down into hers.

'Eliza, I love you. Will you marry me? Do me the honour of becoming my wife?'

She didn't hesitate. 'Yes, Jake, yes. Nothing would make me happier than to be your wife. I love you.'

Now was the time to kiss. He gathered her into his arms and claimed her mouth. She wound her arms around his neck and kissed him back, her heart singing with joy. She loved him and she wanted him and now he was hers. No way would she be alone in that palatial guest apartment tonight.

Jake broke away from the kiss. Then came back for another brief kiss, as if he couldn't get enough of her. He reached inside his jacket to an inside pocket. Then pulled out a small embossed leather box and flipped it open.

Eliza was too stunned to say anything, to do anything other than stare at the huge, perfect solitaire diamond on a fine platinum band, glinting in the faint silver light of the new moon. He picked up her hand and slipped the ring onto the third finger of her left hand. It fitted perfectly.

'I love it,' she breathed. 'Where did you get—?'

'In London.'

'But—'

'I was planning to propose in Sydney. But then Tristan invited me here.'

'Back to where it started.'

He kissed her again, a kiss that was tender and loving and full of promise.

'Can we get married as soon as possible?' he asked.

She paused. 'For the baby's sake?'

'To make you my wife and me your husband. This is about us committing to each other, Eliza. Not because you're pregnant. The baby is a happy bonus.'

'So what happens about the contract once we're married?'

'That ill-conceived contract? After I left you at the elevator I went back to the meeting room and tore my copy up. Then I fired my lawyer for giving me such bad advice.'

She laughed. 'I put my copy through the shredder.'

'We'll be brilliant parents without any need for that,' he said.

'I love you, Jake,' she said, rejoicing in the words, knowing she would be saying them over and over again in the years to come.

'I love you too, Eliza.' He lowered his head to kiss her again.

'Eliza, are you okay? We were worried—'

Andie's voice made both Eliza and Jake turn.

'Oh,' said Andie. Then, *'Oh...'* again, in a very knowing way.

Gemma was there too. She smiled. 'I can see you're okay.'

'Very okay,' Eliza said, smiling her joy. She held out her left hand and splayed her fingers, the better to display her ring. 'We're engaged. For real engaged.'

Andie and Gemma hugged her and Jake, accompanying their hugs with squeals of excitement and delight. Then Dominic and Tristan were there, slapping Jake on the back and hugging her, telling her they were glad she'd come to her senses and that they hoped she realised what a good man she'd got.

'Oh, I realise, all right,' she said, looking up at Jake.

'I couldn't think of a better man to be my husband and the father of my child.'

'You got the best man,' said Jake with a grin.

CHAPTER SIXTEEN

THE BEAUTY OF having your own party planning business, Eliza mused, was that it was possible to organise a wedding in two weeks flat without cutting any corners.

Everything was perfect, she thought with satisfaction on the afternoon of her wedding day. They'd managed to keep her snaring of 'the Billionaire Bachelor' under the media radar. So she and Jake were getting the quiet, intimate wedding they both wanted without any intrusion from the press.

It had been quite a feat to keep it quiet. After all, not only was the most eligible bachelor in Australia getting married, but the guest list of close family and friends included royalty.

Andie had found a fabulous waterfront house at Kirribilli as their venue. The weather was perfect, and the ceremony was to be held on the expansive lawns that stretched right down to the harbour wall, with the Opera House and Sydney Harbour Bridge as backdrop.

It really was just as she wanted it, Eliza thought as she stood with her father at the end of the veranda. Andie had arranged two rows of elegant white bamboo chairs to form an aisle. Large white metal vases filled with informal bunches of white flowers marked the end of each row of seats.

Now, the chairs were all filled with guests, heads turned, waiting for the bride to make her entrance. Everyone she cared about was there, including Jake's mother, whom she'd liked instantly.

Ahead, Jake stood flanked by his best man, Dominic, and his groomsman Tristan, at one side of the simple white wedding arch completely covered in white flowers where the celebrant waited. On the other side stood her bridesmaids, Andie and Gemma. A jazz band played softly. When it struck up the chords of the traditional 'Wedding March', it was Eliza's cue to head down the aisle. On the back of a white pony named Molly—her father's wedding gift to her.

Her vintage-inspired, full-skirted tea-length gown hadn't really been chosen with horseback-riding in mind. But when her father had reminded her of how as a little girl she had always wanted to ride to her wedding on her pony, she had fallen for the idea. Andie had had hysterics, but eventually caved in.

'I really hope we can carry this off, Dad,' Eliza said now, as her father helped her up into the side saddle.

'Of course you can, love,' he said. 'You're still the best horsewoman I know.'

Amazing how a wedding and a baby could bring families together, she thought. Her father had mellowed and their rift had been healed—much to her mother's joy. Now Eliza was seated on Molly and her father was leading the pony by a lead-rope entwined with white ribbons down the grassy aisle. There was no 'giving away' of the bride as part of the ceremony. She and Jake were giving themselves to each other.

Her entrance was met with surprised delight and the sound of many cameras clicking.

Jake didn't know about her horseback entrance—she'd kept it a secret. 'Brilliant,' he whispered as he helped her off Molly and into his arms. 'Country girl triumphs.'

But once the novelty of her entrance was over, and her father had led Molly away, it was all about Jake and her.

They had written the words of the ceremony themselves, affirming their love and respect for each other and their commitment to a lifetime together as well as their anticipation of being parents. Her dress did nothing to disguise her bump—she hadn't wanted to hide the joyous presence of their miracle baby.

Everything around her seemed to recede as she exchanged her vows with Jake, looking up into his face, his eyes never leaving hers. Their first kiss as husband and wife went on for so long their friends starting applauding.

'I love you,' she whispered, just for his ears.

'For always and for ever,' he whispered back.

* * * * *